THE
INSIDER

D0813662

Also by Craig Schaefer

The Charlie McCabe Thrillers

The Loot

The Daniel Faust Series

The Long Way Down
Redemption Song
The Living End
A Plain-Dealing Villain
The Killing Floor Blues
The Castle Doctrine
Double or Nothing
The Neon Boneyard

The Revanche Cycle

Winter's Reach
The Instruments of Control
Terms of Surrender
Queen of the Night

The Harmony Black Series

Harmony Black
Red Knight Falling
Glass Predator
Cold Spectrum

THE WISDOM'S GRAVE TRILOGY

Sworn to the Night
Detonation Boulevard
Bring the Fire

THE
INSIDER

CRAIG SCHAEFER

THOMAS & MERCER

This is a work of fiction. Names, characters, organizations, places, events, and incidents are either products of the author's imagination or are used fictitiously. Any resemblance to actual persons, living or dead, or actual events is purely coincidental.

Text copyright © 2020 by Craig Schaefer
All rights reserved.

No part of this book may be reproduced, or stored in a retrieval system, or transmitted in any form or by any means, electronic, mechanical, photocopying, recording, or otherwise, without express written permission of the publisher.

Published by Thomas & Mercer, Seattle

www.apub.com

Amazon, the Amazon logo, and Thomas & Mercer are trademarks of Amazon.com, Inc., or its affiliates.

ISBN-13: 9781542093200
ISBN-10: 1542093201

Cover design by Kaitlin Kall

Printed in the United States of America

THE
INSIDER

ONE

From the heart of Medford, caressing the hip of the Mystic River, WRKO delivered talk radio and strong opinions to the greater Boston area. Stronger ones than usual today.

"You think he's for real?" Charlie asked.

Charlie McCabe had been pacing the carpet, one eye on the big round wall of floor-to-ceiling glass that looked out onto the parking lot. The lobby of One Cabot Road was done up in shades of bone ivory and forest brown, echoes of nature but lacquered, synthetic. Big abstract paintings hung on the walls to add chaotic splashes of color. The art said nothing to her. Neither did the endless word salad of an interview drifting over the speaker system.

Charlie was dressed for business and mobility this morning, clad in a dark linen pantsuit and storm-gray trainers. The slim box of a radio rode on one hip; on the other, she carried an ID badge marking her as a duly sworn agent of Boston Asset Protection Ltd. The badge gave her as much legal authority as the building's janitor, but she'd learned how an official-looking document and a little show of confidence could open doors all over town.

"Who's for real?" Beckett asked. "Gable?"

Her partner stood like a statue in a strategic corner, silent as he watched the world move by. Charlie still wasn't sure if Beckett was his first or last name; nobody at the company seemed to know, and the big man greeted the question with his usual philosophical nonchalance. He was a broad-shouldered wall in a tailored black suit, the perfectly cut cloth just a few shades darker than his skin. His scalp shone under the lobby lights, perfectly smooth, with the sculpted V of a goatee framing his tight-lipped mouth.

"Just wondering if he actually believes a word he says. The whole extremist-provocateur shtick."

"I take the view," Beckett said, "that character is defined by action. Doesn't matter if the man's motivated by belief or his bank account; we're obliged to take Mr. Gable at his word, accept the face he chooses to present to us, and react appropriately."

Charlie gave him the side-eye. "Appropriately?"

"Under present circumstances—since we're taking his money in exchange for protecting him from the many, many people who would enjoy ruffling the man's haircut—shielding him from harm and ensuring he can deliver his message to the world is the appropriate action."

"And what does that action say about *our* character?" she asked.

He wore the faintest ghost of a smile.

"That," Beckett said, "is an exercise left to the student."

Lincoln Gable was on a book tour promoting his latest magnum opus, *You Know I'm Right*. Somewhere along the way he'd realized he had two audiences: the fans who ate his culture-war diatribes with a spoon, and the haters who took to the internet to exhaustively debunk and dissect every paragraph. He earned the exact same amount of money for every copy he sold, whether the customer was going to praise the book or burn it. And so, savvy businessman that he was, he'd started his tour by doing everything in his power to whip both sides into a frenzy.

When someone had put a rifle round through the windshield of his parked Mercedes, he'd hired Boston Asset Protection. The bullets hadn't helped his behavior any. Now he thought he was immortal, protected behind a wall of bodyguards, and he acted like it.

Charlie's radio squawked. She plucked it from her belt.

"Go."

Dominica Da Costa was outside, monitoring the scene. Her voice washed across the radio on a bed of static.

"We got trouble. Protesters coming your way, about two dozen of 'em."

Charlie did her best work on the front line; she'd traveled from Boston to Fort Bliss to Bagram and back again, finding a battle at every stop, and the front lines were where she felt most at home. Beckett was too big to work anywhere else, though the man had an uncanny knack for turning chameleon when he really needed to. Dom's specialty was overwatch; she was their guardian angel, their eyes and ears.

Dom was capable up close. At range, she was lethal. She'd proved that on the toughest day of Charlie's life, a death match in a junkyard twenty miles from nowhere. She, Charlie, and Beckett had passed through the fire together and come out as the last ones standing, bound together by a secret, a trunkful of corpses, and $90,000 in stolen diamonds. A perfect three-way split.

"The hell?" Dom's radio warning turned Charlie toward the wall of glass. She could see a small pack of people marching through the parking lot, streaming in fast.

"What'd they do, take a bus?"

"Separate cars," Dom said. "They showed up all at once, like a flash mob."

Not for the first time. "And you checked social media this morning?"

"Facebook, Twitter, political forums—all the places where people get together to talk about how much they want to smash Gable's face in." Dom let out a frustrated puff of breath. "Nothing. Not a word. These people have to be coordinating over a private mailing list. How's the interview going?"

Charlie held the radio up to the nearest speaker.

"Sir, that is slander," Lincoln was telling the increasingly flustered host. "Never once, in my entire book, do I use the word *Jew*. What I said was we have to do something about the globalist elites who control Hollywood and the nation's economy. Now, if you think I was talking about the Jewish people, I think that tells your listeners who the real racist is."

Charlie lowered the radio. "Pretty much like that."

"He's on fire today. Alas, not literally. Okay, I'm out here ready to extract; you call the shot."

It sounded like Lincoln was about to wrap things up or get thrown out of the studio headfirst. Either way, they needed to move. Charlie looked to Beckett, a question in her eyes.

"Also an exercise left to the student," he said.

Charlie was still earning her stripes. This was her second big assignment with the company, and the company was her first home since coming back from Afghanistan. Beckett was a learn-by-experience kind of teacher: he was letting her take lead on the job, watching and gently correcting from the sidelines when she stumbled.

The protest mob was marching in and would be stationed in full force by the time her team left the building. Charlie measured about twenty feet of pavement outside of One Cabot's revolving door, in front of a U-shaped driveway. If the protesters moved all the way up, she'd have to run a packed but brief gauntlet on the way to the escape vehicle.

On the other hand, just one or two stragglers standing out in the driveway could form a human barrier and make it impossible for their ride to even get close. More distance to walk, more danger, more chances for somebody to do something stupid.

"Move up now," Charlie said. "Pull the SUV as close to the doors as you can manage, and keep it idling. There are two dozen companies working out of this building. If anybody asks who you're waiting for, just make up a name. We'll ping you when we're coming out."

"Roger," Dom said.

Beckett showed his approval with stone-faced silence. The radio host's voice had gone up two octaves in the last ten seconds while Lincoln kept up his smooth, smirking patter.

"There you go again," he said. "I never once said the words *African American*, and you can replay the tape for yourself. White people can wear saggy pants and listen to rap music, too, you know. And who doesn't enjoy fried chicken? Any mention of race was purely your imagination, and I have to say, your liberal bias is really showing here."

"I'm a *Republican*—" the host said, sounding like he was about to jump over the table. "No, you know what? Sally? Cut his mic. We're done here. Cut his mic."

"I love this job," Charlie muttered.

Beckett made a sound in his throat, a tiny *hn*.

"What?" she said.

He studied her, inscrutable.

"You really do, though," he said.

She looked to the wall of glass and the gathering crowd beyond the revolving door. They were pumping each other up, ready to vent their righteous rage. Some brandished signs, mottoes like **NO HATE IN MEDFORD** and THIS IS NOT THE LAND OF LINCOLN.

Most protests ended without a single violent incident. Most of them, but you never knew which one would careen off the rails until the moment it was going down. Just like most of Charlie's patrols, back in the lethal dust bowl she still caught herself, now and then, calling *home*. The old familiar feeling surged back now, the adrenaline-charged vigilance, the electric wire in her veins. She knew this sensation of surfing a wave of pure chaos, mastering the flow while it bucked against her board and tried to throw her into the abyss.

She answered Beckett with a small toothy smile.

"Hn," he said, folding his arms.

Lincoln Gable emerged from the back hallway, looking like a politician on a smash-hit reelection campaign. Charlie half expected him to hold up his hands and flash victory signs.

"Was I amazing," he said, "or was I amazing?"

Mission time. Charlie snapped to attention, and Beckett was already moving, angling for the revolving door.

"Mr. Beckett will take the lead," she told Lincoln. "Sir, you stay close to me. I'll be at your left shoulder at all times. The SUV is waiting out front; he'll open the back door, you'll get inside, and he'll follow you in while I circle around the vehicle. Understood?"

"Yeah, sure, got it. But honestly, wasn't I great?"

She clamped a hand on his shoulder and steered him to the exit.

They saw him coming. A chant went up from the crowd, the sound bubbling up like water getting ready to boil. Beckett used his body like a moving wall. He emerged from the lobby and bulled the protesters back with his sheer force of presence. Charlie stood five feet, two inches; she had to make up for her lack of size with attitude. As the crowd parted, forming a tight gauntlet on either side of the pavement—*punching range,* she calculated, *stabbing range*—she held up her ID card.

"Make way," she called out over the chant, strident. "Anyone interfering will be arrested for trespassing and assault and prosecuted to the full extent of the law."

Asset-protection work was a bluffing game. Bodyguards weren't cops; they were private citizens with no special powers. Then again, she hadn't said *she* would be arresting anybody. As they waded through the crowd, the SUV idling at the curb twenty feet ahead, Charlie checked hands and faces. Mostly the faces. She figured these were good people doing what they thought was right, but crowds were dangerous creatures. Crowd energy could push a person over the top, make people do things they'd never do alone, turn anger into action.

Not all the shouts and abuse were for Lincoln. People were shoving fingers into her face, telling her she was complicit, a fascist. The words washed off her like water; she couldn't even hear them as she slipped into mission mind, the sounds taking on the high-pitched whine of searing eardrums after a bomb blast.

She broke the world down into perfectly divided segments, wedges of a pie. Each wedge was a stream of data points and indicators, trends in motion, pinpoint signals buried in static noise. Charlie had been trained for this. The same hyperfocus that had taught her to spot IEDs in Afghanistan and go head-to-head with professional bombers went to work on the crowd, hunting for threats and putting her body and mind in reaction mode. Different battlefield, same set of skills. The average assassination attempt lasted five seconds from start to finish. When things went wrong, they went wrong fast.

Movement at ten o'clock, ahead and to the left. Things were going wrong, right now, and the five-second stopwatch was ticking.

His face stood out from the rest. Grim, determined, silent. He had the expression of a man who'd made a decision and committed himself to it, no matter the consequences. He cut through the crowd like a surgeon's scalpel, not looking at the people he shouldered aside as he made a beeline straight for Lincoln Gable.

He had a tube in his hands. Foot and a half long, white plastic, his hands clutching it in a shaky white-knuckle grip.

The idea of anyone hating a hack pundit to the point of wanting to die with him was insane, unthinkable, but Charlie had to work with the facts in evidence, not the facts she wanted. The facts said *pipe bomb, PVC, homemade*. The facts told her how much of a payload a device that size could carry and what its shrapnel could do when it ripped through a tightly packed crowd, especially if he'd mixed broken glass or nails in with the powder.

Battlefield math. If that weapon detonated, most of the people in this crowd would never go home again. Charlie didn't make a conscious decision. There was only one choice to make, the one that shoved Lincoln aside, shouted a warning to Beckett, and propelled her through the crowd like a torpedo in water. She hit the bomber in a full-on tackle and hauled him down to the pavement.

The pipe nestled hard against her belly. Maybe she had enough flesh and bone to muffle the explosion and save everyone else. She'd die, but twenty people would live. Battlefield math. She clenched her jaw and braced herself, preparing for the blast.

Two

The pipe bucked under Charlie's stomach, and one end blew free, the PVC cap hitting her chin with the force of a boxer's punch and slicing open a cut. Then the world turned hot pink.

Glitter. A whirlwind torrent of it, blasting in her face, whipping all around her in a shimmering tornado.

Later, back at headquarters, they'd deconstruct the device. It was surprisingly sophisticated: a spring-loaded cap on a timer, a battery-powered fan to drive the payload, concealed blow-open vents all around the tube to ensure maximum dispersal. Charlie's act of heroism guaranteed that most of the glitter—two pounds—unloaded all over her.

She knelt on the pavement in a neon-pink puddle, stunned, clutching the empty tube while blood from the cut on her chin trickled down her neck.

The crowd's energy burst like the glitter bomb, spraying in all directions. People who'd thought they wanted blood lost their appetite now that they actually saw a little. Others, on the edge of the scene, had mistaken the bang of the tube for a gunshot; they were running, stampeding across the parking lot in all directions while building security swarmed from the glass doors. Charlie's vision was a wet blur. She saw someone in a brown uniform shirt grappling with the glitter bomber, twisting him into a headlock.

Dom had gotten out of the SUV. Breaking regulations, but the rule book was officially out the window. All she cared about now was getting her team out of there. She was throwing punches, her jet-black ponytail whipping the air, as she cleared a path and hauled Charlie up by one arm. Thirty seconds later they had all piled into the vehicle, Beckett and Lincoln in back, Charlie riding shotgun and leaking glitter everywhere. Dom stomped on the gas and pulled out with a squeal of tires.

"Beckett," Dom said. "Tissue?"

He passed up a folded cotton handkerchief. Dom pressed it into Charlie's shaking hand.

"Here. Chin, hon. You're bleeding."

She had barely noticed. She had just been down on the pavement getting ready to die and couldn't quite believe she was still breathing.

"I thought it was real," she said, her voice coming out as a whisper.

"I know you did." Dom shot her a feral grin. "Crazy bitch."

Charlie pushed the handkerchief against her chin, stanching the cut. Pink shimmers clung to the cotton like an invading virus. She rubbed her other hand against her leg. The glitter refused to budge, coating her in a neon field of stars.

"Wow," Lincoln said, staring at her. "Thank you."

She tried to muster a few scraps of dignity.

"Glad to be of service, sir."

"I mean," he said, breaking into a shaky laugh, "you look *ridiculous*. God, imagine if that happened to me—it'd be all over the internet. I'd be mortified."

"Sir—" Beckett said.

Charlie's lips pursed. She could taste the glitter. Dom shot a razor-edged glare at the rearview mirror.

"It's going to take you hours to get that off. And they were all recording. You're probably going viral right now—"

"Sir," Beckett said. "I need you to stop talking now, for your own safety."

Lincoln tilted his head. "My safety?"

"Yes, sir. Because if you don't stop talking, we're going to pull over. And I'm going to hold your arms while my partners take turns punching you. Then they're going to hold your arms while I punch you."

Lincoln blinked.

"You . . . ," he said, as if his words were treading on ice, "can't . . . talk to me like that."

Beckett stared at him, dead silent.

"I'll drop you off at home," Dom said to Charlie.

Home had a way of shifting out from under Charlie's feet. Overseas, her talents as an explosive-ordnance specialist had been in high demand; the army had shuffled her from one forward base to another, never letting her linger long enough to get used to the local sights. Then she'd come home and landed in her childhood bedroom as a guest under her father's roof. Her friend Dutch had told her she needed to get some city around her, that she was a turtle without a shell. He wasn't wrong.

So a week ago she'd gone hunting, and she'd signed the lease on a one-bedroom apartment in Allston that same afternoon.

Allston was a college neighborhood. One of her neighbors, a scruffy kid with a man bun, was lugging a broken-legged chair out to the curb. He caught a glimpse of her, turned, and stared.

"Must have been a hell of a party," he said.

"Oh yeah," Charlie said, trudging past him and leaving a trail of pink sparkles in her wake. "Epic."

The apartment building, just off Brighton Avenue, had gone up in the forties. Her unit was aggressively beige, with faded hardwood floors and light sconces shrouded under scalloped, flowery glass. A vintage steam radiator squatted at the edge of the living room, and if she wanted air-conditioning, she'd have to wrestle a window unit into place.

Decorating was a low priority, someplace behind buying actual furniture. The only thing in her bedroom was a cheap standing lamp and an air mattress.

She tracked more glitter into the kitchen, where she grabbed a yard-size trash bag and stood on it while she shucked her clothes off. Everything went into the bag; she'd figure out how to decontaminate her outfit later. Her next stop was the bathroom. Twenty minutes of scrubbing sent a stream of pink swirling around the drain like the shower scene from *Psycho*. Charlie got out and rubbed a towel through her blonde hair, feathery and cut collar length, regulation short out of habit. She stared at the streaks of glitter left behind and got back into the shower for round two.

While they kept a small office in the city for entertaining clients, Boston Asset Protection made its real home on the back stretch of an industrial park out in Cambridge. A parking lot snaked between lanes of big warehouses. Most of the buildings had their faces bare, nothing but a number over the door and a discreet company logo in one corner of the eaves.

Charlie's engine made a dangerous wet cough as she pulled into a spot and killed the ignition. She'd been driving her father's ancient pickup until it had breathed its last. She'd traded in a chunk of her savings down at a used-car lot, and the only solution she could afford wasn't much of an improvement. Her new ride was a silver 2009 Nissan Sentra; the chassis trembled in fear when she pushed it over seventy miles an hour, but at least the car got her around.

Headquarters was built for function over form. The lobby furniture came from hotel sales, each chair from a different establishment. At some point the owners had ordered a renovation of the building's shell and then frozen progress when the money had gotten tight. That was five years ago now, and half of the drywall shells were still torn down, exposing wooden ribs and bare wiring along the entry hall. The receptionist, a young woman with cornrows and sharp almond eyes, looked up from her paperback novel and gave Charlie a wave.

"Hey," Charlie said. "Dom and Beckett get back yet?"

"Couple of hours ago. I think Dom's on the shooting range. Beckett's in Jake's office. They've got a potential client."

Charlie furrowed her brow. "Here? They didn't take 'em to the *nice* office on Newbury?"

"Guess it's super serious." She put on a stern face and pressed a finger to her lips. "Super secret. Shh."

"My lips are sealed," Charlie said. She delved into the labyrinth. The corridors of HQ were a trackless mess, without any signage or sense of direction, the mostly empty rooms given random purpose whenever they were needed. Learning the construction debris was the best way to get around. She'd memorized, for example, the big spool of bright-blue wire lying on the dusty carpet at the end of one particular T junction. Left went to Jake's and Sofia's offices, the sibling owners positioned across the hall from one another, and right led to the range and the semiofficial briefing room.

She turned right. She'd taken two steps before a door swung open behind her, and Beckett poked his head into the hallway.

"Little Duck," he said. "Need you in on this."

He closed the door behind her. She knew three of the four people in Jake Esposito's office. Jake sat behind his slim, spartan desk—no knickknacks or family photos on the dark-grained wood, just business. The only family he needed was sitting in a chair in the corner. Sofia had a legal pad on her lap, and it looked like she'd already written a book's worth of notes. Beckett preferred to stand, towering next to a battered filing cabinet.

The newcomer was a woman in her fifties, hair gone the gray of railroad steel and pulled into a bun. She was razor thin, and the shoulders on her blazer could cut glass. Her gaze swept over Charlie, one brisk head-to-toe glance, like she could take the other woman's measure in a heartbeat.

"This is Sergeant Charlene McCabe—" Jake said.

"Retired," Charlie added. Her gaze dipped to the floor.

The woman gave a firm nod. "Thank you for your service."

"Charlie helped us with a very delicate job involving a mining-company executive facing multiple assassination attempts," Jake said. "The situation was resolved with no loss of life."

Not true. The final tally was more like two dead by gunshot, one impaled on a rusted fender, and one blown to pieces by her own bomb and scattered across a stretch of desolate junkyard. But none of the victims was the client, and the client only had nice things to say about Boston Asset Protection.

The fact that they could have sent him to prison for the rest of his life with a single phone call might have had something to do with that. At the end of the day, clean or dirty, a win was a win.

The woman extended her hand. She had a firm, dry grip.

"Shannon Poole," she said. "District attorney for Suffolk County."

Super serious, the receptionist had said. That was one way to put it. Charlie held her silence and stood in Beckett's shadow, trying to fade into the scenery.

"I'll bring you up to speed," Poole said. "Are you familiar with the East Boston Three?"

Charlie didn't see how anybody couldn't be, not unless they were living under a rock. The story had been front-page news for two weeks running.

"Sure. Three cops, all Easties. Running a strong-arm ring in their off hours. Started by knocking over backroom poker games; then they graduated to hitting stash houses."

"Then they graduated to murder," Poole said. She reached down to the alligator-skin attaché at her side and slid out an unlabeled folder. She lined her side of Jake's desk with glossy photographs, the ghosts of a crime scene. Charlie wasn't fazed by the dead bodies, the spatters of blood drying on a filthy gray carpet. She'd seen more than her share of violence out in the world, up close and personal. Each shot captured a corpse or two, maybe five or six in all, a few from multiple angles. She had to count by the victims' clothes since some didn't have faces anymore. The man slumped in the doorway with most of his head gone, nothing but broken-bone confetti and gray jelly, didn't bother her too much.

The two teenage girls, laid out side by side with their hands zip-tied behind their backs and their throats slit—that was a little harder to take.

"Dealer's house on Saratoga Street," Poole said. "The gang's MO was to hit their targets under the guise of delivering a no-knock warrant. They wore raid gear, full uniforms and vests, with balaclavas to hide their faces. Nothing strange, not to the kinds of people they targeted. They surrendered without incident, expecting to be arrested, and watched the cops walk away with their cash. Same method, every single time."

"Until . . ." Beckett said.

"Until Saratoga Street. They'd inflicted some damage before, beat up any victims who resisted, pistol-whipped one and gave him a skull fracture, but never anything like this. Our best guess is the victims put up a fight and managed to pull one of the perps' masks off."

"They couldn't risk being identified," Charlie said.

"Exactly," Poole said. "So they took control of the house, rounded up the survivors, including a pair of high school students, bound them, and executed them."

"You caught up to 'em, what, a month later?" Jake asked.

Poole nodded. "That was good detective work. Our people focused on the drug angle. We weren't sure the perpetrators were really police, or just thugs wearing fake uniforms—we thought, *hoped*, they were impersonators—but we knew they'd have to turn the stolen property into cash."

A new photograph slid over the others. Where it fell, it almost blotted out the dead girl on the floor. Almost. One scarlet-spattered sneaker stayed in view, poking at the corner of the tilted frame.

The man in the mug shot hadn't been sleeping, judging from his bloodshot eyes and drooping, stubble-flecked face. He wore his hair in a careless shag.

"Informants pointed to this man, Hayden Cobb. Cobb is a local dealer, strictly small time, mostly selling weed to a college crowd; he ran a grow operation in his basement."

"Pot's legal, though," Jake said.

"An *unlicensed* grow operation," Poole said. "Recreational marijuana may be legal in Boston, but you still have to pay your taxes. At any rate, he had been asking around, trying to find a buyer to take a bindle of heroin off his hands."

"Let me guess," Charlie said. "The dealer on Saratoga Street was into heroin."

"According to Cobb, yes. We took him in, sat him under a heat lamp, and he rolled over in a heartbeat. Cobb admitted he was the ring's inside man, their source for underworld targets. He'd scout out juicy opportunities and pass them along. If the heisters grabbed any drugs, he'd sell them and split the cash. Cobb gave up Lieutenant Gimondi, his point of contact. We kept it quiet and checked out everybody close to Gimondi, mostly watching their bank accounts for inexplicable deposits or splashy purchases. That gave us Kellogg and Vargas, the other two officers in the gang."

Poole's thin hand slid across the photographs. She racked them up like a dealer squaring a deck of cards, then made them vanish back into her folder.

"The East Boston Three are facing a joint trial," Poole said, "and it begins next week. Cobb has agreed to testify in exchange for immunity and relocation."

"He set up a home invasion that ends in multiple homicides, and he gets to walk?" Sofia asked. She'd been scribbling down notes, circling key words in boxes.

"He says he didn't know they'd ever get that violent, and I believe him. Yes, in an ideal world, he'd be going down right beside the others, but what matters isn't what's right. What matters is what I can sell to a jury. What we have, without Cobb's testimony, is a platter of circumstantial evidence. Compelling, but circumstantial. He can make my case a slam dunk."

"So where do we come in?" Charlie asked.

"What I'm going to tell you does not leave this room."

It wasn't a request. It was a certainty, delivered in a tone that tolerated no dissent. Poole rested her hands flat on her knees.

"The East Boston Three is actually the East Boston Four," Poole said. "There was a fourth member of the ring, never identified, presently at large. And with his accomplices' futures hanging on Hayden Cobb's testimony, he has every reason to kill the man. I need you to keep Cobb alive until the trial, by any means necessary."

THREE

"It's not that we *can't* do the job," Jake said, cagey now.

Charlie knew how much he hated turning away business. When she'd joined up with the company, Boston Asset Protection had been on its last legs, down to a single client and looking at closing up shop. Their success with Deep Country Mining had brought in a batch of new work; Sean Ellis, Deep Country's founder, had been singing their praises all over town. The word *blackmail* had never been spoken, but the fact that Charlie could send him to prison with a single phone call had ensured his glowing reviews. That said, they weren't all the way out of the red just yet, and every contract mattered.

"But isn't this more of a witness protection thing?" his sister added. "You mentioned relocation—"

"I had to dangle a few plump carrots to get Cobb's full cooperation," Poole said. "WITSEC was one of them. He gets a clean slate, the full relocation package, a new name, and a new life selling doughnuts in Albuquerque, *after* he testifies. Up until that point I can yank the deal at my discretion. He's terrified for his life right now, which is exactly where I want him: more afraid of me than he is of his former partners."

Something must have shown on Charlie's face. The DA gave her a sidelong glance.

"The citizens of Suffolk County don't pay me to be nice," she said. "They pay me to get results."

"You need us to babysit your witness and deliver him to court on time," Sofia said.

"After which I hand him over to the US Marshals, and he is no longer our problem. Normally I'd assign this to the Bureau of Investigative Services, but you see my dilemma."

"You've got a fox in the henhouse," Jake said.

"The fourth man is a police officer. Most likely working out of District A-7 in East Boston, like the other three, but there's no guarantee of that, and I can't risk it, which is why I'm here. Until the fourth man is identified—and I can't tell you how much I hate saying this—I can't entrust Cobb's safety to anyone wearing a badge. Can you help me?"

Jake and Sofia shared a glance. Something wordless rippled between them, sibling telepathy. Jake looked to Beckett.

He responded with what might have been a nod. Almost too small, too quick, to notice.

"We can help," Jake said.

"You've got no leads on this 'fourth man'?" Charlie asked. "How do you know he exists?"

"Witnesses from the earlier crime scenes," Poole said. "These guys wore balaclavas, moved fast, aimed for maximum chaos, but victims reported seeing four masked cops on the scene. One covered the exit; one covered the victims; the other two scooped up the loot. Once we brought in the three we could identify, they all clammed up tight. You can't break veteran cops like you can break a civilian: they know all the interrogation-room tricks because they use them for a living, and they also know the score. The absolute best they could get by rolling on each other is a reduction in their sentences. They get out of prison in fifty years instead of a hundred and twenty. Not a great deal. On the other hand, if they stay quiet, and if their buddy manages to put Cobb in the ground before he testifies, decent chance they all walk free. I'd roll those dice."

"We're going to need to pull a disappearing act," Sofia said. "I assume we'll be reporting to you and you only?"

"Me and one other," Poole said. "ADA Felton is handling second chair for the prosecution, so we'll both need access to Cobb for trial prep. No worries, he's been with me for years. He's rock solid. No one else, not even other people from my office, and absolutely no one in the Boston PD, is to know Cobb's location."

Beckett broke his silence. "Where is he now?"

Poole looked like she'd bitten into something sour.

"My house, out in Brookline. Safest place I could stash him in the short term, which doesn't mean it's safe. If it's possible to relocate him today, that'd be for the best."

"Today?" Jake's eyebrows lifted. "I mean, I suppose we could possibly arrange coverage by . . ."

He looked to Beckett.

"Two hours," Beckett said.

"Two . . . hours?" Jake echoed, uncertain.

Beckett held up a pair of manicured fingernails.

"Okay," Jake said. "He says we can start in two hours. Better let them get to it. Ms. Poole, if you'd like to step into the other office with me, we can go over the contract and billing paperwork . . ."

He eased her outside. As soon as the office door closed again, Sofia tugged down her cat-eye glasses and fixed Beckett with a hard stare.

"Two hours? Really? For planning, prep, staffing, and execution?"

"Diamonds are forged under pressure," he replied.

"That's just great, hon. You should have warned me—I would have jammed a lump of coal up my ass before we started this meeting, and I'd be rich now."

"The client's unusual, but the job isn't," he said. "I already know a place we can stash Cobb. It's a spot I've used before. Quiet, out of sight, and the owner knows a trick: he goes deaf and blind if you pay him twenty dollars."

"Neat trick," Sofia said.

"And a rare one. We can get moving right away, and me and Charlie can handle the first shift. That buys us another eight hours of fine-tuning the plan and working out the details."

"You make it almost sound reasonable."

"I'm a reasonable man."

"What about the Lincoln Gable assignment?" Charlie asked. "We'll have to hand that off to somebody else."

Beckett's chuckle had a basso rumble to it. A momentary flare of hope sank with the sound.

"Oh, no, Little Duck. Gable only needs minding when he's out on his book-tour stops, and he doesn't have another one for a couple of days. Plenty of time for us to sort out the staffing and make sure we have coverage on Cobb. We'll pull a double shift and take care of both assignments."

"But . . . we *could* hand him off," she said.

"Start a job, finish the job."

"What do you need from me?" Sofia asked.

"A solid team. We keep two ops on him at all times, rotating shifts, we can do it with"—Beckett glanced to one side and down, calculating the hours—"let's say eight people, to pad in some emergency backup. Me, Charlie, Dom—just need five more. Nobody else at the shop should even know we got this job."

"Agreed. Anybody you *don't* want on the roster?"

Charlie and Beckett spoke at the same time: "Malloy."

"He used to work out of the A-7 before they kicked him out," Charlie said, "and he still brags about his friends on the force. For all we know, he was chummy with these guys."

Sofia's lips pursed in a tight line.

"But you want Dominica," she said.

"I do," Beckett told her.

"Who also used to work out of the A-7."

"If we handle this right, Malloy will never find out. And if he does, and he squawks about it . . . well, if he's unhappy about the preferential treatment, maybe he shouldn't have gotten Dom fired in the first place."

"Boston PD's loss *was* our gain . . ." Sofia sighed. She turned to Charlie. "Sweetie, did you get your LTC renewed?"

"Came in two days ago," Charlie said. "I'm fully licensed to carry."

"Good. You're all going armed on this job. That's a direct order, from me."

"I'll get her kitted out," Beckett said.

"Do it quick," Sofia said. "Clock's ticking."

Charlie and Beckett kept their voices low as they navigated the maze of twisting hallways. There weren't many employees on site—almost everyone was out on a job or at home, waiting for a call-up—but they didn't want to blow the game before the opening whistle.

"Thinking about something," Charlie said, shooting a glance over her shoulder. "There's a problem with the setup."

Beckett's silence hung in the air between them, inviting her to fill it.

"Discovery," she said. "Each side in a criminal trial has to reveal their witness list. If the East Boston Three—Four—didn't already know Cobb snitched on them, they do now. If they have any kind of inside reach, avenues of intel inside the DA's office, the mystery fourth man could already be watching Poole's house. And considering Poole wants total compartmental security, even she thinks her office might be compromised."

"Watching, waiting for us to move him to a softer spot, make him an easier target," Beckett rumbled.

"I know you've got a secure place to stash him, but it's only as secret as the road to get there. We have to make sure our tracks are covered."

"Step ahead of you," he said.

"Figured you were, but I wanted to bring it up."

"Glad you did," he said. "You got a solution to go with that problem?"

"Sure, but I figure you already have one."

Beckett turned left at the next T junction. The doors to the firing range were up ahead, double thick and muffled with sound insulation.

"I want to hear yours," he said. "If it's a better plan than mine, we'll use it. If not, I'll tell you why."

They pushed through the double doors and into the vestibule. A plywood rack hung on one wall, orange plastic hearing protectors dangling from a dozen hardware-store hooks. They both grabbed a set and pulled them on before stepping into the range proper.

The crack of a bullet rang out through the cool stillness, turned flat and swallowed up by the gray acoustic tile lining the walls and ceiling. Dom was alone, standing in the middle of the three plywood booths, cradling her bolt-action rifle and taking a paper target apart one limb at a time. Charlie tasted the tang of gunpowder, hanging in the air like invisible smoke.

Crack. The headless, one-armed target lost a hand. Dom looked over from her work.

"Look who's all deglittered," she said.

"Almost," Beckett said.

One thick finger swiped at Charlie's bangs with a feather-light touch. A tiny dot of pink shimmered on the pad of his fingertip. She stifled a groan.

"We got a new client," Beckett said. "Want you on the team."

Dom shouldered her weapon, interested now. "Does that mean we get out of the Gable assignment?"

"Nope."

"Double shifts. You're talking about double shifts, at least two nights this week. I want to do that why? Don't say overtime, because hiring a babysitter eats most of that."

"It's an armed-carry job," Beckett told her.

Her dark eyes lit up. "I get overwatch? Long range?"

"Short range, small arms, close protective duty. But it's armed carry. If everything goes right, it's a cakewalk of a job. If anything goes wrong, good chance you get to shoot somebody."

"You're telling me it's a win-win."

As a general rule, Boston Asset Protection's employees didn't carry firearms. Beckett had laid down the law on Charlie's shakedown cruise: without the protection of a badge, professional bodyguards were just as criminally liable as any civilian—sometimes more so—if the bullets started flying. Outside of rare and special cases, it was safer to work without the risk.

This was a rare and special case. For Dom, who studied calibers and penetration ratings like some people studied baseball statistics, the assignment was like catnip.

Beckett ran Dom through the job while she put up her rifle and policed her brass, scooping up stray crumpled rounds and depositing them in a recycling bin.

"The stash pad," she said. "You're thinking about that no-tell motel in Southborough, just off the turnpike?"

"The tried and true."

"Quiet spot, easy to reach, half-decent Chinese takeout in walking distance . . . yeah, we can play babysitter for a week or so. That checks out." She looked to Charlie. "You get your papers in order?"

"LTC in good standing."

"I assume you need a loaner for the time being."

"Had a nice weapon," Charlie said. "Couple of 'em, in fact, but the army makes you give them back when you leave. They're particular about that kind of thing."

Dom waved her over to a long cabinet set into the back of the range, a combination-locked door shrouding a wall of firepower on wire hooks. The combo wheels spun under her fingertips with practiced speed.

"That's what you get for following the rules. Okay, I've got two suggestions for you, and you can't go wrong either way."

The lock's shackle popped open, and the doors swung wide. She gestured at a pistol on the far left, slim and sleek in shades of cool brown, like wet summer mud.

"You used to pack an M9 in uniform, right? Meet the Beretta M9A3. Same great flavor, slightly refined over the old A1. Universal slide, Picatinny rail for the optics system of your choice, and a seventeen-round magazine. If, on the other hand, you'd like to try something new . . ."

Dom's hand swept across the sea of steel, settling over a fatter, bulkier sidearm in midnight matte black.

"SIG Sauer P320. This one's chambered for .45 ACP, and it hits like a truck. My personal favorite, when I have to carry something for close-quarters protection."

Beckett peered at her. "When are you not carrying?"

"I mean professionally, for a job. My purse gun doesn't count. Neither does my ankle piece. Or my pigsticker. That's just an everyday self-protection loadout."

Charlie didn't hesitate. She pointed to the earth-tone pistol on the left.

"I'll take the Beretta. No time for training, and I want a weapon I'm familiar with."

"And sold," Dom said, "to the lady in the fashionable pink glitter. And speaking of 'no time' . . ."

Beckett's expectant gaze fell upon Charlie, waiting to hear her plan of attack.

Four

DA Poole did all right for a public servant. Her street in Brookline was paved with old money, and her house, a two-story gray stone Tudor with a circular driveway, had the feel of a family hand-me-down.

Dom's voice crackled out over the radio: "Prowl car reporting in. Street's clear, no movement. Convoy ready?"

"Convoy lead here," Beckett replied. "Convoy is go. We're stationed two blocks south."

"Evac ready?"

Armstrong was a lifer. He'd gone from security guard work to asset protection, and he'd probably be with the company until he was too old to walk. He wasn't a master of any particular skill, but he was a workhorse and game for anything.

"Evac lead here," he said over the radio. "Got some eager gentlemen in the foyer with me, all lined up and ready to roll. Say the word."

"Convoy," Dom said, "green light. Go, go, go."

"ETA one minute," Beckett replied. Then radio silence.

Sofia had scrambled a team, not the final roster for minding Hayden Cobb, just a motley crew of any employees they could call up on short notice. Most of them didn't need to know what they were doing here, and they were professional enough not to ask questions. One by one, a convoy of SUVs, picked up at the last minute from a Dollar Car Rental place near HQ, rolled up to the crest of the driveway in tight precision.

Charlie was driving the third vehicle. Kirby, one of the newer hires, rode shotgun. She didn't know a lot about the small, wiry man, but he'd worked a couple of jobs with Beckett, and Beckett said he was solid. He didn't make a lot of small talk, and she appreciated that. She was in mission mind, on patrol and on high alert as she eased to a stop in the driveway. They were sitting ducks out on the wide suburban street in civilian vehicles that might as well be made of paper if someone started shooting.

The house door flung open. Charlie's grip tightened on the steering wheel. If the fourth man had staked out Poole's house—if he'd found a sniper perch and was waiting, patient as a spider, for an easy shot at Cobb—this was the moment of truth.

Poole had lent a hand to pulling this plan off, bringing in two of her interns and a filing clerk who worked down the hall from her office. The criteria were simple: they just had to be men, Caucasian, in their twenties or thirties, with a roughly similar build. Armstrong sprinted out with the first one, bowed down low to make a smaller target, a windbreaker draped over his head with its empty sleeves flapping in the wind. Armstrong threw him into the back seat, and Beckett punched the gas, squealing out of the driveway and taking a hard right turn onto the street.

The convoy was already moving. Armstrong ran relay, back to the house, back out again with a second man under a second jacket to hide his face. The second SUV rocketed off, taking a left and veering off in the opposite direction.

Charlie's turn. She stomped the brakes right in front of the house. Kirby jumped out, opening up the back door just in time for Armstrong to shove their passenger inside. Three seconds later they were rolling. In the rearview, Charlie saw the final ringer sprinting to the final SUV, the finishing touch on the four-way evacuation.

"Did I do okay?" Hayden Cobb asked, head still covered in a baggy jacket. He lay flat along the back seat, like Armstrong had told him to.

"You did fine, sir," Charlie said. "Please stay down. And hold on; this is going to get a little bumpy."

It was almost her original plan. She'd proposed using multiple cars, to give anyone watching the house a serious problem. Now there were four vehicles on the move, each one with a maybe Cobb in the back seat, each going in a totally different direction, and a potential assailant would have to pick which one they wanted to chase. Beckett had pointed out a fatal flaw: her initial thought was to use their own personal vehicles.

"Opposition's a cop," he had reminded her. "Cops can look up license plates. He won't have to chase anybody: he can sit there, run all four, find out where we rest our heads at night, and come pay a visit at his leisure."

Going for rentals, paid for on a company card, added a second layer of insulation. Charlie's driving skills were the third. She knew how to throw a tail. She wound a serpentine path through the streets of Brookline, mixing up her turns, doubling back, scouting for familiar cars and faces trailing in their wake. It wasn't until she was 100 percent satisfied—and then another twenty minutes after that—that she hooked a right onto the four-lane stretch of Boylston Street and followed it west and then northbound, away from Boston, until she could jump onto the Massachusetts Turnpike half an hour later.

Beckett was already at the finish line. The plan had been for him to throw any tails of his own, drop his befuddled passenger off at the closest train station—with a hundred bucks cash in his shirt pocket, hazard pay—and meet up at the motel. Painted smoke wreathed the mountaintops on an embossed plastic sign out front, below mint-green script advertising the Pocono Motor Inn.

"Aren't the Poconos in Pennsylvania?" Kirby said. The first words he'd spoken all afternoon.

Charlie looked around as she pulled into a spot out front. One-story motel, flat land, grassy fields, and vacant lots. The only scenery around was the turnpike.

"Maybe they're going for irony," she said.

Beckett loomed in the doorway of room twelve, down at the far end of the lot. They scouted the scene one last time, then hustled Cobb inside. Once they got him behind closed doors and tight, dusty curtains, the only light coming from a dim lamp by the side of a queen bed, they gave him permission to take the jacket off his head.

He looked more or less like his mug shot. A couple of days scruffier and five years older, with sagging dark rings under his eyes. Being marked for death had a way of aging a man before his time. His gaze jumped around the room while his fingers played jittery piano chords on his hips.

"We cool?" he said.

"Will be. Have a seat."

Beckett gestured to a round side table and a couple of chairs. The decor was motel Americana, and everything that wasn't beige had faded flowers on it. A framed print on the wall depicted a mountain range in wispy oil. Maybe Mount Pocono. Charlie had never been there.

"This," Beckett told him, "is your world for the next week. You do not leave this room. You do not answer the door. You will be supervised twenty-four seven, and if you need anything, we will obtain it for you. The only way we can guarantee your safety is with your absolute compliance. Do we have it?"

The dealer's head bobbed, jerking on his scrawny neck.

"Yeah, I mean . . . yeah, of course. These guys are stone killers. I'm not looking to end up like those kids."

Cobb homed in on Charlie, carrying the edge of a plea in his voice. She wasn't sure why. Maybe he thought the only woman in the room would be a source of sympathy.

"I had no idea," he said. "I mean, I knew they could knock heads together; that's part of running a strong-arm crew. But I never thought they'd murder anybody. I never woulda shook hands with somebody like that. That's not me."

Charlie kept any hint of human feelings bottled down deep, professional distance clear from the tone of her voice. "We're not here to judge you, sir. Our job is to protect you until your trial date. Nothing more, nothing less."

"I'm just sayin'." He sagged a little in his chair. "That's not me."

Charlie thought nothing was more boring than stakeout duty. Babysitting duty proved her wrong. Being out and on the move with a client kept her brain engaged and her senses sharp; here, there was nothing to do but kill time. The minutes dragged on while Cobb watched daytime television, some kind of courtroom reality show where neighbors sniped at each other over petty offenses. Kirby read a dog-eared paperback, a lurid fantasy novel with a knight in green, curlicued armor on the cover. Beckett leaned against the wall and became part of it. A statue, motionless, eyes fixed on some invisible plane.

"Meditating?" Charlie asked him.

"Was," he said.

"Sorry."

Her phone rang. Dom on the line.

"Coming in," she said. "Got ADA Felton with me. All good?"

"All good," Charlie said, moving to the door.

Knocks, even distinctive ones, could be imitated. More importantly, an operative could be pressed into compliance with a gun to their back. *All good* was more than friendly familiarity; if Dom had ended with the words *Everything all right in there?* instead, it would have been a signal that she was under duress and the room's occupants needed to brace for a fight before opening up. If Charlie had changed her own wording, it would be a signal for Dom to fall back and call the authorities in.

She brought Felton in with her. Felton was *brisk*. Fast stride, fast eyes, his every movement calculated and spare. He opened up his briefcase and commandeered the motel room's table without a word, snapping his fingers at Cobb with one hand while laying out a stack of folders with the other.

"Mr. Cobb? Prep time. I need two hours, three at most. Today we'll go over groundwork for your testimony. I want to drill you on the basics of cross-examination so we can spot any trouble points and see what we need to work on."

As far as Felton was concerned, the bodyguards were invisible, irrelevant. He didn't ask for introductions, and Dom didn't offer him any. "You still need me to take over until next shift?" she asked Charlie.

"Is that okay? I've just got that errand . . ."

"Go," Dom said. "Long as you get back on time. The day care place charges me by fifteen-minute intervals if I'm late picking up Natalie. Worse than my damn divorce lawyer."

Charlie took the SUV back to headquarters and changed cars, hopping behind the wheel of her Nissan. It gave her a vaguely jealous sputter as it ferried her farther from the city to the rolling woodland and small-town ambience of Spencer. Down the block from the library, the old red brick pregnant with childhood nostalgia, stood the gray clapboard spire of a Presbyterian church. She found a spot at the curb, pulled up, and idled, waiting. The services in session weren't meant for her eyes to see.

Eventually the front doors opened, and a small pack of people, maybe eight or nine, filtered out into the afternoon sunlight. Her father ambled down the steps, hand cupped over his eyes, uncertain. She gave him a wave, and he spotted her, flashing a bashful smile.

This was hard for him, she knew. And he would have driven himself if his pickup hadn't breathed its last, ending its long life of service as a pile of rusted scrap. She was happy to help, but that didn't make asking for a hand any less embarrassing for him. All she could do, she figured, was stay supportive. All she had to do was drive; the real work was on his end.

He climbed in and gave her a quick one-armed hug. His face was still a patchwork of faded bruises gone saffron yellow, a couple of long scratches making railroad tracks across the bridge of his nose. Keepsakes from the leg breakers who had beaten him into a hospital bed over his unpaid gambling debts.

She'd taken care of the problem. He didn't know what she'd done, and he didn't ask. Someday they might talk about it. But not yesterday and not today.

"Things go all right?" she asked, checking the side mirror and pulling away from the curb.

"Eh, you know what they say. One day at a time. Y'know, we're not supposed to repeat anything that gets said in there—"

"Then you probably shouldn't," Charlie said, catching a faint glimmer of mischief in her old man's eye.

"But this lady. Swear to God. Scratch-off lottery tickets. Not thousands, not hundreds, just five a week. Five bucks' worth, every Friday afternoon like clockwork. I'm thinking, *Lady, the support group for obsessive-compulsive disorder is down the hall.* We already feel shitty enough about our past mistakes."

"One person's crisis," Charlie said. She figured there was another half to that saying, but she didn't know it, so she hoped the words spoke for themselves.

And he was saying *past mistakes*, not *present behavior*. That was something. Of course, he'd said those words before, on and off for most of her childhood and into her adult life. He was always done gambling for good until he got the itch again.

She couldn't afford cynicism this time. Not when he needed her most. She kept a smile on her face, even if she didn't feel real joy. For his sake.

"Need anything on the way home?" she asked. "Groceries?"

"Any chance we can stop at the packie?"

She gave him the side-eye. He flashed a smile, showing off his new dentures.

"Hey," he said, "let me beat one vice at a time."

They stopped on the way. Twice, once to pick up a case of beer, and once to stock up his kitchen pantry, over his protests. Charlie wasn't entirely sure her father knew how much food he really had, and she wasn't going to be able to take him shopping for another few days. She had double shifts to pull, two clients to juggle. At least one of them, if they'd done their job right today, wouldn't be any trouble at all.

She had just enough time to swing by her apartment, crash out on the air mattress, and steal a few hours of sleep. She had a long night ahead of her.

FIVE

Charlie pulled into the Pocono Motor Inn's parking lot five minutes ahead of schedule. She called ahead and confirmed it was all good, and Dom met her on the doorstep. She held up a hand, easing Charlie back. Then she closed the door behind her, muffling the sounds of a sitcom.

"Watch him," she said, voice hard.

"Which 'him' are we talking about?"

"Cobb. He says he's fine, he says he doesn't partake beyond a little bud, but I know the signs. He gets high on something harder than that."

"Is he itchy?"

"Highly, and he's just smart enough to know to try and hide it. I impressed upon him how little his life is worth right now, out on the street. Doesn't mean he still won't try to slip out and find a little arm candy if you give him half a chance."

"Never trust a junkie," Charlie said.

"Exactly. On the plus side, trial prep went fine—Felton left an hour ago—and other than him and Poole, looks like nobody in the world knows where Cobb disappeared to. Clean snatch. We keep it clean, we keep it quiet, and in one week, we get paid."

"Your lips to God's ears," Charlie said.

Dom kissed her fingertips and held them up to the darkening sky.

Kirby left early, called off to another assignment. Beckett had seen the same signs as Dom. He was trying to keep Cobb's mind occupied. Smart, but a losing proposition.

"This game is screwed up," Cobb was saying as Charlie came in. He fidgeted in his chair. "I mean, it looked simple, there's only one kind of piece, but this is some chess-level head game shit."

Beckett held up a single black stone.

"There are more possible moves in a game of Go," he said, "than there are atoms in the observable universe."

"How's anybody supposed to learn all those moves?"

"You aren't." Beckett placed his stone on the grid-lined board between them, boxing one of the white stones on all sides. He removed it from the fight. "This is a game of emergent strategy. Of adaptation to changing circumstances and working with the resources you have."

Cobb obviously wasn't a strategist. He drifted over to the bed, perching on the edge of the mattress with the TV remote in his shaky hand. Beckett and Charlie shared a glance. He knew Dom had talked to her outside, passed on the warning. They'd take shifts through the night, nothing she hadn't done a hundred times on patrol in the sandbox. She'd been smart this time and brought a deck of cards with her.

"You game?" he asked her, clearing the board with a slow sweep of his hand.

"Teach me how to play?"

He held up two stones, one white, one black, as she took Cobb's vacated chair.

Beckett didn't believe in taking it easy on a newbie. He let Charlie make mistakes, threw an army of stones to punish every misstep, then made sure she saw where she'd gone wrong. The first game was a muddy cluster at the heart of the board, a trench battle where her forces died in waves. She got more adventurous the second time around, sparking brushfire wars across the board in pockets of blazing white and black, forcing Beckett to manage five strategies at once. He still won, but she made him work a little harder for it.

"Rematch?" he asked, clearing the board.

She checked the time. Night had fallen. The curtains were drawn tight across the rectangle picture window, darkness beyond.

"Armies can't march on an empty stomach."

"Armies can't," Beckett said. "Soldiers can."

"True, but all the same, dinner?"

"Yes please," Cobb piped up from his perch on the mattress. He'd been glued to the TV set since he'd sat down.

"The ayes have it," Beckett said. He produced a long, thin paper menu. "Chinese place, not far from here. I've eaten there before."

"Good?" Charlie asked.

"It's fuel," he said.

Beckett jotted down their orders and left her in charge. She turned to the television screen. Cobb was watching a reality show, something about Staten Island housewives who were apparently all very rich and best friends, though much of the show involved screaming and throwing glasses of wine at each other.

"You, uh . . . do this a lot?" Cobb asked her.

"Hang out in strange motel rooms?"

"The bodyguard thing. You know. People like me."

Charlie half smiled at that. "You're in good hands. Don't worry. We'll keep you safe."

He fell silent. She thought he'd gone back to watching the show, but he was just looking for something to say.

"I really didn't want this," he said. "None of this. When I went into business with these guys, I . . . I didn't imagine it would turn out this way."

She didn't have anything to tell him. One of the first things Charlie had been taught, her first day on the job, was that generally only three kinds of people needed professional bodyguards: celebrities, scumbags, and celebrity scumbags. Learning to let go of moral judgments—or at least to swallow them down and keep them buried until the end of the gig—was a mandatory skill.

All the same, something in his eyes, something desperate and lost, made her dig for an answer.

"You can't undo what's been done," she said. "Those kids, the victims from the stash house on Saratoga . . . they're dead. They aren't coming back. That's forever. And you're going to have to find a way to live with that."

She was talking about his dead, but she was thinking about hers.

Charlie's first kills had been an ocean away. She couldn't even say how much blood was on her hands because she didn't really know. There had been a handful of engagements, spread across the course of her career on the battlefield. They'd all gone down the same: a flurry of movement, of rattling fire, throwing lead at blurry shadows in bombed-out buildings. Sometimes the fight had ended when she and her element had piled into Hummers and booked it for safer streets. Occasionally they'd hung around long enough to secure the territory. They'd counted the bodies, but bullets didn't have name tags. Charlie didn't know which of hers had landed in pockmarked concrete and which had found a home in a dead man's heart.

It was her job. She'd thought she was done with all that, coming home. Then she'd fallen into the Deep Country mess, caught between a man with a secret and a pack of aging revolutionaries, and discovered the job wasn't done with her. Maybe it never would be. Her life hadn't changed, just her flag of authority. Charlie was a mercenary now.

She was okay with that.

Cobb stared at the carpet. "I just . . . ," he said. Like there was supposed to be something after that.

"But here's what you can do," she told him. "You can testify. You can tell the truth, and you can put these guys away for a very, very long time so they can't hurt anybody else ever again. I won't say it'll make you feel better. Maybe it will; maybe it won't. And I sure as hell can't say it'll expiate your sins. You want expiation, talk to a priest or a therapist. But it's something you can do, and nobody else can."

That didn't seem to make him any happier, but she hadn't expected it would. *Happy* was a vague and nebulous thing. Duty was duty. Hard, tangible, real.

Her phone rang. Beckett, she expected, calling in for the check and countercheck before he approached the motel-room door.

"Trouble," he said.

She was up and moving, grabbing Cobb by the shoulder and pulling him to his feet.

"Bathroom," she told him. "Go in; close and lock the door behind you. Lay down in the bathtub, flat as you can, and stay there until I call you out."

Cobb had a hundred questions in his eyes, but he was smart enough not to waste time asking. The bathroom door swung shut behind him. The flimsy lock turned with a faint click.

"Was coming back with the food, spotted a prowler in the parking lot," Beckett said. "Might just be checking door handles, looking for an unlocked car with something easy to steal inside."

"But . . . ," Charlie said.

"It's just a feeling."

He didn't have to explain, not to her. Intuition was a gift. So was fear, and listening to that tiny voice saved lives.

"I'm circling around," he said. "If this is our guy and we can grab him tonight, I want him grabbed. Going to find a spot to park and move in on foot."

Charlie set aside the obvious burning question—*How the hell did he find us?*—and shrugged back her blazer, reaching for her calfskin shoulder holster. The pistol was new but felt just like her old service piece, a familiar and reassuring tool.

"What's my play here?" she asked.

"Sit tight; stay with the primary. Leave the phone on speaker. I'll let you know when I'm about to make a move."

She could do that. She set the phone out on the table.

Something moved behind the curtains. A shadow, rippling black on black.

Charlie hit the floor on both knees, going low and out of range. The lamp by the bedside turned the motel room into a light box: anyone in the parking lot would see a rectangle of glowing white behind the thin, chintzy curtains, with the silhouettes of anyone moving inside the room.

Her first instinct was to kill the light. Even out the battlefield, darkness on both sides of the window. But if she did that, the creeper would know he'd been made. If he was smart, he'd be long gone before Beckett circled back around. Besides, her partner might be counting on that light to pick out his target.

And if she could keep the stranger looking this way, trying to scope out the room, he'd be easier prey. Charlie scramble-crawled across the carpet, over to the bed. She snatched one of the pillows. Then, easing her way to the edge of the mattress and staying low, she held the pillow up in her outstretched hand.

To someone outside the room, it would be a murky blur, maybe a person, sitting on the mattress and then bending as the pillow flopped in her hand. Charlie waggled it like a red flag in front of a bull, fighting to hold the intruder's attention.

The bull charged with a black-powder roar, a basso high-caliber boom. A bullet plowed through the heart of the window, glass cracking like thin winter ice as the curtain tore, spitting strands of dusty fabric across the faded carpet. The slug ripped the pillow from Charlie's hand and landed a kill shot on the television screen. The TV shorted out in a blurt of squealing static and acrid gray smoke.

Charlie didn't return fire, not without being able to see what she was shooting at. She ripped the bedside lamp's plug from its outlet, drenched the room in darkness, and lunged for the door.

She had been hearing double, the boom of the gunshot matched by its tinny, softer twin rippling from her phone on the table. Now the speaker let out rustling sounds, heavy running footsteps.

"I'm in the lot," Beckett whispered, "hunkered down behind the minivan over by the manager's office. Check your fire."

"Movement?" she whispered back.

"Nothing."

Charlie pressed her back to the wall, right beside the door, and reached for the dead bolt.

Six

Charlie flipped the dead bolt, grabbed the door handle, and braced herself.

She cracked the door, just an inch. She pressed herself pancake flat inside the doorway, the smallest target she could make herself, and angled the barrel of her pistol at the opening. All she saw were parked cars, the glow of the plastic mountains on the hotel sign, a few lonely headlights cruising along the turnpike. Down a few dozen feet, another door rattled open.

"*Sir,*" Beckett hissed from his firing position, "go back inside. Stay down. Police are on their way."

Sort of true. Even if nobody had called yet, they'd be here eventually. The shooter would know that too. She perked her ears, focused now, listening for footsteps in the murky dark. Nothing, just sparse, distant traffic and the rustle of the wind.

Her move.

She pushed the door wider, darkness at her back, and leaned out just far enough to scan the lot. She spotted Beckett's wide shadow off to the right, huddled behind the hood of a minivan. She had a horizontal slice of the lot in her sights; he had the vertical. Nowhere for the shooter to hide.

They weren't hiding. They were running. And with open fields and vacant lots surrounding the motel for a quarter mile, they had their pick of escape routes. She stayed put a little longer, a sentinel statue, just to be certain.

Lights flashed in the distance. Someone—another guest, the manager—had called the cops. If the shooter wasn't long gone, they would be now. Charlie figured they had five minutes, six tops, before the first squad cars rolled into the lot. That was five minutes to gather any intel they could and sort out an emergency plan.

Intel first. Charlie snatched up her phone and held her breath as she stepped out into the lot. She clicked her light on and scanned the scene, strobing her beam along the fractured window. Then the parked cars, the black asphalt, hunting for anything out of place.

Beckett jogged up. His beam of light joined hers, falling into synchronicity.

"Primary intact?"

"He's fine," she said. "Any idea which way the shooter ran?"

"He didn't get past me, so—"

The far side of the motel, then. Charlie muffled her light against her chest, pausing at the corner where the pavement wrapped around the rough brick wall. She scouted a quick look, careful, before stepping around.

"Only two people knew, besides us," Charlie said.

"Poole and Felton. DA's office has a leak."

"And it could be the DA. Think she set us up to fail?"

"Looking for a motive, but I'm not seeing it," Beckett said.

"Somebody's got one."

Charlie's light fell upon a fallen gun.

The shooter had abandoned their weapon, dropping it to the pavement as they fled into the night. It was a dull and tarnished .38, a fat revolver with walnut grips. And it was completely wrong.

"Don't touch it," Beckett warned her. "Leave it for the police."

"Why a .38?" She looked to her partner.

"Why leave it behind?"

"No," she said, "why that gun? You can't put a sound suppressor on a revolver. It's loud, it's crude . . . that's not a hitter's gun."

"It's a cop's gun," Beckett said.

"You know the last person in the world who would drop their weapon in a panic?" Charlie said. "A cop."

Sirens now, coming in fast, slicing down the time they had left. No time to debate. She let the gun hover in the back of her mind, a piece of the wrong puzzle, something to deal with later.

"Southborough PD's got nothing to do with the fox in Boston's henhouse," Beckett said, "but word travels fast. Our primary gets taken in for questioning, anything could happen by the time we get him back in our hands."

She knew what he was asking her to do. Trusting her to do. She also knew that fleeing the scene of an attempted murder was a crime.

All part of the job.

"Cover for us?"

"I was here all alone, all night," Beckett said.

"Alone," the uniform said to Beckett. "All night?"

"All night."

They stood in the doorway of the abandoned motel room. More cops were out in force, combing the parking lot, questioning the other guests. They'd already found and bagged the fallen .38. Light flashed in the corner of Beckett's eye, a crime scene tech snapping photos of the broken window.

"All night," the uniform echoed.

"Securing the room, waiting for a client to be delivered. The shooter jumped the gun; if he'd waited another hour, his presumed target would have been here."

The uniform looked past him, to the Go board and the mounds of colored stones.

"You usually play board games by yourself?"

"Keeps me sharp," Beckett said.

"I saw the bags in your car. That's a lot of food for one person."

Beckett leaned in a little. He had two inches of height on the cop and was probably twice as wide.

"I'm a growing boy," he said.

"And you're going to tell us who your client is."

It wasn't a question. Beckett answered by offering up a business card.

"That number gets you my employer and his legal counsel," Beckett said. "Which brings us to the end of our conversation."

Charlie drove as far east as Newton—a few miles west of downtown, in the shady tree-lined shadows of Boston College—before she ditched her car. There was a parking lot halfway down a sleepy restaurant-lined street, machine metered. She fed it her debit card and punched in eight hours' worth of time.

"Calling us a ride share," she said. Her phone said a Lyft could be there in three minutes. *Thank God for night owls.*

Cobb squinted at her. "We're parking your car and . . . taking another car?"

"The shooter had free rein of the parking lot. Which meant he had time to note down every plate number and VIN there, including mine. We need some distance."

"Where are we going?"

Good question. Almost as good as the one that had sent them fleeing their first safe house: *Who talked?* The fourth man, the last and only loose member of the strong-arm ring, had somehow known where to find them. He'd known Cobb would be in that room, and he'd come aiming to silence him before he could testify against his buddies. The evac from Poole's house had gone flawlessly, and Charlie knew damn well she hadn't been followed to the motel. The only answer was that somebody, somebody on the inside, had given them up.

She could trust—she had to trust—that everyone at the company was solid. Besides, they'd scrambled the mission in two hours flat. She didn't feel 100 percent sure about anyone but Beckett and Dom, but if there was a traitor inside the house, they wouldn't have had time to find the mysterious fourth man and sell Cobb out.

That left the DA's office. Poole or her assistant, Felton. Of course, that didn't mean they were knowing conspirators. One loose-lipped conversation, one email sent across a compromised server, and they might have betrayed Cobb without even knowing it.

They needed to find the source of the leak, one way or another, or this would just happen all over again. And next time, the shooter would be more careful.

First things first. She needed an answer to Cobb's question. While they waited at the curb, her sharp eyes fixing on every late-night car that prowled past, she was hunting for a place to stash him.

The car showed up. She hustled Cobb in back and followed him in.

"I need to change our destination," she said. "That okay?"

It was, only grudgingly. She told the driver to bring them to Farlow Park.

He dropped them off at the edge of the grounds. Farlow was a wide, lush green surrounding a softly burbling pond; the lawns wrapped around a colonial-style church at the far corner of the lot.

"We're not sleeping on a park bench," Cobb said, sounding like he wasn't so sure.

Charlie had abandoned the idea of sleeping tonight entirely. She led him along the sidewalk, taking a right at the church and heading north.

"Just in case somebody gets access to the driver's records," she said, "I didn't want him dropping us off at our final destination. From here, we go on foot."

They headed two blocks north until the sky vanished under the looming shadow of the turnpike. On the other side, they made it to the warm glow of the Crowne Plaza. The long, thin hotel bore oddly lopsided stonework, rooms recessing and jutting out here and there like a twelve-story game of Jenga. The lobby was warm, everything in shades of butter and brown, and the night clerk greeted them with a questioning smile.

"We need a room, please, for . . ." Charlie paused. She wasn't sure whether to plan on keeping Cobb locked down here for the rest of the week or if staying mobile would be safer. For now, she split the difference. "Two nights."

The clerk smiled and checked her screen. "Excellent. We have a standard room with a king, or—"

"Two beds, please."

Part of her was still standing on the pavement outside the Pocono Motor Inn. The abandoned pistol nagged at her. Not nearly as much as the knowledge that they'd been set up. Cobb wasn't done with trial prep. Maybe as soon as morning, the DA's office would come calling, expecting to know his new address.

"Actually," Charlie said, "could I get two rooms?"

"Adjoining? I can see what we have."

"Separate. At least two floors apart from each other."

The clerk's eyes drew an uncertain line between her and her silent friend. Cobb was shifting his weight from foot to foot, one hand scratching his hip, antsy. She looked back to her screen and typed a few keystrokes.

"Sure," she said. "We can do that for you. We have one room on the seventh floor and a second one on the fourth, both double queens."

Charlie slid her debit card across the counter.

"Don't want to seem ungrateful or anything," Cobb told her, alone in the elevator, "but we never did actually get to eat dinner."

She'd been too fired up, fed by adrenaline, to notice. In the aftermath of their escape, fresh hunger crept its way in. There was a restaurant downstairs, but she couldn't take him with her—Cobb needed to disappear, now more than ever—and she couldn't risk leaving him alone while she went out to find food.

"Room service," she said. "We'll see if they have room service."

They did. Up in room 7017—comfortable, clean, more shades of warm brown and gold, and a view of the turnpike's winding ribbon from their darkened window—they glanced over a paper menu. The kitchen was open for another hour. Charlie winced at the prices—*fourteen bucks for a salad?*—and her new friend wasn't helping.

"I'll have the braised short ribs," he said.

"Do you *want* the short ribs," Charlie asked, "or are you just ordering the most expensive thing on the menu?"

"Can I get the herb-and-parmesan free-tays with that?"

Frites, she thought. *Sure, it's only an extra seven dollars. Company had better be reimbursing me for this.*

She was still deciding what she wanted when she phoned the order in. She was tempted to go the opposite route and grab the cheapest snack on the list to keep her card from burning up, but her body needed fuel, and there was no telling how long she'd have to stay in motion. Or when she'd have the time and opportunity to eat her next meal.

"Could I also get the bacon-bleu burger?" she said to the kitchen receptionist. "Do fries come with that? Great. And a Diet Coke, please."

"That stuff'll kill ya," he said as Charlie hung up the phone.

She stared at him.

"Preservatives," he said. "You know the preservatives in diet soda are, like, one molecule removed from formaldehyde? Same stuff they put in dead bodies."

"I'm not sure that's true." She started to turn, then paused. "Also? You're a drug dealer."

He almost looked hurt. "Hey, marijuana and mushrooms are pure and natural. They come from the earth. They're *organic*."

"Watch some TV and sit tight," she told him. "I need to check in with the boss."

SEVEN

Charlie stepped outside and shut the door behind her, muffling the sound of the television set. The hallway was a long, groomed stretch of empty road. She called Beckett and kept her voice down.

"One sec," he told her. "Patching Jake and Sofia in."

She heard a click. Sofia's voice washed over the line. "Oh. My. God. How ya doing, honey? Fingers and toes? Everything still attached?"

"I'm fine; primary is fine. I've got him stashed at a hotel. I also rented a decoy room—"

"Hold it," Jake said. "*Don't* tell us. We've got some kind of info leak here, and until we track it down, I want everything compartmentalized."

"The leak's not coming from our house," Beckett said. "You know exactly where it is."

"I know where we all think it is. Until I can run a sweep on the office lines, make sure we haven't been tapped, better safe than sorry."

"Charlie," Beckett said, "when we disconnect, text me a location. Hotel address, not room number. I'll be there directly, and I'll meet you in the lobby."

"Did the police give you any trouble?" Charlie asked.

"Trouble is like a gift. Someone can try to give it to you, but you're not always obliged to accept."

Room service came around. The man pushing the wheeled cart was young, lanky, draped in a white waiter's jacket with sleeves that hung a little too far past his wrists. Charlie was on high alert. She patted him down with her eyes, watching his hands as she jotted her signature on the bill. She kept him outside the room and sent him away with a cash tip. Charlie brought the trays in by herself and wouldn't let Cobb dig in until she'd checked them both for any sign of tampering.

"I don't think somebody followed us, disguised themselves as kitchen staff, and poisoned our food all inside an hour's time," he told her.

"You don't have to think," she said. "Thinking is my job."

She bit into her burger. Warm beef, a toasted bun, bleu cheese and bacon adding savory flavor as the patty's juices burst across her tongue. Nope, no poison here. She had to pace herself; she hadn't realized how hungry she was. The fries were thick and freshly made, topped with a sprinkling of parmesan, grated herbs, and a whisper of salt.

Her phone buzzed. Beckett had arrived. She wiped her mouth with a stiff paper napkin and left her meal half-eaten on the tray, rushing for the elevator.

"You did good," he said on the ride back up. "Decoy room was a smart choice."

"Well, figured we're going to have to give Poole *something* tomorrow. Worst-case scenario, we can arrange for Cobb and ADA Felton to do their warm-up routine in the room on the fourth floor. The DA's office doesn't have to know where we're really keeping him."

"Felton," Beckett said.

Charlie's partner was a man of few words, and she was getting better at hearing the ones he left unspoken. Felton had come over to the motel for trial prep. Felton knew exactly where Cobb was, and just a few hours after he'd left—long enough to sell him out—a killer had come around. Felton needed some hard looks.

"Could still be Poole, setting us up to fail," Charlie said.

The elevator chimed. The doors rumbled open onto the seventh-floor hallway, fresh-cleaned carpet under soft lights.

"But . . . ," Beckett said.

"She's got too much to lose. Only reason anyone in the DA's office would give Cobb up is because they took a bribe. Agree?"

"There are other forms of motivation," Beckett said as they stepped off, walking side by side. "Blackmail, leverage over a loved one. But Occam's razor says that good old-fashioned cash is usually the answer."

"This is a massive case. Big press coverage, and it's only going to get bigger next week when the joint trial gets rolling. Picture this: the star witness is murdered and the East Boston Three take a walk. Poole is up for reelection soon. How big of a bribe would it take to make her willingly blow this case?"

"And tank her own career? There's not enough green in the whole wide world," Beckett said.

"But Felton? He's an appointed prosecutor, and all he's expected to do is the best he can with the resources he has. As long as nothing connects him to Cobb's murder, losing this trial won't hurt him one bit."

"Could still be someone close to either one of them," Beckett said. "For that matter, could be somebody down in the IT department reading their interoffice emails. We have no idea what kind of internal discipline they're working with."

They came to the hotel-room door. Charlie waved her plastic card and beeped them in.

"Poole sounded pretty serious about security," she said.

"People can *sound* serious about anything," he replied. "What they do is what counts."

Having a second room gave them an added benefit when it came time to lock everything down for the night. While Cobb slipped off to dreamland behind the door of 7017, Charlie and Beckett threw rock-paper-scissors to see who took the first shift. Charlie picked scissors. Beckett picked rock and ambled down to 4205 for four hours of shut-eye while she stood sentry in the hall. This late at night the corridors were desolate, quiet save for the low and steady thrum of the air-conditioning. On the rare occasion some weary traveler came around the corner, Charlie used a technique Beckett had taught her: one quick eye frisk to check for obvious trouble, and then she kept her head down and her thumbs tapping at her phone. Just another piece of the landscape, carrying on an imaginary conversation in texts while she kept the passerby in her peripheral vision and watched their body language.

Eventually Beckett came back around. They swapped places. Charlie was bone tired. She kicked off her shoes and flopped onto the closest bed, not bothering to pull back the covers. Then she was gone. One of the military's unexpected gifts, not part of her official training, was the ability to fall asleep almost anywhere, anytime, in short and concentrated bursts. Twenty minutes on a bus? Sleep. Sitting on a bench, in a "hurry up and wait" situation? Sleep. A rare and precious commodity, and only fools squandered it.

Back in Basic, you could always spot the soldiers who hadn't mastered the skill yet. They were the ones who showed up at PT looking like sacks of wet cardboard, moving at half speed and just begging for one of the army's new and improved, kinder and gentler drill sergeants to come over and tear their heads off. Charlie had made that mistake only once. Maybe twice. She was a fast learner.

It felt like the alarm on her phone went off two seconds after she closed her eyes. She splashed some water on her face and headed back upstairs. It was seven in the morning, the hotel coming to life, morning light streaming in from the hallway windows. Beckett was two doors down, standing guard outside the wrong room. She asked a question with her eyes.

"Empty suite," he said. "Little extra camouflage never hurts."

"Somebody coming to relieve us?"

"I got in touch with Dom. She and Kirby are coming around noontime."

Unspoken words again. "But . . . ," Charlie said.

"Under the circumstances, I want more security on our primary. I also *don't* want to expand the team and bring more potential leaks into the mix."

"You want us to pull a double shift?"

"Are you particularly attached to the idea of a day off?" Beckett asked.

"Nope. My dad knows I'm on call this week, so I can't drive him around; his pantry's stocked, and I've got nothing to go home to but an air mattress and a lamp. I put in enough overtime, maybe I can afford real furniture."

"Try a futon," Beckett said. "Fold it, it's a sofa. Unfold it, it's a bed. Two of your basic needs met in one utilitarian piece."

Charlie stood beside him, standing guard at the door of an empty suite.

"Sometimes," she said, "I try to imagine what your apartment looks like."

He made a questioning sound in his throat. She glanced sidelong at him and folded her arms.

"I'm still trying," she said.

Beckett took his phone out. He listened, silent, then turned it in his hand and tapped the screen.

"Putting you on speaker so Charlie can hear."

"Great," Jake said. "And morning, both of you. How's our primary?"

"Sleeping like a baby," Beckett said.

"I've got DA Poole on the line with me."

"You people are earning your pay," Poole said. "I'm impressed. Also, I have good news. I just got positive confirmation from Boston PD: they caught the guy."

"The fourth man?" Charlie asked. "Was he another officer from the A-7?"

Poole's upbeat mood soured a bit. "Not the fourth man, no. Your shooter was a hired gun, and the weapon from the crime scene was registered in his name. He's a career scumbag, more time behind bars than out on the street, and he's got a long history of doing dirty deeds for cash. Not only can he not provide an alibi for where he was last night, he didn't even try: he lawyered up right on the spot."

Charlie looked around. From where she was standing, there wasn't any good news in sight. Just warning bells, ringing louder than a fire alarm.

Using a .38 revolver for a hit job was amateurish. Didn't mean it couldn't happen. Criminals did stupid, amateur things all the time. Even pros. But pros didn't panic and drop their weapons at the scene of the crime. And they didn't use a legally registered gun, tied to their real name and address, to commit a murder for hire.

This had every sign of a frame-up job . . . except the unlucky framee had clammed up and demanded counsel instead of proving his innocence. None of this made sense. Charlie met Beckett's eyes. He was thinking the same thoughts.

"We're glad to hear that," he said. "All the same, we're doubling our security here as a precaution."

"Good," Poole said. "That's exactly what I wanted to hear. Don't relax: the fourth conspirator is still out there, and now we know he's willing and able to recruit hired help. Stay vigilant and keep up the good work."

Spoken like a woman who was on their side. Also a woman in a unique position to check into her ADA's financial situation. Charlie pursed her lips, not sure if she should speak up, or if she'd be tiptoeing through a minefield. Beckett caught something in her eyes. He gave a tiny headshake, and she held her silence.

"I have some things to finish up with Ms. Poole," Jake said. "Beckett, I'll call back and catch you up in a few."

Beckett ended the call.

"No need to bring it up," he said. "She knows."

"About the leak?"

"That it came from her shop."

"Can we trust her to do anything about it?" Charlie asked.

"We can trust her to try. What that means, I couldn't say."

"So," Charlie said, "assume nothing good will happen and this is all on our shoulders."

"Always," he said, sanguine.

Around eight, Jake called back. ADA Felton needed another sit-down with Cobb to go over his testimony.

Charlie tried to keep her teeth from gritting. It was the perfect deniable excuse: If Felton was on the up-and-up, he genuinely needed to prepare his witness for trial. If he wasn't, they couldn't prove it and didn't have any choice but to hand over Cobb's whereabouts.

Until now, anyway. Beckett gave him the number for the backup room on the fourth floor.

"Do me a favor," Beckett told Charlie. "Go down there and put out the do-not-disturb sign so the maids don't go in."

She followed him. "So that when Felton arrives, he'll see a lived-in room with rumpled bedsheets and assume Cobb's locked down in 4205."

Inspiration hit her. She slipped into the real hotel room, padding through the muffled dark as Cobb snored in his bed, and grabbed one of the room service trays from last night.

"A little set dressing," she told Beckett and earned a nod of encouragement.

She brought the used plates and silverware downstairs, catching some curious looks on the elevator, and was artfully messing up the room when her phone rang.

"Hey, Dad," she said. "I'm at work, can't talk long. What's up?"

"Can . . . can you come home?" he asked.

His voice was wrong. Slurring a little, uneven. *Drunk?* she thought. *Not this early in the day.*

"Can't, stuck on a double shift. Remember, I told you this week was going to be a little intense?" She yanked a curtain aside, flooding the room with light. "Do you need something? I can pick it up and run it over. It'll just be a few hours yet."

He started to talk, went tumbling over his own words, took a breath, and tried again.

"I need help with something, here at the house. I really need you to come home. Right now."

Charlie froze with her hand on the second curtain. The coarse brown fabric slithered loose from her fingertips.

"Dad?" she said. "Are you alone in the house?"

"No," he said.

"Are they listening to you, right now?"

"Yes."

"Are you in danger?"

"Yes."

"Do you want me to call the police?" Charlie asked.

"No." He caught his own vehemence. She could hear him swallow hard, regrouping. "I mean, I'm sorry, I know you're at work, but I already tried to get hold of both my neighbors, and nobody's home, and I'm kind of in a jam here. Can you come home? Please?"

She looked to the hotel-room door. If she left right now, it would take her a little over thirty minutes to get to her father's place.

"Tell them I'll be there in an hour," she said.

EIGHT

"It's a trap," Beckett told her. "And if they don't want him—"

"They want me," Charlie said.

"It's a sloppy trap. That's bad. Sloppy people make dangerous mistakes."

"I'll have to be smart enough for everybody, then."

"You packing?"

She pulled back her blazer, just far enough to show the calfskin holster and the earth-tone Beretta riding at her side.

"And?" he asked.

Her hand dipped into her pocket, and she showed him her key ring. Not the ordinary kind. Beckett's welcome-aboard gift, back when she'd first been hired on, had been an ASP Key Defender. The discreet black metal shaft, textured for a sure grip, could turn her keys into a medieval flail. More powerful was what the Defender packed inside: six bursts of police-grade OC spray rated at two million Scoville heat units. Blinding, breath-stealing pain at the press of a button.

"Good girl," he said, but he still looked dubious. His gaze shifted two doors down. Cobb was sleeping in, making the most of his mandatory vacation. "I can't go with you."

"I know."

"You need backup."

"I'm a step ahead of you." Charlie had her phone out, sending out the distress call with two taps of her finger.

Dom picked up on the third ring. Charlie heard traffic noises in the background, the muffled bleat of horns.

"Hey, already told Beckett I'm on my way, ETA around noon—"

Charlie gave her the rundown. Dom let out half a curse, then caught herself.

"I've got Natalie in the car," she said, "taking her to day care before my shift starts, and I'm about twenty miles in the wrong direction. Can you hold out for another hour?"

She wasn't sure her father could.

"It's okay. Get over here as soon as you can. Beckett's going to need backup too." She ended the call and looked up at him. "You really are. And fast. Trouble's coming this way."

"Sure. Odds are the fourth man got your license plate number from the motel lot last night. He ran your plates, learned all about you. You and me are supposed to panic and rush to your dad's rescue. Leave Cobb all alone and unprotected."

Charlie shot a look over his shoulder, to the elevators.

"You see the timing here, right?"

"Sure is convenient, this out-of-nowhere crisis happening not one hour after we tell Felton where his witness has been relocated to. Still don't like sending you out alone. You trust Kirby? He might be close enough to make a detour."

"I trust him fine. But if this is a big distraction play, you're going to need him more than I will."

After all they'd been through together, all they'd trusted each other with, Beckett and Dom were as close to Charlie as any of her blood relations. They were family now, with a bond that went beyond the company and the job. But that didn't change the motionless, frozen glacier at the core of Beckett's soul, his multiple-choice past, or his carefully carved Stoic mask. She was allowed inside his life but only so far.

Every now and then, though, in rare moments, the mask slipped. Moments like these, where she could see the worry in his eyes, the sign of a beating pulse under the ice. He put his hand on her arm.

"Calling the police is still the smart play, here."

"It's my dad," she said. He understood. She knew he would.

He weighed his words for a moment, and then he tilted his head. "Little Duck. One thing."

"I'm listening."

"If that's what this is, most likely you're going to find nothing but one tied-up and confused old man, sitting all alone in his living room."

"Sure," she said. "Because whoever jumped him, they're on their way over here to murder Cobb. It's one big distraction."

"If we're wrong? And that's not what this is?" His eyes flicked, for the tiniest, most-deniable second, to the bulge under her blazer. "No jury in the world convicts a woman for using deadly force to protect her father from a home invasion. Remember that. If I find out you got hurt because you were trying to resolve things peacefully, you and me are going to have words."

"That won't be a problem," Charlie said.

Home from the service or not, civilian or not, making her father a target meant Charlie was playing by Afghanistan rules now. In her old life, being fast on the trigger wasn't something you apologized for.

It was part of the job.

Charlie's father lived outside of Spencer, far enough for the highway to disappear, the small-town ambience to fade, and the woods to close in. Her wheels kicked loose asphalt against the belly of her car, pinging like hail on a tin roof. She slowed down as she got close. She was thinking about what he'd said on the phone, about his neighbors being gone.

Maybe it didn't mean anything, just an excuse to get her to come over, but she wasn't so sure.

Dad's closest neighbors were the Wilkinsons, almost a mile down the road. The flap of their mailbox was down, the box stuffed with at least two weeks' worth of junk mail. Newspapers piled up in a rough, dirty pyramid on their porch mat. They were gone, all right, off on a trip somewhere. Their battered old Jeep wasn't parked in the driveway.

It had been replaced by a black Mercedes sedan, freshly washed and polished to an onyx mirror shine.

They parked here, Charlie thought. *Approached the house on foot so Dad wouldn't see anybody coming.*

Good tactic. She pulled into the gravel driveway right behind the Mercedes, boxing it in.

Sound carried out in the woods. Charlie stepped out of her car and gently shut the door behind her, just a tiny hip bump so the latch would catch. Then she drew her Beretta and checked the magazine. Safety off. She held the weapon low, braced in a two-hand grip, index finger running parallel to the trigger.

Charlie had grown up here. As a kid, she'd played just beyond the tree line, and she knew how to follow it home. Fallen leaves crunched under her shoes as she darted around gnarled towers of ash-gray bark, staying low, her silhouette a wraith flitting through the woods. A hundred feet of open, overgrown grass lay between the trees and the back of her father's house. She saw her old swing set, rusting away, rooted to the earth. Beyond it, a couple of bedroom windows—both curtained, no clue what was lying in wait—and the back kitchen door. Dad always left the kitchen door unlocked.

Movement. Charlie took a knee, dropping down behind the scarred bulk of a dead stump. A stranger was rounding the corner of the house, out in the open. Skinny, a long scar on one cheek, and the cool breeze pushed his windbreaker back far enough to bare the gun on his belt. Both of his hands were on his phone, though, along with his undivided attention, and both thumbs tapped at his screen like he was going for a high score.

Intel. Now she knew some things. One, he wasn't alone. Two, someone had put him on patrol, watching the exterior of the house, when he didn't have the patience or the discipline for the job.

Three, she could take him.

She bit back a surge of anger. Her father was in that house, scared, maybe hurt, all because some assholes wanted to get her attention. Well, they had it.

Stow that, she told herself, clamping down on her emotions. *Could* didn't mean *should*: she could cross the open distance, buffalo him with the butt of her gun, and take him quietly, but one slip, and this would turn into a firefight. The drawn curtains and the empty Mercedes were unknown factors. No telling how many shooters were holed up in the house, and they'd have the tactical edge if things went sideways.

She let him pass. Staying low, waiting, motionless, until he turned the next corner and faded from sight. Then she made her move, hustling across the open yard, pistol aimed down but held ready. The drawn curtains worked both ways: she couldn't tell how many intruders were inside the house, but they were blind on this side. Charlie's footfalls were a faint, rasping rustle in the overgrown grass, all the way to the kitchen door.

She gave the handle a slow, experimental twist. It moved under her curled fingers. Dad's yard work needed help, but he was serious about home maintenance. He kept his hinges oiled. The door glided open half an inch, not a whisper.

No movement in the kitchen. She opened it a little farther, expanding the pie slice of vision. Nothing out of place, no sign of a struggle. Breakfast dish and a coffee mug sitting out next to the sink. He hadn't had time to wash up.

She stepped sideways across the threshold, toes touching down on faded linoleum, and eased her way into the house.

Charlie raised the gun. She braced it close to her chest as she moved toward the open archway, every step slow, deliberate.

"Might as well step on out, lass," said a man's voice, tinged with an Irish brogue. "Been keeping us waitin' long enough already."

She knew the man sitting in her father's armchair, his bulk poured into it, dressed in tailored slacks and a white silk shirt with french cuffs. She had hoped—expected—that she'd never see him again.

"Before you do anything foolish with that steel," Jimmy Lassiter told her, "bear this in mind: I might not look like much of an athletic marvel, but I can press a button faster than you can shoot."

He showed her the box in his hand. It looked like a walkie-talkie that had been modified on some mad mechanic's lab bench. Fat yellow plastic, with a squat antenna wrapped in black rubber. Charlie had no idea what it was for, but that wasn't the top question on her mind right now.

"Where's my father?" she demanded. She fought to hold her discipline, to keep her finger off the trigger until she was ready to open fire.

He ignored her question. Instead he turned to one of the two behind him, a pair of bruisers who didn't bother hiding the chromed automatics on their hips. She knew one of them: Reyburn—tall, lumpy, vulture eyed, part of the two-man team who had put her father in the hospital. His partner, Grillo, had been replaced by a skinhead whose arms were a pictorial history of faded prison ink. He wore his years of bad decisions and boredom for the world to see.

"You owe me a sawbuck," Jimmy said to Reyburn. "I told you she'd slip right past MacGill. Arsehole's probably playing with his phone again."

"Where," Charlie repeated, "is my *father*?"

"I'm hopin' you find this charmingly ironic," Jimmy said. "See, after you left that little C-4 surprise under my chair, I kept it for a souvenir. Got one of my boys to wire it up again, except this time, he rigged this little remote control thingamabob. I push the button, plastic explosives go boom."

He fixed his gaze upon her as his easy smile faded. His eyes turned to cold steel.

"I'm hoping you can connect the dots here," he said.

Charlie was back in the sandbox. Back where she'd earned an honorary doctorate in the university of bomb building and taken her laurels in Terrorism 101. *Modified Motorola walkie-talkie,* she thought, mind racing as she studied the yellow plastic curves. *Hiking model, long range. Can send transmissions up to twenty-three miles. Half that, out in the boonies, and halve it again for safety. Between the phone call and now, wouldn't have had time to move Dad far. They would have stashed him and the explosives out of sight, but far enough from the detonator that if Jimmy pushed the button, they'd be clear of the blast radius and any flying debris—*

Charlie's heart sank. The Wilkinsons. They'd broken into the Wilkinsons' place. She had been *right there,* a heartbeat from her father, and gone off in the wrong direction. She could have saved him.

"We had a deal," was all she managed to say, blurting out the words.

He gaped at her, incredulous.

"Aye. We did, didn't we? I bent over backward to be nice to you, because I thought we had a little something in common, you and me. I even took it on the chin when you pulled that stunt with the bomb under my chair. And that stung—don't you think for one second that it didn't. But I let it all slide. Water under the bridge."

Charlie's grip tightened on the gun. Her finger ached for the caress of the trigger. His hovered over the detonator.

"Then why," she said, "are you attacking my family?"

He blurted out a laugh, turning to Reyburn.

"Why am I . . . do you even believe this crazy bitch? Do you? Are my ears deceivin' me right now?" He looked back to Charlie. "Why are *you* attacking *mine?*"

She blinked at him. "What the hell are you talking about?"

"My man Grillo," Jimmy said. "He's sitting in lockup, held on remand and looking at a prison stretch. Because you framed him."

NINE

The world was spiraling out of control, slipping from Charlie's grasp. All she had left, the only thing that was solid, stable, real, was the gun in her hand. She clung to it like an anchor in a storm.

"I have no idea what you're talking about," she said.

"It took me a minute," Jimmy said, shooting a hard look at Reyburn. The thug leaned from foot to foot, staring at the carpet, guilty. "Took me a minute to get the whole story. After you gave Reyburn a shiner, they went to see your old man about the money he owed me. They ran into you out in the driveway. This ringin' any bells?"

Like it was yesterday. Her father had owed Jimmy $20,000 in unpaid gambling debts. He'd had only ten days to pay up, and Charlie had been hunting for a solution. Grillo and Reyburn hadn't come looking for the cash, not really: they'd known her father didn't have it. They'd just wanted to dish out some payback for how Charlie had humiliated them in front of their boss.

"I remember," Charlie said.

Reyburn hadn't been shy about it. They'd been going to beat her down, maybe do worse than that, and tell Jimmy that she'd thrown the first punch after they'd come in peace. She'd been thankful for Beckett's welcome-aboard present. She'd blasted Reyburn in the face, blinded him, and then disarmed his partner before Grillo could gun her down. She'd gotten a faceful of the OC spray herself when the wind had shifted. The fight had broken up with the leg breakers staggering away and Charlie stumbling into her father's kitchen, pouring milk in her eyes to cut the searing burn.

"You took Grillo's gun."

"He was trying to shoot me at the time," Charlie said. "And like I told them, I could have put them both in the ground, and I wouldn't have spent one minute behind bars for it. I let them walk. That was a kindness."

Jimmy leaned forward in her father's armchair. His grip tightened on the detonator.

"Oh. A kindness. Is that what you call it? Because the cops kicked Grillo's door down this morning and dragged him out of his bed. See, that gun, the one that *you took from him*, just happened to appear at the scene of a crime. They're saying he tried to murder a man out in Southborough last night. Thanks to you. And I want to know why."

And in a flash Charlie was back outside the Pocono Motor Inn, standing under a yellow sodium light, staring at the abandoned weapon on the pavement. The .38 revolver. The gun that didn't make sense.

"I was there," Charlie said, her voice soft.

"Now tell me something I don't know."

"No," she said. "I was there. Inside the hotel room, with the man they say Grillo wanted to kill. Protecting him. When the shooter opened fire, he almost hit me."

Jimmy had spent a lifetime judging people, weighing their motivations, reading them like a gambler read cards. His eyes narrowed to a razor-thin squint.

"You're not lying," he said.

"I couldn't have planted that gun, because I wasn't the last person who had it." She wanted to push the dawning implication back, but she couldn't argue with the facts. "I know the man who did."

Jimmy set the detonator down, resting it on her father's end table, next to an empty can of beer.

"I'm going to leave this here," he said, "and you're going to holster that steel. And you and me, we're going to take a walk together."

A cool wind ruffled the overgrown grass. Jimmy and Charlie strolled along the tree line. Jimmy walked with a cane, a stick of simple, elegant ebony, leaning into it as he navigated the uneven, muddy ground.

"Reminds me of home out here," he said. "You ever climb these trees?"

"When I was a kid? Sure. They couldn't keep me on the ground."

He chuckled. "Me too. I was a little monkey, back in my short-pants days. So. I have a problem. I have a deep-rooted need to hold the best cards at any particular table. With what I know right now, I can't even put together a measly two pair. Deal me in."

"What do you know about the East Boston Three?"

"Pack of miserable shitgibbons," he said. "Two of those backroom poker games they knocked over were *mine*. Not going to lie, when they were taken down by their own, I warmed myself to sleep imagining their first day in general population. Nobody has a worse time behind bars than a crooked cop, not even a short eyes."

She ran him through the basics. The new client, the primary, the faceless fourth member of the gang. The motel, the gunshot.

"Hayden Cobb?" he said. "I've heard of him. Small time. No capital-*F* family ties to speak of. Nobody who would shed too many tears if he washed up dead on Carson Beach. Nobody who cares enough to put him there either. He's the linchpin of the case?"

"Everything else they have is circumstantial. Strong circumstantial, but . . . you know how that goes."

Jimmy flashed the ghost of a smile. "That I do. But this brings me no closer to grasping why my man's gun was at the scene of the crime."

"After I took it from Grillo, I started carrying it. Things were . . . tense. And I didn't know what else to do with it. Anyway, I had it on me when the police picked me up."

He gave her a dubious glance. "You think I haven't checked you out? You've never been arrested in your life."

"I wasn't. Just questioned. Long story. Let's just say I was in the process of getting the money to pay my father's debts."

"All right."

"I had met this detective," Charlie said. "Riley Glass, working out of the A-7. He was . . . well, the first time we met, when I had to ID a suspect, he gave me his phone number."

"Heh. Do go on."

"It wasn't my gun, and I wasn't licensed to carry one anyway. So, trouble. He . . ."

Her voice trailed off. She *liked* Riley. He seemed to like her. And the next words from her lips were going to ignite a firestorm of trouble. For him, for her, for everyone involved.

"He made the problem go away," she said. "No paperwork, no charges—he just made the gun disappear."

Jimmy was silent for a bit. Thoughtful, as his cane dug furrows in the mud, pulling him along at her side.

"Plainclothes cop," he said. "Working out of the same station as the other bad Easties. Makes an inconvenient gun disappear. He couldn't check it into evidence, not without a crime to tie it to, so he likely kept it for himself. Maybe stuck it in a shoebox for a rainy day. Lots of cops do that. Never know when you'll need a drop piece. But last night, somebody took a shot at your witness with that very same weapon."

He turned his head, studying Charlie's face.

"You ask me, I'd say you just found your fourth man."

Charlie didn't want him to be right. She didn't want the facts to be facts. She had enough presence of mind to catch herself in denial.

He didn't seem the type. She kept coming back to that. Charlie wasn't naive. She knew that people lied, that they showed you the face they wanted you to see while keeping the real one buried deep. But Riley had felt like a guy doing his best, looking out for his neighborhood, and trying to do the right thing by everyone he met. She compared that to the nightmares in DA Poole's folder, the bound and throat-slashed teenagers from the massacre on Saratoga Street, and she couldn't make those images line up.

She was biased. She had to be honest with herself about that. In the service, dating meant navigating an ocean of red tape, rules, and regs about who could fraternize with who. Then there were the unspoken rules; she had earned her rank with dedication and sweat, but she knew that rank and authority were two different things, and being seen as "just one of the guys" was a key part of maintaining authority. So she'd put any notions of romance in a tiny box and locked it away for years.

Now she was out, her own woman, and she could do whatever she wanted with whoever she wanted. And Riley was the kind of man—honorable, with a strong spine and a good heart—she might want to do something with. That was the impression he gave, anyway, and she wanted it to be true.

"Tell me something," Charlie said. "How did they tie the gun to Grillo?"

Jimmy snorted. "'Cause it's his. I mean, the man has guns for days, but that one's his true-blue legally registered firearm. Carries it . . . well, carried it . . . when he was makin' the rounds for me."

"You're saying he never killed anyone with it."

"You know what I do for a living, lass."

"You're a bookie," she said. "And a loan shark. Among other things. Dead men don't pay their debts."

"That's it in one. The gun was for Grillo's protection, in case some rogue tried to jack him while he was carrying a fat wad of cash. He registered it so the cops couldn't hassle him neither."

"So there aren't any other crimes tied to that gun, and he wasn't at the motel last night. When Poole told us they'd busted the shooter, she said he clammed up and demanded a lawyer the second they asked him for an alibi. Why can't he just tell them where he really was? If he can prove it, they'd have to let him go."

Jimmy's cane dug into the soil. The fingers of his free hand curled, tugging at his shirt collar. He wafted the white silk to catch an incoming breeze.

"He was otherwise indisposed at the time of the shooting," Jimmy said.

"'Indisposed'?"

"He was tending to a bit of private business. Handling a job for a friend of a friend."

Charlie didn't follow, at first. Then the other shoe dropped.

"You're telling me that his only alibi," she said, "is that he was committing a *different* murder last night."

He shot her a look. "I didn't say 'murder.' For your information, it was more of a . . . well, it was the unlawful acquisition of several delivery trucks out by the airport, as well as the contents of those trucks."

"Same situation. The only way he can get off on the attempted-murder charge is by confessing to a different crime."

"Not the only way," he said.

His tone had changed, and she didn't like it. She waited for him to fill in the blanks.

"Seems to me," he said, "you're in a perfect position to see that justice is done."

"What do you want me to do? Get a meeting with the DA and tell her about the gun?"

"Reckon it would help?"

She thought about that.

"She'd listen, but Poole is careful. Methodical. Even if she decides Riley Glass is the fourth member of the East Boston Three—and I don't think he is—"

"Despite the facts in evidence."

"Despite that," she said, "the most she'll do is quietly put his life under a microscope, and she'll take her time doing it. She's not going to slap cuffs on him until she has absolute proof positive that he's the man. The kind of proof she can bring to a jury. The East Boston Three trial is a career maker for her. That means it can be a career breaker too."

"Well then, it's a good thing she has such a motivated and industrious little helper on the street. Someone who can get things done and dig up the truth. Someone the mysterious Detective Glass is sweet on."

"You want me to expose him," she said, her voice flat.

"Loyalty is a rare and valuable commodity in my line of work. Now, Grillo? He's meaner than my dearly departed grandmother, and that woman was *mean*, and he's dumber than a sack of hammers, but he's loyal. And I reward loyalty. I need him sprung loose. You're a creative lass. I've seen that much, firsthand. Sort it out."

"You realize," Charlie said, "that the only reason this was able to happen in the first place was because him and his buddy tried to beat the shit out of me."

Jimmy pressed his hand to his heart and gazed upward to the skeletal boughs of the trees and heavens beyond.

"I have sad, sad news for you, my dear. Life . . . is deeply unfair. Look, I'm not asking you to do anything you shouldn't already be wanting to do yourself. You need to keep this Cobb fella alive, yeah? Nailing the villain trying to do him in would make your life a hell of a lot easier. Help yourself, and help me at the same time. And help your da."

Charlie's eyes narrowed. "Meaning?"

"Your father's going to be my personal guest until you get this sorted. Grillo walks, he walks." Jimmy fluttered a hand at her. "Please, no squawking. I'm not going to have the man tied up in a basement with a gag in his mouth. I'll give him a telly with all the sports channels and a twelve-pack of beer. It'll be so close to his current standard of living he might not even notice anything's changed."

Charlie entertained some dangerous thoughts. Jimmy gave a slight nod, catching it in her eyes.

"Number one," he said, "you know me well enough to know we aren't *really* alone out here together."

She had felt something, now and again, since they'd left the house. That crawling, tingling feeling at the back of her neck, telling her she was being watched. Through binoculars, maybe. Or down the scope of a rifle.

"Number two," he said, "this is a win-win all around, if you play your cards right. Like I said, loyalty matters. I help the people who help me."

"And if I can't prove that Grillo is innocent?"

Jimmy played off the question with a wave of his hand.

"Let's not dwell on the negative," he said. "I've every faith in you. Simply remember one thing. You know what you said back there? About how dead men don't pay their debts? That's exactly right. It doesn't make any sense at all to murder a man who owes you money."

He stopped walking. So did she. He leaned with both hands on the head of his cane as he turned to face her.

"Your father doesn't owe me a single red cent," Jimmy said. "You made sure of that."

TEN

"*Fucking* Irish," Dom snarled.

Charlie was back at the Crowne Plaza, up in the room on seven. Cobb was gone for the moment. He'd been relocated to the dummy room on the fourth floor, under the watchful eye of Kirby and another relief operative, who were standing guard outside while the witness went through another round of trial prep with ADA Felton.

Beckett stood silent and thoughtful, stoic while Charlie outlined her encounter with Jimmy Lassiter. Dom paced the carpet like a panther.

"A few years back," she said, "the Five Families up in New York almost went to the mattresses with the Accardos here in Boston. Know how worried I was about becoming collateral damage, given my blood relations? I wasn't. Know why? Because as far as they're concerned, I'm a civilian, and going after civilian relatives *is not done*. There are rules, and rules are what separate us from the animals."

Charlie sat on the edge of a rumpled bedspread, hands on her knees.

"Maybe I should have blown him up back when I had the chance," she mused.

"No." Some of Dom's fury ebbed, her shoulders unclenching. "No, I told you not to, and I'm glad you listened. Jimmy Lassiter's the kind of scum who has friends in high places. He goes missing or dead, his friends are going to come around asking questions, and you don't want that."

"He's also not entirely wrong," Beckett said, breaking his silence. "At this moment, our primary is finishing up his sit-down with Felton. If our collective hunch is on the money and Felton's the mole inside the DA's office, that means we can expect a follow-up visit from a hired gun in short order. Fastest way to put this nonsense to rest is to lay hands on the one calling the shots."

"I don't think Riley is the fourth man," Charlie said. "And yes, okay, you don't have to tell me. Yes, all the evidence says it's him, and also I'm biased because, well . . . I mean, I like him. But I think I'm a pretty good judge of character. I just don't see it. He's not a killer."

Beckett folded his arms. He leaned back against the golden-brown wall.

"Whether he is or isn't, we still have to establish how that stolen .38 navigated its way from his possession to the pavement outside the Pocono Inn. You say he's not a killer, I believe you, but that gun has a story to tell."

"And if Riley Glass doesn't know it," Dom said, "he can tell us who does. It's just a matter of getting the truth out of him."

"There're a few ways to do that," Beckett said.

"Sack of oranges usually does the trick."

"We are not," Charlie said, "beating a police detective with a sack of oranges."

Dom tilted her head. "Because he's a cop or because you think he's cute?"

"Charm may be cleaner," Beckett said. "You have the man's phone number."

Charlie knew what had to be done. She had thought about it on the highway, all the way back to the hotel. She had been planning on calling him, when work was less busy, when life was less crazy. Just dinner, nothing serious. Funny how a single bad day could change your perspective on a man.

If she called him now and went to him, she'd be going with a mission on her mind and a hunt on her agenda. And if she was wrong about him, if he really was the fourth man in the East Boston Three, willing to kill to protect his dirty secrets, her life would be in danger the second she walked through his door.

"I have to think about this," she said.

"If you're going to call him or not?" Dom asked.

"Oh, no," Charlie said. "I'm calling him. What I need is a solid plan. And an escape route, just in case I'm wrong about him."

She checked the time.

"First things first. Cobb should be just about done. Let's wait until Felton leaves the hotel, then hustle the witness back up here."

"And brace for the fallout," Dom said.

"And Felton is . . . out." Dom's voice crackled over the radio nestled in Charlie's hand. "Watching him long range. He sat out in his car for five minutes, texting somebody, maybe checking his emails. Just got rolling, and he hit the on-ramp for the turnpike."

"I'm on four," Charlie said, "going radio silent."

The radio disappeared into her shoulder bag. They'd tried an experiment this time. When ADA Felton had called to ask for the location, they'd only given him the hotel address and told him—like Charlie had done with Beckett the night they'd arrived—to meet her down in the lobby. He was brisk on the phone, agreeable and blunt, like he was billing by the quarter hour. Charlie had searched his words and his tone for some sign of treason, and he'd given her nothing in return. She'd escorted him up to the decoy room on the fourth floor personally.

There was still the remote possibility that Cobb's location had leaked the first time around due to a tap on Felton's phone or somebody compromising the office's emails. This time, the only person at the DA's office who knew the room number was Felton himself. If the shooter came around hunting for Cobb, they'd know exactly who to trace the leak back to. That would prove Felton was either complicit in the plot or criminally negligent; his boss could figure out which.

But first they had to wait for the shooter to show their face.

They pressed Cobb for information, gently, once they got him back up to the real room on the seventh floor. They didn't want to get him jumping at shadows, not any more than he already was.

"I mean, nothing felt weird about it or anything," he said. "Just the same questions, over and over again. Just like when the cops questioned me, but with extra interruptions."

"Sounds like typical trial prep," Beckett said. He folded his arms, studying Charlie. "You taking first watch, Little Duck?"

She was. She'd brought a change of clothes from home. A T-shirt, an old pair of acid-washed jeans, and her running shoes, as far away from bodyguard chic as she could get. If and when the shooter came around, she didn't know if he'd try to be subtle or go in guns blazing, like he had back at the motel. Given his idea of an assassination was taking potshots at shadows with a .38 revolver, stationing guards outside the door was too dangerous.

If the opposition was reckless, they'd counter by going subtle. Charlie strolled the fourth-floor hallway, walking a casual circuit around the decoy door, past the elevator bank, down to the ice machine, and back again. To all appearances, just another hotel guest, coming or going on a sunny afternoon.

Time slowed to a crawl, as steady and monotonous as the pattern on the hallway carpet, the perfectly measured space between the overhead lights. Every now and then the elevators would let out a soft electric bing, and she'd brace herself. Then an elderly couple would emerge, or a little kid swooping down the hallway with his arms out wide, making airplane noises, and she'd go back to sentry duty. She floated in a state of casual alert, noticing everything, feeling nothing.

Next one off the elevator was a maintenance worker, overalls, lugging a grainy metal toolbox. She followed him at a distance. He didn't notice his new shadow, and Charlie trailed the man until he unlocked a utility hatch at the far end of the floor and crouched down, getting to work. Nothing more dangerous in his toolbox than a socket wrench.

Time slipped by. She was about to call up to take a break and swap places with Beckett when she saw the room service guy. Not the same one from last night, but that was no surprise; they probably had a dozen working at any given hour. He was in his twenties, deep tan, draped in an ivory coat that was too big for him; the sleeves draped down to the first knuckles of his white-gloved hands as he pushed a rolling cart along. He checked a delivery ticket, hunting for a room number.

He stopped outside of 4205. He rapped his knuckles on the decoy-room door, patiently waiting, one droopy sleeve hovering near the covered dish on his cart.

Charlie's hand slipped into her shoulder bag and found the radio, right next to her gun. Two clicks sent a message upstairs: she had movement, maybe trouble.

There was always the chance he was a real employee and the clerk downstairs had made a mistake on his ticket. She wasn't going to pull a gun on him based on nothing but a hunch. Like Beckett often reminded her, they were private security, not cops. If she pulled a gun on an innocent civilian, she'd most likely end up in handcuffs. She kept her steel out of sight and made a casual approach. He gave her the once-over as she walked up the hall. She wasn't sure if he was frisking her with his eyes or checking her out.

He had a familiar posture. The man stood like she did when she was waiting for action: relaxed but ready, parade rest. Maybe he was ex-military. Maybe she was reading too much into it. She was thinking about the motel and the bullet that had missed her by inches.

By the time she closed the distance between them, she'd come up with a test that would prove his intentions. She held up her key card.

"Oh," she said, looking surprised. "Room service."

She couldn't read his expression. "Yes, ma'am."

She waved her card over the lock. It clicked and flashed green.

"You got here faster than I expected. Sorry if I kept you waiting." She pushed open the door with one hand, keeping her other one free and ready. "Please, come on in."

If he was an innocent room service clerk with a bad ticket, he'd bring the food inside. If he was the shooter, covering his approach with a stolen jacket that didn't fit and a cart he'd grabbed when no one was looking, he'd know she hadn't placed an order. Either that, or he'd lucked out with a lottery-winner level of coincidence. Either way, backup would be here in less than a minute.

He hesitated. Just for a second, maybe not even that long. She saw the flicker of uncertainty in his eyes, the flicker that wouldn't have been there if this were his real job.

He read her face, same as she read his. He knew he was blown.

He whipped the steel serving-tray cover loose and threw it in Charlie's face. She swung an arm, batting it away, sending it clanging off the wall.

A black nine-millimeter automatic, stubby tube of a sound suppressor screwed to the barrel, nestled in the dish. He went for the gun.

Charlie ran the numbers; they flashed through her mind, computer fast. It would take her two seconds to get the pistol out of her shoulder bag. In two seconds, a competent shooter could empty his magazine.

She used the bag as a weapon instead, swinging it down, slamming it across his wrist. Then she grabbed the edge of the cart and hauled it over. Silverware scattered across the carpet, the dish shattering, pistol bouncing out of reach. He threw a right cross. His knuckles cracked against her cheekbone, cutting it open, blood trickling hot and sticky as she dodged back from a second punch. She ducked and shot out a pinpoint kick, aiming for his kneecap. The sting along her cheek threw her aim off. Her heel was a piston against his shin, knocking his leg out from under him.

He hit the floor and grabbed for the fallen gun. She stomped down, and he yanked his hand back before she could fracture it. Then he went for the closest weapon he could reach, a butter knife, and launched himself at her like a torpedo. The knife was dull. Didn't matter, not in trained hands, and he had the training. She danced backward as he punched at her ribs, each knife thrust riding on a hiss of breath.

He went high, swooping in for the kill. She made an X with her forearms, catching his wrist, holding him back as the tip of the knife strained toward her eye. He broke the clinch with a sweep of his leg and sent her tumbling to the hallway carpet.

Instead of pressing the advantage, he dropped the knife, broke, and ran, hurtling toward the stairway door at the end of the hall. Charlie scrambled back to her feet, pausing just long enough to grab her radio.

"Hitter on the move," she gasped, breathless as she chased him down. "Headed for the stairs. Circle around and cut him off on the ground floor."

She hit the swinging door with her shoulder and barreled through. He was already halfway down the stairs, boots pounding, ripping off the over-size waiter jacket as he ran. The man threw it over his shoulder and sent it billowing in his wake. He was wearing a sweat-stained tank top underneath, muscled arms bare and pumping, ink on his right bicep: Charlie made out a familiar motto, an eagle perched on a globe. *Marine,* she thought.

Two doors were at the bottom of the stairs. One led to a hall just off the lobby. The other, warded by a metal push bar and a warning sign, opened onto the hotel back lot. The Klaxon of a fire alarm wailed as he threw himself against the bar and out into the sunlight.

She was five seconds behind him. Charlie bounded down the last few steps and followed him through the door. The alarm wailed in her ears, drowning her sense of hearing, and the sun glittered in her eyes.

She didn't realize he'd stopped running, that he'd pressed his back to the wall, just left of the doorway, until a rock-hard fist plowed into her gut and knocked the breath out of her. She doubled over, blinded. Then his clenched fists came down between her shoulders, driving her to the ground. The hot black asphalt scraped her left arm raw, pinpricks of blood welling up, joining the howling sandstorm of pain.

Someone was shouting, running. Charlie blinked, trying to get her senses back and fill her lungs again. Someone else had her shoulder now, gentle but firm, easing her up until she was sitting on the pavement.

"Can you walk it off?" Beckett was asking her.

She answered by giving him her hand. He hauled her up to her feet. Now she was hurt, bleeding, and pissed. She should have braced for an ambush, should have waited for backup, should have—

"You're thinking about your father," Beckett told her. "Got distracted."

She'd been too hungry, too eager to lay hands on the man who could set her father free. She'd gotten sloppy. Just for a second, but one second of sloppy was all it took.

"Yeah," Charlie said, sinking into the shame.

"You made a mistake," Beckett said, "but it's a mistake anybody would have made."

"Would you have?" she asked him.

He raised his radio to his lips. "Got anything?"

The radio clicked. "Gone," Dom said. "We chased him through the parking garage; asshole turned into smoke. We're checking all the cars now, just to be safe, but I think he's in the wind."

"I'm going to head back upstairs," Charlie said. "Going to secure the scene before the cops get here."

"And?" he said, catching the words unspoken.

"I want to take a look at what he left behind."

ELEVEN

The gun was right. And that felt all kinds of wrong, in a way that lurked at the edges of Charlie's mind. She didn't touch it. The shooter had been wearing gloves, but there was always the remote chance he'd slipped up while getting ready for the kill. Crouching over the fallen weapon, her feet squared in a clutter of broken porcelain and scattered silverware, she could see all she needed to.

Nine-millimeter semiautomatic, polished and clean. Titanium sound suppressor, not a cheap one. If he'd managed to fire a shot, it would have sounded like a slamming door. He could have gunned down Cobb and anyone with him and slipped out without making a fuss. The pistol's serial number was a pale scar of blurry metal. He'd stripped it with acid.

This was a hitman's gun. Exactly the weapon she'd have expected him to carry. And that was a problem. Because at the motel, he'd come for Cobb with a loud, janky .38 revolver, the wrong tool for the job. His style had evolved from amateur to pro literally overnight.

The police came, cordoned off the hall, hustled everyone down to a quiet corner of the lobby. She told her story, then told it again. Then a third time, each repetition to a man with more stripes on his uniform sleeve. Dealing with the cops was a lot easier when she didn't have to lie. They let her drive her own car down to the station house. She gave them a description, challenging her own memory every step of the way, and they had her browse through photo arrays to see if she could spot her attacker. Fat books of them, with a six-pack of usual suspects glaring out from every page. He wasn't hiding among the riffraff.

"What about the other guy?" Charlie asked, seizing on a glimmer of hope.

"Other guy?" the sergeant asked her.

"They arrested someone the other night, out at the Pocono Motor Inn, because he was the registered owner of the gun that got left behind there. Doesn't this prove he couldn't be the shooter? They'll let him go now, right?"

He said he'd make a few calls. He ambled off to do that while she hunted through a fresh set of six-packs. No luck. No hope either. He came back and said Grillo was staying put.

"No proof it was the same guy," he explained. "Could be there's two people want your client dead. Better safe than sorry, until we get it all sorted out. This Grillo, he a friend of yours or something?"

"I just don't like the idea of someone being locked up for a crime they didn't do."

"Well, if he wasn't at the motel, he was somewhere else, right?" The cop gave her a fatherly smile. "Don't worry. I'm sure they're checking his alibi."

An alibi he didn't have because he'd been out hijacking a truck at the time. Charlie followed a fruitless trail through the mug shots, hunting a ghost, leaving empty handed. On her way out the door, a kid in his first uniform tried to give her a card for a crisis counselor. She stared at him, not following.

"When someone's been the victim of a violent crime," he said, "it can help to talk to a counselor."

Charlie still didn't follow. She hadn't been the victim of a violent crime. She'd been doing her job.

Out in the parking lot, she checked herself in the rearview mirror. She wore the scab of a healing cut on her chin, a fresh bandage on her cheekbone. Mostly she looked tired. Tired of getting knocked around this week and itching to return the favor. It was dark. She was done for the night. Nothing to do but go home and collapse.

Instead, she drove back to the Pocono Motor Inn. Her car was the only one in the lot. The motel had been sparse before, and now it was stone dead. Gunshots had a way of driving off the clientele.

No police tape over the door to room twelve, but the broken window wore a shroud of plastic, held in place at the corners with thick blue strips of electrical tape. It caught a gust of cool night wind, billowing. She walked into the front office and flashed her Boston Asset Protection ID card at the clerk.

"You know," he told her, "we're still tryin' to find out who's covering the damages. Everybody tells us to call somebody else. Police said we can rent the room out, but somebody's gotta pay for the window and the TV set."

"Sounds like that'd be an insurance claim," she said.

"Boss says our insurance doesn't cover 'acts of gun.'"

"Sounds like you need a better policy," she said. "Still have that television set?"

He jerked a thumb over his shoulder.

"Tossed it, soon as the cops gave the all clear. Should still be in the dumpster out back. Why?"

"Trying to catch the guy who pulled the trigger," Charlie said. "I find him, you can sue him in small-claims court. Sound good?"

"Whatever."

Around the back of the motel, a lonely dumpster stood at the edge of a puddle of light. Charlie hauled back the lid and wrinkled her nose. A gust of foul air washed over her, smelling like dirty diapers and rotten scraps of fast food.

"I love my job," she said, snapping on a pair of disposable latex gloves. She repeated it, a devout mantra, as she carefully lifted herself up onto the edge of the dumpster and lowered herself into the trash.

Broken-down cardboard and overstuffed bags of garbage shifted under her shoes.

◆ ◆ ◆

"Damn shame," Dom said, "the things people throw away these days. Haven't they heard of recycling?"

Waist deep in the dumpster, Charlie shot her a look.

"Got your message, but you didn't tell me you were moonlighting as a trash panda."

"Chasing a hunch," Charlie said.

"Straight into the garbage. I can relate."

"Thanks for coming out. Here, help me with this."

She hoisted a television set, screen shot through with jagged cracks and a bullet in its heart, onto the corroded steel rim of the dumpster. One corner glistened under the yellow light.

"It's *wet*," Dom said.

"Just . . . hang on to the dry end while I climb out."

They wrestled the TV down onto the dirty pavement and laid it flat. Charlie brandished a pair of tweezers like a surgeon.

"I keep thinking about the sound," Charlie said.

"Being shot at tends to do that to a person."

"No, it was . . ." She gestured off to her side. "Beckett was in the parking lot, hunkered down. He had me keep my phone on speaker. I left it on the table in the motel room, and then I got low, down behind the bed. I knew the shooter could only see shadows behind the curtain, so I drew his fire with a pillow."

"The shooter was amateurish as hell," Dom said. "He had no idea who he was firing at, no line of sight to his target."

"That guy at the hotel, today?" Charlie glanced up as they crouched on opposite sides of the TV. "He wasn't an amateur."

"You think two different hitters are after our guy?"

"Not exactly. Okay, so . . . the sound. I heard it from two sources: the actual boom of the .38 going off outside the window, and the distant, muffled version from Beckett's end of the parking lot, piped over my phone's speaker."

"And this acoustics lesson means . . . what, exactly?"

"I'm not positive. Like I said. Chasing a hunch. Get a light on this for me?"

She worked away the bits of shattered screen, peeling back the chipped remnants of the LCD display and baring the slender guts of the television. Dom angled her cell phone at the wreckage, shining a spotlight. The prongs of the tweezers gave off raspy, scratching sounds as Charlie hunted for her prize.

She held it up to the light. A rough mushroom circle of brass. Even crumpled and deformed by the impact, they both knew what it was.

"That's . . . ," Dom said, her voice trailing off as the implication set in.

"A nine-millimeter slug. Either the hitman fired his nine and then deliberately dropped the .38 on his way out—"

"Or there were two shooters," Dom said.

"Follow me. I want to check something out."

They circled the building. Charlie was doing geometry in her head. Lines of attack. She stood in the middle of the parking lot and eyed the billowing plastic over the busted window, mentally reconstructing the motel room in her mind's eye.

"From the angle of impact, the shooter with the nine had to be standing right about here."

She moved over to the side of the building, where they'd found the abandoned revolver. She made a gun with her fingers, cocking her thumb back, and drew a second invisible line across the parking lot.

She followed it, Dom jogging in her wake, to the far end of the motel, where the building curved in a faded brick L. The light from her phone slowly strobed across the wall. Over and down, back and forth, until it settled on a crater of crumpled stone. Charlie crouched low and dug around with her tweezers, the prongs catching on a buried brass meteorite.

"It's stuck in there. But if we could dig it out, you know what we'd find."

"Round from the .38," Dom said.

Charlie pointed back to the parked cars.

"Our hitman, the one from the hotel today, was closing in, hunkered down in the shadows. At the same time, shooter number two was hiding near the side of the building."

"The guy with the revolver wasn't here to kill Cobb," Dom said. "He was here to kill the hitman."

"I didn't hear the echo of a single shot over the speakerphone. I heard two gunshots—one loud boom from the .38, one pop from a sound-suppressed nine millimeter—going off at almost the same moment. Maybe the hitman wasn't even taking aim at the window. Maybe he was closing in, planning on getting through the door before he opened fire. Either way, I figure he had his finger on the trigger. Bad discipline. I'd expect a Marine to know better—"

"Maybe it's his first contract job," Dom said. "Nerves. But I can see it. Guy with the .38 takes a shot at him, misses; his hand jerks back, squeezes off a reflex shot. That's the bullet that hit the window."

"And both of them make a run for it. The shooter with the .38 dropped his weapon. Pure panic move. The one with the nine, well, he was expecting to be the killer that night, not the target."

"I'd run, too, get some distance until I could figure out what was going on." Dom tilted her head, studying Charlie. "You sure it was panic?"

"What's your take?"

"We keep coming back to Riley Glass. He was the last person, as far as we know, who had that gun. And he knew the gun could be tied to a leg breaker working for a local mobster."

"You think he deliberately framed Grillo?"

"Maybe he just wanted to start a fight," Dom said. "Get these guys stomping each other while he stays safely out of the spotlight."

"Considering I have to clear Grillo's name . . ." Charlie sighed. She glanced down at her phone. "No time like the present, is there?"

Dom reached over and squeezed her shoulder. "I've got your back." She called Detective Glass.

She expected to get his voice mail. He picked up after four rings, breathless.

"Hey, sorry, had my phone on the charger, I was in the other room—" He paused, his tone shifting like the subtle bend of a night breeze. "Charlie! I mean, hi there. Hey."

"Hey. Is this a bad time? I can call back . . ."

His voice dropped a little. Smooth now, collected.

"Not at all. Not for you. Is this a business call, or . . . ?"

"Sounds like you're hoping it's not business," Charlie said.

"Maybe just a little. What's up?"

"I seem to recall vague discussions, at some point in the nebulous future when we weren't both insanely busy, about possibly having dinner?"

"Still insanely busy," Riley said, "but for you, I can make an exception."

"Same."

"Do you like Italian?"

"Sure. You know a good place?" Charlie asked.

"I do. My apartment."

"You cook," she said.

"I cook. Catching bad guys and cooking are my only two real skills. That and being devastatingly handsome."

"You're really too pretty to be seen with in public," Charlie deadpanned.

He mirrored her tone. "Hence why you should come over to my place, tomorrow night. You can bask in my glow while I cook pasta. Seven-ish?"

"Seven-ish," Charlie said.

She got his address and hung up the phone. Dom nodded her approval, one hand resting on her hip.

"That went well," Dom said.

"Sure," Charlie said. "I've got a date with a cop who might have used a stolen gun to try and start a gang war. And we're not any closer to figuring out who the fourth man in the East Boston Three is."

"You've got a date with a cop who knows who our shooter is," Dom said. "Hey, look on the bright side: it's not like this situation's going to get any worse."

TWELVE

The windows of the Nashua Street Jail were stark inverted Vs, facing inward like a stern command for self-reflection and penance. The building squatted alone on a broad boulevard, the far side running down to the bank of the Charles River. Nowhere to go, nowhere to run. The jail was maximum security, for holding prisoners before trial. Segregated cells and silent, cold hallways offered a taste of the future.

The doors of a mantrap—ten feet of corridor between two slabs of reinforced steel—buzzed for Oscar Pembrose's passage. The guards knew his face. He'd built a thirty-year reputation as one of Boston's best defense attorneys, a bulldog who fought tooth and nail for his clients, winning at trial more often than he lost.

Of course, that assumed a case was winnable. Sometimes the scales of justice needed a helpful fingertip on one side to steer the weight in the right direction.

A stone-faced turnkey let him into an interview room. His client was waiting. Lieutenant Gimondi's uniform and medals had been traded for a jumpsuit. His hands were folded, wrists cuffed to a length of chain looped through a ring on the steel table.

"Thank you," Oscar told the guard. "I just need some time alone with my client. Preparing for trial."

The guard shot Gimondi a look that could curdle milk. He grudgingly shut the door, sealing them inside.

"Tell me you got some good news," Gimondi said.

"There are . . . complications," the lawyer replied, sitting down at the table. He popped the latches of his designer leather briefcase. His fingers trilled along the Italian stitching, a nervous flutter.

"Don't tell me about complications. You got any idea what it's like in here? I'm in ad seg. That's twenty-three hours a day alone in a cell. They let me out just long enough to hose me down and stuff me back in."

"I'm sure you'd prefer that to general population."

"Got a lot of time alone with my thoughts." The chain rattled as Gimondi pointed a finger at his temple. "It's not good for a man, having that much time to think. What kind of complications are we talkin' about here?"

"The district attorney retained a private firm to keep Cobb under lock and key until he testifies. They're good."

"I'm pretty sure that's your guy's job to deal with. I mean, can he whack him or—"

"Keep your voice *down*," Oscar snapped.

"What? This is privileged communication."

"Discussing the active commission of a crime is not covered under attorney-client privilege. Hiring me as your lawyer buys us a little privacy"—Oscar waved his hand, taking in the room—"but that's it. You haven't been discussing . . . our arrangement with the others, have you?"

"Kellogg and Vargas? Nah, I ain't seen either of 'em since they brought me in. I know they're being held somewhere in here, but they keep us separated. Private accommodations."

"Good. Keep it that way. And don't use the telephones. All calls are recorded, and I guarantee Poole has someone hanging on your every word. If they do give you a roommate, assume he's an informant."

Gimondi rolled his eyes. "Like I don't know this. I wrote the book on that trick. Look, there's only one thing I care about right now: Can your guy get the job done or not?"

"He's never let me down before. That said, you need to prepare for every possibility. You know, you can still offer up a confession and flip this on Cobb. You'd have to tell them everything."

The disgraced cop fell silent for a moment. His fingertips rapped against the interview table.

"The retirement fund," he said.

"That's right," Oscar replied.

"I do that, I have to confess to what really went down on Saratoga Street. All of it."

"That's right."

"And I get . . . what, maybe ten years off my sentence for cooperating with the DA?" Gimondi's lip curled in a sneer. "Hell with that. Still means spending most of the rest of my life up at Cedar Junction. Then what choices do I got? I can go nuts in solitary or get shanked in gen pop. I got a better idea: do your damn job."

Oscar held up his open palms. "I'm just saying, no matter what you choose, success is a roll of the dice."

"From where I'm sittin'," Gimondi said, "I don't see too many options. I'm all in."

Night drifted over the city. A wind rippled across the Charles, carrying a musty, greasy smell. Oscar shot a glance over his shoulder as he hustled through the parking lot, winding around sparse rows of mismatched cars in the dark.

You're being paranoid, he told himself. This was hardly the first trial he'd gone above and beyond to fix for a client. Hardly the highest-profile one, either, though it was close. He was careful. Kept himself insulated. But three little words chased him from the interview room, haunting his footsteps.

The retirement fund.

When his new client had come clean for the first time, behind closed doors, Oscar knew he should have walked. Washed his hands, gone to church, forgotten Gimondi's name. The lure of easy money kept him on the hook.

I'm insulated, he thought. The doors of his BMW unlocked with an electronic squawk.

He slipped behind the wheel, tossed his briefcase onto the passenger seat, and loosened the knot in his tie. The engine purred to life at the press of a button, doors locking, sealing him in. Safe.

Then a shadow moved in the back seat. It lunged for him. An arm—smooth, muscled, like marble wrapped in silk—curled around his throat and squeezed. His head slammed back against the headrest. He felt breath, steady and warm, wash against his neck.

His eyes shot to the rearview mirror. All he could see was the edge of a hard-angled face and a slash of midnight-blue lipstick.

"Where is it?" she asked him.

No clarification. He didn't know who the woman was, but he knew what she wanted. She knew that he knew. He breathed as deep as the arm clamped against his throat would let him.

"I'm just the defense attorney," he rasped, fighting for his last shreds of calm. "I'm not the person you want. But I'm . . . I'm engaged in the situation, and I can be useful—"

Something glinted in the woman's other hand. She held it up in front of his face, inches from his right eye, giving him a good close look.

A sewing needle. Two inches long, polished brass.

"You—you want the insider," he said. "Hayden Cobb. Look, I have someone working on the problem as we speak. We can make a deal."

The woman made a tongue-clicking sound. Quick, dry, like the tail of a rattlesnake. The tip of the needle swayed in her fingertips.

"I'll tell you anything you want to know," Oscar promised.

The needle fell away. Her arm relaxed, just a little. He closed his eyes and breathed a prayer of thanks to whoever might be listening.

She let go of his neck. Then her hand clamped down over his mouth. His eyes shot open, bulging.

"Oscar," the midnight-blue lips whispered in his ear. "I want to *meet* you."

The tip of the needle poked at the slope of his neck, not far from his spine. Hunting for one particular spot.

Then it slid in, and his world exploded in liquid fire. Her hand trapped his screams, keeping them locked inside his chest, as his heels hammered the floor mat. His hands twitched, contorted into claws, his arms paralyzed. The tip of the needle scraped against bone. She left it there, only a tiny nub sticking out from his flesh, a ruby of blood welling around the metal.

Now she showed him what she had in her open palm.

Another five needles. Each one a different length, each one polished and gleaming.

THIRTEEN

Come sunrise, the relief team was watching Cobb. So was the Boston PD, from a safe distance: they'd added a couple of patrols to the streets around the hotel, bringing a conspicuous presence. Charlie wasn't sure if that was a positive or not.

"They don't know who the target really was," Beckett told her, leaning back in the rear seat of the SUV. "And they don't need to."

Dom was driving. Charlie had shotgun, leaning into her armrest and squinting at the morning light.

"The opposition," Dom said, "meaning our hitter, and whoever's paying for him, probably realizes we used a decoy room. That leaves a few hundred possibilities, and they can't search the entire hotel. We've still got trouble, but at least Cobb's safe for the moment."

"Until the ADA calls and demands another meeting," Charlie said.

"Until then."

"Felton's our leak," Beckett said. "He gave Cobb's location up twice and failed twice. Way I see it, he's got to be one thin inch from a full-on panic attack right now. We get our hands on the shooter, he's got no reason not to give Felton up."

Dom nodded. "My question is, Who's paying *Felton*? Because I'm not seeing any motive beyond money for him. Anyway, either he's going to back off, give up, and pack it in if we're lucky, or he's going to pull something dumb and desperate."

"Always bank on dumb and desperate," Beckett said.

"But that's a problem for later. Which gives us the entire morning to take care of . . ."

They pulled into the artfully cobblestoned driveway of Lincoln Gable's four-bedroom, three-garage house. He had another radio interview scheduled for nine sharp.

"This asshole," Dom said. "This asshole right here."

"I love my job," Charlie said.

Onyx lenses concealed Beckett's eyes. His face was a stoic mask.

"Any squawking online?" he asked.

Dom threw the SUV into park, gave the horn two quick, angry taps, and glanced back over her shoulder.

"Just like last time," she said. "Grousing, hate mail, obscene tweets by the bucketload, but nothing calling for a protest."

"And yet, last time, a protest showed up. We any closer to figuring out who organized it?"

Dom pursed her lips. They twisted into a scowl.

At least it was a smaller venue. AM radio, a hole-in-the-wall studio over in West Roxbury, where the halls were lined with seventies-era dark wood paneling and the carpet was some mutant form of faded orange shag, like the surface of an alien moon. The lobby smelled like mothballs. Lincoln was all smiles and raring to go, and they gave the studio a quick once-over before passing him over to the show host. The host was a burnout case in an olive army jacket and a woven headband. Charlie wasn't sure who was going to have a worse time in there.

"Five bucks," Dom says. "Five bucks says the interview is over in ten minutes or less."

"I'll take that action," Beckett replied.

Charlie arched an eyebrow. She glanced back over her shoulder.

"You kidding? There's an autographed photo of Hillary Clinton behind the reception desk. These guys are going to tear each other apart."

"What do radio stations sell, Little Duck?"

Charlie shrugged. "Advertising?"

"And advertisers are drawn to listener attention. Attention is a form of currency. So is outrage." Beckett pointed his thumb up the paneled corridor. "I've got a five-dollar bill that says the host stretches this out for a good twenty minutes. Thirty, if he takes callers once they're good and lathered up. He wants a show they'll be talking about for weeks, and so does Gable. They might be natural enemies in the wild, but they feed on the same red meat."

He wasn't wrong. The trio got front-row seats for the show, thanks to the tinny speaker over the reception desk. Charlie was already feeling sick to her stomach. This time yesterday she'd been charging to her father's house, off to the rescue, only to find Jimmy Lassiter waiting. And her father . . . he needed her. She trusted Jimmy wouldn't hurt him, so long as Charlie was useful.

And her usefulness hinged on her "date" with Riley Glass tonight. Everything was riding on her shoulders. She thought about calling Jimmy, giving him a status update, but she didn't have anything concrete to tell him—yet—and he wasn't in the market for excuses. It would keep until after she met with Riley and got the truth out of him, one way or another.

"And these . . . I'll be honest," Lincoln was telling the host, "I'll be honest and call them animals, which is what they are, unhinged animals, attacked a woman protecting me at my last appearance."

"The glitter bomb," the host said with a chuckle. "Yeah, saw that on YouTube."

"See? You think it's funny. She was injured, her face cut open, and let me tell you something, Phil. Let me tell you something. This woman, Charlene McCabe, is not only one of my dearest friends and supporters—I've known her for years—she's a veteran of the United States Army."

Charlie's jaw dropped.

"Oh, he did fucking *not*," Dom hissed. She took a step toward the studio door, and Beckett stopped her with one hand.

"This woman served her country with distinction and came home, only to be assaulted by Neanderthals. And for what? For standing up as a loyal American and saying yes, Lincoln Gable is *right*."

"Wait," the host said, "weren't you just saying women have no place in the military?"

"And now you're trying to change the subject and pull a gotcha. Phil, I stand by my love of the troops. You won't shame me for that."

"I'm going to stomp him into a mud puddle," Dom said.

"*Tigrotta*—"

"You don't get to *tigrotta* me today, Beckett."

"Trouble," he said, nodding toward the lobby windows.

A line of cars snaked into the parking lot, seven or eight in all. The last were pulling into spots near the exit while the first arrivals popped their trunks and started passing out picket signs. Charlie zeroed in on the signs. Familiar colors, familiar lettering. THIS IS NOT THE LAND OF LINCOLN in Comic Sans font on white pasteboard.

"Same signs," she said. "Same people as the crowd in Medford."

"It's nine a.m. on a weekday." Dom crossed her arms. "Do these people not have jobs?"

Beckett made a faint sound in his throat. *Hn.* Dom nodded at him, sharp.

"On it," she said.

She headed out before the crowd could assemble, slipping through the lobby doors and jogging to the SUV. Charlie felt numb, digging her short-cropped fingernails into the meat of her palms. Lincoln had just named her on air, lied, and invited every pissed-off antifan to dox and harass her at will. Now the protesters were here, and her father was sitting in a basement somewhere, under the gun, and she had a date tonight, and—

"Little Duck," Beckett said.

She turned, jolted from her downward spiral. A gust of wind pushed up against her smoking wings.

"It's all right to be under stress," he told her. "Long as you process it, flow through it, keep swimming until you're out and free. The only wrong reaction, under stress, is to shut down and freeze up."

"Got it," she said.

"Even your blood's under pressure. That's what keeps it moving."

The interview had gone from a rapid-fire back-and-forth to shouting, and somebody was pounding his fist on the broadcast desk, punctuating his words with percussion. Charlie plucked the radio from her belt.

"Dom? Get ready for exfil. Sounds like they're wrapping up."

They were. The second the station cut to a commercial break, Lincoln emerged, going from red-faced bluster to a silky-smooth smile like flicking a switch.

"Now that," he said, "is how it's done. Honestly, AM radio is terrible for exposure, but once people rip a few choice clips and upload 'em to social media, that's what draws the real clicks. Hey, looks like my adoring public is here."

Charlie forced her hands to unclench. They were feeling a little too much like fists. *Be polite, be professional,* she told herself. *Be polite, be professional.*

She was the first out the door, holding up her badge, pushing the crowd back with a bubble of authority. They were packing the lawn, standing out on the grass as they waved their signs, a chant going up. The SUV was curbside, fifteen feet ahead. Smirking, Lincoln tried to flash a victory sign at the mob. Beckett caught his wrist and gently but firmly pushed it down.

They must have been listening to the interview on their car radios. Charlie caught as much heat from the protesters as Lincoln did, shouts and abuse pelting off her back like stones. She kept her mind on the mission, chin high, checking for threats with her lips pursed in a bloodless line. The words were just a froth of hate, meaningless; movement was what mattered.

Movement like the sudden churn in the pack on her right. She signaled to Beckett, and he grabbed Lincoln's shoulder and hustled him past while she bodychecked the sudden surge of protesters. Dom was out of the SUV and circling around, yanking open the back door. The mob broke like a wave, the ones in front giving cover for the real incoming threat.

A fat cardboard cup went spiraling through the air like a football pass, spinning, plastic lid and straw coming loose in midair. The supersize cup hit Charlie in the chest and burst. Suddenly she was drenched, freezing, her blazer and blouse painted in vanilla milkshake. Spatters of the icy treat caught in her bangs and drizzled down her cheek.

Charlie rode shotgun. She tried not to dribble onto the seat. She stared into the distance like a prison-yard convict, a thousand miles away.

"I want you to know how much I appreciate—" Lincoln started to say.

"No," Beckett told him.

"But I—"

"No."

He shut up after that. Charlie sank into the gulf of silence, lost in the drone of the engine, the thrum of the wheels against the road. Under normal circumstances, the milkshake would be a mild annoyance; now it was one stone too many piled on top of her mountain of trouble, and the collective weight squeezed the breath from her lungs.

She knew what to do. She always did. Left foot, right foot, one in front of the other, until she marched through the storm and out the other side. She just had to keep moving. Keep thinking, keep fighting.

They dropped Charlie off at home. She stripped down in the kitchen and trudged to the shower.

She was rummaging in her closet, digging for something to wear, when her phone rang. She didn't recognize the number.

"Ms. McCabe? Lincoln Gable gave me your contact information. I'm the producer for *Eye on Boston*. He'll be on our program in a couple of days, to promote his new book?"

"Right," Charlie said, bracing the phone against her shoulder while she wriggled into sweatpants. "If this is about his security detail, Mr. Beckett should be contacting you shortly."

"No, actually, this is about you. I . . . don't know if you're aware, but 'Fascist Gets Milkshaked' is racking up a ton of views at the moment—"

Charlie bit her bottom lip. *Just keep moving. Push through the stress.*

"We'd actually like you to come on the program, alongside Mr. Gable, so you can have a platform."

"A platform," she echoed.

"To openly discuss your views. As one of Mr. Gable's closest friends and supporters, we think you could bring a unique perspective to the discussion."

She bit her lip harder this time. Anything to keep the torrent of things she wanted to say far, far away from her mouth. Boston Asset Protection was still getting back on its feet. They needed this contract, they needed Gable's money, and more importantly, they needed a reputation for rock-solid reliability. No matter what. Jake and Sofia—and her friends and partners—were counting on her.

"I am a security professional," she told the producer. "I don't *have* personal views, not when I'm on the clock. Anyone who contracts with our firm, no matter who they are or where they stand on the political spectrum, can expect the exact same level of dedicated service. That's my only statement. Thank you."

She hung up. She finished getting dressed. A numbness was setting in, like cold gel just under her skin. Emotional numbness didn't do much to help with the aching in her ribs and her left shoulder from her fight at the hotel. Ibuprofen would have to take care of that. Her movements were mechanical; she bagged up her suit, grabbed her keys and wallet, and headed back out. She'd found a good dry cleaner a couple of blocks from her new apartment. They were still working on the glitter. Now she had a second suit with a fresh challenge for them, and her professional wardrobe was running out fast.

When she emerged from the dry cleaners, Dom was waiting for her. She drove a sleek white Continental tricked out with full leather and trim, the kind of car that no one could afford on a bodyguard's salary. The first time Charlie had seen it, Dom had explained that she'd actually bought the ride six years ago, during her short-lived prior career.

Charlie hadn't pointed out, at the time, that a rookie cop couldn't afford a car like that either.

Dom leaned toward the open window. "Hey."

"Hey," Charlie said, surprised to see her.

Dom nodded at the empty passenger seat.

"Get in, loser. We're going shopping."

Fourteen

An hour later Charlie was reclining on a plush chair at a strip mall day spa, cotton puffs spacing out her freshly painted toes, while a technician gave her right hand a vigorous manicure.

"Aren't you supposed to be watching Cobb?"

Dom had cucumber slices on her eyes.

"Beckett talked one of the B-team guys into pulling a double shift," she murmured, her voice faintly dreamy. "Also, before you ask, Sofia's paying for the mani-pedi."

"And she's doing that why?" Charlie's stomach tightened. "Wait, is she afraid I'm going to quit? I don't quit."

"Oh my God, Charlie. Please. No, Beckett and I just thought, considering you're understandably a little high strung at the moment, you could use a little relaxation therapy. And Sofia agreed, especially after we filled her in about tonight."

"Right," Charlie said, sinking into her chair. "Date night."

"And I came, because if we just gave you a gift certificate or something, we all know perfectly well that you wouldn't use it. By the way? Jake called Gable and read him the riot act for endangering one of his employees. I was in the room; it was pretty impressive. Jake doesn't raise his voice often."

"I don't suppose I should expect an apology."

"Guys like Gable don't apologize," Dom said. "However, he was chastened enough to offer a sizable addition to his contract fee, along with a promise to keep our names out of his mouth going forward. His one request was that you stay on his security detail."

Charlie's brow furrowed. "Why? If he can't use my military service for a prop, what difference does it make?"

Dom reached up, languid, and pulled back a single slice of cucumber. She gave Charlie a sly, one-eyed stare.

"I think he's got the hots for you."

"Oh." Charlie winced. "Oh. *Ew.*"

"Hey, if Detective Glass turns out to be an attempted murderer who planted evidence at a crime scene, now you have a fallback option. Romance is in the air."

The woman working on Charlie's nails gave Dom a look.

"Yeah, this is gonna be my year," Charlie said. "I can feel it. Mr. Right is coming my way."

Their next stop was a boutique in the Back Bay, on a street outside of Charlie's price range.

"Don't worry about it," Dom told her, reading Charlie's face.

"Sofia's paying for my date-night outfit?"

"No, but I know the owner."

Charlie figured that was the broad-shouldered woman behind the counter, who wore her hair in a rockabilly bouffant. Her contoured makeup made her look like a forties pinup model. She squealed as Dom came in and rushed around the glass-topped counter to drag her into a bear hug.

"Little Dommie! Where have you been?"

Dom air-kissed her cheeks. "You know, work and more work, like I do. Gotta keep my divorce lawyer fed."

"I swear, that no-good *figlio di puttana* ex of yours—"

"He'll get his. Carmela, this is Charlie. She's a friend of mine."

Charlie was next in line for a hug, whether she wanted one or not.

"A friend of yours is a friend of ours, always." She held Charlie at arm's length and looked her up and down. "And what is this? Sweats? Gray flannel? Honey, you brought your friend to the right place. This is an emergency."

"She's got a hot date tonight," Dom said. "Figured we could use your expertise."

"It's not really a——" Charlie started to say, but Carmela was already taking her by the sleeve and hustling her across the brightly lit store. She ended up in a changing room with an armload of dresses to try on. Outside, Dom called over the door.

"Hey, Charlie, you don't speak Italian, right?"

"Nah, just two years of high school French."

"Okay, cool."

She and Carmela started to talk in rapid-fire Italian. Charlie rolled her eyes and undressed. Nothing fit right. Then she had to ask herself if she just didn't *want* anything to fit right, if this was her subconscious way of digging her heels in. She was alone in the tiny changing booth with nothing but her thoughts, staring at herself in the mirror.

She breathed. Regrouped. Everything—her father's life, Hayden Cobb's life, the truth about the motel shooting—was riding on her shoulders tonight. *And that's fine,* she told her mirror image. *I've got strong shoulders. I'll deal with it.*

She reached for the next hanger, tried on the next dress, and it fit like it was made just for her.

She emerged from the changing booth. Carmela was across the store, helping another customer, while Dom tapped at her phone. She glanced up and flashed an eager smile.

"Perfection," she said.

"You think so?" Charlie glanced over her shoulder, to the mirror, getting a look at herself from the back. The tea gown was light and breezy, ruched at one side with a frilled hem, a constellation of white dots on midnight black. The neckline plunged somewhere just a quarter inch short of dangerous.

"I think your date won't know what hit him," Dom said. "Which is great, in case things go wrong and you need to, you know. Hit him."

Charlie checked the tag and blanched.

"Oh damn. I should have looked first." She showed Dom. "I can't afford this."

"Sure you can. Trust me."

"No, I mean I just had to lay down advance rent and a deposit on my new place. I can't go spending four hundred bucks on a designer dress—"

Dom put her hand on Charlie's arm.

"Trust me," she said.

At the register, the dress rang up as twenty dollars. Charlie started to say something, and Dom poked her in the ribs.

"You give my regards to your father," Carmela said to Dom, handing Charlie's debit card back.

Back out on the sidewalk, Charlie gave Dom the side-eye.

"What just happened in there?"

"Family pays wholesale," Dom said. "Come on, you've seen my Prada bag. You really think I paid full price for that thing? Anyway, it's not like Carmela even paid that much, so everybody wins."

Charlie lowered her voice to a near whisper. "Did I just buy a stolen dress?"

Dom pretended to be mildly shocked by the question.

"Nonsense. My cousin operates a perfectly legitimate business. It's just that, you know, things happen. Sometimes a mailing label gets mixed up, or a delivery truck takes their packages to the wrong store. By accident."

"Uh-huh," Charlie said.

"And as a consequence, some insurance company's loss is your gain. C'mon, you need accessories to go with the dress. New earrings."

"I have earrings."

"It's date night. You need *new* earrings."

"No word from ADA Felton?" Charlie asked.

"Nothing," Beckett said. He sat behind the wheel of the company SUV, fingers light on the dark plastic curve. He'd pulled over at the curb, one block shy of Riley's apartment building. Dom was in back. The dashboard clock said it was almost showtime.

"Lending credence to my 'realized he was about to get caught and decided to back off' theory," Dom said.

"That's not a theory; that's a hope," Beckett replied. "We have to sit on Cobb for a few days yet. These woods are long and deep."

"I'd say *one crisis at a time*, but life never really cooperates." Charlie fidgeted with the neckline of her new dress, which she'd been doing since she'd gotten in the truck. Her wrist carried the faint scent of orchids.

"Stop fussing," Dom told her. "Got a game plan?"

"If I confront him directly, good chance he'll clam up. I'm going to play it subtle and try to figure out what he knows."

"Like, does he know that you know the gun you gave him was used in a recent crime?" Dom asked.

"That, and does he know I was inside that motel room. Even if Riley was there, and he fired and dumped the .38, there's a good chance he doesn't know we were contracted to protect Cobb. As far as we know, he, or whoever had that revolver, was there to murder the hitman. And that raises its own mountain of questions. So I'm going to push him a little bit and see how he reacts."

"Just a little?" Dom said.

"Just a little, for starters. We'll see how dinner goes."

"If you decide you need to escalate the pressure . . . ," Beckett said. He left the rest in an expectant silence.

"I know. I'll withdraw, get to a safe distance in case he turns dangerous, and call for backup. If I really need to get rough, I won't do it alone. Where are you going to be tonight?"

Beckett leaned toward the windshield. He peeled down his sunglasses and slowly drew his gaze along the street.

"Well, in about fifteen minutes, tigrotta and me are going to be inside that gyros place right over there. Then we'll be back here again. Eating gyros. Providing, of course, that the online reviews check out. I don't know this street."

"I think there's a good Indian place a couple of blocks over," Dom said.

"There you go. We may be eating Indian instead of gyros. Speaking only for myself, I find a good home-cooked dish of *mattar paneer* to be nothing short of delightful."

Charlie turned in her seat.

"You know this is going to take a while, right? Like, he's making dinner. I could be in that apartment for hours. You don't have to stick around."

"After we've enjoyed our meal," Beckett said, "I may search for a local gelato shop."

"We passed a Baskin-Robbins a couple of blocks back," Dom said.

Beckett slid his glasses back over his eyes.

"I didn't say ice cream. I said gelato."

"You're really going to sit down here," Charlie said. "All night. For me."

"Partners," Dom said.

It was all she needed to say. Charlie reached back and squeezed her hand.

"Now, if you do find out he passed the .38 to somebody else and he's totally innocent," Dom said, "a courtesy text would be appreciated.

Especially if you're going to bone him. I don't need to be paying a babysitter for overtime while somebody who *isn't* me is getting lucky."

Heat warmed the pale blush on Charlie's cheeks.

"I don't . . . I mean . . . not on the first date."

Dom's eyelashes fluttered, all innocence. "Oh, me too. I never, *ever* go down to pound town on the first date. Never once in my life. I completely agree."

"Are you carrying protection?" Beckett asked.

Charlie squeezed her black clutch purse, squirming in her seat.

"I mean, yeah, always, of course, but I'd hope he's responsible enough to have—" Charlie caught the look he was giving her out the side of his glasses. "And . . . you were talking about weaponry."

Dom snorted.

"Can't really tote my pistol in this thing," she said, patting her clutch, "or in this dress. I've got my ASP, though, and I loaded a fresh cartridge of OC spray this morning."

"Then I believe you are officially ready for date night. Keep us posted."

FIFTEEN

If places had jobs, Riley's apartment building would be a beat cop, or maybe a night watchman. It felt like the anchor of the block, a four-story slab of old bronze-tinged brick that had gone up sometime in the forties, with exposed piping in the vestibule and wooden stairs with vintage banisters. The linoleum floors had faded over the decades. Charlie imagined the original colors must have been vibrant, once, but now the deco scallops looked like the mush of an overripe banana.

But the front door was sturdy, and the brickwork held fast, and the boiler thrummed steadily somewhere under her feet. The building was an old, reliable workhorse, and it would still be here after she was dust and bones. She hunted for Riley's number on the intercom—304—and pressed the button. He buzzed her through the security door.

The door to 304 swung open as she rounded the landing, and there he was, trying to conceal his nerves and failing. He had a little energetic bounce, leaning into the toes of his freshly polished loafers, and tight shoulders under a crisp mint-green button-down. Riley Glass looked like a fox. He had a sharp face and a sharp nose, bright eyes, and his unruly ginger hair curled in the faint impression of a woodland mane.

He reached out, caught himself, paused. "Do you hug?"

"I do," she said and gave him a squeeze. His muscles were like steel cords under the pressed cotton of his shirt. Riley was lean and quick, far from a buffed-up gym rat, but he took care of himself. He led her inside with a flourish and an anxious smile.

Riley's place was breezy and open, hardwood floors, one long gallery from the living room to the kitchen separated by a broad archway. The walls were the color of sunbaked mud. His furniture had a college thrift shop aesthetic; somehow, she wasn't surprised to see a big black beanbag chair in front of his wide-screen TV, sitting out next to a solitary PlayStation controller. An acoustic guitar leaned against his television stand.

"You play?" she asked, nodding to the guitar.

"Eh, sort of." He shut the door behind her and flipped the lock. "Learned when I was in college."

"You mean, you learned so you could pick up girls."

"I mostly played at dorm parties," he said, sheepish. "I know five songs by heart. Three are by the Dave Matthews Band."

Charlie put a hand over her heart. "Oh no. You're that guy."

"I'm that guy. The fourth song is 'Your Body Is a Wonderland' by John Mayer."

"I may have to leave," Charlie said. "Please don't tell me the fifth song is 'Hey There Delilah.'"

"Ma'am, I have my pride."

He scooped up the guitar, cradled it in his arms, and strummed the strings with practiced grace. The opening chords of "Hotel California" rippled across the apartment, quick and delicate and dark. He could play.

"Okay," Charlie said, "now I'm staying for dinner."

He laid the guitar down and led her to the kitchen. Past a couple of closed doors, past a wall adorned with sparse photographs. There was a shot of an older man, bearded, in hip waders, holding up a trophy fish with a little boy on his knee. Even as a kid, Riley looked like he should have been running wild in a forest somewhere. Then another picture of an elderly couple, wedding rings gleaming, posing for their anniversary.

A wide portrait, framed in black plastic, snapped her out of date mode and back to the mission. Riley's graduation photo from the Boston Police Academy. He was up in front, head high, wearing his first uniform cap and white gloves. Charlie's gaze drifted across the ranks.

DA Poole knew there was a fourth member of the smash-and-grab ring. A fourth corrupt cop, one who'd escaped scrutiny when they'd rounded up the East Boston Three. At first it had looked like Riley was the number one suspect. Now, after what she'd found at the motel, the signs that the man with the .38 had been there to kill the killer, she wasn't so sure.

"Anyway," he said, "this is my place. I won't show you the bedroom."

She glanced to the closed door and imagined a rumpled bed, clothes on the floor, stray socks. His kitchen was immaculate. Old fixtures with a refrigerator that softly rattled and faded backsplash tiles, but he kept it operating-theater clean. At least on date night. The tools of his second trade were laid out along the counter: a cutting board, chef-grade knives, and a jumble of fresh peppers and peeled cloves of garlic.

"Nice to actually cook for someone else for a change," he said, running his hands under the tap. "When I cook for myself, I end up with leftovers for days, and the third or fourth night of microwaved tortellini gets a little old."

"I've been living on takeout since I got my new place," Charlie said. She thought about her empty cupboards, bare shelves. Her first moving-day purchase had been a coffee maker. Everything else would have to wait until her next paycheck.

Riley filled a pot with water for the pasta. The sound and his turned back gave Charlie a few seconds of cover. She stepped out of the kitchen, framed the graduation photo in the rectangle of her phone, and snapped a quick picture. She attached it to a text and fired it off to Beckett and Dom. Riley's grad pic. See any of the EB3 with him?

Riley made his sauce from scratch. The kitchen filled with a robust, hearty aroma as oregano, basil, and thyme joined sautéed garlic in a pan, tomato paste turning rich and dark.

"I've got to run to the little boys' room," he said. "Do me a favor and stir this for me? Just keep it moving so it doesn't burn."

He passed her the wooden spoon, and she took over at the stove. The bathroom door thumped shut. This was a chance to poke around, maybe the only one she'd get. Charlie looked back over her shoulder to the bedroom door. No. Too close to the bathroom; there was a chance he'd hear her. She kept the sauce moving, stirring with one hand while she stretched out and checked his kitchen drawers with the other. She wasn't expecting to find a signed confession hidden with his silverware, but she couldn't let the opportunity slip by.

He kept a junk drawer by the fridge, stuffed with the floating detritus of everyday life. Spare change, loose AA batteries, a handful of instruction manuals for kitchen appliances. An old, dead TV remote. And a pair of keys, bound to an unlabeled red plastic tag.

Spares. She shot another look at the bathroom door. They looked like house keys; for his apartment or someplace else? They'd been nestled at the bottom of the drawer, so either he hid them out of habit or he just didn't use them often. Out of sight, out of mind.

She slipped the keys into her purse. The drawer slid shut as the toilet flushed, and she stirred the sauce while he washed his hands.

He took over at the pan, she chopped scallions for him, and they talked. About college, their jobs, the getting-to-know-you banter that skimmed over the surface of their lives. The truths Charlie needed were deeper, down in the lightless depths of Riley's forest.

He served up the food at his kitchen table. One bite, and Charlie could have fallen in love. The linguine was firm, robust, the sauce a perfect balance of sweet and savory. He'd even made garlic bread, heavy on the butter.

"I'd love to say I had some dramatic reason for joining the force," he was telling her, pouring a second splash of red wine into her glass. "Instead, I have to blame a steady diet of cop shows as a kid. Thought I'd get to spend all my time solving mysteries and putting away bad guys."

She took a sip of her cabernet. Grocery store table wine, cheap but good.

"The real job's not as glamorous, huh?"

"It's a lot of paperwork, a lot of rules, and a lot of . . . community management, I guess. We spend a lot of time trying to talk knuckle-heads into not being knuckleheads and getting people to be less shitty to each other."

"That sounds impossible."

"Who was the guy from the myths who had to roll a boulder uphill, and every time he got to the top, it'd just roll back down again?"

"Sisyphus," Charlie said.

He pointed his fork at her. "That's the one. And you know, on TV, there's always a twist. The mystery's always more complicated than it looks, and there's always some big third-act revelation."

"The real thing, not so much?"

Riley shrugged. "You walk into a place; there's a dead woman on the floor. Know who did it? The husband or the boyfriend. Case closed. Walk into a liquor store, dead clerk, empty cash register. Know who did it? The idiot over on the next block, wearing brand-new kicks, who bragged to all his friends about it. And they'll all line up to roll on him, because 'honor among thieves' isn't a real thing."

And there was the opening she'd been looking for.

"I don't know about that," she said. "I mean, I don't want to bring it up if it's a sore point . . ."

He eyed her over his wineglass, curious now. "What?"

"Well, you work out of East Boston. I follow the news like every-body else."

Riley looked sour. She wasn't sure if she caught more than that in the flicker of his expression, something else buried under the surface. Nothing that gave him away, either: he looked angry, tired, the same emotions she'd expect any cop working out of the A-7 to be feeling right now.

"Nothing worse," he said. "Nothing worse than a bad cop. People don't respect cops. They don't *like* cops. We have to bend over backward to get an inch of trust, and that trust is what helps us keep people safe. Then these guys come around and burn it all down, just to line their own pockets."

"Did you know them?"

"The East Boston Three?" Riley shifted in his chair. "Just enough to match their names to their faces. I knew 'em from roll call; that's about it. I mean, those guys were tight. Insular. That's how they got away with it as long as they did."

"Just the three of them?"

"That's how I understand it. I'm just hoping they go away for the long count. Won't make up for all the damage they did, but at least it sends a message."

He sounded sincere. Then again, Charlie knew a lot of gifted liars.

The conversation was a train running out of track. She had until the end of the meal to get something out of him, something she could use. Confronting him about the .38 was too risky. She thought it over between bites of pasta, using the momentary silence to hunt for an angle.

"I shouldn't tell you this," she said.

His eyes brightened. "Oh, that's always the setup for something good."

"You know that guy, Hayden Cobb? The star witness?"

"Think I read about him," Riley said.

"Local dealer. He flipped on one of the East Boston Three, to save himself from being tied to those murders on Saratoga Street. He was their insider, the one lining up all the heists."

"See what I mean?" Riley said. "No honor among thieves."

"The district attorney hired my company to keep him safe until the trial."

She studied his face. New interest, the lift of an eyebrow, the slightest flare of his nostrils. Nothing unexpected; again, it was the same reaction, casual curiosity, that she'd expect from an innocent man.

"That sounds like a dangerous assignment," he said.

"They usually are. Nobody pays for a security detail if they don't need one."

"True," he said. He gazed into her eyes and sipped his wine.

"So this is the part I shouldn't tell you. We were keeping Cobb at this cheap motel in Southborough, the Pocono Motor Inn. First night there, somebody came and took a shot at him."

"No way," Riley said. "Is he all right?"

He was a good liar, but not that good. His posture shifted with his attitude, going from genuine curiosity to a counterfeit copy of the real thing. He had the face of a man who had already heard the story she was telling but wanted to look interested.

Because you were there, she thought. *Here's the part I don't think you know about.*

"He's fine. I almost wasn't."

His brow pinched. "How's that?"

"I was there," she said. "In the motel room, by the window. The shooter saw my shadow behind the curtain and mistook me for the witness. If I hadn't caught a glimmer of movement and hunkered down, that bullet would have killed me. My partner showed up, and the guy took off running. He even dropped his weapon. Must have panicked."

He tried to clamp down on his emotions. Too slow. Riley was feeling the panic, too, and while some of it might have been for her, worry for her well-being, he understood the situation.

She knew about the .38 at the crime scene. And if Poole was keeping her in the loop—if Charlie had found out that Grillo had been arrested for the attempted hit—she knew that gun had passed from Grillo's hands to hers to Riley's. She could pin it on him with a single phone call.

Now you have a mystery of your own to solve, Charlie thought. *How much do I really know? Am I a threat? And what are you going to do about it?*

She reached for the bottle. She topped off his glass of wine, then her own. The pulled muscle in her left shoulder twinged. She didn't mind. The pain helped her keep a poker face while Riley was losing his.

Sixteen

Charlie had to give Riley credit: he bounced back fast. He buried his flash of fear and put it all on her, playing it off as friendly concern.

"That had to be terrifying," he said.

"I've been shot at before. Occupational hazard."

"I'm just imagining it." His shoulders gave a little shiver. "So I assume they took you off the assignment?"

"Why would you assume that?"

"I don't know. Just seems wrong that they'd make you stay on after that. This guy . . . he dropped his gun when he ran?"

There it is, she thought. *Can't help yourself, can you? You need to know what I know.*

She had no doubt now. Riley had been there, the shooter with the .38. She didn't know why he'd abandoned the stolen weapon or why he'd been trying to murder the hitman in the first place, but he hadn't known Charlie was fifteen feet away when he'd pulled the trigger. If he had, she figured, he never would have dumped the gun like that.

But he had, and now he had to consider the consequences.

"That's right," she said. "We're not thinking this guy was much of a professional. The weapon was this janky old revolver, not exactly a James Bond kind of gun."

"Have you heard anything else?" he asked. "Do you know if they have any leads?"

"I haven't heard," Charlie lied. "But obviously, we want to know. My boss asked the DA to call him if anyone gets arrested, and I assume he'll tell me, but . . . well. Private security. We never have half the intel we need. If they can even manage to tie the gun to an owner, it could be a month before I hear about it."

He relaxed a little. Giving himself away, one move at a time. His shoulders unclenched, and he reached for his glass.

"Any idea who it was?"

"Hired gun, most likely. The way I hear it, Cobb has the receipts on the East Boston Three. He testifies, they go down. He dies first, they probably walk. Let's be honest—there are ways to hire a shooter from behind bars, if you have the connections and know how to game the system."

"Wouldn't be the first time," Riley said.

"On the other hand, there're . . . the rumors."

He froze in midsip. Glass tilted back, red wine a fraction of an inch from his lips.

"Rumors?"

"It wasn't in the papers, but when she brought us on, DA Poole said some of the witness reports talked about *four* masked cops. I mean, they were confused, some of them were roughed up, the robberies were all blitz attacks—"

"You can't always trust an eyewitness," Riley said. "Memories lie."

"Exactly. But if they're right, that means there's a fourth member of the gang. Still out there, on the loose."

"Doesn't seem like his problem," Riley said. "I mean, the Three won't even point fingers at each other, let alone a mystery partner, and it sounds like Cobb either can't or won't ID him. What does he have to gain from killing the witness?"

"Maybe he's trying to save his buddies' lives. Maybe there *is* honor among thieves."

"Maybe," Riley said.

"The only good news is now that there's a weapon in evidence, there's a solid lead. *If* they tie that gun to a police officer, especially one working out of the A-7, like the other three . . . well, I imagine a jury would convict on that alone."

Charlie twirled her fork, capturing the final strand of linguine. She gave him a second to let her words sink in, then added a little punctuation.

"Whoever he is, that guy is screwed," she said.

Riley set his glass down. He looked a little pale around the edges.

"I wouldn't want to be him," he said. "But if the fourth man is real, he can't be someone working out of my house."

"How's that?"

He gave a faint chuckle. "IA's had us all under a magnifying glass since they arrested Lieutenant Gimondi. I mean, that's how they caught Kellogg and Vargas: they were both going on spending sprees. Kellogg bought a Corvette with his stolen cash."

"Not too bright."

"He never was. But trust me, they were combing through our lives and checking our bank accounts down to the last penny. If one of us stole a nickel back in grade school, Internal Affairs would have found out about it. It was like getting a month-long prostate exam and about as much fun. But one thing I can safely say is, thanks to the investigation, every cop left in my house is one hundred percent true blue. Not a dishonest badge in the bunch."

He had a point. She had to imagine IA and Poole's entire office were working overtime to ferret out the bad apples. None of them had been able to put a face or a name to the fourth man in the gang, which said he was working another squad house, in another part of Boston.

But. Charlie played Riley's words back in her mind, keeping them fresh, making sure she hadn't misheard him. He'd just shown her a card that he should have kept hidden.

"I'm sorry," she said, taking out her phone. "I have to check this. Work phone."

"Oh, I get it. One thing we've got in common, we're both on call twenty-four seven."

She pulled up an old text message, pretended to read it, and slipped the phone back into her clutch.

"Damn. One of our operatives called in sick at the last minute, and they need me on the job. Like, as of fifteen minutes ago. I have to run."

He wiped the corner of his mouth with a napkin and slid his chair back.

"Hey," he said, "I get that too. Different vocation, shockingly similar lifestyle. You have no idea how many movies I've had to walk out of halfway through. At least you're not going to work hungry."

She had to smile. "I am not. That was *really* good. You weren't kidding when you said you could cook."

He escorted her to the door, through the living room and past his leaning guitar.

"Yeah, but you're missing dessert. And then I was going to serenade you with the eternal, dulcet tones of the Dave Matthews Band."

She gave him a sidelong glance. "I'm escaping in the nick of time."

"Would you prefer John Mayer?"

He opened the door for her. They hovered together, on the apartment threshold, separated by a strip of wood and a few inches of open air.

"Seriously, though," he said. "Would you think about doing something for me?"

"Having dinner again sometime?"

He flashed a boyish smile. "Yeah, definitely that, but also . . . do you think they could move you to a different assignment?"

"Why?"

"Look, I'm nobody to tell you how to live your life. You've been in an actual war; I've never fired my service weapon outside the range—"

"But," she said.

"But this is dangerous. Somebody's out there trying to kill your client, and it doesn't sound like they care about collateral damage."

"That's the job," Charlie said.

He withdrew from his own smile. It turned wan, fading from his eyes.

"I guess," he said. "So. Another time?".

"Another time."

They lingered a little longer. She pulled him into a close hug, feeling his breath on her neck, and let go.

"I'll text you," she said.

She didn't hear the apartment door click shut until she was halfway down the stairs.

On a different night, under different circumstances, she might have kissed him goodbye. But Riley had given too much of the game away. She still didn't know what his motive was, but he had been at the motel, he'd planted Grillo's gun, and he'd set off the chain reaction that led to her own father being held hostage. And for his protests that he barely knew the East Boston Three, he'd let something slip when Officer Kellogg's name had come up.

"Not too bright."

"He never was."

"You think he's the fourth man?" Beckett asked.

They were back on the street, curbside in the company SUV, one block south of Riley's apartment building. The interior of the truck smelled like fresh-baked naan and Indian spices.

"I don't want him to be," Charlie said.

"Not what I asked."

"I know. Just . . . let me be disillusioned, a little. I thought Riley was one of the good guys. At the very best, he planted evidence and got my dad jammed up. At worst, he was part of a gang of crooked cops."

She was thinking about the photographs from Poole's briefing. The crime scene shots from the house on Saratoga Street. The bound wrists, the slashed throats.

"And he's got a tighter connection than just working out of the same house," Dom said from the back seat. She had her laptop open. It was a Toughbook, its rugged black shell engineered for outdoor conditions and field engineering. She turned the screen so Charlie could see.

The graduation photo from Riley's apartment was up on the screen, blown up until it started to distort. With a swoop of her finger, Dom painted ragged red circles around two of the white-gloved cadets.

"Kellogg. And Vargas. Riley didn't just work with them; he went to the academy with two members of the East Boston Three. They trained together, came up in the ranks together . . . even if he's not the fourth man, he's lying when he says he barely knew 'em."

"I'm still stuck on a motive," Charlie said.

"For the drop piece?"

"For the shooting," she said. "The hired gun was at the motel to kill Cobb. Riley took a shot at *him*. Why would the fourth member of a gang protect the witness who could send the other three away for life?"

Beckett answered his buzzing phone.

"Mm-hmm. Got it. I'm here with Dom and Charlie, putting you on speaker."

He tapped the screen. Jake's voice filled the cabin of the SUV.

"Hey. Poole just got in touch. New development in the case."

"Let me guess," Dom said. "ADA Felton needs another meeting with our primary, which is certainly not an attempt to leak his location for the third time in a row."

"That's what I expected, but no. It's about Oscar Pembrose. Guy's a big shot defense lawyer, and he was heading up the joint defense for the East Boston Three."

"Was?" Charlie said.

"He never came home last night, and this morning the cops found his car abandoned in a rental lot at Logan Airport. No blood, no signs of a struggle, but in a few more hours he officially goes on the missing-persons list."

"This could delay the trial." Charlie glanced at Beckett. "More time, more opportunity to take Cobb out before it's too late. Think these guys are desperate enough to have their own lawyer killed?"

"That was my thought, too," Jake said, "but Poole talked to the judge. Pembrose was just the face of a bigger team; his whole staff is briefed and in the loop, and their second chair is ready to roll. Defense didn't even *ask* for a delay. All the same, something seriously weird is afoot. So, uh, out of idle curiosity? You three aren't scheduled to be on duty babysitting Cobb for another few hours yet. Why are you all together? Social occasion?"

"Working some unpaid overtime," Beckett said.

"What are you three working on?"

"An angle."

"Do I want details?"

"You do not," Beckett said.

Jake didn't miss a beat. "Great, I never asked. Carry on."

The call ended. Beckett's phone disappeared into the tailored folds of his blazer.

"We know what Detective Glass did," Beckett said. "The question of the hour is why he did it. Best source is the man himself."

"Meaning we're all on board with my sack-of-oranges idea," Dom said.

"I've got a better idea." The keys Charlie lifted from Riley's rummage drawer jingled in her hand, dangling from the red plastic tag.

"How about before we do anything we can't undo, I see if he left any clues behind?"

Dom's eyebrows lifted. "You snatch those?"

"His spares. I mean, I think they're his spares. Won't know until I try."

"Does he have an alarm system?"

Charlie shook her head.

"I checked for a panel by the door on my way out. It's an old building; they've got a security door with a buzzer, and that's about it. I figure we pull our babysitting shift tonight, and when the B-team takes over in the morning, we swing on by. All I need you to do is cover the street, just in case he comes home early."

"And if he does?" Beckett asked. "Bearing in mind that the man already tried to kill someone, he carries a gun for a living and could legally shoot you if he caught you ransacking his castle."

"We improvise," Charlie said.

SEVENTEEN

One thing the three could agree on was that improvisation, while sometimes necessary in the field, was no substitute for a solid plan. They spent the night watching Cobb two at a time and going over the details, while the third partner caught a couple of hours of shut-eye down in the decoy room. Then they'd rotate. The shooter didn't make an encore appearance, and the night passed without a new call from Felton. Whoever was pulling Felton's strings, and whatever they were paying him, it was starting to feel like he knew he'd pushed things too far by leaking Cobb's location twice in a row.

Or maybe he was just shifting tactics.

The relief team showed up at five minutes to nine. Charlie was refreshed and ready. She hadn't gotten anything resembling a full night's sleep, but catnaps and strong black coffee, fresh from the café just off the hotel lobby, would power her through. That and the growing sense of anxiety, the tingling pressure at the nape of her neck that could turn into a shot of adrenaline at any moment.

"Tell me something good," Jimmy said in her ear.

Charlie was on the move, striding down the sidewalk and homing in on her target. She'd called Lassiter on the way.

"I'm about to get some answers."

"*About* to," he said. "Oh. About to. So you're coming to me empty handed why exactly?"

"I want to talk to my father."

"Sure thing, lass. Sure thing. Hold on, I'm *about* to hand him the phone."

He hung up on her.

Charlie gritted her teeth and kept walking.

Dom had found a fire escape she could reach from the alley, across the street from Riley's building. She clambered up until she found a vacant apartment, bare floors and stripped walls on the other side of the grimy window, and made her nest on the balcony. Leaning against the old ironwork, an unlit cigarette nestled between her fingers, she looked like any other bored city dweller slipping out for a secret smoke.

Beckett took the sidewalk outside Riley's front door. He blended. Charlie still couldn't figure out how he pulled it off, but the big man had a knack for vanishing in a crowd. He became a part of the urban landscape, flowing effortlessly into the background.

Hey, Charlie texted to Riley, thanks again for dinner last night. I didn't leave my travel umbrella over at your place, did I?

In seconds, ellipses rippled on her screen, showing Riley composing his response. She wondered if he'd been waiting to hear from her.

Don't remember seeing you with one, but I'll check as soon as I get home tonight. Can't really talk right now, working a scene, but it was great seeing you! Maybe dinner again next Friday?

I'd like that, she replied. I'll check my schedule and let you know.

He was gone. She made her move, casually strolling up the apartment steps and into the vestibule.

She tried the first of the spare keys. It stopped short, jammed less than a centimeter into the lock. No fit. The second one slid in, a little bumpy, like old glass. The lock clicked and the door swung wide.

Charlie made her way to the third floor. Her heart wanted her to hustle in time to its staccato beat, nerves pushing her to jog up the stairs, run along the faded hallways. She forced herself to breathe deep and take it slow. She didn't want to give the residents anything unusual to remember her by, not even an out-of-place sound; if she did everything right, Riley would never know she'd been here.

The last of the spare keys opened his apartment door. She hesitated on the threshold, holding it open, just a crack. He'd told her he was at work, but considering he'd already lied to her face at least once already, she couldn't take that as gospel.

"Riley?" she called out, her voice drifting into the silent apartment. "Is everything okay? Your door was open. I'm coming in, all right?"

She was talking to herself. She shut the door behind her, standing in his empty living room. The beanbag chair and the video game controller had migrated a few feet to the left, and his guitar was on the other side of the room, but otherwise the space looked just like it had last night.

His bathroom door hung open. Bedroom, still closed tight. Charlie pulled on a pair of disposable latex gloves, snapping them tight at her wrists. Her fingerprints were already all over the apartment, with a perfectly valid reason to be there, but she was about to enter unknown territory.

She checked the hall closet, right next to the bathroom. Mostly bare shelves, a dead and dusty minivac, a few spare towels in mismatched colors. The bedroom door was next.

It swung open to the expected. A queen bed with rumpled, heavy covers the color of a damp meadow, stray socks on the floor, crumpled receipts and spare change on the nightstand. A closet's sliding door hung halfway open on the opposite wall, exposing dress shirts and slacks dangling from plastic hangers. Then she stepped across the threshold, glanced to her left, and froze.

A long aluminum-framed corkboard hung on the wall, facing the foot of the bed. He'd turned it into an evidence board. An evidence board for her case. A candid, telephoto-lens shot of Hayden

Cobb shooting a nervous look over his shoulder as he stepped out of a fast-food place squatted at the center of a spiderweb woven from thumbtacks and string. There were photos of Gimondi, Kellogg, and Vargas—professional shots of the East Boston Three, taken from their ID cards—festooned with sticky notes stuck to the borders. Each note was a list of dates, connections, observations scribbled down with the furious devotion of a paranoiac.

Thread linked Gimondi to an older man with jowls and a bulldog glare. Charlie didn't recognize him, but a business card tacked to his photo, gold leaf text on soft cream, identified him as Oscar Pembrose. Twin strands of black thread tied the defense lawyer to DA Poole and, beneath her, a scrap of paper with a big red question mark drawn in Sharpie. *Shooter,* he had written, *not necessarily a pro. Known to Gimondi? Someone he let off the hook once, maybe turned into a confidential informant like he did with Hayden Cobb?*

A second question mark, this one in deep purple, hung from threads to the East Boston Three like an anchor. *Fourth man,* Riley's notes began. *I've cleared everyone working out of the A-7. Need to dig into Gimondi, learn more about his contacts with neighboring precincts. Charlestown cop?*

The bedroom kept Riley's evidence board out of sight and away from the eyes of guests like her, but she couldn't miss how he'd positioned it. It would be the last thing he'd see at night before closing his eyes and the first thing he'd see in the morning when he woke.

Riley's keys rattled in the front door. He stumbled in, bone tired, a stubble shadow darkening his high cheekbones. It was close to eight o'clock, and he'd plowed through his shift and beyond with nothing but an energy bar and some cheap convenience store coffee. He reached over, muscle memory guiding his hand to the light switch. The overheads clicked on.

Charlie was leaning against the wall, over by the windows, arms crossed. Waiting for him. He didn't recognize the dark-eyed woman in his beanbag chair or the heavyweight in the hall by the kitchen.

"The hell is this," he said, thrown too far off balance to put any force behind the question. His hand edged toward his jacket.

Charlie gestured to his open bedroom door.

"We need to talk," she said.

"You broke into my apartment." Not a question so much as a statement of disbelief.

"You should have been honest with me."

"Honest with—" His mouth hung open. "You *broke* into my *apartment*. You realize I'm pretty much obligated to arrest you now, right? You and . . ."

"These are my associates. Beckett, Dom . . . Riley Glass."

"That's Detective Glass . . ."

"The beanbag is cute," Dom told him. It rustled under her as she pushed herself to her feet. "But seriously, you *are* allowed to buy new furniture when you graduate from college. It's kind of a rite of passage for adulthood."

"I know you're not the fourth member of the East Boston Three," Charlie said. "Your evidence board told me that much. I'm pretty sure you're trying to be one of the good guys here. That said, you're not only investigating without your department's go-ahead; you've gone full vigilante."

He rode out a hurricane wind of emotions. Fear, indignation. He felt invaded. He put one hand on his hip and threw up a wall of attitude.

"What's it to you?"

Charlie unfolded her arms and pushed herself away from the wall. She stalked toward him like a panther.

"What's it to me? I'll tell you. You came to the Pocono Motor Inn, playing Batman. You were hunting for the hunter, the man who was there to murder Hayden Cobb before he could testify."

"And I'm sorry you almost got hurt," Riley said. "I swear, I had no idea you were even there. I knew Poole had hired outside protection, since she can't trust the police to keep Cobb safe, but I had no idea who. I was trying to keep everyone safe."

"I'm aware. I'm aware you didn't know I was there. Because if you had, you probably wouldn't have used the .38 you took *from me* as a drop piece."

The blood drained from his face.

"No," he said, "you don't need to worry about that. I never checked it into evidence or filed a report. It came home with me the afternoon I confiscated it from you. No one can tie that gun to you. I never would have put you at risk."

"Now I get it," Dom said, glancing over at Charlie. "You have a type. You like your men young, cute, and dumb."

Charlie took a deep breath.

"The police can't tie it to me. Considering I took it from one of his men, Jimmy Lassiter sure as hell can. And did."

"Oh," Riley said.

"Oh," Charlie echoed. "And now he's holding on to my father, as collateral, until I can get his man Grillo out of jail. That wasn't a throw-away gun like we both thought; it was his legal, registered piece, and you led the cops straight to his doorstep."

"Can't . . . can't he alibi himself out?"

"His only alibi is a different felony he was committing while you were trying to murder someone with his gun on the other side of town. So no. He can't. You know, I'm not even angry that you drew me into your mess. I'm being paid to keep Hayden Cobb alive and breathing, so I'm already pretty much neck deep in it anyway."

She stood before him, eyes blazing.

"But you got my *family* involved," she said. "So now you're going to tell us everything, and I mean everything. And then we're going to put our heads together and figure out how to make this situation right."

He nodded, slowly, his gaze drifting to the floor at her feet.

"Let's move this to the kitchen," he said. "I don't know about you, but I need some coffee. Got a feeling it's going to be a long night."

Eighteen

Riley was silent, pensive, until the first mug of coffee was in his hands. He passed out mismatched cups from his cabinet. Charlie took hers black, like him; Dom, with a splash of hazelnut creamer from his softly rattling refrigerator. Beckett stood in the doorway, empty handed, his granite stare giving the silence a cold and heavy weight.

"I never meant for any of this to happen," Riley finally said.

"Funny," Charlie said. "Hayden Cobb told me almost the exact same thing. You know what they say about the road to hell, right?"

"Trust me, there were no good intentions involved."

He leaned against his counter, tilted his head back, and closed his eyes. Charlie felt like she was watching a man play tug-of-war with himself, using his own soul for the rope. Pulling it, digging his heels in as it twisted and frayed in his white-knuckle grip. Dragging the truth out one stubborn inch at a time.

"I lied to you," he said, "about not knowing them. Gimondi, Vargas, Kellogg."

"I know," Charlie said.

"I went to academy with Vargas and Kellogg. When we got our first assignment, I met Lieutenant Gimondi. He was a sergeant then, working out of the A-7."

"Was he dirty then too?" Dom asked.

Riley nodded, took a sip.

"Gimondi had friends all over the place and a sympathetic ear buried deep in the rat squad. He knew every trick; nobody gave him a second glance, but in the rare event anyone was looking his way, he knew about it before IA could even open the books on an investigation. Meanwhile he was bringing in cash on the street—mostly payoffs for looking the other way, letting petty stuff slide—and building a workforce of confidential informants out on the street. Not for *solving* crimes so much as pointing out juicy opportunities."

"Insiders, like Cobb," Charlie said.

"Like Cobb. Anyway. We went through a reorganization, and for about five minutes the brass was hot on the idea of free-floating task forces. Self-directed go-getters, out fixing community problems."

"Can't say Gimondi wasn't a self-directed go-getter," Dom said.

"In all the wrong ways. So the four of us ended up on a detail together. I was thrilled. I mean, I was fresh to the job, so wet behind my ears I was squeaking, and all I could see was that detective shield dangling out in front of me like a carrot on a string. I was willing to do anything for a little clout on my record, anything to make me look better for promotion, up to and including washing the commissioner's car. I mean, if he asked me to."

He lifted his coffee cup, stared into its depths, and fell silent.

"Riley?" Charlie said. "What happened?"

"Fuck it," he muttered. He set his cup on the counter. "I knew. I knew Gimondi had a rep. Nothing anyone could prove—he was too slick for that by miles—but I knew he wasn't a good guy to be around. I knew he wasn't the kind of cop I wanted to be. But I wanted to get ahead. So I ignored my brains, and I ignored my gut, and I took the duty assignment. The city was having issues with one particular patch of Eastie, over by the airport; disproportionate complaints compared to the rest of the neighborhood were turning it redder than Rudolph's nose on the crime-statistic maps. They wanted it pacified."

"What did you do?" Charlie asked.

He pursed his lips, bitter as the coffee.

"Pacified it," he said. "Thinking back . . . it's funny. Mostly, I remember the smell."

Charlie tilted her head. "The smell?"

"This one night in August. Hot as hell. It smelled like bug spray and citronella and sweat. Even now, I catch a whiff of that smell, and it takes me right back."

Riley stared down at his hands. He flexed his fingers, clenching and unclenching, putting his thoughts in order.

"I didn't know what Gimondi had planned. Figured we were just up for a routine patrol, show some muscle, remind the local bangers we had our eyes on 'em. Then he passed out the balaclavas and told us to lose our badges."

"That didn't sound any alarms for you?" Beckett asked.

"All of them, ringing loud and clear. But I was wet behind the ears, standing in this patch of no-man's-land under a broken streetlamp with three guys who were up to no good, and Vargas was getting a shotgun out of his trunk."

Beckett understood. "Didn't feel like a healthy time to ask questions."

"This was Gimondi's plan, and Kellogg and Vargas were already in on it. All I could do was go along and hope for the best."

Riley paused. He pursed his lips. Gave a little headshake to the kitchen floor.

"No. That's bullshit. I *told* myself all I could do was go along with it. Anyway, the target was this guy, Trujillo, low-level dealer working out of a motel. He was protected by one of the local gangs, and Gimondi wanted to make an example, show everybody that their 'protection' wasn't worth jack if Boston PD decided to roll in heavy. So we kicked the door in. Caught Trujillo with his boxers around his ankles and a teenage girl bouncing on his lap."

"Easy bust," Dom said.

"Yeah, well, I was reaching for the cuffs when Gimondi told me to put them away. We weren't taking him in. Then he asked Trujillo where his stash was. He clammed up, pretended he couldn't speak English. So Gimondi told Vargas and Kellogg to beat the language into him."

Riley kept flexing his fingers. Rhythmic, conjuring some old touch memory, his gaze a thousand miles away.

"They broke his ribs, six of his fingers," he said. "They beat him until he pissed himself. Eventually he gave it up. He'd done a big deal earlier that night. Gimondi already knew, care of one of his confidential informants. Trujillo had a fat wad of cash hidden in his mattress."

Charlie put it together. "The real reason you were there. I'm guessing that wasn't the first time either. Gimondi was using the duty assignment as an excuse to steal from the local dealers."

"Not nearly the first time," Riley said. "So I ended up in a booth at this dive bar, squeezed in between my new 'partners,' and Gimondi's counting out the cash like it's a routine deal. And he gives me a stack. Came out to three hundred dollars and change, for each of us. And up until that point . . ."

He trailed off. Charlie put her hand on his arm. She gave him time. He took a deep breath, puffing up his chest. Then he let it out, deflating in front of her.

"You don't know what you're really made of until somebody puts you to the test. When I sat at the table, I had this fantasy in my head. Like I was going to refuse the cash, make some dramatic stand on principle, march straight to Internal Affairs, and confess everything. Be the noble, heroic cop I thought I was all along."

He glanced over, meeting her eyes.

"Then I saw how they were looking at me. Hyenas, on the prowl. And I knew there were two ways that night could end for me. Only one of them guaranteed I'd see sunrise."

His gaze fell back to the kitchen floor.

"I took the money," he said.

NINETEEN

"After that," Riley said, "I asked for a transfer out. Hell, I wanted out of the house entirely, never wanted to see those guys again, but that wasn't in the cards. I kept my head down and my mouth shut."

"They let you go?" Charlie asked. Her mug of coffee was cooling in her hands.

"Sure. I took the money. I was just as guilty as they were. What was I going to do, turn them in? And I knew . . . I mean, they never threatened me, not openly, but they didn't have to. Anyway, two months later, the entire program got shut down. Nothing Gimondi did—it was just more bureaucratic reshuffling. So at least I knew that was over and done."

"Did you think they suddenly stopped being corrupt?" Dom said.

He looked sick to his stomach. Pale tinged with green, like deli meat gone bad. A faint glimmer of sweat appeared on his forehead.

"No, obviously. I . . . I figured they'd be on the take, sure, but nothing on that scale. I didn't realize they'd get a taste for it. I guess eventually they figured out they didn't need the pretext of a police raid to rip off their targets. They could just cowboy up after hours."

Beckett had been silent, weighing Riley's story against the tone of his voice, calculating. Now he spoke up.

"But you weren't invited to that party," he said.

"No. I mean, they weren't stupid. We had a truce—I kept my mouth shut and so did they—but they knew I wasn't their kind. I had no idea they were pulling smash-and-grabs, not until IA came in and slapped Gimondi in cuffs, right at his desk. Kellogg and Vargas weren't far behind him."

"And the fourth man in the gang?" Charlie asked.

"No clue. The witnesses are right. There's too much collaboration to doubt it. There were definitely four cops in the ring. But like I told you at dinner, it *can't* be someone working out of the A-7. The investigation would have rooted them out for certain. What about Cobb? Can't he put the finger on anybody?"

Charlie shook her head. "He was Gimondi's informant, and that was his only point of contact with the gang. Cobb didn't even know about Kellogg and Vargas—he was never allowed to meet anybody else. Whenever they stole drugs on a raid, Gimondi passed them to Cobb, who turned them into cash."

"Which is how they got caught in the first place," Dom said. "Cobb dealt to a high school and college crowd. Soft stuff. They gave him a bindle of heroin, and he was out of his league. He tried selling it to an undercover officer."

Riley's brow furrowed. "That's weird."

"Why?"

"Because I'm pretty sure he had someone who *could* sell heroin for him. Like I said, Gimondi cultivated a small army of CIs, and I know for a fact he had at least two dealers on a string. Why risk giving it to Cobb?"

"Sounds like Gimondi wanted to keep things tight," Beckett said. "Everyone insulated from everyone else. Safer that way."

"Maybe," Riley said.

"But none of this tells us what you were doing outside the Pocono with a gun," Charlie said.

Hé needed time to line up his thoughts, gather his words. She gave it to him. He started slowly.

"I've been carrying a weight around, this . . . lump in my stomach, like I swallowed a rock, ever since I helped Gimondi rob that dealer. I told myself I could work it off. That the more good I did out there, as a cop, the more people I helped, the more it outweighed what I did that night. I got to a place where I could almost stop thinking about it. Then the busts went down and the story broke."

Riley pushed himself away from the kitchen counter. He paced across the tiny span of vinyl flooring, face tight. When he turned to Charlie, his eyes were glistening.

"If I had come clean, gone to Internal Affairs and owned up, if I'd been enough of a man to face the music and take the consequences, if I'd just *said something*, Gimondi and his crew would have lost their badges. And because I didn't? Those people, the victims in that house on Saratoga Street . . . they're dead now. They're dead because of me."

"You can't know that," Charlie said. "You don't know what might have happened—"

"They're dead because of me. And I'll have to carry that weight."

He wiped the heel of his hand across one eye. His arm dropped limp to his side.

"I know Gimondi," he said. "I knew he was looking at spending the rest of his life behind bars, and he'd do anything to get out of it. He'd kill his own mother if it meant getting a walk. Once I heard the DA's office had a star witness, somebody who could nail him to the wall, it wasn't hard to guess how he'd react. I also knew the lawyer, Pembrose, would be the man in the middle setting it all up."

"How do you figure?" Charlie asked.

"Access. The East Boston Three are all in lockdown at the holding facility on Nashua Street. The whole place is maximum security to start with, and corrupt cops are like pedophiles: they're automatically put into administrative segregation for their own safety. Alone in a cell, one hour of sunlight out of every twenty-four. Gimondi knows people on the street who can get things done, but that doesn't help him any if he can't get the word out."

"But his lawyer can," Charlie said, putting it together.

"Attorney-client privilege," Riley said. "Pembrose gets unmonitored, private visits with his client to prepare for his impending trial. Gimondi gives the orders; the lawyer coordinates on the outside. I checked into this guy. He's got a history."

"Of killing witnesses?" Charlie said.

"Pembrose is a very lucky man. Not always—he doesn't win every time he's up at bat—but he's followed by a storm that never fails to rain in the right direction. Pieces of key evidence going missing, witnesses suddenly developing amnesia. He's a good lawyer, real good, but if that isn't enough, *allegedly* you can pay him a little something extra to press a finger down on the scales of justice."

"He's also missing," Dom said, "and it looks like the kind of 'missing' that'll get upgraded to 'dead' as soon as the body turns up. That doesn't track. If he hired a hitman, why would that same hitman turn around and take him out?"

Riley lifted his eyebrows. "Pay dispute? I mean, sane and well-adjusted people don't commit murder for a living. Guy could have snapped over anything. Or it could have been the fourth man, the one who slipped free."

"Motive?" Charlie said. She'd had that same thought, asked herself the same question, and come up empty.

"I got nothing. All I know for certain is that a hitter was in play, and the lawyer hired him."

She eyed him. "And how'd you find this out?"

"I paid a visit to Pembrose's office," Riley said, looking bashful now. "Posing as a prospective client with a brother in jail. I, uh . . . planted a bug. Stuck it to the underbelly of his desk while his back was turned."

"You bugged a defense attorney's private office," Charlie said.

"I couldn't change what happened that night on Saratoga Street. Couldn't bring those people back to life. All I could do was make damn sure Gimondi and his buddies went down. So yeah. I bugged the office. Didn't do me a whole lot of good. He was barely ever there, and when he was on the phone, I could only hear his side of the conversation. But once, just once, he popped in while he was on his cell phone, talking to the hitter."

Riley paced the kitchen, pantomiming an invisible phone next to his ear.

"He wasn't explicit," Riley said. "It was all cloak-and-dagger talk, about 'picking up the package,' that kind of thing. Criminals always think they're being smart, talking like that, but it stands out from a real conversation like a sour note on a tuba. I read between the lines and copied down the address."

"For the Pocono Motor Inn," Charlie said. "How did Pembrose know about it?"

"Near as I can tell? He's gotta have somebody in the DA's office feeding him info. I thought it might be Poole, but I couldn't figure a motive for her to tank her own case."

"ADA Felton," Beckett said, stroking his goatee as he traced the connections. "The lawyer was the middleman, every step of the way. He paid Felton for Cobb's location, then passed it to his hired gun."

"Twice," Dom said.

"I'd love to tell you I had a plan that night," Riley said, "but I only heard the playback half an hour before the hit was supposed to go down. I grabbed that .38 out of my dresser and raced to the scene."

"You took the .38 so it couldn't be tied back to you," Charlie said. "That was your solution, to make sure Cobb testified and took Gimondi down. You were going to kill the hitman."

"Spur of the moment. Wasn't thinking straight. Wasn't thinking much at all. There I was, hunkered down at the edge of the parking lot. I saw him; he didn't see me. I lined him up in my sights. Perfect kill shot."

"Then what happened?" Charlie asked.

His gaze went distant, like he was seeing through a window and looking at himself two nights ago, gun in hand. He didn't like what he saw.

"I started thinking," he said.

"You told me," Charlie recalled, "that you've never fired a gun outside of the shooting range."

"Never but that one time. I was just thinking . . . yeah, it's for a good cause, but . . . murder's still murder. I thought about showing myself, announcing, busting him on the spot and making it a legal takedown, but how the hell could I explain being there? It'd all come out, from the illegal wiretap all the way back to that goddamn three hundred bucks I took when I helped Gimondi rip off a drug dealer. I'd be the one going behind bars, and since I managed to taint all the evidence, the hitter and Pembrose would probably both walk free. Only way to do it was the ugly way."

"You missed," Dom told him.

"I decided Gimondi made me a criminal." Riley lifted his sagging chin, just a little. "But he didn't make me a killer."

Charlie put it together.

"You missed on purpose," she said.

"Split-second decision. I saw him making his move, and I had to choose, right then and there: kill him or don't. I took the middle option. I parted his hair and sent him running. I had to run too. But first I wanted to really throw some fear into this guy, scare him off the contract entirely."

"That's why you dropped the .38," Charlie said. "Considering where it came from, good chance a ballistics report would tie it to some gangland business. An unsolved murder or two."

"And if word got back to the shooter, well . . . think about it. Not only does he get ambushed on one of his jobs, maybe now it looks like the Irish mob wants him dead? If I was him, I wouldn't stick around to ask questions. I'd be on the first train out of Boston."

"Professional killers," Beckett said, "real, actual professionals you can rely on, are rare as diamonds on the ground. The lawyer wouldn't be in a position to find a replacement, not fast enough to stop Cobb from testifying."

Riley nodded at him. "My thoughts exactly. All I needed to do was throw a wrench in the works and stall the situation out until he took the stand."

"You threw a wrench in the works, all right," Charlie said.

His shoulders tensed like a steel spring. He couldn't quite look her in the eye.

"If I thought, for one second, that any of this could blow back on you and yours . . . if I even dreamed—"

"I know," Charlie said. "I know. And I'm not angry at you. You were trying to do the right thing. But now we have to deal with the fallout."

"I have to," Riley told her. "You mean *I* have to."

He took a deep breath. She watched him steel himself.

"I'll talk to my captain, right now."

Charlie's eyes narrowed. "And?"

"Confess," he said.

TWENTY

"Confess," Charlie said, like she wasn't sure she'd heard him right.

"It's the only way," Riley said. "I'll come clean, tell them everything, all the way back to day one. This guy, what's his name?"

"Grillo."

"Once I take responsibility for the .38 and walk them through it, step by step, they'll have to let him go. He walks, your dad is safe, right?"

"And you'll be arrested for . . . how many crimes, exactly?" Charlie asked.

Riley quirked a humorless smile.

"I've got a good union rep," he said. "Maybe they can get me off on the smaller charges."

Charlie took a quick eye contact poll. Beckett was his usual onyx wall, quiet and serene; he didn't have an opinion, wouldn't have one until it was time to act. Dom looked like she'd bitten into a lemon. Charlie knew her. She didn't like this any more than Charlie did.

"We're not doing that," Charlie said.

"It's not your call," Riley told her.

"Sure it is. Because I'm not letting a good cop go down just to spring a scumbag who honestly belongs behind bars. That's the easy way. It's not the right way."

"But your dad—"

"We'll figure something out," she told him. "Look, with no witnesses, Southborough PD treated the motel shooting as open and closed. They had a gun, they had a bullet hole, done. They didn't dig the slug out of the television set and figure out there were two different-caliber weapons at the scene. That was all me and Dom. And we haven't told anyone."

"Meaning," Dom said, "if we find the hitman . . ."

"We find him, we prove he was at the scene, and we hand him over to the cops with a pretext—a *legal* pretext, not one based on wiretapping a lawyer's office—to arrest him for it."

"And we pin the .38 on him," Dom said.

"Hey, he really was there, and he really did fire the shot through the window. It's not exactly a frame job if he's guilty."

"I'd say our next stop should be Pembrose's pad," Dom said, "but with him going missing all of a sudden . . ."

"The one guy who could expose anyone and everyone involved," Riley said.

"Which gives everyone involved a reason to take him off the board," Beckett pointed out, "if they thought he might be getting cold feet. But unless he makes a miracle reappearance, that door is closed. What else have we got?"

Dom ran down the list. "Even if we could get an interview with Gimondi, he won't talk. Neither will his jailbird buddies. What about Felton? If this hitman is still on the job, he'll need help tracking his target down. And if he knew the ADA was leaking information to Pembrose, he might go straight to the source. I doubt Felton cares where his bribe money is coming from; a payoff is a payoff."

"I think tomorrow," Charlie said, "we need to do some digging into Mr. Felton's personal life."

"And until then?" Riley asked.

"You? Get some sleep." Charlie yawned into her hand, then looked to Beckett and Dom. "Same goes for you two. Tomorrow's going to be a long day. I've just got one more stop to make."

Dom tilted her head, curious. "Where at?"

"Visiting an old friend."

Charlie rolled up on the Crab Walk right around last call. There was still a scattering of rust bucket trucks in the narrow strip of parking lot, alongside a couple of vintage Harleys gathering dust beneath the yellow electric glow of a bug zapper. Boat netting, adorned with petrified starfish, draped along the corrugated metal eaves of the ash-gray shack.

Charlie's boots rustled on the asphalt. She pushed through the tavern door, greeted by the warm smell of beer and a Pink Floyd song playing on the old Seeburg jukebox. A seventies deep cut, something bluesy with a wailing sax. As she came in, the house lights flickered on and off with the toggle of a switch.

"Closing time," Dutch called out. "You don't have to go home, but you can't fall asleep on my porch. Talking to *you*, Lester. Drink up and hit the road."

Dutch lived behind the bar. He stood six five, a living patch of bad weather in a tank top and cargo pants. He spotted Charlie and flashed a tombstone smile.

"Got time for a beer?" she asked.

"Got time for two," he said. "One for me and one for you."

He reached under the bar, rummaged around in the cooler, and came up with a pair of bottles. Brown glass, white labels, stark and tiny type. The caps popped loose under Dutch's old and tarnished bottle opener. Charlie slid onto the hard curve of a wooden stool and tilted the bottle, giving the label a dubious eye.

"'Woods and Waters'?"

"I've been on an IPA kick lately," Dutch said. "Maine Beer Company brews some righteous shit. Cheers."

They clinked bottles and downed a swig. Charlie squinted, studying the wash of nutty, chewy flavor.

"Is that . . . pink grapefruit around the edges?"

Dutch raised his bottle. "And pineapple, with hints of garlic and onion."

"When did beer turn into wine?"

"Beer is God's perfect vehicle. It can be a cheap old beater, a work-horse of a truck, or a Ferrari supercar. Either way, it'll get you where you're going."

"I'm just saying," Charlie replied, "don't go hipster on me."

Dutch grinned. He ran his fingers across his faded buzz cut.

"Imagine me with a man bun."

"I'd rather not."

He hustled across the bar, scooping up a few soggy bills and change, sending another drunk stumbling out into the darkness with a clap on his shoulder.

"Your dad came in the other night," Dutch said. "Hadn't seen him in a dog's age."

"How'd he look?" Charlie asked.

"Good. He looked good. Gathering you took care of his little debt problem."

"Long as he stays on the straight and narrow," Charlie said. "He's going to meetings."

"I've known your old man for a long time. He's *been* to meetings."

Charlie tilted her bottle back.

"I know," she said. "I know. But he's got some motivation to change now."

Dutch studied her face. "Because he doesn't know what you did to lay hands on twenty thousand dollars on short notice. He only knows he doesn't want you doing it again."

"I told him I wouldn't bail him out again. If he starts gambling, whatever happens, that's on him. I won't save him."

"Yeah," Dutch told her, "but we both know that's a lie."

He cashed out another customer while Charlie drank her beer.

"So how did you get the cash, anyhow?" Dutch asked, swinging by again. "I didn't hear about any unsolved bank robberies."

"You wouldn't have heard about this one. It happened back in '69."

"Charlie Mac, time traveler extraordinaire."

"Something like that," she said. "But there's a complication."

"What kind?"

"The kind named Jimmy Lassiter. I paid him off, but there's been some unexpected blowback."

"Blowback usually is. Hold up a second." He nodded at a couple of grizzled bikers in the back, down to the dregs of their pint glasses. "Lemme clear these guys out and lock up. Sounds like we're about to have a capital-*C* conversation."

Dutch closed up, locked up. Half of the house lights powered down, draping the back of the tavern in darkness. A string of Christmas lights above the bar glowed green and warning red. Dutch cleaned the bar, dumping unused garnishes and quartered limes into a trash can while Charlie walked him through the case.

"I'm seeing a problem," he told her.

"Just one? I'm seeing five or six."

"No. Long term, with Lassiter. You ever train a dog, Charlie?"

She shook her head.

"You get the behavior you reward," he said. "He's making you play errand girl because you're already hip deep in this mess. But what happens after that mess is all cleaned up? What's stopping him from dropping in and sitting on your old man every time he wants you to take care of some dirty business for him?"

Charlie hoisted her beer and tossed back another swallow. "What can I do?"

"Make him gone," Dutch said.

"Thought about it," she said. "Dom says it's a bad play. Lassiter is connected from here to New York. If I thought putting a bullet in the guy would solve my problems, I would have done it already."

Charlie stared at the label on her bottle. Not reading it, her vision sliding just out of focus. The words became runes, a foreign mystery.

"It's weird," she said.

He grabbed a dishrag. "What's that?"

"After the hitter jumped me, at the hotel, I had to file a police report."

"Did you tell them how bad he kicked your ass?"

"Funny man. I'd laugh, but my ribs hurt. Anyway, this rookie cop, had to be fresh out of the academy, was trying to . . . console me."

Dutch raised an unkempt eyebrow.

"Was he hitting on you?"

"No," Charlie said. "He was sincere. Gave me a card for a counselor so I could talk to someone about being the victim of a traumatic attack or something like that. And I didn't get it. It didn't click, until I was out in the parking lot. I'm supposed to be upset."

"You're not?"

"Sure. I'm upset because the jerk blindsided me and got away. But the actual violence . . . I mean, dealing with that is just part of my job." Charlie frowned. "You ever get in a conversation with somebody, somebody who hasn't been where we've been, and just realize you're not . . . *like* them?"

"Kid, we underwent a very rigorous, scientifically engineered regimen to rewire our brains when it comes to matters of violence." He paused, sly. "I mean, I did, as a Marine. I understand you army types get the little-baby training wheels version, but I'm sure it's really tough and scary for people who can't hack *real* boot camp—"

Charlie blurted out a laugh, waving her bottle at him. "And fuuuck you."

"But seriously. People aren't machines. You don't stop being a soldier just because you left the service. And just because you're stateside doesn't mean you left the war. What matters isn't that you handle violence different than a civvy." Dutch tapped a finger against his temple. "What matters is staying healthy. You keep support around you, close. A family."

"I've been mending bridges with my dad," she said. "Trying to."

"And that's good, but that's not the kind of family I'm talking about. You need people who know where you've been. People who think like you do, who really get it when everything's twisted up inside and you need to let it out."

"I got you," Charlie said.

A fresh couple of bottles clinked down on the bar.

"When you're here," he said, "you're family."

She stared up at the year-round string of Christmas lights. "This place is the worst excuse for an Olive Garden I've ever seen."

"In the immortal words of one Charlie Mac," Dutch said, grinning, "fuck you."

"No breadsticks, no salad . . ."

"And the service is lousy, I know. So your long-term Jimmy problem aside, what's your next move here?"

"That's what I came to ask you about," she said. "I know you set guys up with jobs sometimes. Veterans looking to make a little cash."

"Worked out fine in your case, it sounds like. Security work looks good on you. I figured you'd take to it."

"Not that kind of job," she said.

Now he eyed her, taciturn.

"You're really jumping into the dark side with both feet, aren't you?"

"More like I got pushed, but I'm not asking for me." She nodded at Dutch's arm. "The hitter had a Marine Corps tattoo. Eagle and globe, just like yours. I'm wondering if anybody's been around lately looking for work."

"Thing you gotta understand is, I'm not the black-market want ads. I know a few people who occasionally need a helping hand; I know some vets who occasionally need some quick cash and don't mind getting down and dirty. Every once in a while, I play matchmaker. Lining up murder for hire isn't my usual gig."

"Sure," Charlie said. "But I'm thinking this guy might have come to you and left empty handed before he found employment elsewhere."

He raised his bottle. "Good thinking, but nah. Sorry, it's been a dry season, and the last two matches I made don't fit your description at all. Whoever your hitman is, he hasn't graced my fine establishment. Something does occur to me, though."

"Yeah?"

"This shyster, Pembrose, you said he's got a rep for this kind of thing?"

"He doesn't normally go this far," Charlie said, "but yeah, word is he'll do just about anything to clinch a win if you pay him enough."

"Working with criminals is always a risk. Say he hires a burglar he's never met to pull a B and E, and the guy turns out to be an amateur. He gets caught, rolls over for the cops, and now Pembrose is screwed. He's not stupid; he'd want a very small list of tested, proven associates he can really count on when it comes to farming out his dirty deeds. People he knows can get the job done and won't go shooting their mouths off."

"This hitter," Charlie said, "it's not his first time up at bat."

"Go back far enough, you'll find this guy in Pembrose's orbit. Odds are they've been working together for years. And remember, the lawyer has access to the greatest hiring pool around."

"What's that?" Charlie asked.

"His client list." Dutch set his bottle down. "How do you find a stone killer, get to know him better than his own family, and learn what he's really capable of?"

"Defend him in court," Charlie said.

"And get him off the hook. I guarantee this twisted little business relationship started in a jailhouse visitation room. It might not have been a murder rap, but this guy got caught doing something violent. And remember, Pembrose isn't a public defender."

"He's top tier," Charlie mused. "That means top-tier prices. Meaning the hitter has money or comes from money."

"There you go."

"This'd be a lot easier if Pembrose was around. That's the part I can't suss out."

"Who profits from making him disappear?"

"The hitman's being paid by Pembrose, and so is ADA Felton," Charlie said, ticking names off on her fingertips. "The East Boston Three need his help to beat the charges. The fourth member of the gang, whoever he is, doesn't have a horse in this race. Out of all the players on the field, *nobody* benefits from hurting Pembrose."

"What does that tell you?" Dutch said.

"That there's another player out there, one we don't know about. One with their own agenda."

That was one possibility. Another occurred to her, but she didn't want to say it out loud. Dutch did it for her.

"Watch your back out there," he warned her. "And don't assume you only have *one* new player in the mix. Could be a whole damn team."

TWENTY-ONE

Felton wasn't sleeping.

He'd never been a good sleeper. Most nights it took a glass or two of scotch to put him down for a few restless hours, tossing and turning in storm-gray sheets, with the moonlight streaming in through the picture windows of his Back Bay condo. Tonight he put away half a bottle. He lay half-awake, half-drifting, feeling the darkened bedroom turn in slow, nauseating circles.

He had called Pembrose to tell him they were quits. He didn't mind sticking his neck out a little, considering how much the lawyer paid him under the table, but after two misfires, even a child could see that he was the leak in the Cobb case. He'd covered his tracks, laid down a careful shield of plausible deniability, but the floors of his office had turned to sheer ice. With every step under DA Poole's all-seeing gaze, he felt like he was going to slip and fall or just break through, plunging into the frozen and lightless deep.

He couldn't deliver the message, because Pembrose was missing. Wiped off the face of the earth, vanished. Somewhere out there was a burner phone with Felton's number on the call list. That and Pembrose's poison pill, his just-in-case contingency plan for a situation like this. He had let it slip once, after a night of heavy drinking: if one of Pembrose's enemies took him down, everyone went down with him. Payback from beyond the grave.

"Don't worry about it," the lawyer had assured him. "*You're* not in the file."

Felton didn't believe him. Not then, not now. And there was nothing he could do about it but sit and wait for the ax to fall.

He had spent most of the night slouched at his laptop, half-blind on expensive scotch, googling methods of painless suicide. He didn't want to die, but he'd still choose the self-checkout option over going to prison. Felton found the research oddly soothing. He'd lost all control over his circumstances; deciding how he was going to die, paging through methods and means like he was browsing a seasonal menswear catalog, gave him back a little feeling of power.

Sleep wasn't happening. He shoved the tangled covers back and rolled off the bed, standing on wobbly legs. He stumbled into the living room. His laptop was out, powered on, a lozenge of pale blue turning the glass-and-chrome expanse into the surface of a distant moon.

Didn't I shut that off? he thought, rubbing the bristle on his cheeks.

He stood at the picture window. He had a view to kill for, high and wide and gazing out over the span of the river. Light sparkled off the black waters. Across the span he could see the MIT campus and the distant city sprawl, the urban expanse a shining diamond web in the midnight dark.

"Maybe I could just disappear," he mumbled. "Just up and vanish, like Pembrose did."

A shadow moved.

Just a flicker in the corner of his eye. A trick of the gloom. He turned, frowning as his booze-soaked brain tried to process the data.

Then he heard the clicking. The dry snap of a tongue off the roof of a mouth, soft and dangerous as a rattlesnake's tail.

"What is . . ." He let the question dangle as he shuffled across the room. Felton reached for the standing lamp in the corner, suddenly craving light.

A hand clamped down on his throat.

Then he was flying backward off his heels and crashing down onto the coffee table. The wood shattered under his back, and the table collapsed. He hit the floor, groaning, nestled in the debris.

A nightmare in black launched toward him, billowing from the shadows. A knee plowed into his belly as it landed on him. He couldn't breathe, couldn't see, couldn't think. The shadow pinned him flat. All he could see, through the blur of tears, was lipstick.

A savage slash of midnight blue.

"You're—" he stammered, struggling for air, "you've got to be Pembrose's hitman. Look, whatever happened to him, I had nothing to do with it. I don't even know where he is."

Her fingers found his neck in the dark. Not squeezing. More . . . kneading, her fingers and thumbs like a cat's paws.

"I have money," Felton said. "I—I mean, I can pay you. Not just for my life. I know you want Cobb. I can't give him to you. I'm already on the verge of getting caught; it's too dangerous. But I need some people killed, to make sure they can't trace me back to Pembrose. You understand? I'll pay you, whatever your rate is. And then some."

The fingers kept kneading, hunting. Her middle finger traced a bulging vein like it was a river on an antique map.

"Well?" Felton gaped at her. "*Say* something, damn it!"

She held something up, close to his eye, so he could see it. A long, slender brass needle. It swayed in her grip as she clicked her tongue.

"Felton," she said.

Then she leaned in, moving her knee so she could straddle him, and put her lips against his ear.

"I want to meet you," she whispered.

Charlie made it home, eventually. She could have swapped stories with Dutch all night, but the chance for more than two hours of sleep in a row was a rare luxury this week, and she couldn't count on getting another shot before the case was all over. She crashed on her air mattress, safe behind blackout drapes, and drifted away to the sounds of a city by night.

Six hours later she was back on her feet, as close to refreshed as she could be, drinking in the morning sunlight outside her apartment building's door. She called Riley while she was sitting in traffic.

"Pembrose's client list, of course," Riley said. "I should have thought of that."

"I mean, you are a detective and all."

"I would have gotten there eventually."

"Can you do some digging?" Charlie asked.

"On it. I've got your description of the hitman from the police report, but I might need you to look at some mug shots later."

"Send me anything you find," Charlie said. "I'm doing nothing but babysitting Cobb today."

"Sounds exciting."

"Bodyguard work is a lot of standing around and waiting for something terrible to happen while hoping it doesn't. Basically just like Afghanistan but not as many IEDs. Usually."

"Careful," Riley said. "Just because Pembrose is off the grid doesn't mean this guy isn't still out there looking to finish the contract."

Charlie wasn't worried. Concerned but not worried. She knew what the hitter looked like; he knew it too. No chance he'd risk showing his face again unless he had a bulletproof plan of attack. And Cobb was safely ensconced in a room far from the decoy suite, three floors up and a world away. Plus, if the lawyer had either gone into hiding or been taken off the field, that sliced the lines of communication. As far as they knew, the leak went from Felton's lips, through Pembrose, and to the assassin's ears.

Which was why she was surprised, two hours later, when Felton got in touch. He had reached out directly to Jake, who patched the call through to Beckett's phone. Beckett set it on speaker so Charlie and Dom could listen in.

"I apologize for the short notice," Felton said, "but as you know, we're coming up on the trial date fast. I'm going to need access to Mr. Cobb, just for an hour or two, so we can brush up on some weak points of his testimony."

Charlie locked eyes with Beckett. Dom started to say something, and Beckett made a gliding motion with his hand, silencing her. *Smooth,* the flow of his palm said. *Play it smooth.*

"Of course, sir," he said aloud. "We'll be happy to facilitate that for you. Sometime tomorrow?"

"This . . . this afternoon, actually," Felton said. Charlie caught a strange hitch in his voice.

"Short notice," Beckett said. "It would have been better if you had contacted us yesterday."

"I know, I just—I didn't anticipate." That hitch again, almost a stammer. "I'll need him at one p.m. sharp. Are you ready to write down the address?"

Beckett's eyebrows lifted.

"Sir? If you're asking us to move the primary out of hiding, I must strongly advise you to reconsider."

Jake was still on the line. "Listen to the man, Mr. Felton. Beckett's my best operative. If he says it's not safe to move him, it's not safe."

"I saw the police report," Felton said. "The thug disguised as a room service waiter? I'm not meeting with Mr. Cobb in that room again. *That's* not safe."

"We can find another secure room on this property," Beckett said.

"No. I'm not setting foot in that hotel."

Charlie spoke up. "With all due respect, sir, you aren't the assassin's target. There's no reason to believe you're in any danger."

Especially if you're the leak in the first place, she thought, aching to say it out loud.

"This isn't negotiable," Felton said, getting his hackles up. "We have a location, away from my office, that we use for this sort of thing all the time. It's secure."

"Whether it's secure or not," Beckett said, "and I wouldn't venture that without checking it out myself first, there's still a risk involved with moving your witness in and out of cover."

"This. Isn't. Negotiable."

He gave them an address. Dom wrote it down, scribbling on a scrap of hotel stationery.

"That's the waterfront," Beckett said.

"The Sapphire Hotel. Room twenty-seven. Just knock; I'll already be there when you arrive. I'll only need him for a couple of hours, and then we're done. I shouldn't have to meet with him again until the morning of the trial."

A click double echoed across the shared line.

"Boss?" Beckett said.

"Right here," Jake replied.

"He gone?"

"Line's clear. Speak your minds."

"This," Dom said, "is bullshit."

"Huh," Jake said. "You know, I was just doing my morning cross-word puzzle, and I was looking for an eight-letter word for *trap*."

"We need Poole to intervene, shut this down," Charlie said.

"Sofia's already on her cell phone, pacing a trench in my office floor," Jake said. "And . . . she's shaking her head. Now she's making a hand gesture. Not going to describe it—you can use your imagination."

"Poole's backing him up?"

"He's her golden boy," Jake said. "He's smart, covered his tracks, probably scattered blame over a half dozen of his coworkers the second any suspicion swung his way. I'm betting they really do use that place when they need to meet a witness away from prying eyes; that way, the request wouldn't seem strange to her."

"So tell her what we know," Beckett said.

"We don't *know* anything," Jake told him. "We have strong hunches and circumstantial evidence. And while that feels like a lot of ammo, Felton's got a solid record of service going back over a decade. Ten years of being the DA's perfect angel, day in and day out. They're not just coworkers; they're friends. Tight. She's not going to hear otherwise, not until we bring her some solid proof that he's dirty. What about the hotel? Can you make this work?"

"It's not the hotel I'm worried about," Charlie said. "It's the there-and-back-again. Short of plastic surgery or CIA-quality disguise work, the shooter's cover is blown. As long as I'm around, he can't get anywhere near Cobb without being spotted."

"Blitz attack?" Dom suggested.

"If he wants to die with us. Look at the profile: This guy isn't a suicide bomber dreaming of martyrdom. He's a professional killer. He's not looking to take any crazy risks, and at the end of the day all he wants is to get paid and get away clean. There's only one way to do that now."

"Long range," Dom said.

"Waterfront's a sniper's playground," Beckett said.

"What's the word?" Jake asked. "Want us to keep working on Poole?"

"Negative," Beckett said. "I'll call you back."

He tapped the screen. The phone went dead.

"Now for the conversation we *don't* need the bosses listening in on."

"I'm seeing two possibilities," Charlie said. "Either Pembrose isn't dead, just hiding for some reason—"

"Or the hitter got in touch with Felton directly," Dom said.

Charlie nodded. "Either way, this is his last chance at baiting us into an ambush. And our best chance, maybe our last chance, at getting our hands on the hired gun. We do that, my dad goes free."

"Hell," Dom said, "if we can prove Felton's the leak, we can take both of these guys down and wrap the whole job up in a bow by dinnertime. Think the DA will pay us a bonus?"

"Don't go counting the money just yet," Beckett said. "There's a wide divide between *if* and *maybe* and seeing the job through. There's also about a hundred different ways this ambush can go down. We know the man's coming, but he still gets to throw the first punch."

As the line clicked, the silent woman plucked the phone from Felton's trembling fingers. His other hand clutched a legal pad. She'd written out his lines for him, everything to say, every counter for every possible argument. He was sitting on his sofa in his underwear, ruins of the shattered table and his broken laptop at his feet. His white Y-fronts were still stained, cold, and damp from when he'd pissed himself three hours ago. She hadn't let him move since.

Dark-blue fingernails closed on the scruff of his neck. Pinching, lifting, like a mama cat with a wayward kitten. He bit back a whimper as he rose.

She steered him into the bedroom, to the open closet. She pointed to one of his freshly pressed suits dangling from a cedar-and-brass hanger on the end. He picked it up.

Their next stop was the bathroom. She took the hanger from him and draped it from the hook on the back of the door. She pointed to the shower, expectant.

TWENTY-TWO

Sailboats skimmed along the sun-kissed waves of Boston Harbor, while ivory yachts and tour boats hugged the shore. The endless Harborwalk curled along the coastline; tourists and locals thronged the path, filling the benches along the broad wooden walkway, leaning against the pale-blue railing to take pictures of the distant harbor islands.

"Sapphire Hotel's a boutique spot," Beckett said, gathering the team in the decoy room for an impromptu briefing. Charlie, Dom, and the relief squad for backup were on hand, along with Kirby and two other men, tight-lipped faces Charlie knew only in passing. "Sixty rooms, cheapest one is four hundred bucks a night."

"They've got the right idea," Dom said. "We should start using this place instead of the motel in Southborough."

"I don't think we're welcome back there anyway," Charlie said.

Dom pulled up a map on her laptop, magnified it, and drew sharp red lines along the screen.

"These two roads cross the hotel from the north and south. They are the only approaches by vehicle."

Kirby, still half-asleep, raised a groggy hand.

"But he doesn't know which one we'll take. Could set up a sniper perch at either end, and if he guesses wrong—"

"He won't guess," Dom said. "He'll do what I would do."

She circled the hotel, a block of salmon-pink pixels.

"He's going to set up somewhere with an unobstructed view of the main entrance. *If* he's going with a sniper approach. If he's got something else planned, he could be planting a surprise inside the hotel itself as we speak. Felton set the meet, and he's got Felton's cooperation, which means he's got a head start and the home field advantage."

"Decoy target?" another of the backup guards suggested. "Like when we moved Cobb to the motel?"

Charlie shook her head. "Too risky. If this guy opens fire, whoever he hits—decoy or the real Cobb—ends up just as dead. You're not far off, though."

"We're going to give this guy something to focus on," Dom said. "Just not something to shoot at. And while he's distracted . . ."

She drew a curving line along the Harborwalk, separated from the hotel by a thin strip of parkland.

"The primary will be taking an alternate route."

They had just enough time to go shopping. Charlie swapped her black blazer for a Red Sox jersey and cap and hid her pistol inside a shoulder tote emblazoned with a silhouette of the city skyline. She blended right in with the tourist crowds on the Harborwalk. Cobb walked alongside her, his face shadowed by a hat with a floppy foam brim. He grimaced down at his extra-large **I Heart Boston** T-shirt, the hem draping halfway to his knees.

"I feel like an asshole in this outfit," he said.

Flanking him, wearing garishly oversize green plastic sunglasses, Dom shrugged.

"Fair enough," she said. "You look like an asshole too."

Charlie moved with a controlled pace, setting the stride for all three of them. Not too fast, not too slow—nothing that would make the three of them stand out from a distance. A little girl bolted across their path, squealing, chasing pigeons as they fluttered across the wooden slats.

There were too many towers lining the harbor, too many windows, too many angles of attack. Their best defense was to keep moving and fade into the scenery.

"I'm gonna get shot out here," Cobb groused. He bounced when he walked, hands fidgeting at his sides. "What was Felton *thinking?*"

They hadn't shared the fact that Felton was almost certainly trying to get him killed. They knew Cobb wouldn't be able to keep quiet about it when the two of them came face-to-face again. Safer to keep him in the dark.

"If he shoots, he'll miss," Dom said.

"How can you know that? How can you possibly know that?"

"Because I am a missionary of the Goddess of Superior Firepower."

He stared at her. Dom gazed straight ahead, serene.

"Bullet Karma," she told him, "is real. This guy trying to kill you? He's sloppy. He has bad trigger discipline, he's reckless, and he probably doesn't police his brass at the firing range. All of these things accrue Negative Bullet Karma. Ergo, his most important shots will never land on target."

Cobb turned to Charlie. "Is . . . is she serious?"

"As a heart attack," Charlie told him.

At least they wouldn't have to worry once they'd delivered him to the suite. Felton wouldn't sign off on any plan of attack that might catch him in the cross fire. He'd had a fairly reliable MO until now: visit Cobb, get his location, then pass it on to the assassin once he was far away from the action. No reason to think he'd break the pattern now.

That left two windows of threat: arrival and departure. They'd already planned their evacuation route, a system of car switches and decoys that should throw off any tail, and they weren't bringing Cobb back to the Crowne Plaza. Beckett had lined up a new motel to stash him in, five miles outside of town.

This was the hitter's last chance. Charlie couldn't imagine he'd let the opportunity slip by.

Up ahead, on the right, a long rectangle of parkland stretched from the edge of the Harborwalk to a two-lane street. Just past the road stood a curling row of waterfront hotels. And there was the Sapphire, scalloped shingles and edging blue as its name, rich blue detail set into ivory stucco.

They broke from the pack of roving tourists, leaving the safety of the crowd, to cross the rolling green.

Through the smoky tinted glass of the company SUV, the motionless figure in the back seat might have been Cobb. Anyone sighting him from a distance would see exactly what they expected: a man, sitting, waiting to be escorted into the hotel. The SUV had pulled up to the curb five minutes ago; the hazard lights were on, strobing across the black asphalt.

A sniper couldn't ask for an easier target. And from a distance, through the tint, they'd never realize it wasn't a person at all. Just a bundle of pillows and blankets, propped up and bound together with a couple of bungee cords, draped in a gray flannel hoodie with the hood pulled low.

After stepping out from behind the wheel and shutting the door behind him, Beckett stepped closer to the hood. He wanted to give the shooter the best angle he could. His gaze trailed along the hotel towers, the condos in the near distance, hunting for open windows or the telltale glint of a scope.

Come on, he thought. *Take the easy shot. Show me where you're hiding.*

A blitz attack was still in the realm of possibility. He could be hiding in a doorway, just around a corner, waiting with a shotgun or a Molotov cocktail. He could rush in, unload, and sprint away, vanishing in the boardwalk crowds or jumping into a waiting boat. Beckett plucked his radio from his belt. He held it off center instead of holding it to his mouth, and he talked loudly: he wanted to make sure the shooter had a chance to hear him or to read his lips if he was watching from a window.

"Reporting in," he said. "I've got Mr. Cobb, and we're right outside the hotel. Waiting for the secondary team to move up and provide backup before I bring him inside."

His response was a crackle of static. That was Kirby's signal. He cruised up in his personal car, a green Hyundai with a front bumper that looked like chewed-up gum, and pulled in behind the SUV. Beckett pretended to loiter, counting to fifteen under his breath. On cue, Kirby thumped on his horn. The sudden blast sent pigeons scattering to the air.

The Hyundai's window slid down. He leaned out, glowering. "Hey! Move your damn truck already."

"Go around," Beckett told him.

Dressed in a faded T-shirt and jeans, civilian camouflage, Kirby hopped out of his car. He slammed the door behind him.

"What'd you just say?" he demanded. "What did you just say to me?"

Beckett held up his ID card, standing like a wall. People turned in passing. A few hung back, starting to watch the show.

"Sir," Beckett said. "You need to get back in your vehicle. This is a matter of hotel security."

"Move. Your. Truck."

"Last warning, sir. Get back in your vehicle."

Now onlookers were stopping, pointing, bringing their phones up to record the action. A passing car stopped, brakes jolting, as Kirby stalked right in front of it, oblivious to the horn blaring at his back.

"That's it," he snarled. "I'll take your damn keys and move it myself."

Kirby charged. He sprinted at Beckett, one fist curled and cocked back to throw a roundhouse punch.

"Now," Charlie whispered.

Fifteen feet away, Beckett hoisted Kirby into the air. He brought the smaller man down onto the pavement with a thud that drew gasps and shouts from the gathered crowd. Behind their backs, unnoticed, Charlie led Cobb into the air-conditioned stillness of the hotel lobby. A few patrons were standing at the windows with their hands cupped over their eyes, glued to the glass, and a clerk behind the counter was putting in a nervous call to the manager.

"Fun fact," Dom murmured, bringing up the rear, "Kirby's in an indie pro-wrestling league. He wrestles on weekends as 'the Celtic Destroyer.' Loses almost all his matches. He's not great at handing out a beating, but he can pretend to *take* one like nobody's business."

Cobb was still fretting, staring back over his shoulder while his hands tugged the hem of his tent-size shirt.

"Great. That got us inside. What are you going to do when we have to leave again, stage an encore?"

"Relax," Charlie told him. "We have everything covered."

"How am I supposed to relax? You tell me that. How? There's a psycho out there who tried to kill me twice already, and he ain't just gonna give up and go home. I was safe back in my room, but no, I had to go all the way across town—"

Charlie pulled him aside as they left the lobby. Just beyond the check-in desk, a hallway was carpeted in soft sapphire, the glossy wallpaper striped blue and white. She put his back to the wall and looked him in the eye.

"Listen to me," she said. "You want to know how to relax right now? Really?"

His head bobbed.

"I've been in some hairy places," she said. "A lot hairier than this one. And what I learned was the best way to keep your head, especially when people are trying to put a bullet in it, is to focus on your job."

He squinted at her. "Case you haven't noticed, I'm unemployed at the moment."

"Wrong. Do you remember that first night at the motel? You told me how bad you felt about everything that happened. You told me you never meant for anyone to get hurt and how you never would have played the inside man for those guys if you knew how it would have ended up. Is that still true?"

"Well, yeah—"

"Then you have a job to do. Your job is to prepare yourself, in every way possible, to testify. You have an obligation to the people who died in that house on Saratoga Street. You have an obligation to their friends and families. That's where your head and your heart need to be right now. One hundred percent committed. Can you handle that?"

His jaw clenched. He gave a tiny nod. Hesitant, but something shifted in his eyes.

"Yeah," he said, voice soft. "I think so."

"Good. You focus on trial prep; let us focus on keeping you safe. Everything is going to be okay."

Room twenty-seven was on the second floor, midway down a string of gold-numbered suites, where the corridor bent in a soft-lit L. Charlie scoped the floor plan fast; only one elevator, at their backs, and a stairwell fifty feet down the other side of the bend. Nook with an ice machine at the far end of the corridor, empty. One door for a utility closet. Charlie checked the knob, and it held firm under her hand, locked.

She held Cobb back while Dom knocked on the door. It opened a second later, Felton standing on the threshold with drooping bags under his eyes and his hundred-dollar haircut mussed. *Somebody had a long night,* Charlie thought, eyeing the crooked knot of his silk tie.

"You're late," he said.

"We had to arrange safe transport," Dom told him. "You wouldn't want anything to happen to your star witness, would you?"

His lips pursed. One corner of his mouth gave an irritated twitch.

Charlie checked the suite as a formality. She knew she wouldn't find anything. A window looked out across the park. She peeked out through the corner of the drapes, then pointed to the swaying blue fabric.

"These stay closed at all times," she said.

"I'm aware," Felton said, crossing his arms tight. "I told you, my office uses this place all the time. I don't need you to teach me basic security."

Charlie found herself hoping, in her heart of hearts, she'd be there to see Felton's face when they slapped the handcuffs on. *Getting ahead of yourself*, she thought. *We have to prove he's dirty first.* She bit back a dozen retorts, each sharper than the last, and forced herself to smile.

"Of course, sir," she said. "Will there be anything else, sir?"

He pointed to the exit.

"Watch the hallway. I'll call you if I need you."

Felton and Cobb disappeared behind the door. Charlie stood out in the hallway, Dom at her side, on cautious alert.

"This is going to come as a shock to you," Dom said, "but I'm starting to really not like that guy."

"Which one?"

"Both of them, but mostly Felton." Dom glanced her way. "I'm still not sure about the exfil plan."

Neither was Charlie, but they had time to work on it. They had nothing but a couple of hours' sentry duty ahead of them, watching a bending, empty hallway, waiting for Felton to finish stalling.

The attack was going to happen on their way out. The hitter had ignored the decoy in the back of the SUV; he hadn't sniped his target, and he hadn't run up for a close-range attack when the "fight" out on the street had given him a golden opportunity.

"I'll tell you what's going to happen," Charlie said. "Felton's going to pull something when we try to leave. He'll suddenly demand we take Cobb to his office downtown or to a bogus meeting somewhere—"

"Something that forces us to change our plans at the last second." Dom hooked her fingers, drawing air quotes. "Ten bucks says he gets a 'phone call' that he says is from Poole, but he hangs up before we can hear for ourselves."

"Makes sense. Even if Felton doesn't realize we're on to him, the shooter isn't stupid. He'll know we wouldn't show up here without a plan. Only way he can kill Cobb and get away clean is by derailing it and forcing us to improvise."

"How do you want to play it?" Dom asked.

"Beckett's call, but if you ask me? Tell him to pound sand. We stick to the plan, we do not deviate, and he's welcome to throw a hissy fit over it. Felton's not our client; Poole is."

"Agreed." Dom nodded at the door to the suite. "Did you get a look at the guy? The stress is eating at him."

"Good," Charlie said.

Beckett strolled up the corridor, smooth and unflappable, not a rumple in his tailored black jacket.

"Who won the fight?" Dom asked.

"I did." He took up a station with his back to the wall, right beside her. "The Celtic Destroyer is what they call, in the parlance of sports entertainment, a jobber."

"You ought to take up pro wrestling sometime. Might be a fun sideline."

Beckett gave her a sidelong glance. "Who says I never have?"

"Was that before or after you were living in a Zen monastery?" Charlie said.

"Who says it wasn't at the same time?"

"Someday," Charlie said, "I'm going to get a true story out of you."

He turned his gaze, holding it steady on the hallway.

"Who says I'm lying?"

They fell into a companionable silence.

Charlie listened to the distant rumble of the ice machine, the faint hum of the air-conditioning. And something else. She couldn't catch it at first, not until her thoughts had gone still, lulled in time with her slowing heartbeat. Not until she faded into that old place of relaxed alertness, calm but ready to move.

It was a faint mechanical clacking sound, plastic slapping on plastic, just under the AC's thrum. Her brow furrowed. Beckett caught it.

"What've you got there, Little Duck?"

She held up a hand. Listening. Charlie's mind was a catalog of machines. The army had been Charlie's first teacher, but the Taliban had been her second. They'd shown her a hundred ways to hide murder in the mundane, to turn pressure cookers and paddle mixers into weapons that could wash a street in flame. She had heard this sound before, and as she slowly prowled up the corridor, she rifled through the pages of her memory, trying to match it up, to remember.

Then she turned back, breaking into a run, pointing to the door of the suite.

"*OUT!*" she shouted. "Get 'em out, right now! We have to *go*—"

Behind her, the door to the utility closet blasted open with a cannon roar and a gout of flame. A concussive heat wave hit her like a fist, throwing her to the carpet, broiling the air. Her ears rang in time with the warbling shriek of the fire alarm. The overhead spigots erupted, raining cold chemical foam.

TWENTY-THREE

Charlie pushed herself to her feet. She couldn't hear, couldn't do much more than put one foot in front of the other as her vision swam. She staggered along a wall charred black, flames guttering and dying in spots on the sodden carpet while the emergency sprinklers unleashed a storm in the hallway. The acrid tang of chlorine mingled with the stench of smoke and melting plastic.

The utility closet was a smoldering, blackened pit. Her shoe came down unsteadily on scorched shards of wood and a twisted door hinge. She saw all she needed to see, the pieces clicking together. Remnants of a mounting bracket, midway up the wall. A bit of severed wire.

Shaped charge, on a timer. He set it up before we got here. Distraction.

The door to the suite was locked. Beckett hit it in a full-on charge, ramming his shoulder against it. The lock buckled and broke, snapping as the door burst inward. Charlie and Dom were right behind him.

Cobb was gone. Felton lay sprawled out on the carpet, not moving. Dom ran over, crouched down, put her fingers to his neck, and felt for a pulse. Charlie's eyes shot to the door on the other end of the suite. A connecting door. It hung open, just a crack.

He rented two suites. He was waiting in the next room, waiting for—

Beckett was a step ahead of her. He barreled through into the adjoining suite. Charlie had a different idea. She drew her gun as she ran back into the hallway. She shrugged off the shoulder tote, shedding the extra weight, and held her weapon close as she rounded the L bend of the corridor.

One way was the detonation, scorched wall, spray cascading down from above. Through her blurred vision she made out the elevator door. Opposite direction. Three suite doors before the stairwell.

He took out Felton, grabbed Cobb, and walked him through the adjoining door, she thought, breaking into a sprint. *Then he waited for the detonation and slipped past us. He went right while we were looking left.*

The method fit; the motive didn't. The East Boston Three and their hired gun needed Cobb dead. Why kidnap him instead of killing him on the spot? He would just slow the shooter down and make it that much harder to escape. No time. She had to act now, puzzle out the details later.

Charlie thundered down the stairs, taking them two at a time. Down on the first floor, employees were supervising the evacuation, escorting a line of anxious guests—some sopping wet—out through the lobby. Calls to stay calm, to stay orderly, fought to be heard over the shriek of the fire alarm.

Not through the lobby—too slow, too open. The shooter would have to keep Cobb under control and make sure he didn't shout for help. She looked the other way, to a pair of swinging doors marked **EMPLOYEES ONLY**.

She hit the door with her shoulder, plowed through, and found herself in a changing room. Lockers lined the walls, staff names written on strips of tape, a couple of jackets and a stray maroon tie draping over a long wooden bench. A waiter for the house restaurant was coming out while she was coming in, and she almost knocked him flat. He got a look at her gun, and his eyes bulged.

"Security," Charlie shouted over the siren, flashing her laminated badge. She pointed to a door on the far side of the changing room. "What's past that?"

"Service tunnel," he said.

"Did you see anyone come through here just now?"

"Y-yeah, man and a woman. I shouted that they had to turn around, leave through the lobby, but—" He waved a helpless hand at the speaker grille high on the wall, his voice almost inaudible over the Klaxon.

Charlie darted around him, through the door, and down a flight of stairs into gathering shadows.

◆　◆　◆

Felton's pulse throbbed, weak but steady, under Dom's fingertip. The ADA groaned, wincing as he arched his back and shifted on the floor. His eyelids flickered.

"What happened?" she said. "What did you see?"

"Nothing, I—I just felt a needle, must have . . . must have dosed me with something. Never got a look at his face."

My kid lies better than you, Dom thought, *and she's in kindergarten.* At least the groan was real. She was pretty sure he'd been drugged just to keep the charade intact, but he delivered the words like he'd rehearsed them all morning.

She left him on the floor and chased after Beckett. She found him in the next room over. No sign of Cobb or his attacker. He was in the bathroom, standing stock still.

"Beckett?"

He was staring at the bathroom mirror.

She had seen the big man angry before. She'd seen him troubled. She'd seen him cry once, just once, at the end of a day they'd agreed to never talk about again. But she was pretty sure she'd never seen him scared. Not until today.

The shooter had left a doodle behind, drawn on the mirror in dark-blue lipstick. It was a pair of ducks: a mama being followed by a waddling baby.

"Beckett?"

"We have to find Charlie," he said, turning, pushing past her. "We have to find her *right now*. She's in danger."

Dom shook her head, not following. "Why? The guy was after Cobb. Probably already shot him and stuffed him in a closet somewhere. He's got no reason to stick around."

He was already sprinting for the stairs. His shout echoed over the wail of the fire alarm and the rattling downpour from the hallway sprinklers.

"Charlie is the target!"

The service tunnel was just that: a wide, high-arched tunnel running down below the belly of the hotel, the curve of the ceiling lined with rattling pipes, walls built from blocks of rough stone. Every ten feet, a fat utility bulb lit the way for the hotel's staff.

Glass crunched under Charlie's heel. The first bulb had been smashed. So had the second. The third, up ahead, cast a circle of bright-yellow light that divided the tunnel into walls of shadow.

Charlie pressed her back to the wall and gripped her pistol with both hands, easing her way forward. The distant sound of the fire alarm, beyond the stairwell door, faded into a muffled drone.

Stalling tactic, she thought. *If I want to chase them, I'll have to step into that light, make myself an easy target. Maybe the shooter is somewhere up ahead, waiting for me to expose my position so he can take me out. Maybe he's long gone. I'm supposed to take my time, worry about it.*

She had a better idea.

She framed the bulb in her sights, held her breath, and squeezed the trigger. The bullet plowed through the light with a deafening crack, echoing like thunder down the tunnel, and plunged her into darkness.

Unless you brought night vision goggles, Charlie thought, ducking low and charging ahead, *we'll call this handicap even.*

She felt her way with one hand, following the ridges of rough stone, occasionally wading across puddles of broken glass. A glow appeared, coming from beyond a gradual bend in the tunnel, luring her onward.

Cobb waited for her at the tunnel's end. One light had been left intact, the last one, at the foot of a metal staircase. The stairs led to a pair of wide doors, sealed by a key-card lock. A sign read **DELIVERIES/ ALLEY ACCESS.**

Cobb had been carefully positioned at the far edge of the light. Just far enough to hide the figure standing behind him, the one with the slim barrel of a .22 pistol pressed to his skull. Their other arm wrapped tight around his throat, holding him still and turning him into a human shield.

Charlie brought her weapon up, spread her footing, bracing like she was on the firing range. Warning bells rang out, strident and loud: this situation was all wrong. *Why are you still here?* she thought. Had the shooter dragged Cobb down here for reasons she still couldn't work out only to discover they needed a staff key for the door? Were they cornered now, trapped one door away from freedom?

No. They rigged up a shaped charge inside a locked utility closet. They have *staff access to the entire hotel. This was deliberate.*

It was all deliberate. The timing, the lights, the staging. Every last detail.

And it wasn't the shooter, not the one she'd confronted outside the decoy room at the Crowne Plaza. The arm around Cobb's neck was muscled but smooth, hairless. The stranger's head moved behind him, poking just into sight. Charlie made out hard, angled cheekbones and midnight-blue lipstick.

Charlie adjusted her aim. The figure flashed a smile, holding still, as if daring Charlie to take the shot. Cobb was pale. His face dripped with sweat, one knee starting to shake uncontrollably.

No shot. Not at this distance, not with a gun to the primary's head. Even if she could nail a perfect bull's-eye, death reflex could yank the woman's trigger finger and take Cobb down with her. Charlie couldn't risk it.

"Let him go," she called out, bluffing. "Let him go, or I *will* shoot you."

The smile became a cheshire grin in the shadows. She didn't move. Bluff called.

What are you waiting for? Charlie thought. The woman would need to free one hand to swipe a card across the lock and open the alley door, but she could control Cobb with the gun alone. Backup was coming, and so were the police. She had to know that the longer she waited, the narrower her odds got.

Charlie advanced. Two brisk strides, bringing all the authority she could muster.

"Listen to me," she said. "You're not getting out of here, not with him. That explosion is bringing EMS in force. You know what they're thinking right now? Terrorism."

The woman didn't respond. Didn't move.

"That means the police aren't going to play games with you. There will be no negotiations. They'll roll in here, they'll roll heavy, and they will roll *over* you. Your only hope of survival is to let your hostage go, right here, right now. Live or die. Make a choice."

The deep-blue smile grew an improbable notch. Charlie felt like she was on a dissection table under the woman's steady, curious stare. Or naked in an art studio, posing for the class, her every flaw and imperfection on display.

Then, apparently, she'd seen enough of Charlie. The figure crouched down behind Cobb's back.

She shot him.

The .22 slug ripped across Cobb's inner thigh, and he fell to the floor, clutching his leg. He let out a strangled shriek that turned into a long, keening whine. The woman danced back, feather light on her feet, and promptly threw the gun down. It went clattering across the concrete. She held out her open palms, showing them to Charlie.

Charlie's finger brushed against the trigger. She had a perfect kill shot.

No.

She didn't know what made her fingertip jerk away, like she'd brushed it against a hot stove. Training, ethics—she didn't know, but she couldn't do it. A gunfight was one thing; the woman was unarmed now, and if she pulled that trigger, it would be a cold-blooded murder. Charlie couldn't even justify a kill shot by saying she was protecting Cobb. The .22 was gone, off in a corner of the tunnel, out of anyone's reach.

"Freeze," she shouted. "Don't move!"

The woman turned her back. She nonchalantly waved a plastic card. The lock clicked, and the door swung wide, light streaming in from the alley. She paused, for just a moment, and nodded at Cobb. He was down on the ground, clutching his leg and hissing through gritted teeth. Rivulets of blood drooled between his clenched fingers.

Finally, she spoke.

"You'd better save him, Charlie."

Then she vanished. The alley door swung shut in her wake, blotting out the sunlight.

TWENTY-FOUR

Charlie ran in and hit the floor on both knees. She set her gun aside and pressed her hands over Cobb's, adding to the pressure. His blood was hot against her palms, and he'd stopped screaming because he didn't have any air left. His eyes rolled back, sunken in his fish-belly-white face.

"*Need some help over here,*" Charlie shouted over her shoulder, as loud as she could. "Stay with me. Hayden? *Hayden.* Stay with me. You're going to be all right."

Help was coming. The strobe of a flashlight arrived just ahead of thundering footsteps. Beckett whipped off his blazer, grabbed both arms, and twirled it into a lumpy rope. He got down next to Charlie and fashioned a makeshift tourniquet while Dom and a hotel employee got the alley door open.

"Over here," Dom called to someone in the alley. "We've got injured here! GSW, he needs immediate evac!"

Paramedics raced in, hauling a collapsible stretcher. Cobb was trying to talk. The plastic bubble of an oxygen mask swallowed his last words. He fell unconscious as they hauled him out.

Charlie followed, out into the open air, squinting against the wall of strobing emergency lights. Police cars blocked off the street. Fire trucks and ambulances formed a snaking steel conga line. She just stood there, perplexed, feeling outside of herself as she tried to parse what had just happened.

"You've got something to say," Dom told Beckett.

The paramedics were racing the primary and a groggy ADA Felton to Massachusetts General. The alarms had fallen silent, the spray of the sprinklers reduced to faint, slow drips onto sodden carpet, the blue fabric soaked to a murky black that sucked at Charlie's heels. Firefighters prowled the hallways, studying the charred remains of the utility closet and hunting for danger.

Charlie stared at the lipstick doodle on the suite mirror. Two ducks.

"I'll explain on the way to the hospital," Beckett said.

Dom stood in the doorway, blocking his path.

"You'll explain it now."

"On the way," he said. "You know why she shot him on the inside of his leg?"

Dom shook her head, stone faced.

"Femoral artery—inner thigh—is one of the biggest pathways for blood in the body. Sever both femorals, you bleed to death in minutes. Surgeons are going to find that .22 slug lodged just about an inch shy of his femoral. Scary wound, but not a fatal one. On purpose."

He took hold of Dom's shoulder and firmly, gently moved her aside.

"She knew she wouldn't be able to sneak Cobb out of here, and she couldn't risk us hiding him somewhere off the grid, so she changed the battleground. Now he's cornered in a hospital, and she knows exactly how and where to get at him. At her leisure."

"How do you—"

"Because it's one of her favorite tactics," Beckett said. "Wound the prey, bleed the prey, get them moved to a hunting ground that she controls, move in for the kill. She's a lioness. Pursuit predator."

He locked eyes with Charlie.

"*Apex* predator," he said. "And she's got her sights on you. We need to move."

◆ ◆ ◆

Charlie drove. At her side, Beckett sank into himself. *Haunted,* she thought. He put his dark glasses on while he gathered his thoughts. Shielding his eyes, opening up everything else.

"You wanted to learn something real about my history," he told her. "Today's your lucky day. This is as real as it gets."

She didn't feel lucky.

"Her name is Nina," he said.

"No last name?" Dom asked, sitting in back.

"If she needs one, she invents one. Nina's just the name I knew her by. She's probably had a dozen others since." He tilted his head, capturing Dom in the rearview mirror. "You know I've done some overseas work."

"*We've* done some overseas work."

"Before I knew you," he said. "Nina . . . she taught me everything I know about this business, and at the time we parted ways, she had a lot of lessons left."

Charlie frowned. "Wait. She's a *bodyguard?*"

"She's a mercenary. A hired gun, working for the highest of bidders. Nina's known for a very particular specialty: the acquisition and/or termination of targets under high security."

"That sounds like a euphemism for 'kidnapping and murder,'" Charlie said.

He answered her with stony silence.

"She's . . . the anti-us," Dom said.

"She penetrates security systems," he said. "Gets people who can't be got. She once abducted the CEO of an oil company. Man knew he was wanted with a six-figure price on his head. He'd gone to ground inside a fortified mountain compound, and she snatched him out from under thirty armed guards."

Dom whistled. "How'd she pull it off?"

"Spent three months studying him. Another two months to compromise the service that supplied food to his fortress. Then she bided her time, waited for him to host his annual company gathering. More executives on the scene, all with their own security details. She made sure the meals for the shindig were contaminated. Now it was a compound full of VIPs with full-blown food poisoning. Major medical emergency, and more importantly, all those security details were arguing with each other, trying to coordinate ten different responses at the same time, everybody shoving their own primary to the front of the line."

He cracked his knuckles.

"Then she disguised herself as a medevac pilot, flew into the chaos on a stolen helicopter, picked up her man, and left. She was across the Venezuelan border before anyone noticed anything was wrong."

"Damn," Dom said. "Have to ask—why'd the band break up?"

"Job in Cuba went bad on us. Butch-and-Sundance levels of bad. The whole thing was a setup from the start. First time I'd ever been shot. Not an experience I recommend to anybody. Nina saved my life, got me out of there, stashed me in a private hospital in Geneva, and footed the bill. I spent about a year in rehab while she went halfway around the world and hunted down the client who did us dirty. She left coordinates behind, latitude and longitude to pick up her trail and meet up once I was back on my feet."

"And?" Charlie asked.

"I had a lot of time to think, laid up like that. Makes a man philosophical. Decided on a change in lifestyle."

"So the mirror, that . . . weirdness down in the tunnel," Charlie said. "What was that all about?"

"She wanted to meet you." She felt his eyes behind the onyx wall of his glasses, studying her. "Nina believes you only truly know a person when they've been placed under conditions of absolute stress. The way you behave under said conditions reveals your true character. The closer a person comes to their pain threshold, physical and emotional, the more genuine they become."

Dom sagged back in her seat. "Great. So now we have *two* hitmen chasing our primary, and one of them is a sadistic psycho."

"Not so," Beckett said. "For one, she's not a sadist. Torture's just a tool to her. And she's sociopathic but not psychotic, not delusional. Nina loves puzzles. Security systems are puzzles to her. So are people. And puzzles exist to be cracked and unraveled. She's . . . *curious.*"

"Why is she curious about me in particular?" Charlie asked.

"Because I took you under my wing. The quality of a student reflects on the quality of their teacher. She taught me; I'm teaching you. So she wants to put you to the test."

"This is . . . her twisted way of getting closer to you," Charlie said.

"I feel like I should be jealous here," Dom said. "I mean, I'm not. At all. But I feel like I should be."

Beckett turned in his seat. "What you and I have, that's different. You know this, tigrotta. She does too."

"I could have killed her," Charlie said. "I had the shot."

"She *gave* you the shot," he said. "Two kinds of people: the kind who can shoot an unarmed woman in the back and the kind who can't. Now she knows what kind you are. She also knows you won't open fire if the primary could get hurt. That thing with the one light she didn't smash? She wanted to see how you'd tackle a suspected ambush: if you'd hold back or charge in or play it smart and find another solution."

"She's building a profile," Charlie said. "On me."

"Do we even know if she's involved in this mess?" Dom said. "I mean, is it possible she just decided to walk back into your life and picked a random client to screw with?"

Beckett shook his head, firm.

"Nina doesn't roll out of bed for less than a hundred grand. No. Somebody hired her. And it's not the East Boston Three."

"What about the fourth man?" Charlie asked. "There's still a member of the crew the police couldn't catch, out and running loose."

"He couldn't afford her. And I'd be amazed if a Boston cop had the juice to find her, let alone know the back channels to float an offer."

"Whoever it is," Charlie said, "there's another wrinkle. She wasn't there to kill Cobb. She was there to kidnap him. Why?"

"Bet he can tell us," Dom replied.

Charlie drove in troubled silence. She kept thinking about the lipstick doodle on the mirror.

Did you give me a hand-me-down nickname, Beckett? Were you Nina's Little Duck, once upon a time?

And did she really come to test me, or is she aiming to get you back under her wing?

TWENTY-FIVE

From a distance, Massachusetts General looked more like a block of mismatched office buildings than a hospital. Up close, the clashing styles of dark-red brick and tall, vertical slices of glass meshed together around a central tower, rising up in a majestic curve. It was the biggest hospital in the state, one of the biggest in the world.

That didn't feel like good news to Charlie. The bigger the territory, the larger the staff, the more holes you could poke in any building's security. *And Nina wants him here*, she thought. *Like Beckett said: she chose this battleground. She chose it for a reason.*

Cobb was in surgery. The prognosis was good. Charlie pestered nurses until someone gave her an update on the ADA. Felton was fine, resting up, making a swift recovery from whatever he'd been injected with.

"She got at him," Beckett murmured. They stood and waited in a lobby lined with pale tiles. "This had nothing to do with the other two setups or the hitman working for the East Boston Three. She got at him, forced him to set up the meet, arranged everything just right before we ever showed up. The drugging was to give him deniability, make him look like a victim."

"Why not just kill him?" Dom asked.

Beckett shook his head. "She doesn't kill if it's not the smartest play. Don't get it twisted: the woman puts less value on human life than she does on her morning Starbucks latte; she just doesn't like to waste someone who might be useful down the line. And a corrupt ADA in your pocket is a nice thing to have for a rainy day."

Riley stepped off the elevator. He came up fast, reached for Charlie, almost hugged her, then dropped his arms to his sides. He was like a train trying to ride three tracks at the same time.

"I dropped everything, soon as I heard. Are you okay?"

"Little shaken is all," she said.

"I might have something. I spent the whole morning working the lawyer angle, digging through Oscar Pembrose's past clients and trying to match up anyone who fit your description of the shooter."

He brought up his phone and started flipping through photographs. The first was a near miss; the man in the mug shot was a little too old, his eyes a little too small.

"Not him," she said.

The next photo was a little closer—right age, right general shape—but he still didn't match the man in her memories. Charlie pointed to the corner of her eye.

"My guy didn't have a tattoo. I would have noticed the teardrop."

The third picture brought her right back to the Crowne Plaza. The young, hard-eyed man glaring from Riley's phone was the same one she'd confronted outside the decoy room's door, disguised as a room service waiter with a silenced pistol under his serving tray.

"That's him," she said. "That's our guy."

Riley broke into a grin. "We've *got* him. I mean, we don't have him, yet, in custody, but . . . but we will, now."

"Who is he?" Dom asked, leaning in at Charlie's shoulder to get a closer look.

"Guy's name is Angel Strickland. He did a stint in the Marine Corps straight out of high school; then he came home looking for a fight. Found one at the Tabby Cat Gentleman's Club, over on Lagrange."

"Bar brawl?" Charlie said.

"He killed a guy with a broken bottle. Pembrose took the case, got him off when the club's security footage vanished in a mechanical malfunction. None of the witnesses could agree on who started the fight, and there was enough mud in the water to give Angel a walk."

This was it. All they needed to do was bring him in, tie him to the .38, and that would fix everything. Grillo would be back on the streets, and her father would be coming home, safe and sound.

"Where is he?" she said, a new fire in her eyes. "Right now? I want him."

Riley put the phone away. "Hey. You are not going after this guy."

"The hell I'm not. This is about my *dad*—"

"And unless the law changed in the last half hour or so, when last I checked, that laminated ID card doesn't have the same authority as my badge. You aren't a cop, Charlie. You can't arrest anybody, and if you go chasing this guy down on your own, you could screw up the case. No vigilante business. We do this clean. Promise me."

She pursed her lips. He was right. She hated it, but he was right.

"Then what are *you* going to do?" she asked. She didn't mention that the whole mess with the .38 was his fault in the first place. From the pained look on his face, she didn't have to.

"He's got a Jeep registered to an apartment in West Roxbury. I got a couple of friends who work out of the E-5 district; I'm going to give them a call, right now, and ask them to check his place out. From there, we'll work out a game plan. I know you're aching to get this done, but we have to take it slow and careful, or Angel might bolt."

"Do it," Charlie said.

"Detective Glass," Poole said, standing behind him. "What brings you here?"

Riley turned, startled, and straightened his tie.

"Oh, uh, ma'am. Yes, ma'am. I mean, I'm following up with Ms. McCabe on a police report. Unrelated to . . . to present circumstances."

"I see."

"I should be going." Riley looked to Charlie. "I'll be in touch as soon as I know more."

He hustled to the elevator like the tile floor was a bed of hot coals.

"You two know each other?" Charlie asked.

The district attorney nodded, sharply. Poole had gray clouds behind her eyes, a thunderstorm brewing.

"He's a bright young man." She turned to Beckett. "Talk to me."

"Prognosis says Cobb lost a lot of blood, but he'll pull through. He's in surgery now, say it could be another few hours yet."

"When I retained your firm, Mr. Beckett, I was assured you could see this job through. Was I incorrect?"

"No, ma'am." He folded his arms. "We assured you that Hayden Cobb would be kept secure to the extent of our ability. We also asked that we be entrusted with full authority over the operation so we can do what we do best."

"And you were," she replied.

"No, ma'am," Charlie said. "We absolutely were not."

Poole turned to face her, one razor-thin eyebrow lifted in surprise. "Excuse me?"

Charlie swallowed hard. She stood at parade rest, chin high, and met the DA's icy stare.

"We were ordered to move the primary from a safe and secure location. We warned Mr. Felton that it was too dangerous, we told him it was unnecessary and reckless, and he overruled us. If we had full authority over this assignment, today never would have happened."

Poole's gaze bored into her. The woman was a courtroom shark. Charlie had the sense that she was swimming through Charlie's words, hunting for any lapse, any inconsistency or fault she could sink her teeth into.

"Interesting," she said. "Mr. Felton advised me that the Crowne Plaza was unsafe."

"If I may—" Charlie hesitated, catching a look of warning from Beckett. Then she pressed forward. "If I may, also? This is part of a pattern."

"Do tell."

Charlie counted each bullet off on her fingertips.

"First, we provided the primary's location to Mr. Felton. That night, an assassin put a bullet through the window of the motel room he was staying in. The next day, we provided Mr. Felton with a deliberate decoy location."

Poole's eyebrow lifted a millimeter higher. "Decoy?"

"They met in that room, but Mr. Cobb was actually being kept in a secure location elsewhere in the building. The assassin didn't come to the real room. He came to the fake one, the one that your assistant knew about, the one we'd carefully set dressed to give the impression that Cobb was sleeping there."

She heard her own voice rising, felt her cheeks getting hot, but she couldn't stop now. She leaned in a little, shooting the DA's laser glare right back at her.

"In other words, there's a leak. And if the leak was on our end, the killer would have known the right room number. The only person who didn't know that room on the fourth floor was a decoy and that Cobb wouldn't be there was *your* man."

"If you're accusing—"

"I'm not finished," Charlie said. In fact, she knew she might be, if this got back to Jake and Sofia, but she was done holding her silence. "Today, with the full knowledge that a contract killer is actively hunting for your star witness, Felton demanded that we take him out of hiding and ferry him all the way across town, exposing him to attack. The attacker didn't just make a move at Felton's handpicked site; she *controlled* it. She had closet keys, employee pass cards, access to an adjoining room. The entire attempt was set up and orchestrated long before we arrived on the scene."

"Let me be very clear on something . . . ," Poole said.

Then she fell silent for a moment. Making Charlie wait for it, playing the tension in the air like a violin.

"Are you formally accusing my assistant of setting Hayden Cobb up to be killed?"

"No, ma'am," Charlie said. "I'm formally accusing your office of having a leak. Could be anyone. But Mr. Felton is the most likely suspect, and I think you'd have to be willfully blind not to be putting his life under a microscope right now."

That silence again. Poole allowed Charlie only the slightest glimpse behind her mask, hidden in a twitch of her narrow chin.

"And me?" she asked. "Do you suspect me as well?"

Charlie held her ground.

"It's my job to suspect anyone who we know was capable of leaking the information, and Felton reports to you. So as it stands, yes, ma'am. Yes, I do."

"Good," Poole said. She turned to Beckett. "This one's a keeper. I hope you realize that."

Charlie's stomach unclenched. A little bit.

"As it happens," Poole said, lowering her voice, "I came to the same conclusion on my way over. Said microscope is being put in place as we speak. I trust you can all hold your silence and pretend that nothing's wrong?"

"Discretion is part of our basic service package," Beckett told her.

"You'll be dealing only with me going forward. If Felton calls you, pretend to agree; then contact me immediately for your real instructions. And as for my witness, I don't even want you to tell *me* where you're taking him once he's discharged: if by some miracle Felton is innocent, that means there's a much deeper problem in my office. Silence is our best policy right now."

"You can count on us," Charlie said.

Poole looked her up and down, gave her a nod, and walked away. They stayed quiet until the elevator doors rumbled shut, whisking her away.

"Sorry," Charlie said.

"Why?" Beckett replied.

"Talking out of turn like that."

He waved an open palm, unconcerned. "And if it had been the wrong play, we'd be having words right now. It wasn't, so we aren't."

"I think she likes you," Dom said to Charlie. "I mean, as much as she likes anybody."

Beckett wrinkled his nose.

"That's not 'like.' That's respect. Respect is more valuable than being liked any day of the week. Now that we're all being straight shooters, let's decide on our next move." He stared down at Charlie. "Which does not include going out and hunting down Angel Strickland. I can feel you itching to do it, and you're not wrong, but neither was your new boyfriend. You make one false move, and you'll taint any evidence on the scene, hand Angel a get-out-of-jail-free card. Or worse, he'll end up dead, because he *will* put you in a kill-or-die situation, and we'll have nobody to pin that .38 on."

"I know," Charlie said. She let out the rest of her breath in a leaden sigh.

"Food for thought: an active mind and busy hands help to keep unwise temptations at bay."

"Why did she try to steal him?" Dom muttered, almost to herself. She glanced up. "We know why Angel wants to murder Cobb."

"Because Pembrose hired him," Charlie said. "Cobb dies before he can testify, his clients go free. That's not complicated."

"Who *is* Hayden Cobb, anyway? He was the insider for a gang of corrupt cops, steering them toward backroom poker games and rip-off targets. Grew pot in his basement. He's a nobody. Who hires a world-class mercenary to kidnap a guy like that?"

Beckett stroked the V of his goatee, thinking. "Could be he's not the main target. Could be he knows something or somebody. Could be he has some kind of access that Nina needs to get her real job done."

"What access?" Dom said. "The guy's a schlub."

"What about the fourth man on the crew?" Charlie asked.

They both turned her way.

"The police couldn't catch him," Charlie said. "He's the odd piece out. We don't know who he is or where he is or how he slipped the dragnet when his three pals all got popped."

"Cobb never met him," Dom pointed out. "He didn't know who the other two cops were either. His only point of contact with the crew was Lieutenant Gimondi."

"Does Nina know that?"

Charlie's gaze went distant. She was back in Poole's crime scene photographs, in the aftermath of a massacre.

"I keep coming back to that house on Saratoga Street," she said. "It doesn't fit the pattern. We know how they operated: Cobb found a juicy target; the crew masked up and went in like it was a no-knock police raid."

"Kept the targets docile until they realized they were being robbed," Beckett said.

"Exactly. Then . . . Saratoga Street. They rounded up everyone in the house. Then they executed them. Nobody died in any of their other raids. Roughed up, but nobody died, not even once."

"Poole's theory works," Dom said, thinking it through. "Somebody got their mask pulled off in the fight. Couldn't let any witnesses live."

"It's *a* theory," Charlie said.

She didn't have an opposing theory to counter it with. Not yet.

"I want to check that house out. I want to see where it all happened."

"I'm in," Dom said.

Beckett nodded. "You two go. I'll stay and wait for updates."

"It's going to be a few more hours, probably," Charlie said. "Nina's not going to make a move until he's out of surgery. I mean, I think."

"I need a little time," he said. "Have to gather my thoughts."

TWENTY-SIX

"Did you know about Nina?"

Dom laughed.

"Just because me and Beckett have history," she said, "doesn't mean I know all of *his* history. We protect each other's business, and we mind our own."

They'd stopped off at HQ. Dom always kept a change of clothes in her locker, in case of emergencies, and Charlie had started following her lead the day after the glitter-bomb attack. Her tourist disguise was banished, replaced by her last clean pantsuit. Back in professional mode. Dom drove from there, laid back behind the wheel of her Continental.

"He seemed pretty shook," Charlie said. "I mean, by Beckett standards."

"Becket makes like nothing can break his stride," Dom said, "and in truth, not much does. But a blast from the past like Nina? That'd knock anybody off balance."

Charlie gave her a sidelong glance.

"So how do we help him?"

Dom's lips curled in a tiny smile. "This psycho's got you in her sights, and the main thing you're worried about is how to help Beckett."

"Yeah, I mean . . . yeah."

"You're a good friend, Charlie."

"I try to be," she said.

"He's going to do what he does."

"Be silent, brooding, and inscrutable?" Charlie asked.

"More or less. We can help him by giving him room. Trust me: when he wants our help, he won't be shy about asking. And I think he's going to need it. He learned from Nina's playbook. That means she knows all of his moves. His techniques, his tricks, his old reliables—she *taught* him that shit."

"But she doesn't know us."

"Got that right," Dom said. "You, she's trying to figure out."

"That's about Beckett too," Charlie said.

"How do you figure?"

"Beyond the whole twisted relationship dynamic there, which I can't even begin to untangle, this could be her way of figuring out if he's learned new tricks since they split up. I'm learning the ropes from him, so if I do something she doesn't expect, that's a giveaway."

"Don't think that's it," Dom said.

"No?"

Dom flicked her turn signal. She leaned low in her seat, neck craned, hunting for street signs as the roads became a tight, knotted tangle.

"You're learning from him, but you're not the same person. You brought your own training to this gig. Your own baggage too. Beckett's teaching you, but you've got your own style." Dom accelerated into a turn. The Continental swayed as a front tire hit a pothole. "Down in the tunnel? He would have shot her."

"In hindsight, I'm assuming she was wearing a vest," Charlie said. "Nina's not suicidal. She studied me, which means she knows my background and how I was trained. She knew I'd fire for center mass. If I hit her, it would have hurt like a mother and left her a bruise to remember me by, but she'd survive."

"That's *why* he would have shot her."

They found their address on a patch of bad road, more cracks than pavement. The street had been born long before the age of housing-association rules and cookie-cutter suburbs; every house was different, a faded flower in a wilting bouquet. Their destination was the yellow of a dead sunflower, and gray wood showed through fallen flecks of paint. A sign out front, nailed into the overgrown yard, read **FOR SALE BY REALTOR.**

Stray pebbles lay scattered on the narrow concrete walk. The wooden slats of the porch groaned under their footsteps. The front door was old, grainy wood, with three recessed deco diamonds that made Charlie think of an oversize playing card.

"A lot of older houses, they've got these fancy doors," Dom said with a glance over her shoulder. "Cover me?"

Charlie turned, facing the street. No attention from the locals, no movement from the neighbors' windows. Just a few stray parked cars and some kids playing street hockey down the road, their shouts drifting with the summer breeze.

"Anyway," Dom said, "these wood details are usually held in with carpentry pegs. Glued in place. Thing is, you go fifty, sixty years . . ."

She pressed her palm against the middle diamond and leaned in, rocking her palm back and forth. The detail slowly gave. It creaked as it wobbled inward and then fell, the wood panel dropping to the floor beyond.

"Good carpentry. The wood's still solid. The glue isn't."

Dom reached in, curling her arm through the hole, and unlocked it. Charlie heard the rattle of a chain sliding out of place.

"After you," Dom said, opening the door wide.

It was hard to tell anyone had lived here. It was impossible to tell they'd died here. The house had been emptied out: no furniture, no mess, just open, empty cabinets and bare floors gathering dust in the sunlight. Doors opened onto sad and silent galleries, yellowed laminate, then naked floors where the carpet had been professionally stripped away. It was hard, getting bloodstains out of old carpet. The eggshell walls wore patches of too-bright white in spots, the colors not quite matching up where they'd painted over the spatter.

"So much for clues," Dom said. "I'm guessing the bank stepped in when the owner kicked it and hired a cleaning company so they could get this place back on the market. There are outfits that do that, specialize in sanitizing crime scenes. Want to take off?"

"Not just yet," Charlie said.

She was hunting for something. Maybe the soul of the place, if it still had one, if it hadn't been scrubbed and scoured away along with the history of everything that had happened here. She matched up spots of flooring to her memory of the crime scene photographs, picturing where the bodies had fallen.

"This is where they were killed," she murmured, standing in the heart of what might have been a dining room.

Dom's brow furrowed. "Something special about that?"

"Middle of the house. The invaders would have spread out, the four of them, and moved fast. They killed a couple of people when they first came in. Then they rounded up everyone else, dragging them back here, tying their wrists. Doesn't fit the narrative. If there was a fight when they first arrived and somebody pulled one of the robbers' masks off, they could have—would have—killed the witness, remasked, and that would be the end of it. They didn't have to do this. Nobody in any of the other rooms would have seen their face."

"They had another reason."

"They had a mission," Charlie said. "The massacre wasn't an accident. It was part of the plan."

"But they didn't kill anyone at any of the other robberies. I mean, they knocked over at least one backroom poker game run by the Irish mob. If there's anybody they *should* have killed for their own safety, it was those guys, but they let them live. They clearly weren't worried about their victims coming back for revenge. So why get all blood hungry at some random drug dealer's pad?"

Charlie had run out of answers. She hovered on the threshold of a bathroom that was snug against the back of the house. Someone had left a message behind.

A tiny *X* drawn in the bottom right corner of the bathroom mirror, in midnight-blue lipstick.

"She was here," Dom said.

"After the place was scrubbed down and cleaned out," Charlie said. "So, recently."

"What do you think it means? *X* marks the spot?"

"Or *X* for rejection. *X* instead of a check mark." Charlie pointed to the mirror. "This is for us. She knew we'd come here. She wants us to know that she was here first."

"I'm not seeing a reason."

Neither was she. Was it a message? A taunt? *Maybe she's trying to confuse us,* Charlie thought. *Maybe she's just saying hello.*

She fixed the front door, shoving the pegs of the fallen diamond back into their wooden holes, and they left.

One of the neighbors was outside, wearing a sun bonnet and spraying water across her scraggly lawn with a garden hose. She was old and dark, with bags under her eyes like tree rings. As they stepped out onto the porch, she gave them a friendly wave.

"You the bank or the police?" she asked. "Figure it's one or the other, dressed like that."

Charlie held up her company ID card and then put it away. Too fast to see it wasn't a badge, too far to read.

"Did you know the people who lived here?" she asked.

"For years. Terrible thing that happened, terrible thing. They didn't do anything to deserve that. I mean, they were a little on the funny side, but they never hurt a fly."

"Funny side?" Dom asked.

"Oh, just young folks being young folks. Playing their music too loud and too late at night, throwing parties at all hours. I went over there more than once, and I told Matias—it was his house—I told Matias, don't *make* me call the authorities. I didn't want that, and neither did he."

"I assume he didn't want the attention," Charlie said. "Being a dealer and all."

The woman put her hose down. She gave an incredulous laugh.

"Dealer? Oh, honey, no. That man smoked so much weed you could smell it all the way down the block, but he didn't sell it. Matias was a short-order cook. He worked up at Maxine's place."

"What about heroin?"

The old woman waved her hand, batting the question away.

"That crowd? Never. Not that I ever saw, anyhow. I would have reported that. Weed, I don't mind. I mean, I was a kid once; I get it." She lowered her voice, conspiratorial. "I have a medical card, myself. Helps my glaucoma."

Charlie and Dom shared a glance.

Charlie took her phone out as she stepped down from the porch, crossing over into the neighbor's yard. She hunted through photographs and turned the screen.

"Did you ever see this man before?"

She squinted at the screen, at Hayden Cobb's picture, then nodded.

"Oh sure, all the time. That's the young fella who brought the party favors." She rolled her eyes. "They weren't exactly subtle about it. Got no idea why someone would buy pot the old-fashioned way now that there's legal dispensaries, but I suppose it's cheaper."

"No sales tax," Dom said.

"So this man and Matias," Charlie said, "they were friends?"

"I don't know about friends, but they were friendly enough. I'd see them smoking together sometimes, out on the back porch. Last time was . . . oh, had to be four, five days before all that awfulness happened. He's lucky he wasn't here that night."

"Yeah," Charlie said. "Lucky."

Twenty-Seven

Back in the car, Dom drummed her fingers on the steering wheel.

"What even *is* this situation?"

"Nothing adds up," Charlie said. "Cobb and this Matias guy were friends. Matias bought his ditch weed on the regular, they smoked out together . . . and Cobb turned around and fingered his house for the East Boston crew. He set the guy up to be robbed."

"Robbed and killed. Guy was a short-order cook in a house full of cheap stoners. What were the odds he had anything worth stealing?"

"That's one story," Charlie said. "Cobb's story is that the guy was a heroin dealer. Just like always, if Lieutenant Gimondi and his buddies found drugs on a robbery, they'd pass them to Cobb to sell."

"But there was no heroin," Dom said.

"And yet that's how Cobb got busted in the first place: picked up trying to move the drugs he *said* came from the house on Saratoga Street. Which led to his full confession, and from there to arresting Gimondi and his gang."

"What the hell was Cobb really doing?"

"Soon as he's out of surgery and awake," Charlie said, "I plan on asking him."

She tapped out a text message.

"In the meantime, I'm getting his home address."

Hayden Cobb lived out in the sticks. His ranch house was a relic of the seventies, with cheap vinyl siding painted forest brown. A big yellow **BEWARE OF DOG** sign hung on the chain-link fence, and there was a kennel around back but no signs of life. Dom jimmied the cheap lock on the patio door.

They weren't the first explorers to cross this territory. Down in the humid, amber air of the basement, thin shafts of light streaming from narrow windows along the upper walls, they looked out across empty tables and trellises stripped bare. Cobb's unlicensed pot farm was a memory. A musky tang still clung to the air.

"Cops," Charlie said. "They must have turned this place upside down, once they brought him in."

Dom waved her hand across her nose. "You can never get the smell out, though. Whoever buys this place is going to have to tear out the paneling."

They had left Cobb's personal paraphernalia behind. Upstairs in the wreckage of his living room, bongs cluttered a low-slung coffee table, next to a couple of dirty ashtrays. More mismatched water pipes, in a rainbow of plastic colors, stood at ease on the kitchen counter.

"Remember that first night?" Dom asked, prowling the sandy carpet. "I thought he was jonesing for a fix."

"I remember," Charlie said.

"I'm thinking that wasn't it. He was twitchy, sure, but now I'm thinking it was nerves." Dom pointed to the clutter. "Know what I'm not seeing here? Kit. He's got gear for smoking weed, and that's it. No needles, no tubing for tying off an arm—"

"He's not a junkie," Charlie said.

"If the heroin he got caught with didn't come from the house on Saratoga Street, and it didn't come from his personal stash, where did he get it? Why did he say it was Matias's when he didn't have to? Cobb *deliberately* tied himself to a massacre. And I'd like to chalk it all up to criminal stupidity, but . . ." Dom held up her phone. "Give me a second; I need to reach out and touch somebody."

Charlie drifted back downstairs. Dom's comment about the paneling had her thinking. She wasn't the first trespasser to take a closer look; tool marks edged the cheap wooden slats, showing where boards had been pried away and then popped back into place. Upstairs, she found tiny rips at the edge of the carpeting.

Someone had searched this place with the meticulousness of a surgeon and covered their tracks. Charlie checked the bathroom. Nothing but dust on the mirror over the sink. All the same, she caught Nina's psychic scent.

You were here, she thought. She crouched to feel along the baseboards, hunting for signs of her passing. *You came here hunting for something. Not Cobb; if you'd been to the house on Saratoga, you already knew that whole story. No, you were looking for something Cobb had, something he would have kept hidden.*

And you didn't find it, so now you want him.

Dom appeared in the doorway. "Called my cousin Sammy. Who—reluctantly, after some arm-twisting—gave me the lay of the land."

"What did he know?"

"A name. Cobb could have bought that heroin anywhere, but it's reasonable to guess he did his shopping close to home. Sammy knows the neighborhood hookup."

"Close?" Charlie asked.

"Five minutes away. Let's go say hi."

Their destination didn't have a jukebox or a TV over the knotty pine-wood bar. It was the kind of place for serious day drinking, and the locals liked it quiet. A tinted window kept the sunlight at bay and trapped the heat, turning the air muggy and desperate. A pall of contemplation hung over the tap house, mingled with self-loathing, and the barflies minded their own business. A monastery for nonrecovering alcoholics.

They found their guy in the back, slouched in the lacquered wooden curve of a booth seat, eyes on his phone. He had a scruffy salt-and-pepper beard, and the patches on his denim jacket marked him as a sworn brother of the Brigands MC.

"Little hot for that, isn't it?" Dom asked him.

He looked up, curled his lip, and flapped the hem like he was flicking off some dirt.

"Ain't about comfort—it's about pride." He gave her the once-over. "Not something you'd understand. Cop."

Charlie held up her ID badge. For him, she gave him time to read it. He stared at her with reptilian curiosity.

"Asset protection? That a real job?"

"Real as yours," she said.

"Sounds made up. Like calling a garbageman a sanitation engineer." He set his phone down and shifted in the booth, just far enough for Charlie to spot the revolver on his belt. "Whatever you're selling, I'm not interested. Do me a favor: shake your ass a little on your way out the door."

Be polite, be professional, Charlie told herself.

"We need you to look at a photograph," she told him. "All you have to do is say yes or no. Either way, we leave, and you never see us again."

"I don't have to do a damn thing."

"No, you don't. We're not cops. But here's the thing: you help us out, we go away. You don't help us out, I call a friend of mine. And he *is* a cop. A detective, actually."

"And he's going to ruin your whole day," Dom added. "Make you get off that comfy bench, go down to the station, stand in a lineup . . . you really want to put yourself through that?"

The biker got into a staring contest with Charlie. He held out for ten seconds of stony silence. Then he backed down, punctuating his defeat with an irritated rap of his fingers against the wooden table.

"Show me," he said.

"Need to know if this is one of your customers," Charlie told him. He eyed the picture of Cobb.

"Once."

"Once?" Dom said.

"Once. Singular. One time. Do I need to say it in Spanish?"

"I'm more fluent in Italian, but take your pick; either's fine."

"I knew that dude from around," he said. "Same road, different lanes; I'd see him up at U of M, selling his cheap-ass weed to the frat boys. I tried his shit once, all stems and seeds. Anyway, he came by my office here, said he wanted some skag. Not a lot, just a twenty. So sure, I sold it to him. I knew he was a first timer, so I asked if he needed any gear or a how-to lecture. He said no, just the chemicals. That was the last time I saw him."

"When was this?" Dom said. "Exactly."

He swept his hand across the table on its way to picking up a half-empty bottle of Bud.

"Lemme just check my day planner here, where I make detailed notes of all my transactions. Oops. Left it at home."

"Try this," Charlie said. "Did you hear about the massacre that went down, over on Saratoga?"

His eyelids went heavy. "That's nothing to do with me. Somebody saying otherwise?"

"No. But do you remember if he visited you around that time?"

The biker leaned back. He squinted into the middle distance.

"Yeah," he said. "Yeah, come to think of it. It was two, maybe three days later."

◆ ◆ ◆

Dom drove Charlie back to HQ. Her car was waiting in the parking lot, in a sea of empty concrete.

"Looks like everybody's gone home," Dom said, glancing at the dashboard clock. "And I've got to go pick up Natalie from day care. How are you holding up?"

"Oh, you know, angry, confused, worried about my dad. Angry and confused are neck and neck right now; could be anyone's race."

"You're seeing the same picture I am, right?"

"Cobb bought that bindle of heroin," Charlie said, "got caught trying to resell it, and when the cops leaned on him, he . . . promptly implicated himself in a multiple homicide and gave up his partners."

"Could be he panicked. People do dumb stuff when they panic." Dom furrowed her brow, thinking. "Or maybe he had a guilty conscience. He didn't know his cop buddies were going to play Terminator on a job that he set up for them. You'd have to be ice cold not to feel some grief over that."

Charlie clicked her seat belt. She leaned against the car door, pulling the handle, and paused.

"But why? Why choose that house in the first place? Matias wasn't a dealer, he didn't have a ton of drugs and cash sitting around, and Cobb had to know that. He called out a worthless target and lied about it; he basically manufactured evidence *against himself* and all but volunteered to destroy his own life the second the cops put the cuffs on."

"He's going into witness protection after the trial. That's not exactly life destroying. He'll end up working a cash register in a small town in the middle of nowhere. Kind of a lateral move for that guy. His buddies, though? They're screwed."

Charlie thought about that, walking across the empty parking lot alone. She waved to Dom as the white Continental rolled out.

There was an angle that almost worked. Cobb, playing the insider, fingered Matias's house for a heist. It went bad, people died, and Cobb felt the guilt. It started eating him from the inside out. Confession was good for the soul.

Know what else is? she thought. *Revenge.* Gimondi and two of his accomplices would spend the rest of their lives behind bars.

The theory held up until it didn't. For one thing, the heist still made no sense: Cobb had sent the gang to raid a worthless target. For another, the scheme was too elaborate. Why go to all this trouble when he could have made an anonymous phone call to the cops? Exact same outcome, and he could have watched it all happen from a safe distance, untouched.

She called Riley.

"It's . . . not great," he said. His sigh gusted across the line and dragged her hopes down to the asphalt. "Good news is a warrant's been issued. Every cop in the city is keeping an eye out for Strickland."

"Bad news being?"

"Well, his apartment was empty, and from the stench in the kitchen, he hasn't been there for at least a couple of weeks. He'd been seeing a therapist at the local VA hospital, but he missed a check-in last month and hasn't been back there either."

"He's in the wind." Charlie cursed under her breath.

"Hey. We'll find him."

That wasn't a promise he could make, but she knew he'd try. She said goodbye, opened up her car to let the pent-up summer heat out, and paced the lot a little while she waited for the steering wheel to cool down. Her next call was to Beckett.

"Dom just called me," he said.

"She shared the weirdness?"

"I'm still parsing it. Meanwhile I'll tell you what I told her: Cobb got out of surgery about an hour ago. No complications, but he'll walk with a limp for a while, once they let him walk. Right now he's doped up and dreaming of a better life."

"I want to take a run at him."

"Tomorrow," Beckett said. "Doc says tomorrow. You ought to go home, get some solid shut-eye. Got a feeling tomorrow's going to be a long day."

"Are you okay?"

"Copacetic," he said.

"There has to be something else I can do."

"There is," he said. "Rest. Rest is a form of restorative action. I plan on getting some myself, once the relief team shows up. Jake's calling in reinforcements too. I wanted a small team, for security's sake, but . . . well. Situation's changed."

"Are you worried?" Charlie asked.

"About?"

"Nina. What if she comes after you?"

"Have you ever read the *Hagakure*?"

"Not that I'm aware of," Charlie said.

"I'll lend you my copy. *Hagakure* is the book of the samurai, a guide to the way of Bushido. The way of Bushido, or so said Yamamoto Tsunetomo, is death. A samurai must be prepared to die in his lord's service at any moment. If he is afraid of death, he will falter and stumble. If he is not afraid, he will defeat any man who is, for he has more heart in the battle."

"We're not supposed to die for our clients," Charlie said. "I remember you and Dom and Jake all strongly explaining this to me. Take reasonable risks, yes. Die, no."

His basso chuckle rumbled across the line.

"That's because we aren't samurai, Little Duck. And the way of the ronin is to stay alive and get paid. But that doesn't mean we can't learn from the past. Let me put it another way. Shantideva, Indian Buddhist from the eighth century: 'If you can solve your problem, what is the need of worrying? If you cannot solve it, then what is the use of worrying?'"

"Good idea, hard in practice," Charlie said.

"Something for you to chew on, instead of fretting over Angel Strickland."

"How do you know I'm—"

"Because you fret," Beckett said. "And you don't like leaving big, important jobs in the hands of other people. You're like me that way. But sometimes we don't get a choice in the matter. This is one of those times. Go home; sleep. Rest up for the next battle."

He was right. His advice made sense. And as Charlie drove, sun setting on the horizon and turning the highway to a winding ribbon of ink, she knew she couldn't take it. She couldn't rest, not just yet. There was one more lead to follow.

This one, she had to chase alone.

TWENTY-EIGHT

As Charlie drove, she sorted the pieces in her mind. There were two threats in play, two vectors of attack.

First, Nina. She wanted something that Cobb had, and she was aiming to snatch the man and make him give it up. How did a six-figure mercenary end up sharing an orbit with a small-time dope farmer? All Charlie could do was guess, and guesses weren't getting her anywhere. She filed the problem and set it aside for now.

Second vector of attack, Angel Strickland. He wanted Cobb dead, and they'd figured out the whole chain of command backing him up. Oscar Pembrose, defense attorney to the scumbag stars, had hired him to get his clients off the hook, and Pembrose had bribed ADA Felton into setting Cobb up for the kill. Simple and clean, at least as clean as a murder-for-hire job could go.

But Pembrose was off the grid now, and so was Angel. No way to know if they were dead or in hiding or why. Only one link in that chain was still standing.

Felton.

She didn't know what she was going to do when she got to his condo in the Back Bay. She had some ideas. Dangerous ones. They percolated down in her stomach, marinating in a slow-simmering broth of anger. Three times, he'd put her and her friends in the line of fire.

He'd sold them out, first to Pembrose, then to Nina, and had the gall to play innocent about it.

She knew his time was coming. The district attorney could smell the rotten fish in her office, and the odor was coming straight from his desk. She'd dig into his life, find the money, make the connections.

Charlie couldn't wait that long.

Not with him being the only tie left to Angel Strickland. Thinking about Angel made her think about her father, held hostage, waiting for her to come through and save the day. Wherever Jimmy was hiding him, her father was counting on her. And she was failing him.

She'd promised she wouldn't go after Angel Strickland, and she would keep her word. But she hadn't said anything about staying clear of the men helping him.

She pulled into the parking lot. A silver Land Rover was pulling out at the same time. She caught a flash of headlights across her windshield, dazzling, and then the shadow of Felton's face behind the wheel. She hooked a U-turn. Then she slid onto the avenue and into his wake, plowing after him in the gathering dark. Careful, at first; she wasn't sure if he'd spotted her. But he didn't speed up, didn't take any evasive action, and five miles down the road, she knew she could breathe again.

She followed him onto an on-ramp. Out on the highway she fell back a little, letting a car slip between them to give her some cover in the flow of traffic. She was right behind him again as he took the next exit, down into a suburban tangle of strip malls and apartment buildings. Felton's final destination was an office complex, one story and shingled with sloping rooftops, signs advertising a neighborhood CPA and a printers' shop and a water-heater repair company.

And a lawyer. Charlie held back until Felton parked right outside Oscar Pembrose's office. She watched as he approached the darkened glass door and let himself in. He had a key. The alarm code, too; she saw his silhouette turn and tap it in.

She left her car near the mouth of the parking lot and moved in on foot. The light flicked on behind a rectangle of glass. She crept close, slipping behind low, sculpted shrubbery, angling for a better look. Between the angled slats of wooden venetian blinds, she saw the ADA storm into Pembrose's empty office. He tossed the place. Starting with the filing cabinet behind Pembrose's big mahogany desk, drawer by drawer, rifling through the files. One or two got slapped on the desk for later reference; the rest he left alone.

The search was methodical. Brisk. *Rehearsed,* Charlie thought as he moved to the desk, hitting each drawer with precision. The top one was locked; Felton produced a tiny key from his pocket without missing a beat. More folders and a few stray sheets of paper joined the growing pile. He had planned for this, and either he was tight enough with the defense lawyer to have free rein over the man's office, or he'd found his own means of access behind Pembrose's back. Either way, Pembrose wasn't here to complain, and Felton didn't look like he was worried about anyone walking in on him.

Charlie thought about doing just that, but she decided to give him a little more rope. His next stop was the back wall of the office, where a pastoral painting hung in a frame too big, gaudy, and gold for the picture it was ornamenting. The lawyer had more money than taste, and he wanted prospective clients to see it on display. Felton took hold of the frame by the sides and hoisted it up, lifting it from the wall. He set it down and carefully leaned it against the filing cabinet.

Behind the painting was the recessed steel door of a safe. Felton knew the code. He punched in a six-digit string from memory, and it clacked, a light on the panel strobing from red to green. He hauled open the door and reached in with both hands.

A thin file folder joined the stack on the desk. He eyed another, opening it, rifling through the pages, then put it back in the safe. Then he took out a stack of rainy-day cash, crisp bills bound with a cardboard band. Charlie watched Felton with the money, hesitating a moment, waffling—then he shoved the cash in his pocket.

He shut the door, hung the painting, covering his tracks. Finishing up. Charlie hustled back to her car. She cruised through the parking lot with her headlights off, turned to face the exit, and waited. A few minutes later, Felton emerged with armfuls of stolen files. He locked up behind him. When he got back on the road, Charlie was right on his tail.

She watched him. Sitting on the edge of the parking lot, headlights off, low behind her seat, Charlie stared at Felton's back as he carried his plunder home. He disappeared into the vestibule of his condo, then behind the sweep of a security door. She waited awhile. Another car pulled up, another weary commuter coming home.

Charlie checked the load in her pistol. The weapon disappeared under the fold of her jacket. She got out and walked, brisk but measured. An old man with an armload of groceries was hobbling into the vestibule. Charlie jogged up, caught the inside door as he opened it with his key, and held it for him. Just another friendly resident lending a hand. He gave her a smile. She entered the building right behind him.

Felton lived on the third floor. Top floor, facing the river. Charlie stepped into the stairwell. She marched all the way up to the second-floor landing before reason overtook her instincts and reined her in.

She could get the answers she needed out of Felton. She could wring him dry if she had to. But to do that, she'd have to cross a line and make a dangerous enemy. Felton was dirty, but she couldn't prove a thing, not in a court of law. He was also an assistant district attorney with the resources and trust of the Boston PD. This could get rough fast, rough in ways she wasn't ready for.

She walked up one more flight of stairs. Then down again, all the way down, back to the stairwell door. The arguments in her head, for and against, became a cacophony of warring voices. All of them hers. She needed clarity.

The first number she dialed, instead of Dom's or Beckett's, belonged to a bar called Deano's over in Charlestown.

"I need to talk to Jimmy," she told the bartender. "Tell him it's Charlie McCabe."

He didn't keep her waiting long.

"Hope you've got good news for me, lass."

"I'm working on it," she said. "Is my father there? I want to talk to him."

"Talk to me first. Your da's fine. Tell me a tale, one that ends with my man getting out of lockup. You check your beau out, the valorous Detective Glass?"

"He was there—"

Jimmy chortled. "Knew it. Bloody knew it."

"—he wasn't the shooter," Charlie said. "He was trying to stop the real assassin."

"Lass, you're deeply confused on something here. I don't give a good goddamn. I don't care about his motives or your client or anything in this situation beyond springing Grillo. If you know Glass was the man with the .38, pin it on him and hand him over. One phone call to the right ear, and this situation's resolved. Your father can be back home tonight, safe and sound."

"I want to talk to him. *Don't* hang up on me. Either I get proof that my dad is okay, or you get nothing."

Jimmy thought about it. He made her wait, while she paced back and forth in the concrete box of the stairwell. Then he let out a sigh. She heard muffled conversation, then a creaking door. Heavy footsteps trundling down. A television was on in the background, and Charlie picked up the roar of a stadium crowd. Then faint and raspy breath.

"Hello?"

"Dad," Charlie said, her heart surging. "It's me. Are you okay? Did they hurt you?"

"No. No, I'm . . . I'm fine," he said.

He wasn't fine.

"Listen," she said, "I don't know what they told you, but I'm working on getting you out of there. Don't worry. I'm going to fix everything."

"Hey. Don't . . . don't get hurt on my account, all right? Don't do anything crazy."

"Everything's going to be all right," Charlie said. She talked fast, feeling the seconds drain away. "I love you."

"I love you t—"

His voice ripped away. Jimmy came back on the line.

"I allowed this momentary reunion," he told her, "in the hopes it serves as appropriate motivation. The next forms of motivation, if you keep dragging your heels? Those won't be quite so friendly."

The line went dead.

Charlie turned and strode up the stairs, all the way to the third floor, her hesitation gone. Halfway up, she drew her gun.

Twenty-Nine

She knocked. She heard him moving around in there, floorboards groaning. She knocked again and put her face close to the wood.

"Mr. Felton? It's Charlie McCabe, from Boston Asset Protection? I need to talk to you about Hayden Cobb. There's been a situation."

Felton cracked his door an inch, looking bleary eyed, a glass of bourbon in his hand. He had a question on his lips. Charlie didn't give him time to ask it. She slammed her shoulder against the wood, blasting it wide and shoving him back, tearing the flimsy security chain from its anchor. Then she jammed the muzzle of her Beretta up beneath his jaw. The glass slipped from his fingers. It hit the hardwood floor and shattered, shards of razor glass and amber droplets spraying like a volcanic eruption.

Charlie kicked the door shut with the heel of her boot. Then she grabbed Felton's shoulder, spun him around, and threw him against the wall.

"You scream, you die," she hissed. "Actually, scratch that. You tell me exactly what I want to know, you hold nothing back, or you're not leaving this room alive."

He gaped at her, eyes bulging.

"Are you *insane*? I'm an assistant DA. Do you have any idea—"

She thumbed back the hammer so he could hear it go click. His words died on a gust of shallow breath.

"We're going to have a chat," she told him. "Try to bullshit me, and my weapon joins the conversation. I'll tell you right now: it will contribute one loud and very final opinion. Nod if you understand."

He nodded. Tried to, with the gun muzzle digging just under his chin.

"I know you set us up. Oscar Pembrose bribed you to give up Cobb's location, which he passed on to his hired gun. You did it twice: once at the motel, once at the Crowne Plaza. Today? That wasn't for Pembrose. That was for Nina."

The blood drained from his face. It took him a second to find his voice again. Fresh fear, now, and not for Charlie.

"She didn't tell me her name," he whispered.

"How much did she pay you?"

"She didn't," he said. "She told me what I was going to do, and then I did it. She said . . . she said she was going to inject me with something when she grabbed Cobb so it would look like I was attacked. She said if I cooperated, it would be a sedative."

"And if not?" Charlie said.

He swallowed, his jaw flexing against the gun.

"Battery acid," he said.

"I don't buy it," Charlie told him. "She had to leave you alone while she set up the snatch attempt. You had all morning to go to Poole, tell the cops—hell, you knew where she was going to be hiding. You could have played along just long enough to bring in a SWAT team."

"You don't understand."

"Make me understand," she said.

"She broke into my condo last night."

He jerked his head, just a little, drawing Charlie's eye to the shattered coffee table and the remnants of a broken laptop. His sofa was stained, and the room stank like dog piss.

"And?" she said.

Tears glistened in Felton's eyes.

"She . . . *did* things to me. She had these . . . needles, and . . ." He swallowed down another lump, his voice breaking. "She made me tell her things, about myself, things nobody in the world knows. Things I've never told anyone."

"So she could blackmail you," Charlie said, thinking she understood.

"*No.* Just . . . random, pointless things. The time I stole a candy bar when I was twelve. The first time I . . ." He glanced downward. "Nothing that could hurt me, nothing anyone would care about. She just wanted to know. Everything."

"How long did this go on?"

"All night. All night." He squeezed his eyes shut. "And in the morning I did what she wanted because I was *scared*. All right? I was scared. Yes, I could have tried to trap her, I could have brought in SWAT . . . but dear God, what if they lost her? What if she *came back*?"

She eased up on the gun. Just a little, just to make it easier to breathe. She wasn't anywhere near done with him yet.

"What were you doing at Pembrose's office tonight?"

"He called it his poison pill," Felton said. "A file with all the details and receipts. All the dirty deeds, all the trials he fixed, all the shady deals he ever made. Oscar ran with a rough crowd, and he knew all their secrets. He figured, one day, one of those guys might decide to shut him up permanently."

"If he disappears, the file leaks."

"Exactly. No way of knowing who would pull the trigger, so the file has everything. It was designed to go supernova. Wipe out everybody in the man's orbit. He promised me my name wasn't in it."

"But you're not stupid," Charlie said.

"No. I'm not. I found a disgruntled paralegal and handed over my entire rainy-day fund. She got a spending spree, and I got the keys to the kingdom. Alarm code, safe code, even the key to his desk drawer."

"Did you find it?"

He looked to the open kitchen, separated from the living room by a bar topped in white quartz. A sea of papers washed over the glittering stone.

"No," he said. "I took anything that looked like it might be anything at all, but . . . no. *She* must have it. I mean, that's how she found me, right? She caught up with Oscar and . . ."

"What about Angel Strickland?"

"Who?"

"The hired gun," Charlie said. "You know, the killer you sent after me and my friends?"

"I never knew his name. Look, it wasn't personal—"

Charlie shoved him back against the wall, harder now.

"You have no idea," she told him, "how personal this is for me. You don't have any way to contact Strickland? Think hard before you answer."

"I swear to God. I don't. And I pray he doesn't have any way to contact me. I don't need any *more* of you nutjobs breaking into my place."

She believed him. She hated that she believed him. She'd gone fishing, stuck her neck out, stirred up more trouble for herself, and came away with nothing for it. She thought fast, hunting for anything she could use.

"Let's talk about Nina," she said.

His head gave a little shake, almost a twitch.

"Did she ask you about anything else?" Charlie said. "Anything about Hayden Cobb or the East Boston Three or the missing fourth man? What about the house on Saratoga Street?"

"That one," he said.

"The house?"

He pointed a shaky finger behind Charlie. She turned him, slow, one hand on his shoulder. A television stand ran along one side of the living room wall and, next to it, a glass-topped desk. A fat file lay open to a crime scene sketch, a map of the house with penciled-in annotations.

"She wanted to see my case file," he said.

"Stand here, hands where I can see them, and don't even *think* about moving."

He didn't argue. She stepped over to the desk and lowered her gun. He was a motionless blur in her peripheral vision. Her hand hovered above the loose pages, touching nothing.

You were here, she thought, talking to the shadow in her mind. *You had already been to the house, left your mark on the mirror. What were you looking for?*

The annotations confirmed her suspicions. The first responders had marked the floor plan with the positions of the dead. One man had died in the foyer, another in the laundry room; both had been armed, suggesting a gun battle, but the crime scene techs hadn't noted any stray shots. Every bullet from the invasion crew's guns had landed on point, and neither of Matias's friends had even had a chance to return fire. One had been shot in the back of the head.

Ambush, Charlie thought. *The cops weren't unmasked or surprised. The four of them went there intending to murder every single person in that house.*

Matias Cruz, along with two teenage girls—one of them his daughter—had been corralled in the dining room, bound, and executed.

Charlie turned back a page, following Nina's trail in reverse. The coroner had reduced Matias's death to prim lines and hard numbers. Stomach contents, toxicology, height and weight, time of death. She glanced over at Felton.

"Says his TOD was four hours after the first death."

"He was the last to die," Felton said.

She studied the diagram again. The drawn silhouettes. Matias bound to a dining room chair. The girls . . .

"Facing him." Her finger fell on the sketch. "They made him watch. They killed his daughter and her friend, and they made him watch."

Felton didn't say a word. Then she got to the medical summary. Matias's wounds weren't fatal, wounds like his broken fingers, his fractured toes. What had killed him was the final cut, a clean razor slice across his throat.

"They tortured him. They spent hours working on this guy." She looked to Felton. "Why?"

"If I knew, I'd tell you. We kept that detail out of the papers, to weed out any phony confessions, but our detectives came up empty on the motive. Gimondi and his two pals won't even admit to *being* the East Boston Three, so asking them is pointless."

Was it the money? Charlie wondered. Cobb had fingered this house for a robbery. They wouldn't have found anything worth taking. Maybe they hadn't believed that Matias was really dirt broke. Maybe they'd tortured him for some imaginary hidden treasure.

Still doesn't explain why they broke the pattern. No one died at any other robbery; this one, they came prepared to go scorched earth on the place.

She turned another page. And another. Witness statements, mostly from a door-to-door canvass. A lot of people had seen a lot of nothing that night. She rapped her fingertip against one of the reports, barely half a paragraph and more notes than transcription.

"What's with this one?"

"Which is that? The Mila Huerta interview?" Felton shook his head. "That was a dead end. She was another friend of Matias's daughter, a classmate. Her family runs a sidewalk-vendor operation in the neighborhood, selling ice cream out of a refrigerated pushcart. She was working that night, and they thought she might have seen something."

"Did she?"

"No idea. Her mom freaked out and shut the whole thing down. She's seventeen. We can't interview a minor if the parents refuse consent, so that was that."

Charlie gave him a look. "You know what that means, right?"

"Means she saw something."

He gave her a "what are you gonna do" shrug. She turned back to the file. Hunting through the past, tracing Nina's path. Trying to figure out what the mercenary had seen hidden among the scattered pages. She set her gun down and took out her phone, angling it to snap a shot of every page. Maybe her partners would spot something she missed.

She was so focused she almost missed Felton starting to move. The hazy silhouette in the corner of her eye slid, slow and smooth as syrup, toward the open kitchen.

She turned her head, locking in on him like a homing missile. Felton threw himself into the kitchen and lunged for a drawer next to the dishwasher. Charlie raced after him, covering the distance in four long strides, closing in just as a chromed pistol appeared from its hiding place.

Charlie grabbed his wrist and brought his forearm down against the edge of the white quartz counter. Then a second time, hard enough to make him drop the gun. He let out a strangled yelp. She wrenched his arm behind his back, grabbing a fistful of hair with her free hand. She doubled him over and drove her knee up, straight into the soft of his belly.

Felton collapsed to the kitchen floor. Panting, red faced, his back to the corner. Charlie scooped up his pistol, popped the magazine, and kept it. She tossed the empty gun onto his lap.

"You have one chance, and only one chance, to survive this situation," Charlie told him.

His shoulders slumped. "Doesn't matter what you do to me. If Oscar's poison pill goes public, I have no chance to survive any of this."

"And I'm headed for a face-off with the woman who probably has it. You've got a lot of resources as an ADA, but they're built for a different battlefield. This one's more my speed."

She knew the look in Felton's eyes when he finally raised his head to meet her steady gaze. He was broken. No fight left in him.

"What do I have to do?" he said.

"If anyone contacts you—Nina, Angel Strickland, Pembrose if by some miracle he's still alive—you call me. Immediately. Same goes for any developments in the East Boston Three case. If you hear anything about the fourth man in the gang, or if any new witnesses show up, I want to know about it."

Charlie walked back to the glass desk, scooped up her Beretta, and holstered it.

"And if Cobb makes it to trial, no thanks to you," she told him, "you'd *better* win. I want these guys behind bars until the sun goes cold."

"Hey, no argument." He didn't sound like he could make one if he tried.

She left him there, on the kitchen floor, with an empty and useless gun in his lap.

THIRTY

"We're going to leave aside any discussion of your questionable decision-making," Beckett said to Charlie, fixing her with a steely stare, "and focus on the here and now."

They sat at a table in the hospital cafeteria. Dom brought a tray over. Just three cups of coffee. None of them had an appetite, especially not after Charlie had shown them her photographs of the crime scene reports.

Beckett was stern. Dom was quietly furious. Charlie thought that anger might be for her, until she saw how Dom kept focusing on the sketches, the outline silhouettes of the dead.

Dom had a daughter too.

"Gimondi and his crew came to that house on a mission," Charlie said. "They ambushed Matias and his friends, killed anyone they couldn't use, dragged the rest into the dining room."

"And tortured Matias until he broke," Beckett said.

"We don't know that."

Beckett sipped his coffee.

"He broke," he said. "They started out with the amateur-night tactics. Snap a man's fingers, he can tough that out, especially if he can find enough hate in his heart to ride out the pain. Some things, though . . ."

His gaze drifted to the phone on the table, to the twin silhouettes facing the dead man's chair.

"Some things, you don't tough out. Whatever they wanted, he gave it to them before he died."

"We know that Cobb and Matias knew each other," Charlie said, drawing the pieces together. "He hung out at Matias's house. If Matias had something, something worth stealing—and we *know* the heroin-dealer story is a lie—he would have seen it there."

Beckett nodded. "What'd the neighbor say? Matias was a short-order cook? Can't imagine he had much of anything."

"This tells me two things," Dom said. "Number one, Cobb's confession was a lie, or at least half a lie. The whole heroin-dealer angle is something he made up for the cops, and he knows Gimondi and the others won't contradict him, because they won't confess in the first place. He can tell any story he wants and get away with it. He saw something in that house, something worth killing for. That's the tip he passed to Gimondi."

"And number two?" Charlie asked.

She blew across the brim of her coffee cup.

"And number two, we should march up to Cobb's room and start giving him a collection of new injuries until he fesses up."

On the elevator up, something else occurred to Charlie. If a short-order cook had somehow laid his hands on something so valuable it was worth killing for . . . maybe somebody out there had decided it was worth hiring Nina to get it back.

"We play this cool," Beckett said, aiming his words straight at Dom. "We got two jobs right now. One, keep Cobb alive and breathing. Two, find out anything that might help the cops catch up with Angel Strickland. Anything beyond the scope of those two objectives is not our problem."

"Gimondi led a kill team into that house," Dom said. "They did it on Cobb's say-so—"

"Not," he replied. "Our. Problem."

Two stone-faced men stood outside the door to Cobb's private hospital room. Another two held their posts at either end of the pristine tiled corridor, the hall smelling of antiseptic. Charlie spotted three more familiar faces walking the floor, dressed like visitors, weapons stowed in gift bags or backpacks as they blended in with the flock.

Sofia could have been someone's mildly worried aunt, sitting on a bench midhallway and pretending to read an issue of *Better Homes and Gardens*. She glanced up and rested the magazine in her lap.

"What's the word?" Dom asked her.

"He's not going anywhere until tomorrow earliest," Sofia said. "Came through surgery with flying colors. He shouldn't need any kind of rehab, but he lost a lot of blood. They've got him on fluids, and they want to keep him under observation."

"You shouldn't be here," Beckett said.

Sofia's eyebrows went up. "Excuse me? Honey, did you forget that me and Jake *did* this job before we started the company? I wasn't always the bean counter in charge."

"Not the point. You're a high-value target. Any operative on this floor, if he had to choose between you and Cobb, would protect you."

"They know better than that," she said.

"They think they know better. What a man thinks he'd do under pressure and what he actually does in the heat of the moment are two different things. Nina knows this."

"We're going to have a longer talk about that," Sofia said. "Later."

"Later," Beckett replied.

"I don't want to know what you three are up to, do I?"

"Also later," he said. "Cobb awake?"

"He is." Sofia turned her head, catching something in Dom's eyes. "Don't hurt him."

"Who said anything about hurting him?" she asked.

"You get a certain look about you," Sofia said.

"What?" Dom shrugged. "That's just how I look. I have resting bitch face."

"You have resting *murder* face."

Sofia picked up her magazine. She flipped it open to a random page and crossed one leg over the other, shifting on the padded bench.

"We just need him alive for two more days," she said. "Make it happen, okay?"

Cobb was awake, laid up in bed, watching *The People's Court* on a wall-mounted TV set. An IV tube slithered down, taped to his pale arm.

"You'd think I'd be tired of hearing about trials," he said.

They clustered around his bed. Charlie took the lead.

"We went over to that house on Saratoga," she said, trying to keep the accusation out of her voice. "Neighbor knew your face. She said you were a friend of Matias Cruz."

He kept his eyes on the television.

"Yeah. I knew just about everybody I put the finger on. That's why Lieutenant Gimondi recruited me in the first place. Him and his boys needed an insider, somebody who could call the best targets, the ripe scores."

His gaze dropped, just a little.

"I didn't think they were going to hurt the guy. I told you, I never would have agreed to that."

Dom stepped around the bed, picked up the remote from the bedside table, and turned the TV off.

"Why him in particular?" Charlie asked.

"He dealt a little on the side. Horse, mostly. He always had stuff laying around, stray bundles of cash. Gimondi was leaning on me, telling me I had to come up with something by Friday, and I figured Matias's place would be an easy in and out."

Lie. And Cobb knew it was a lie. Charlie caught a warning glance from Beckett and bit down on her words. He was right; calling Cobb out would just make him shut down.

"I know I must seem like a rat," he said, "selling out a buddy like that. But you gotta understand. The weed game's the only thing I've ever known, only thing I've ever been good at. When the state opened up for medical pot back in 2012, my income got cut in half. Then recreational went legal in '16, and the dispensaries left me scrounging for spare change. Only way I could compete was by slashing my prices down to pennies on the dollar."

"You could try getting a different job," Dom said.

He waved his arm, then winced as the IV cord jerked like a leash.

"And do what, with my illustrious résumé? I'm barely qualified to be a Walmart greeter. I was already in Gimondi's pocket, one of his CIs. When he came to me and told me what he wanted me to do, it felt like a lifeline."

"Just to make sure we understand," Beckett said, sounding like a lawyer, "the East Boston crew hit Matias's house, recovered some cash and heroin. Gimondi passed the heroin on to you, to sell."

Cobb's head bobbed. "That's how we always did it. They'd split the money and kick a little my way, as a finder's fee. If they scored drugs, I'd turn it into cash and split it with them."

"And that's how you got caught."

"Yeah." Cobb's brow furrowed. "What's with the third degree?"

Charlie considered her approach. Obviously, he was going to cling to his story. The best she could hope for was to catch a stray detail, something he might accidentally drop around the edges.

"We have reason to believe," she said, "that Gimondi and his gang found something else in that house. Something more valuable. Did he . . . say anything to you about that?"

"I don't know if you understand our, you know, relationship. Gimondi was the boss, okay? And he never failed to remind me of that little fact. If he and his boys found something on *any* score that he didn't feel like sharing, he wasn't going to let me know about it. He didn't pay me on a percentage basis; it was more like tossing a treat to a dog."

"We'll let you get back to your show," Beckett said, turning the TV back on.

They stepped out into the hall, holding their silence until the door drifted shut.

"Any chance he's telling the truth on that?" Charlie asked. "I mean, we know he's lying about the heroin, but he *was* under Gimondi's thumb. Unless he felt like bragging, no particular reason he'd tell Cobb anything at all."

Her phone buzzed. She glanced at the screen. Incoming call from Deano's. She felt gravity pulling her down. Another call from Jimmy Lassiter, then, probably aiming to lean even harder on her. She thought about letting it go to voice mail. Then she thought about her dad.

"I have to take this," Charlie said. She walked around the corner, finding a little bubble of privacy.

"Listen—" Jimmy breathed in her ear.

"I am *working* on it," she hissed, keeping her voice low. "You think I'm not motivated to get this done? You've got my goddamn father. I couldn't *be* more motivated right now."

"Listen," he said. His voice was a million miles away.

Five minutes later, Charlie walked back around the corner. Her face was bloodless, pale. The phone dangled in her hand, fingers curled so tight around the case that her knuckles turned white.

"Charlie?" Dom saw the hollow look in her eyes. She rushed over, reached out, held Charlie's shoulders. "What is it? What's wrong?"

"My dad," Charlie said.

Thirty-One

The cellars under Deano's had their own entrance off a back alley. Private club, members only. Past a short flight of stairs and a windowless steel door, it was a warren of nestled chambers set in woolly gray colonial stone. Bare light bulbs dangled down between the old wooden rafters, dim light glowing across cheap, water-stained rugs.

Harry McCabe could imagine revolutionary patriots gathering down here, conspiring beneath the streets of Boston. Maybe they had, once upon a time. Under Jimmy Lassiter's management, a new clientele gathered under the tap house, lounging on the hand-me-down furniture or tossing greasy cards across a folding table. Young men raised on a diet of *Goodfellas* and *The Godfather*, with pistols jammed into their belts.

Harry wasn't afraid of guns, and he wasn't afraid of punks. He'd gotten his fill of both back in 'Nam, and he hadn't been afraid of much of anything since. The only thing that scared him, bone deep, dragging the minutes into hours, was thinking about Charlie.

She'd bailed him out when he'd been in a bind with Lassiter. He didn't know how she'd done it, but she'd done it. And there was no honest way to make $20,000 in less than a week. Whatever she'd done, she'd done it for him.

And now she was out there again, on her own, sticking her neck out on his account. He'd failed her, every day of his life, and she was still out there fighting for him. He didn't know what she'd have to do this time, how far she'd have to go.

And all he could do was sit on a folding chair, watch ESPN on a janky television set, drink cheap beer, and wait.

"Hey. Old man. You want in on this action?"

The asker was Russell, one of Jimmy's leg breakers. He was playing cards with another of his buddies, who'd shown up an hour ago to relieve the last watch. He didn't know the other kid's name and didn't care to ask. Just another punk who thought flashing a pistol made him a man.

He almost said yes. Almost got up, without thinking twice, to join them at the table. For most of his life, that would have been the natural choice, as instinctive as breathing.

Then he thought about Charlie. In his mind's eye she was still his little girl, still a twelve-year-old with messy blonde hair and dirt-smudged cheeks.

Still disappointed in him. Because he kept giving her reasons to be.

"Nah," Harry said. "Thanks. I . . . I don't gamble anymore."

"What, you get religious or something?"

"Or something," he said.

He drank his beer and watched television. A soccer match was on.

Russell's buddy tossed his cards to the felt. Rumpled bills slid across the table. "Swear to Christ, if you're cheating—"

"Catch me," Russell said.

"I gotta drain the lizard." His chair rustled against the water-stained rug. "Back in a minute."

A minute passed. Then another. Then five. Harry had barely noticed—he had a good buzz going, and the grainy image on the TV was starting to go hazy around the edges—but Russell was frowning.

"You fall in or something?" he called out, getting to his feet. Russell turned to the open archway where his friend had vanished. A dangling bulb swayed, casting a moving shadow.

Then a blur fired from the arch and hit him like a bullet. One muscled arm yanked him close. The other rabbit-punched his belly with a stiletto blade, again and again, turning his guts into ground beef. The figure spun him around, twirling him like a ballerina, and the glistening knife ripped his throat open from ear to ear. Blood sprayed across the cellar floor in a red wine arc.

Harry was trying to stand, fumbling, his beer-fogged brain struggling to keep up. The figure rushed him with the knife. Black fabric billowed in its other hand.

A sack fell over his head and drew tight. The world vanished in musty darkness.

Thirty-Two

"An hour ago," Charlie said, pale and trying to keep her hands from shaking. "One of Jimmy's guys went over. He found four men dead, cut . . . cut to pieces. And my dad is missing."

"Nina," Dom said.

"Has to be, but why? He has nothing to do with this."

Beckett glanced up and down the hospital corridor. Then his gaze slid away, down and to one side, as he turned reflective.

Charlie looked up at him. "You know. Why did she take my father?"

"The good news is he's alive. For now."

"Beckett," she said. *"Tell me."*

It still took him a second while he looked for the least bad way to break the news.

"There was a job down in Los Cabos. Nina was contracted to take out this cocaine cowboy with a streak of paranoia and a small army backing him up. No clean way to get at him, not directly, so she went down the chain. She found his lieutenant and snatched the man's kids."

Dom understood. "To make *him* do it."

"What happened to the children?" Charlie asked.

"Nina gave them back, a little shaken but safe and sound, soon as he delivered his boss's head on a plate. And I do mean that literally."

Behind the door, Cobb's hospital room felt like a bank vault. Impregnable and filled with treasure.

"She wants me to hand him over," Charlie said.

"That's the message," he said.

"Why?" She shook her head. "Why the change in tactics? You told us that this is all straight out of her favorite playbook: wound her target, move them to a softer location, then go in for the kill. Why shift gears all of a sudden?"

"I can speculate. Got a couple of notions. First off, she's playing against my team now. She knows what I know, and vice versa. Nina knows I'm expecting her to show up here. The hospital snatch is a lot easier when they don't see it coming. She may have already been here. Could be she checked out the security on Cobb's room and decided it wasn't worth the risk."

"And the other reason?" Charlie asked.

"She wants to see how you'll respond. You've got Nina's attention, Little Duck. And her attention is more like . . . fixation. She wants to get to know you, up close and personal. In her way."

"In her way," Charlie echoed.

She shoved her fears aside. Tried to. Nina wanted her panicked and confused; a cool head was her best weapon right now.

She wasn't the only one grappling with phantoms. A flicker of emotions crossed Beckett's face, a flock of ghosts behind his deep-brown eyes. They battered at his stoic mask, the dam he built between his emotions and the outside world, and Charlie saw the cracks in the wall.

He wrapped his hands around her shoulders, turning her toward him, holding her tight.

"Listen to me, Charlie." He leaned in close, his voice for the two of them alone. "That *will not happen*. Because I'm not going to let her lay a finger on you."

He let go of her. He took a deep breath, straightened his spine, and reached for his sunglasses.

"She left you a message," he said. "Regardless of our next move, we should probably go find it."

"Where would she write a message?" Charlie asked.

"Someplace just for you. Someplace intimate."

The three stood in the bathroom of Charlie's apartment. Nina's message was written on the mirror. Two numbers, stacked one over the other.

"Latitude and longitude," Charlie said.

"Pack a bag," Dom said. "Right now. You're staying with me tonight."

Beckett folded his arms.

"No reason to," he said. "She can get at Charlie anywhere. That's the part she didn't bother writing down. Nina doesn't *want* to hurt her. Not physically."

"Not yet," Charlie said.

"Not until she gets her hands on Cobb."

"And then?" Dom said.

"Then," Beckett said, "is then. Now is now. Let's see where the numbers take us."

They pulled up the coordinates on Dom's laptop, gathering around the bare kitchen counter. It was a truck stop, an hour outside of Boston and snug against Interstate 93.

"Nothing unusual about the place," Dom mused, scrolling through the reviews. "Not as far as I can see. They've got a motel, a twenty-four-hour restaurant, a retail store. Power wash, private showers. Motel's closed for renovations until September, but everything else is open around the clock."

"People coming, people going," Beckett said. "Good place for a trade."

"This isn't about Cobb," Charlie said. "This is about what happened on Saratoga Street. What was taken. Nina can't get at any of the East

Boston Three, not as long as they're behind bars, and the fourth member of the gang is in the wind. Cobb's the weak link."

Dom glanced to the window. "And if Cobb disappears before he can testify? The case collapses, Gimondi, Kellogg, and Vargas probably all walk free—"

"And Nina can scoop them up, one at a time," Charlie said.

"If he has the information she wants, she wins," Dom said. "And if he doesn't, one of the others will, and she still wins."

Charlie was having thoughts. The kind of thoughts she didn't want in her head, but they swarmed around her like gnats.

"What would she do?" Charlie asked. "Nina. What would she do to Cobb? If it turns out he doesn't have what she's really after, would she let him go?"

"The problem is," Beckett said, "she's not gentle when she asks questions."

Charlie thought about the look of terror on Felton's face. One night in Nina's hands, and he was willing to do anything she asked. Anything.

"She'd kill him," Charlie said.

Beckett pondered that. He was careful with his words. Diplomatic. "More like . . . by the time she was absolutely, one hundred percent satisfied that Cobb didn't have the information she's looking for, there might not be much of him left to set free."

They fell into a shared silence. Dom's fingertip rapped against the side of her laptop, keeping time in the stillness. Eventually she spoke again.

"But we're all thinking about it, right?"

Beckett tilted his head. "Handing him over?"

"If it was my kid? If Nina had snatched Natalie, instead of Charlie's dad? I'd do it in a heartbeat. And you'd back me up. Don't say you wouldn't."

He didn't answer her.

"Look, I'm pragmatic," she said. "Let's weigh the value here. Between Charlie's father and a weasel like Hayden Cobb, only one of 'em is going to be missed if they have to go on the chopping block. We don't know *what* your psycho mentor has planned."

"I see this," Beckett said, "as a matter of professionalism. You start a job, you do the job. And we're being retained to see to the man's safety. Beyond that, contemplate the ripple effects."

"Ripple effects?"

"Cobb dies, the case falls apart, the East Boston Three end up acquitted after committing a home invasion and multiple homicides, including two teenage girls. DA Poole is up for reelection, and her career is on the line. She's not going to go quietly into retirement."

"She'll pass the blame," Charlie said, following him. "Make sure the whole city knows that Boston Asset Protection was asleep at the wheel."

"Company can't take that kind of hit."

Beckett fixed her with his gaze, cool and steady.

"But it's your blood in the mix," he told her. "That means the final say is yours. Whatever you decide, we'll back you."

It was easy to speculate, easy to tread close to the line when it wasn't really her decision. Now that she was on the spot, she knew the right answer.

"No," she said. "We protect Cobb. We'll find another way to get my dad back. I'm not handing a man over to be tortured and killed, no matter who he is. I don't want that kind of blood on my hands."

Beckett nodded his approval.

"Fair," Dom said. "What *are* we going to do? I'm assuming if we go to the truck stop empty handed, she's not going to be there."

"Ghost on the breeze," Beckett said.

"We can't give her Cobb," Charlie reasoned, "but there is something else we can trade. All we have to do is figure out what she's really after. We get our hands on that, we've got some real leverage."

"But nobody involved is talking," Dom said.

A memory came to her. Charlie remembered standing in Felton's living room, photographing the pages of his case file. *Her mom freaked out and shut the whole thing down,* the ADA had said. *She's seventeen. We can't interview a minor if the parents refuse consent, so that was that.*

"One person might," Charlie said.

◆　◆　◆

They cruised the neighborhood in Dom's Continental, prowling slowly, turning corners, and leaving a serpentine trail. They found their target a couple of blocks away from Saratoga Street.

"Park at the curb right here," Beckett said. "We'll go up on foot. Gentle. Don't want to spook her."

The teenager pushed an ice cream cart along the sidewalk, occasionally giving a half-hearted flick to a bell on the handle. She looked bored and hot, her skin glistening with summer sweat. The sun had just started to go down, and occasional scraggly trees painted iron bars of shadow along the pavement.

Charlie took the lead. The girl gave her an appraising eye. Charlie could read her expression. She knew they weren't locals, knew they could be trouble, didn't know what kind.

"Mila Huerta?" Charlie asked.

The pushcart jolted to a stop.

"Who's asking?"

Charlie handed over her ID card and gave her time to read it. Mila squinted at the laminated paper.

"What's that mean? You're like . . . a bodyguard?"

Charlie took the card back. "That's right. We're trying to help someone, a client of ours."

"Lady, people in this neighborhood can't afford bodyguards."

"We need to ask about something you might have seen," Dom said.

Mila snorted. "People in this neighborhood don't have eyes and ears either."

"The police think you do," Charlie said. "They think you might have been walking your cart past Matias Cruz's house—"

That got her moving. Eyes forward, lips pursed. The cart let out a little metallic jingle as it started to roll. Beckett stepped around and planted himself in her path.

"We're not looking to cause you any trouble," Charlie said.

"You're causing me some right now," Mila fired back. "A *lot*. If I didn't talk to the cops, I'm sure as hell not talking to . . . whatever you people are. You think I'm looking to get killed? They murdered his family. They'll murder mine too."

"Three members of the gang are in jail," Dom told her. "And we have every reason to think the fourth is long gone. He's not sticking around, and he's not lifting a finger to help his buddies out. Nobody is going to hurt you."

"Easy for you to say—nobody's asking you to stick your neck out."

Charlie put one gentle hand on the cart. Not touching Mila, but close, an offer of human contact. She looked like she needed it. She could see the fear simmering just under the teenager's surface bluster, and something else. Something deeper than that, something desperate.

"Matias's daughter," Charlie said. "She was a friend of yours, wasn't she?"

Mila nodded. Her head drooped, eyes on her gym shoes.

"Her and Jada," she said. "Both of them. Best friends."

"We've got a puzzle on our hands. And if we can't work it out, more people are going to die. What happened to your friends . . . you don't want that to happen to anyone else, do you?"

Mila shook her head. Just a little.

"All we want," Charlie told her, "all we need to know, is what you saw that night. This isn't going into any police report; nobody's going to write your name down; nobody will ever know you said a word. It stays between us."

Mila's gaze lifted. She looked Charlie in the eye.

"You swear?" she said.

"I do. And I get the feeling you've been wanting to talk to somebody. It's hard, carrying a secret around, right?"

A tiny nod. "I thought . . . I mean, Mom didn't want me to talk to the cops. I wanted to, but . . . we were scared. Once I heard they arrested the guys, I thought I'd feel better. But I don't."

"You saw something that night," Charlie said.

"I was there."

"Passing by with your cart?" Dom asked, studying the girl.

"No," Mila said. "I was *there*. Inside the house."

THIRTY-THREE

"I was in the bathroom," Mila said. Her gaze was distant now, looking back, staring at her own history. "That's the only reason I lived. Because I was in the bathroom. I came over after school. The three of us were just hanging out in Isabelle's room, watching TV. I was in the bathroom when I heard the door slam open. Then . . ."

She fell silent. Her fingers curled tight around the handle of her ice cream cart.

"Take your time," Charlie said.

"Then I heard the gunshots. Real quick, pop-pop-pop. Soft, but not."

"Sound suppressors," Beckett said.

"They don't sound like they do in the movies," Mila said. "Anyway, Isabelle's dad was always a big-time stoner. Always. He never let us touch that stuff, but he always had his buddies over, getting high. I could get a buzz just walking through his living room. Back before pot went legal, he carved out a panel in the drywall, made a secret stash spot in case the cops ever tried to bust him."

"In the bathroom," Charlie said.

Mila nodded. "He never bothered fixing it back up. It was tiny, but I'm pretty tiny, too, so . . . I opened the bathroom door so they wouldn't think anybody was in there, and I hid behind the panel. I could keep it open, just a crack, and see down the hallway."

"How long were you in there?" Dom asked, concerned now.

"Don't know. Hours. I saw the guys, four of them. They had cop uniforms, but their badges looked fake to me. You can buy those anywhere. Anyway, once a couple of them took their . . ." She gestured at her face, hunting for a word.

"Balaclavas?" Charlie said.

"Those. I figured pretty quick that it was a home invasion, and once they took those off? I knew it was bad. Home invader shows you his face, he's not letting you live to talk about it. One of the guys—I saw him on the news later and recognized him; he was that lieutenant. He was *pissed*."

Charlie thought about Cobb's story. They knew he was lying about the heroin he'd gotten busted with. Had he lied to Gimondi, too, and told him to expect a score that wasn't there?

"Was it about the robbery?" Charlie asked.

"No," Mila said. "It was one of the guys they killed when they busted in. Mr. Cruz's cousin, Hector."

Charlie thought back to the crime scene report. The victim Hector Ibarra. He'd been the one in the laundry room, ambushed and shot in the back of the head. He'd had a gun in his hand; they hadn't given him time to use it.

"Hector wasn't a local," Mila explained. "He was visiting from out of town. Miami, I think. Anyway, the guy in charge was ranting about how they needed him, the other guy shouldn't have shot him, and the other guy's all, 'We have his cousin. What's the big deal? *Somebody's* gonna give it up.'"

Charlie already knew what had happened after that. She didn't want to take the girl back there, but she didn't have a choice. She rested her hand over Mila's.

"I heard Mr. Cruz scream," she said, her voice gone thin. She sucked her lips in and chewed on them for a minute. "I couldn't see any . . . any of that part. Couldn't hear most of it, what they were saying. Just the screaming. Eventually, I guess, he told them what they wanted to know. I only figured out later . . . I only figured out later that they killed Jada. They cut her throat right in front of him and said Isabelle would be next if he didn't talk. One of the guys left the house for a minute and came back with a sledgehammer."

"It's okay," Charlie told her. "You can take a break if you need to. I know this is rough."

Mila took a deep breath, and then she plowed ahead.

"I heard pounding, real loud, from the far end of the house, like somebody was tearing the floor up. Then laughing, feet stomping, just . . . over the moon. I saw the cops in the hall, lugging these two big black duffel bags. Whatever was in 'em, they looked heavy. One of the guys called it their retirement fund. Anyway, then he asked what they should do about Mr. Cruz and Isabelle. One of the other guys, he . . ."

Her voice trailed off. Charlie leaned close.

"What did he say, Mila?"

"He handed him a box cutter. Then he said, 'Kill him, kill the other little bitch, and let's go out for drinks. We're rich.'"

The trio commandeered a meeting room back at HQ. More like a box of bare drywall with a card table and folding chairs, the air thick with the smell of sawdust, but it would do. Dom hunched over her computer, diving into her research, while Charlie put in a call to Riley Glass.

"Stepping out for a second," Beckett told them. "Need to find out if an old friend is in town."

"Hey," Riley said on the phone, sounding breathless. "Sorry, no new news about Strickland, but the second he turns up—"

"Least of our problems right now. I'm putting you on speaker; Dom's here with me. The Cruz case: one of the victims was a man named Hector Ibarra. He might have been related to the homeowner. Did the police do any digging into his background?"

"Off the top of my head? They know he was Cruz's cousin, Florida resident, think he was from Miami Beach? Rap sheet, but not a big one, all petty stuff. Pretty sure he ran a small business."

Dom spun her laptop so Charlie could get a better look. A seaplane was touching down at the top of the web page, making a big splash above a star-spangled logo: IBARRA SKY TOURS.

"Anything else on him?" Charlie asked.

"Just surface detail. I mean, you've got one guy shot dead the second they busted in, and another one tied up and tortured; it's pretty obvious who the bad guys came looking for. Why? What's up?"

"Not sure yet," Charlie said, though the picture was growing clearer by the second. She just wasn't ready to bring him in, not until she had a plan of action to go along with her mounting suspicions. "Thanks. I'll tell you more as soon as I can, okay?"

Riley's tone of voice told her that he had suspicions of his own. She didn't want him digging around, not until she had the chance to sate her own curiosity first. She promised to call back the second she had anything for him. Beckett came back and shut the door behind him.

"Have to go," he said. "Meeting someone for drinks."

"This seriously feels like a good time for a date to you?" Dom asked him.

"Not that kind of date."

Charlie gestured to the web page.

"They came looking for Cousin Hector. Cousin Hector, who owns his own seaplane, lives in Florida—"

"And suddenly relocated to Boston with two very large duffel bags filled with something very expensive," Dom said.

"Cobb knew," Charlie said. "He knew all along. He went over to the Cruz place on a weed-delivery run, like usual, and met Hector. Maybe he got a look at this 'retirement fund' with his own eyes, or

241

maybe he heard something on the wind about Hector. Either way, Gimondi and his crew knew exactly who and what they were looking for that night."

"Hold that thought," Beckett said. "I'll be in touch shortly."

Dom squinted at him. "Where are you really going?"

"Told you," he said. "Drinks with an old friend."

The murmur of conversation filled the gallery of the Eastern Standard, rising up beneath whirling paddle fans and broad globe lights. A white marble bar ran along one side of the restaurant. Beckett nodded amiably to the bartender, passing him by, sliding into a red leather seat near the far corner.

His guest was already here, sipping a cocktail, with a phone and an unlabeled manila folder in front of her. The phone strobed every ten seconds or so, another text or email pinging in. She didn't answer them. She was lean, with something almost serpentine about her, dressed for business in emerald green. The straight fall of her hair, cropped at her neckline, was so blonde it was almost white.

She acknowledged him with the slightest ghost of a nod and sipped her cocktail.

"What's good?" he asked.

"Cameron's Kick," she said, holding her glass to the light. "Jameson Black and Monkey Shoulder. You still playing bodyguard and atoning for your sins?"

"Atonement's not the issue."

"Like hell it isn't. Nothing sadder than seeing a pro player demote himself to the minor leagues." She gave him the side-eye. "Didn't think they made hair shirts in your size."

"Missed you too, Hawke."

She gestured to the bartender, catching his eye.

"Another Cameron's for me," she said. "And a Brigitte Bardot for my friend here."

"Brigitte Bardot?" Beckett said.

"Tastes like a vacation in paradise. And it's made with your favorite gin."

"You remember."

"I know all," Hawke said.

Her phone flashed again. She kept ignoring it.

"You still batting your eyelashes at those NSA boys, making them all hot and bothered?" he asked.

"No such agency. In this situation, three other capital letters are more pertinent."

Her fingernails caressed the unlabeled folder. She slid it a couple of inches his way.

"D-E-A," she said. "Here. Don't look at this. That would be an illegal breach of several secrecy acts."

He lifted the cover of the folder, just a few inches. The report underneath, laid out in stark Courier font, confirmed what they already suspected. He closed the folder.

"Varela cartel," he said, sliding it back to her.

"Up-and-comers carving out a small fiefdom in the vicinity of Acapulco. Your boy Ibarra flew smuggling runs for them. Cocaine, mostly."

"Past tense," Beckett said, "and not because the man has a bullet in his skull."

"They used him for a few years. He built up trust, took on bigger and bigger runs. Then they decided to open their Miami pipeline like a fire hose. His handlers loaded Hector Ibarra's cargo hold with, according to DEA's intel, somewhere around thirty keys of their finest, purest snow."

Beckett did the math in his head. Thirty kilograms, sixty-six pounds. Enough weight to pack a pair of military-grade duffel bags. Then he did the rest of the math.

"Street value's, what, thirty thousand dollars a key?"

"As is. Cut it, sell it at the gram level, and your fortunes multiply."

"They trusted him with over a million dollars of product," Beckett said.

"And he didn't land at the designated strip," Hawke replied. "Hector Ibarra was a very bad boy. The Varelas will be sending someone to deliver his well-earned spanking and reclaim their stolen property. They'll be pissed to find out he's already dead."

"They already sent someone," he said. "Nina's in town."

The woman winced. She rubbed her neck. The neckline of her emerald top slid a little, showing the trail of an old, pale scar along her collarbone.

"Christ." She raised her cocktail glass and tossed back a swallow. "What kind of body count are we looking at?"

"Hopefully minimal. You know Nina. She's surgical."

"Hell she is." She rubbed her scar again. "I was there in Panama. You remember Panama."

"You know how she works. Once she gets what she came for, she'll go away."

"What about you?"

"What about me?" he said.

"Did she come for you?"

The bartender brought their drinks over. Beckett contemplated his. The gin went down smooth, flavored with notes of lemon and herbs, the taste of a garden on a cool spring morning.

"That's a loaded question," he said.

"You know, if you're ready to drop the noble-protector routine, I do have work that needs doing. Your kind of work."

"I enjoy my present occupation," Beckett said.

"Down in the minors. With minor-league players."

"I like my coworkers too," he said.

"Then you'd better hold them tight," she said. "Because if Nina decides she wants you back, she may feel inclined to purge you of any worldly distractions."

He stared into the depths of his glass.

"Not going to let that happen," he said.

After that, they drank, sharing an old, comfortable, familiar silence.

THIRTY-FOUR

Beckett called his partners on the way back, roping them into a conference call. Charlie was home at last, pacing the floor of her empty living room in her bare feet, listening to the vintage floorboards groan.

"So Ibarra ripped off the cartel; then Gimondi and his crew ripped off Ibarra," Dom said. "They've been playing hot potato with sixty-odd pounds of uncut coke."

"And Nina is in town to collect," Beckett said.

Charlie had an entirely different drug on her mind. Cobb's imaginary heroin score.

"One way or another," Charlie said, "Cobb found out. He told Gimondi. Then he went and talked to his friendly neighborhood outlaw biker, bought a baggie of heroin, got caught trying to resell it, and told the cops it came from that house. That got the dominoes tumbling."

"You're thinking what I'm thinking," Dom said.

"He *deliberately* got caught. Picture this: Gimondi's leaning on him. Cobb gives up the juiciest target he's ever seen. Not only do the rogue cops hit the house, they murder everybody to cover their tracks." Charlie turned, pacing faster now. "Cobb's sitting there, thinking. And the longer he thinks, the worse it feels. He's not going to get a share of the 'retirement fund.' Gimondi gave him small batches of drugs, mostly weed, to sell after their raids, but no chance he's going to trust a loser like Cobb with that kind of a mother lode."

"He gets a dog treat," Beckett said. "Like he told us. And a dog treat isn't much when you're an accomplice to a mass murder *and* ripping off a drug cartel."

"Only a matter of time before one consequence or another comes down like a hammer and squashes him flat," Charlie said. "He did the smartest thing he could manage: got himself arrested, gave a confession that *doesn't* implicate him in the cocaine theft—hence the heroin and the cover story—and gave up Gimondi."

"Granting him immunity on the charges, and he goes into witness protection when the trial's over," Dom said.

Charlie nodded. "Who better to protect him? You were right: for somebody like Cobb, WITSEC is a lateral move at worst. He gets a new identity, he's hidden from the cartel, and he even gets a straight job now that his life of crime is over."

"He gets a do-over," Dom said.

"Assuming he lives that long," Beckett said. "Okay. We know what Nina wants. The cops are clueless about the coke, and none of the East Boston Three had it when they were arrested."

"We need to brace for the worst-case scenario," Dom said.

"Which is?"

"That the fourth member of the crew took off with the loot," Dom said, "which would explain why he's leaving his buddies to rot. Know what's better than a million bucks' worth of coke split four ways?"

"A million bucks split no way at all," Beckett replied.

"That might be how we find him," Charlie said. "I'll catch you both up in a bit. Have to make a phone call."

Riley was head down at his desk, buried in a growing mountain of paperwork. That felt like half his job sometimes, and he'd been letting it pile up ever since the warrant for Angel Strickland had come down.

He'd been bunking at the station, in a crash room with a couple of cots for cops burning the midnight oil. Stopping in just long enough for a status update, fueling up on cheap, burnt coffee, and then hitting the streets all over again.

What had happened to Charlie's dad was Riley's fault. His mistake to fix. So he was going to fix it.

His phone rang. He scooped it up. "Glass."

"Hey," Charlie said. "Got a weird question for you."

"I might have a weird answer."

"So you were telling me that Internal Affairs checked out every cop in East Boston, more or less."

"Checked out, dug in, drilled deep," he told her. "And then I ran my own investigation, off the books. Like I said, the fourth man in Gimondi's crew can't be one of us. My money's still on Charlestown."

"Are any of your coworkers missing?"

He tilted his head. "Missing?"

"Maybe not *missing*-missing, but did anyone take a leave of absence? Maybe they went on vacation and haven't come back yet, or they've been out sick for a while?"

Riley rubbed the back of his neck. He thought it over, taking a mental roll call of the desks all around him.

"Should be easy enough to find out," he said. "Why?"

"Because there's a chance that the fourth member of the gang ran away with the loot."

She walked him through it, step by step.

"Wait," he said, "how's your buddy Beckett getting access to internal DEA reports?"

"He didn't, he doesn't, and you don't know about that part."

"I . . . guess we never had this conversation." He rapped the cap of his pen against the stack of forms in front of him. "Okay. I'll check and see if anybody's not where they're supposed to be, but there's another angle to consider."

"What's that?" Charlie said.

"These guys knew what they were stealing. They knew who it belonged to. Meaning they knew the cartel *would* come hunting for their lost merchandise. They're greedy, but they're not stupid. Well, I mean, Gimondi's not stupid. The other two are dumb as bricks."

"They'd have to sit on it for a while," Charlie said. "Maybe for years, until the heat cooled down."

"Years for certain. What'd they call it? The retirement fund? They'd have to wait about that long to convert the coke into spendable cash and not get their heads chopped off in the process."

"Meaning they'd need a safe place to hide it," Charlie said.

"And Gimondi's not the trusting sort. He's not going to split the coke and hope his partners in crime stick to the agenda. He'd keep it all bundled tight, someplace where he's got the only key."

"There'd be a money trail. Buying land, renting a storage locker . . . there'd have to be a money trail. Can you get Gimondi's financials?"

"That's all under IA's purview," Riley said. "Just because I'm a detective doesn't mean I can pull any jacket I want."

"Is there a *way* to get it?"

Riley thought about that.

He glanced up the hallway to a long office window. Two men in polyester ties were shooting the breeze behind closed doors, one with his square-toed shoe up on the cluttered desk. Riley pursed his lips.

"Maybe," he said. "Let me call a couple of favors in and see what I can do. In the meantime, do something for me?"

"Name it."

"Be careful," he told her. "Secure your doors and windows, and watch your back. Angel Strickland is still out there."

"Like I said, least of my worries right now. I'm not his target, and Cobb's locked down tight at the hospital."

"Not the point," Riley said. "You're the only person who saw him when you two faced off at the Crowne Plaza. Meaning you're the only person who can identify him in a lineup. He doesn't need to get paid; he already *has* a reason to kill you."

Felton was out of his element. He was out of a lot of things lately: time, courage, options.

This cocktail lounge was a roach motel. A last watering hole for lifers and losers. It smelled like spilled nail varnish, and the owner kept the shrouded lights dimmed way down so nobody had to get a good look at who they were drinking with. A girl at the end of the bar, sixteen going on forty and poured into a minidress the color of bubble gum, appraised him like she could count the cash in his wallet.

Out of my mind, he thought. *Out of my damn mind, coming here.*

But the last twenty dollars in his pocket had bought him one final shred of information. A chain he'd been following from rumor to rumor, relentless, ever since Oscar Pembrose had vanished into thin air.

The end of the chain was sitting alone in a booth for four, nursing a bottle of beer. Three empties formed a ragged line to the left, dead soldiers standing at attention. This wasn't the kind of place that offered table service. Felton walked up to the table, heart pounding fast.

Angel Strickland fixed him with his heavy-lidded eyes. His silent stare felt like a heat lamp on full blast, melting Felton where he stood.

"Do you know who I am?" Felton asked him.

"In that suit? Out of your league, champ."

That too. Felton's gaze dropped. One of Angel's hands was on his beer bottle. The other was under the table.

"I'm here as a friend," Felton said. "Just so we're clear on that before I say anything else."

"I didn't ask you to say anything at all."

"I do some work with Oscar Pembrose."

Now he had Angel's attention. And his silence. Angel sipped his beer, studying him, waiting for more.

Felton took a seat on the opposite side of the table. He laid both of his hands flat on the clammy wood.

"I want to hire you," Felton said. "To do what you do for Oscar."

Angel took another swig of beer.

"Oscar's gone," Angel said. "You know anything about that?"

"I might."

"Is he coming back?"

"Don't think so," Felton said.

"Well. Guess I'm up shit creek, then. Was counting on a payday." Angel set his bottle down. "You kill him?"

"No. We have a mutual problem."

He reached for his phone. Angel tensed, his muscles going taut, the arm with the hidden hand making a dangerous twitch. Felton froze.

"Want to show you something," he said. "Okay?"

Angel nodded with his chin, jutting it out.

"Incidentally," Felton said, "you do know there's a warrant out for your arrest, yes?"

Angel spread his hands wide, taking in the scenery. "And I'm going to go where? Boston's a big city. I know how to move around, stay under the radar. Running to strange places, sticking out . . . that's how people get caught."

Felton turned the phone around and tapped the screen. He had the photograph he wanted lined up and ready. Angel stared down at the face of Charlie McCabe, and his drooping eyelids narrowed to slits.

"I'll pay you whatever Oscar was paying you," Felton told him.

"She knows my face."

"All the more reason to take the job. First of several."

Angel lifted his gaze. Steady, silent.

"We're both in the barrel here," Felton said. "I'm going to need some people taken care of. Everyone who might be able to pin anything on me. Nice thing for you is that includes anyone who can pin anything on *you*. We survive together, or we go down together."

"That so."

"That's so. Her name is Charlene McCabe. She's part of the security detail assigned to protect Hayden Cobb—"

"Figured that part out for myself," Angel said.

"And Cobb and I were both brought to Massachusetts General. He was shot, in no condition to be moved."

Angel squinted. "That wasn't me."

"There's another player involved here. Point is Cobb is laid up in a room at General for at least another day, maybe two. That's where you'll find McCabe. You can go in and get her, you can catch her coming or going—I don't care how you do it. Take her out, get paid, and we both sleep a little easier."

THIRTY-FIVE

Come the next morning, Charlie wasn't at the hospital. Beckett had taken the first watch, joining the backup team to stand sentry over Cobb's room, while she and Dom had a less pleasant job ahead.

"Seriously," Dom muttered, "I'd rather deal with the psycho."

"It's almost over," Charlie said.

The next leg of Lincoln Gable's book tour brought them to a television studio downtown. The host of *Eye on Boston*, Ria Fey, was a pixieish woman wearing a peroxide dye job; she greeted the triumphant Lincoln with a hug and air-kisses. Charlie and Dom stood off to the side of the studio, shadowed by a clutter of camera gear and keeping an eye on the back hallway. Crisis or not—and all she could think about was her father in Nina's hands—Charlie still had a job to do.

At least today would be a milk run. No live audience, nobody in the studio but cast and crew, and the company SUV was secured inside a locked-down carport. The studio had its own security force; if the protesters assembled for a third time, they wouldn't get within a hundred yards of their target.

"Who's the new guy?" Dom asked.

Lincoln and Ria were doing show prep up on the soundstage, which was built to look like a cozy 1950s living room with powder-blue plywood walls and a fake fireplace. A newcomer had joined them. The hot studio lights glistened against his bushy mustache as he ran down a checklist on a clipboard. Charlie checked her memory, matching his face against their briefing packet.

"Lincoln's publicist," she said. "Can't remember his name, but he set up the whole tour."

"Is he going to pay your dry-cleaning bill?"

Charlie cracked a smile. "I don't think *that* part was on the agenda. Not that Lincoln's complaining. The more anger he stirs up, the more books he sells."

Today wasn't going to help his agenda, not against an interviewer who was already working his shock-provocateur angle and doing it better than he was. As the cameras started rolling, Lincoln started out off balance and just kept teetering, shaken by Ria's utterly blithe awfulness.

"And the level of homelessness and drug addiction in this country," he was saying, "fostered by socialist policies—"

"Exactly," Ria said, wide eyed and innocent as she talked over him. "I see these homeless people, and I think, Why isn't anyone doing something about this?"

"We need stronger leaders, leaders who aren't afraid to take a bold stand—"

"I mean, why do I have to see those people on my drive to work every day? Can't we put them somewhere? If we rounded up all the homeless people and put them in a work camp, they'd have jobs and a place to stay. And the city would look so much cleaner, which is really what matters here."

Lincoln blinked at her.

"And another thing," she said, looking to the camera. "I think these backward social policies are hurting the wrong kind of people."

Dom clamped a hand over her mouth, smothering a laugh. She leaned against Charlie's arm.

"Interview over," she whispered. "He can't compete with this level of crazy. Only way he can salvage this mess is if he gets up and walks out."

Five more minutes crept past, with Lincoln squirming under the hot lights. His face glistened with sweat.

"And that's why we need to bring public shaming for degenerates back," Ria said, her tone completely casual. "The stocks, whippings, the whole nine yards. It worked for our forefathers, and it will work again. Once we start branding loose women and adulterers, as a warning to others—"

"So, my book—" Lincoln said for the fifth time, squeezing the copy on his lap.

"Right! Dear viewers, I *loved* this book. It was insightful, patriotic, a masterpiece. Let me tell you my favorite part—"

A buzzer sounded. One of the camera operators raised his arm and gave a thumbs-up.

"And . . . that's commercial," he called out.

Lincoln launched from his easy chair. His perfect smile vanished behind a thundercloud, like someone had flicked a switch in his brain.

"I would like," he said, "to go home now. Please."

The publicist scurried to catch up with them. Lincoln read him the riot act as Charlie led the way down the back corridor toward the carport.

"That woman is a lunatic," he hissed. "What were you thinking?"

"Lincoln, baby, it's fine. You did great."

"I know I did great. I'm always great. I *am* great. That's not the point."

One of the stage doors blasted open. A young man ran in, arm drawn back, shouting, *"Eat it, fascist!"* before letting his weapon fly.

The water balloon hit Charlie in the chest and exploded. It wasn't water. Yellow mustard, pungent and bright, splashed her face and soaked her suit. Long rivulets of the stuff dribbled down, spattering her shoes.

"You've been *mustarded*," the kid shouted as a couple of studio guards wrestled him to the ground.

"Tell me we got that on video," the publicist said, the hallway swarming with employees and more guards. "Somebody tell me we got that."

Dom took Lincoln's shoulder and hustled him through the mob. Charlie moved with them, eyes on the new arrivals, staying focused. It was that or start screaming, and she already looked ridiculous. Lincoln glanced at her, started to say something, then caught the simmering fury in her eyes.

This time, for once, he kept his mouth shut.

The publicist caught up with them in the carport, waving a clipboard. He shoved it in front of Charlie.

"Can you sign this?"

She tilted her head. "What is it?"

"A release. Security camera in the hall caught the entire thing."

"And I want to sign this why?"

"To tell your side of the story! Look, book sales jumped after the milkshake thing—"

"My job is to protect Mr. Gable," Charlie said, "not sell his book. That's your job."

"I'll pay you two hundred bucks," the publicist said. "Cash."

"No."

"Five hundred," he said, "but that's my top offer."

Dom had loaded Lincoln in the back of the SUV. Charlie pointed to the passenger seat.

"I have work to do," she said.

Charlie drummed her short-cropped fingernails on the armrest. She was dripping yellow mustard everywhere. She was long past the point of caring.

Behind the wheel, Dom wrinkled her nose. "They could have at least sprung for the expensive kind."

"*You've been Grey Pouponed* doesn't have the same ring to it," Charlie replied.

Lincoln sat in back, very quiet, keeping his head down.

"Drop you off at the dry cleaner's?" Dom asked.

"Actually," Charlie said, "drop me off at the corner, here. I want to go for a walk."

"You're drenched in mustard."

"I really need to be alone with my thoughts right now."

Her thoughts and a growing suspicion, one she couldn't voice in front of the client.

Charlie doubled back, winding down a back alley, jogging between vans in the outside parking lot. Her shoes made squishing sounds. She mapped the place in her mind, trying to figure out how the lone protester had gotten inside.

Past two layers of uniformed security guards, she thought, studying the doors. Guards who had told her they were calling the cops to pick the kid up. Fifteen minutes passed, and no sign of a squad car anywhere.

The timing of the attack had been a little too perfect. Charlie ducked low behind the snub-nosed hood of a television van as the back doors rattled open. And there was Mustard Boy, free and clear, with Lincoln's publicist right beside him.

The publicist handed him a wad of cash and sent him on his way.

Charlie had time to think in the shower, massaging her scalp and watching streamers of yellow mustard spiral down the drain. She got out, toweled off, pulled on a terry cloth robe, and called Dom.

"You have got to be fucking kidding me," Dom said.

"He set the whole thing up."

"All of it?"

"The glitter bomb might have been a real protester," Charlie said, "but after that went viral? Yeah, the publicist is behind it. That guy with the milkshake was looking to hit *me*, not Lincoln. Same with today."

"And there's Lincoln, calling you out by name on the air, setting you up so he can get more attention for his book tour. He's in on it. Has to be. And this is why he was so desperate to keep you on the security detail." Dom took a deep, steadying breath. "Okay. Let's talk about payback."

"I figured we'd call Jake and Sofia and fill them in."

"No, they'll just cancel the contract. I want to talk about *payback*."

"Hold that thought," Charlie said. "Dealing with Nina comes first, everything else a very distant second. I need to stay focused."

"I'm Italian," Dom said. "When it comes to revenge, I can multitask."

While Charlie hunted for something to wear, her phone buzzed. Email from Riley, with a PDF file attached. Don't ask how I got these, the message read.

She was going to ask anyway. With a tap of her fingertip, she found herself staring at Lieutenant Gimondi's financial records. Twelve months of bank statements, line by itemized line. Searching through the file felt like sifting for grains of gold in a muddy stream, but at least her mind had something to do.

It didn't take long to find a connection to two of his coconspirators. Every month, right on the fifteenth, both Kellogg and Vargas were sending *him* money. Sixty dollars each.

What for? she wondered. She felt like she'd been building a house of cards with the clues, and every new piece of information knocked the whole shaky tower to the ground, forcing her to start all over again. Every time she thought they'd uncovered the truth, there was something bigger just behind it, waiting to twist their assumptions into knots.

Assumptions. That was the problem. Charlie knew, down in her gut, that they already had all the facts they needed. There was just something they were overlooking, some fatal assumption blinding them to the truth.

She thought about Lincoln Gable. That had been a fatal assumption, too; they'd believed they were protecting him, when he and his publicist had been running a scam all along. With that one bit of truth, everything snapped into place and suddenly made sense.

She thought about Nina, the cocaine, the massacre on Saratoga Street. The fourth man in the crew of corrupt cops, slipping out from under the police dragnet while his three buddies were facing life in prison.

And there it was. The truth. Right in front of her, all along.

Charlie pulled a windbreaker over her shoulder holster, grabbed her keys, and ran for the door.

Charlie cruised the neighborhood until she found Mila Huerta, out on a scraggly playground with some of her friends. They were lounging by a swing set—only one swing, the other dangling from a broken chain—and killing time. Charlie pulled up to the curb. She left the engine running; this wouldn't take long, and if she was right, she needed to move fast.

"Mila," she called out. "I'm sorry to bother you; I just need your help with one last thing. One last question."

Mila's friends gave her curious looks. The teenager split from the pack, meeting Charlie halfway across the lot. Charlie pitched her voice low and took out her phone.

"You said you saw the men, that night. That they took their masks off."

Mila nodded, shooting a glance over her shoulder.

"Not real well, but yeah. Like I said, when I saw the lieutenant on the TV, I recognized him."

Charlie brought up a photograph.

"Was he there?"

Mila took a stumbling half step back as the blood drained from her face.

"He's the one," she said. "The one who said . . . 'Kill him, and kill the other little bitch.' That's him."

Mustard Boy had made a mistake. Two mistakes. The first had been pelting Charlie with a water balloon filled with mustard. The second had been opening his door for a stranger.

Now he was tied to his kitchen chair, wrists bound behind his back, his body drenched in fear sweat. Dom loomed over him.

"Honestly," she said, "very little in the world pisses me off more than somebody messing with my friends. Which you did. So here we are."

"I'll—I'll give the money back! I'll apologize, I swear—"

"So we're going to have a little talk about ethics. Just you, me . . ."

She whipped her arm down. The heavy plastic bag in her hand slammed down against the kitchen table with a bullwhip crack, loud enough to rattle his cabinets.

"And this sack of valencia oranges."

Her phone buzzed against her hip. She plopped the sack down on the table so he'd have something to think about.

"Hold that thought." She put the phone to her ear. "Yeah?"

"Dom," Charlie gasped, breathless. "Are you at the hospital?"

"No, I'm, uh . . . handling a personal project."

She pointed two fingers at her eyes. Then at the kid. Then at the sack of oranges. Mustard Boy started to cry. *Wimp,* she thought.

"Beckett's keeping watch," she added. "Why, what's up?"

"It was a con from the start, he fooled everybody—"

"Slow down," Dom said. "What's going on?"

"Hayden Cobb. He was there, Dom. Hayden Cobb *is* the fourth man."

THIRTY-SIX

"You're certain," Poole said.

Charlie had the phone on speaker and sitting out on her passenger seat while she fought her way through afternoon traffic. A truck swung out in front of her, and she stomped her foot on the brake.

"There's an eyewitness who can place him at the massacre. We *almost* had the whole story. We knew Cobb had gotten himself caught on purpose. The motive was wrong, though. He didn't do it because he got cold feet or because he was afraid. And he wasn't upset about being cut out of the score. His whole story about being their inside tipster who only fingered the jobs for Gimondi's crew and never got his own hands dirty? That was a lie from the beginning. They must have set him up with a fake uniform and a badge. He was right alongside them for each and every heist, an equal partner."

"And we fell for it," Poole murmured. "Damn."

"He set his partners up. And the beauty of the scheme is they can't say a word. Because the only way they can expose Cobb is by confessing to their own involvement, which guarantees a longer prison sentence."

Charlie didn't mention the rest of his motive. There was a million dollars of stolen cocaine in play, hidden somewhere in the city. Cobb's three partners would rot in jail, and he'd get WITSEC, a whole new life somewhere far away, and the entire haul of loot. With a new name and a new identity, he could sit on the coke for years, decades if he had to, safe and comfortable at the end of an ice-cold trail. His plan was bulletproof.

It just wasn't Nina proof. And right now, Charlie needed to keep Poole and the authorities as far from the truth as possible. Handing over Cobb was one thing; if the cops found the cocaine, they'd confiscate it on the spot. And that meant her father was as good as dead.

"I'm bringing detectives to take Cobb into custody," Poole said. "Sit on him until we get there."

Cobb was walking the halls. Doctor's orders. He was off the fluid drip—and the morphine, much to his chagrin—but it felt good to be up and moving. They'd given him a crutch, but he really didn't need it.

Every step ached like someone was pressing a lit cigarette against his thigh. That would pass. This would all pass. All he had to do was stay cool for one more day, testify, and vanish into thin air. Unexpected bullet wound aside, everything was flowing smooth as glass.

They'd assigned him a minder. Guy named Williams: young, good hair, more interested in making time with the pretty young thing behind the nurse-station desk than keeping an eye on him. Cobb humped it up and down the hallway, back and forth, getting back into shape. He was at the far end when he heard voices drifting down the corridor, punctuated by brisk slaps of shoe leather.

"Beckett says to spread out, find Cobb, and bring him back to his room, pronto. Stay off the radio. We don't want him to know anything's up. The DA should be here with a police escort in twenty."

Cobb's blood turned to winter ice. His stomach plunged like the first hard drop of a roller coaster. He pressed himself to the wall, held his breath, and waited for the two men to pass him by.

He was blown. He couldn't imagine how. He'd accounted for everything, every last detail . . . couldn't think about that now. Had to move.

He clamped down on his panic. *THINK, damn it,* he commanded himself. *Find a way out. Worry about what went wrong later. Right now, find a way out.*

He speed walked to the nurse's station, wincing with every step. "'Scuse me, there a washroom close by?"

"Right down there," the nurse said with a smile, pointing. "Take a left, first door."

Williams pushed himself away from the desk. "I'll come with you."

Damn, damn, damn. Cobb fixed a frozen smile on his face and led the way.

It was a small bathroom, brightly lit and empty, the chemical tang of bleach thick in the air. Williams stepped around him.

"Just have to check these," he said. "Mr. Beckett doesn't think anybody's going to make a move on you, not here, but safety first."

Williams pushed open the first stall door. Cobb suddenly experienced a flash of desperate insight, a peal of wisdom from the heavens, like he was some kind of thug Buddha.

He positioned himself and waited for Williams to check the second empty stall. Then he grabbed his crutch with both hands and raised it high. It whistled down and slammed into the back of the man's head with a bone-jarring crack. Williams slumped to the pale floor, motionless. Blood drizzled from the tear in his scalp and ran along the grout between the tiles, painting a grid of scarlet on white.

Cobb tossed the crutch aside. It landed with a clatter. He rolled Williams over, yanked his jacket open, and grabbed his pistol. *Loaded. Good.* Then he tugged the bodyguard's tie loose and started to unbutton his shirt.

There was a cemetery wind blowing through Felton's office. He could hear the bells and smell the sickly dirt of his own grave.

The bells sounded like a phone call. The one that had sent Poole, visible through the glass across the hall, rocketing to her feet. She'd snapped her fingers at a couple of junior aides, drawing them into her wake as she'd charged out of the office on some kind of emergency. Without him. Without a single word, just a stray glance in passing.

He'd seen that look in her eyes before. Usually when she was staring down a criminal on the witness stand.

She suspected him. That didn't mean she knew anything, didn't mean there was a shred of proof, but Poole was a bloodhound.

This is fine, he told himself. *Everything is fine.*

Once Angel was done taking care of Charlie McCabe and anybody she might have talked to, Felton would have one more name to add to the hit list. It was time for a vacancy in the district attorney's office.

His phone chimed. Felton didn't recognize the number. He answered it anyway.

"Got an eye on the hospital," Angel told him. "No sign of McCabe, but Cobb just left. On his own, no escort, wearing a suit about two sizes too big. You want me to roll up on him, take him out?"

Felton tried to hear his own thoughts over the alarm bells in his head. Cobb had slipped out from under his minders somehow, and it had to be connected to Poole's sudden exit.

"No," Felton said. "Follow him. Stay out of sight. His bodyguards are going to be looking for him. You stay on him long enough, you'll find McCabe."

"And then?"

Only one option, to stay safe, to get my life back under control, Felton thought. *Need a clean slate.*

"Kill them all," he said. "Cobb, McCabe, anyone with her."

Angel snickered. "You know I charge by the bullet, right?"

"Just . . . just do it. Kill them all."

◆ ◆ ◆

They'd found Williams in the bathroom. Five minutes later he was on a crash cart, being raced to the ER.

"Docs say he's got a concussion and a skull fracture," Beckett said. "Lost a lot of blood. And his clothes. And his gun."

Dom threw a frustrated punch at the air. She'd arrived five minutes ago, with Charlie close on her heels.

"*Damn* it. And Poole's going to be here any minute. We look like total assholes."

"It's worse than that," Charlie said. "You know where he's going."

"The retirement fund," Beckett said. "He knows where it's hidden. And if he knows his story just fell apart, he's only got one way to stay out of prison alongside his three best friends."

"Run," Charlie said.

"If he grabs the coke and disappears . . ." Dom shook her head. "No. We're not letting that happen. We've got to beat him to it. Charlie, you have those financials?"

She took out her phone and showed her partners Riley's email with the attached scan of Gimondi's bank statements. They stood at her shoulders as she scrolled through the file.

"Gimondi didn't really trust his partners—" Charlie said.

Dom frowned at the screen. "He should have trusted them *less*."

"Meaning he would have kept the coke someplace under his control, where he could keep an eye on it while they waited for the heat to die down. We know that Cobb didn't relocate it after the bust, because we found signs that Nina searched his house and came up empty."

"No need to take a risk," Beckett reasoned. "If it's stashed somewhere safe and Gimondi is locked up, it's as good as his."

"I keep coming back to this." Charlie tapped the screen. "Every month on the fifteenth, Kellogg and Vargas were each sending him sixty bucks. Some kind of buy-in, like they were splitting a big purchase."

"Or a rental," Dom said. "See any listings for a storage facility? Maybe they were paying for a lockup and hiding the coke there."

"Too much money for that," Beckett said. "You can rent a climate-controlled ten-by-ten for less than a hundred a month."

Charlie hunted for big numbers. Annual payments. Only one stood out, and she recognized the name. Her fingernail rapped against the screen.

"This is a marina," she said.

"Two things cops planning to retire just love investing in," Dom said.

Beckett met her gaze. "Bars and boats."

"We'll take my car," Dom said. "I've got some rainy-day goodies in the trunk. Just in case."

Thirty-Seven

Angel wore a ball cap slung low over his eyes and a pair of dark glasses. A long rucksack dangled off one shoulder as he leaned back in the shadow of an awning and chewed on a toothpick. The Liberty Marina was in Bunker Hill, a long stretch of river walk lined with piers and restaurants. Masts bobbed in the tranquil water, the sun starting to set, gulls squawking and flying lazy circles above a river painted in streaks of gold.

Cobb was dead ahead, hobbling, hunting for something. He was on the far side of a pack of tourists and sailors; the marina was busy, sailboats coming in for a landing or drifting out into the gathering dark, locals making conversation outside a seafood restaurant. Every time the front door opened, Angel caught a gust of chowder and breaded clams. His stomach grumbled.

New arrivals, on the far side of the marina. Angel spat his toothpick out and reached for his phone.

"Felton. You were right. McCabe just showed, got a couple of her friends with her. Little complication, though."

The ADA sounded like he was on the verge of a panic attack. "What is it?"

Angel's eyes narrowed behind his glasses, spotting the man walking up to confront them.

"There's a cop here. I know the guy. Glass, I think his name is. Anyway, looks like he and McCabe are having a close conversation."

"Add him to the list," Felton said.

"I charge extra for doing a cop. That's a lot of heat."

"Add him to the list."

"Fine by me," Angel said. He pushed himself away from the wooden slats, stretching. "But not here. Too many people around. Sit tight—I'll give you a call."

◆ ◆ ◆

"How did you figure it out?" Charlie said.

Riley arched an eyebrow at her, almost looking offended.

"C'mon, I had access to the exact same financial records you did." He waved a hand behind him, at the endless tangle of boats and weathered dock. "I *am* a detective."

She peered past him. "Cobb could already be here."

"Great. I can arrest him, recover the drugs: it's a one-stop shop."

"You can't," Charlie said.

He tilted his head, like he hadn't heard her quite right.

"It's literally my job," he said.

"You can take Cobb," Dom told him. "Not the coke. That's ours."

"Okay." Riley held up a finger. "I *know* you didn't just say what I think you said."

Charlie moved close. Her fingertips brushed the sleeve of his jacket as she looked him in the eye.

"Nina, the cartel's hired gun—she has my dad."

He didn't say a word. Something shifted behind his gaze, a new understanding setting in.

"We're supposed to meet her at a truck stop off I-93, about an hour outside of town. We give her the drugs, she gives my dad back. We don't, then . . ." She trailed off and let him fill in the blank space.

"We can set up a sting," Riley told her, suddenly inflating with fresh hope. "I mean, you know where she's going to be; we can surround the place, bring in SWAT—"

Beckett took a step forward and jabbed a pin in his enthusiasm.

"You'll never see her," he said. "She so much as smells a cop, you'll find nothing but one dead body on the scene, still warm. And it'll be your fault. That's a promise."

Riley's shoulders slumped. He took a step back. Then a step forward, playing tug-of-war with himself.

"Please," Charlie said.

"*Damn* it." Riley ran his fingers through his ginger hair, took a deep breath, and nodded. "Okay."

"Okay?"

"Okay," he said, waving at the marina. "Let's move, already—we're running out of daylight here. As a cop, my number one job is saving lives. So . . . let's go save a life."

Riley flashed his badge at the clerk in the marina's front office. The clerk told him to go and get a warrant.

Beckett flashed a trio of crisp twenty-dollar bills, and the clerk welcomed them back behind the counter with a courtly bow.

"All our rental info is on the system," he said, gesturing to an outdated Mac with a bulky monitor. "I'm going to go outside and take my legally mandated fifteen-minute break."

"Good man," Beckett told him.

Dom paged through screen after flickering screen. The database was old enough to vote, with an interface that wanted to fight her.

"Here we go," she said. She rattled off a few keystrokes. "Names. But . . . nothing for Gimondi. We know he was making deposits on a slip here, but it wasn't his name."

"Wait a second," Charlie said, pulling up Gimondi's bank statements on her phone. "We know what days he made the payments on. Can you cross-reference and see who made a deposit on . . . let's see. The twenty-eighth of April?"

That narrowed it down.

"Thirty records," Dom said, pulling up the list. "Anything stand out?"

Charlie pointed to the screen, midway down.

"GVK Enterprises."

"Gimondi, Vargas, Kellogg," Dom said. "Slip thirty-eight. Boat's registered as the *Inland Wind*."

Charlie led the charge for the door.

"That's where he stashed it," she said. "And that's where Cobb's headed."

She spotted him first. The setting sun turned Cobb into a limping silhouette, hip jerking as he made his way along the pier, pushing through the crowd. Then she saw his final destination: *Inland Wind*, a forty-foot cabin cruiser bobbing gently on the water.

"Hang back," Beckett warned, his voice soft. "The man's carrying a stolen gun, and he's got nothing to lose."

Riley eased his windbreaker back, standing like a gunslinger as he sized up the battleground. Charlie knew what he was seeing: too many lanes of fire, too many civilians in the way. A massacre waiting to happen.

"You go for the boat," Riley said. "I'm going to circle around and take him down, nice and easy. I should be able to get the jump on him if he doesn't see me coming. Charlie, do something for me?"

"Name it," she said.

"As soon as you see me rolling up on Cobb, get out in front of him. I just need a distraction, something to throw him off balance. Two seconds should do it."

Charlie nodded. Beckett broke left, going wide, Dom alongside him. Riley went the other way. Long blocks of concrete planters decorated the edge of the wooden boardwalk, off to their right. He circled around, angling for Cobb's gun hand. Charlie reached under her jacket. Her fingers curled around the textured grip of her Beretta. She watched Riley close the gap from behind, fifteen feet and counting. Cobb had tunnel vision, eyes only for the boat.

Nice and easy, she thought.

Two seconds later, the shooting started.

Thanks to Poole, Riley wasn't the only badge on Cobb's trail. Once he'd gone missing from the hospital, an APB had gone out. Every patrol officer in Boston was hunting for the fugitive, and they'd been warned that he was armed, dangerous, and connected to the Saratoga Street massacre.

So when a beat cop spotted the limping man on the move, practically walking right in front of him, his training kicked in. His hand slapped leather, and he shouted for Cobb to freeze and show his empty hands.

Cobb whirled, stolen gun flashing in the sunset, and opened fire. The cop jerked backward as one slug went wide and the other punched through the stiff polyester of his uniform shirt. The crowds erupted in a stampede, screaming, thundering in all directions along the boardwalk. Riley grabbed the fallen officer's shoulders and hauled him back, dragging him behind the concrete planters.

"Hey. Hey, stay with me. You wearing a vest?"

The cop shook his head, grimacing. A bubble of blood erupted between his lips. Riley cursed under his breath and ripped the radio from his belt. He hunched low, another bullet cracking through the air just over his head.

"We're at Liberty Marina. Have an active shooter and an officer down. I repeat, *officer down.*"

Cobb raced for cover. Charlie raced for the boat.

"Dom," she shouted over her shoulder, "go get the car! Bring it as close as you can!"

Beckett followed her lead. They stormed the pier, leaping onto the back deck of the cabin cruiser. A door barred their way down below; the cheap laminate splintered under Beckett's kick, and the second blow sent fractured particleboard flying across paper-thin carpet.

The cabin smelled musty. Dust coated the bare countertops like a veil. Charlie ripped open cabinets, hunting for the loot.

"Little Duck," Beckett said.

She looked past him, through the open doorway to a tiny bedroom. Two fat black duffel bags sat on the bare mattress, side by side.

Angel didn't stampede with the rest of the crowd. He watched, eyes hard, and rubbed the sweaty stubble on his jaw. His gaze trailed from the two cops, pinned down behind the planters, to Cobb, who had snatched a little cover behind a tall steel garbage can. Cobb was popping out, slinging bullets downwind, not managing to hit much of anything.

Then there were McCabe and her big pal, emerging from the same boat Cobb had been angling for. Each one lugging a duffel, and from the looks of them, they were packed with bricks.

He could have done the math on a cocktail napkin. Cobb needed to disappear pronto. He wouldn't show his face at the marina unless this was where he kept everything he needed for a clean getaway.

Angel didn't know what was in the duffel bags. But he knew he wanted it.

"Hell with it," he said, unzipping his rucksack. "Didn't have anything better to do today."

He strode across the marina as he reached into the rucksack. An ArmaLite tactical carbine, long, sleek, and black as midnight, swung up into his ready grip. Up ahead, Riley poked his head out of cover, trying to get an angle on Cobb. Angel squeezed the trigger. A three-round burst from his rifle peppered the air, carving into the planters, kicking up a storm of stone chips and dust. Angel grabbed Cobb's shoulder and hauled him to his feet.

"It's your lucky day," Angel told him.

He fired from the hip, another burst slicing the air, forcing the cop onto his belly. He dragged Cobb away from the fight. Angel pulled him around the corner of the seafood place, patrons huddled inside, terrified faces peering from the windows, and shoved him up against the wood-slat wall.

"Now's the part where I either save your life or leave you to die," Angel said. "Because Boston PD's coming in hot, and they *will* shoot you. What's in those duffels?"

Cobb was pale, shaking, frozen with Angel's forearm pressed to his neck.

"A million dollars in stolen coke."

Angel leaned in with his arm. "Right now is a real bad time to mess with me."

"I'm serious," Cobb croaked. "It was the score from the Saratoga heist. A million dollars' worth. Swear to God, I'm telling the truth."

Angel looked to the parking lot. It was a nightmare tangle, everyone trying to flee at once, the incoming police sirens faintly rising over a symphony of car horns. A trunk slammed. His gaze darted to the sound. McCabe and her friends were piling into a dusty white Continental.

"Fifty-fifty split," Angel said. "This is nonnegotiable; decide right now. Live or die."

Cobb's head bobbed, frantic. "Fifty-fifty."

Angel made his rifle disappear back into the rucksack and zipped it tight.

"C'mon, partner. Gonna take 'em a few minutes to get out of the lot. My Jeep's parked right down the block."

"Where are we going?" Cobb said, breaking into a run at his side. The sleeves of his stolen jacket, too big for him, flapped in the hot summer wind.

"Wherever they're going. Hopefully someplace nice and quiet. I've got two fresh mags in my sack, and I was already getting paid to take McCabe and her buddies out."

Take you out too, Angel thought with a sidelong glance at Cobb. *But we'll sort that out later. After you help me.*

THIRTY-EIGHT

Halfway home, Charlie thought, riding in the back of the Continental.

She and her partners shared a pensive silence until the last siren faded into the distance, the last squad car lights vanishing around a bend in the road. They'd gotten away with the loot.

Now they just had to deliver it.

"Where are we supposed to go when we get there, anyway?" Dom said. "She gave us the coordinates for a truck stop. That's . . . not real specific."

"Won't be the meeting place anyway," Beckett said.

They rolled to a stop at a red light. Dom turned and gave him a look that could cut glass.

"Number one, why are you just mentioning this now? Number two, this place is an hour away, so if it's not the right spot, why are we going there?"

"Standard Nina operating procedure," Beckett said. "Whenever she does a handoff, she sends the other party to a set location. Once they arrive, she checks them out from a distance, and if things seem on the up-and-up, she redirects them to the real staging ground."

"So if they bring cops with them, she'll know?" Charlie said.

"Or if they're breaking any rules. Like if she says to come unarmed and they show up strapped, she'll know they're not playing right. In which case she packs up and leaves them behind like a stood-up prom date."

"She didn't tell us to come unarmed," Dom said.

"Think we all know that'd just be a waste of time."

The light strobed green. She stepped on the gas.

"Driving around Boston with enough cocaine in the trunk to send us all to prison for life," she muttered. "Goddamn right we're not showing up without guns."

"What's the plan?" Charlie said.

"There is no plan," Beckett told her. "We arrive, park ourselves someplace conspicuous, we get comfortable, and we wait. She'll send us a message. Maybe a phone call, maybe a bike courier. Maybe it'll be nestled in a fortune cookie. Then we go where she says to go and do what she says to do when we get there."

Charlie shifted in her seat. She stared out at the city as it rolled on by. She caught the ghost of her own frown in the glass.

"She's in control."

"The entire time. That's the point of doing it like this. Nina holds all the cards, and we either play along or we don't."

She had another question. She held it trapped, pinned behind the tight line of her lips, because she didn't know if she really wanted an answer. Eventually, like she knew it would, it wriggled loose.

"Is she really going to let my dad go?"

Beckett had to think about that. She didn't like how long it took him.

"Under normal circumstances," Beckett said, "yes."

"Normal circumstances," Charlie echoed.

"If this was one of her average jobs, trading a ransom for a hostage? Always. Nina doesn't damage the merchandise. She's not fair, but she's professional, and she prides herself on being a professional."

"But," Charlie said.

"But her average jobs don't involve her own former student and the woman he's mentoring in a career that just happens to be the mirror image of her own. That makes the situation . . ."

"Unpredictable," Dom said.

Beckett gave her a nod.

Charlie looked into the side mirror. She could see the edge of Beckett's face, stoic, staring into the middle distance. She caught something in his eye, the momentary twitch of one stony cheek.

"You weren't just her student, were you?"

He didn't answer.

Charlie's anger was a rough-winged bird beating its wings inside her rib cage. It wanted out. It wanted to lash out at someone, anyone, and she bit her tongue before she vented it on Beckett.

She knew it wasn't his fault. He hadn't brought Nina here, hadn't invited her psychotic obsession. And whatever he'd done in his youth, whoever he'd been when he'd stood at Nina's side instead of standing with her and Dom, Charlie knew he wasn't that man anymore. His past sins were exactly that. Past.

But old, buried sins had a way of coming back around.

"What does she want from you?" Charlie asked.

"If she wants me to know, she'll tell me. And she'll do whatever she's going to do."

Beckett turned, meeting her gaze in the mirror.

"Go with the flow, improvise, and adapt," he said. "Be ready for anything. Those are the rules of engagement for tonight."

He turned back to the windshield and to the winding road ahead.

"Those are the *only* rules tonight."

The city faded away. One moment they were in a canyon of stone and steel; then there was nothing but the highway and the hills and the rolling green. An endless tangle of trees encroached on the left side of the road, and as the sun went down, the forest's boughs chewed at the golden sunlight, making it flicker like a dying film projector.

Then the sun went away, and the headlights clicked on, and there was nothing but the highway.

They crested a hill, and lights came up from below, the bend of a valley powered by diesel and caffeine. The towering, star-spangled plastic sign, glowing in the dark, read **Big America**. The lot was the biggest part, the heart of the truck stop, where semis camped along the slanted yellow lines and slumbered in the dark. Two sides of the lot were lined with buildings; the other two were open to the forest and the hills. Dom flicked her turn signal, pulled onto the off-ramp, and stared at the sea of shadows.

"Perfect sight lines," Dom murmured. "She could be anywhere out there."

"That's why she picked the spot," Beckett said.

Charlie was hunting for an angle, a scheme, some way to twist the odds and get the upper hand. She wasn't seeing one. For now, at least, they had to play it straight. And trust in the benevolence of a sociopath.

The truck stop was a village. Dom rolled slowly through the lot, cruising on high alert, easing past trucks and RV campers and the stray, odd airport limousine. The east side of the compound was for services; Charlie spotted a Verizon kiosk, closed for the night, next to a general store that offered products and goods for life on the road. Phone chargers and beef jerky and magazines. Then there was Alice's Big 24, still open for business. Soft lights shone behind a long row of plate glass windows looking in on a rustic, lonely restaurant. Alice's had empty tables, gingham tablecloths, and a half-sold pie under a plastic dome next to the cash register.

On the north face of the lot, a cavernous garage stood dark and empty behind the gas pumps. The nozzles of power-wash hoses dangled over bays sized for tractor-trailer rigs, and big orange brushes stood ready to scrub the road dust away. Then there was the motel. Charlie zeroed in on it.

"Feel you looking," Beckett said.

Hard not to. The motel was under heavy renovation. Rough fencing strung along leaning, haphazard posts encircled half of the three-story building, and a chunk of one side was open to the elements, concrete hammered down and the interiors stripped bare. The balconies along the second floor were missing railings, and all the windows were gone, replaced by drapes of plastic sheeting or just left as open, dark portholes into shadow. A dirty yellow excavator sat parked next to the motel, the mouth of its scoop bucket curled and still.

"Feels like a trap," Charlie said.

"The motel?" Dom asked.

Charlie sat back and drummed her fingers on her knee.

"All of it."

Dom made one more full circle around the lot, like a bird swooping in for a landing, and parked at the farthest edge. The headlights went dark. The engine died.

"I like absolutely nothing about this," Dom said. "Where are you two going to make camp?"

"Alice's Big 24 looks fine to me," Beckett said. "Might try some of that pie."

Dom popped the trunk, and they got out, circling around back, stretching after the drive. Charlie gave Dom a curious look.

"'You two'?" she said. "You're not coming with?"

Dom hoisted one of the black duffel bags from the trunk and passed it to Charlie. It yanked down on her shoulder, stuffed to bursting.

"Playing target is your job." She passed the second duffel to Beckett. He lifted it like it was weightless. "Playing guardian angel is mine."

Dom leaned deep into the trunk. She pulled out a long, hard plastic case and a folded oilcloth tarp before slamming the lid shut. She gestured up to the forested hills, the deep olive darkness.

"I'll be on overwatch," she said.

"You do realize," Beckett told her, "that Nina's expecting that. She knows me; she's studied Charlie. Guarantee she's studied up on you too."

"Yeah, but you're the one she wants to play with. How is she with a rifle?"

"Capable," Beckett said.

"If I spot her before you do," Dom said, "I'll make sure to say hi."

Angel Strickland had learned half of his lethal trade in the service, the other half on the streets. He'd never had much patience for what he considered "spy-versus-spy bullshit"; he'd learned from experience that you could walk right up to a man in a crowded bar and blow his brains all over his dinner date, and a hundred witnesses would give the cops a hundred different descriptions. Disguises had their purpose, but the quick and dirty kind—grabbing a room service cart and a waiter's jacket, or pulling on a valet's red vest to steal a set of car keys—worked just as well as any *Mission: Impossible* antics.

So when it came to tailing a target, he was at a loss. He knew the ideal tail used three or more vehicles, coordinated by radio, working in unison. He was one man driving a battered Jeep Cherokee on the open road. His new partner wasn't helping.

"Hang back," Cobb said. "They're going to spot you."

"I know what I'm doing," Angel said for the third time in a row.

His task was easier once the sun went down, even easier once they got onto the highway. Nobody thought twice about sharing the highway with the same handful of cars for an hour; they were all going the same way. When the Continental took the off-ramp, Angel slowed things down. Easy to tell they were headed for the truck stop, the only electric lights for a mile in any direction. He hung back, gave them a little lead, taking his time for caution's sake.

"Careful now," Cobb told him. "Don't get too close."

Angel was thinking about killing him here and now. He stayed his hand. He was feeling good about his odds tonight, but one against three was still a risk. He could use Cobb as a stalking horse, draw his targets' attention while he took them out from a distance. Safer that way.

Also, scrubbing blood out of car upholstery was a stone bitch.

He cruised through the lot, slow and easy. He spotted McCabe and her partner, the big guy. They were on foot, each one lugging one of the duffels, headed for the lights of an all-night diner. Angel frowned.

"Where's the third one?" he muttered.

Cobb turned in his seat, looking out all the windows, sticking out like a sore thumb.

"I don't see her," Cobb said. "What are they doing here, anyway?"

Meeting someone. Angel could tell that much. Nobody walked around with a million in coke if they weren't doing a deal.

"My guess is they found a buyer."

"Impossible," Cobb said.

Angel asked a question with his eyes.

"There's no way they knew the coke *existed* before today," Cobb said. "Nobody has the juice to set up a sale this big this fast. Nobody."

"You got a better explanation?"

Cobb slumped in his seat.

"No." His bottom lip jutted out in a sullen pout.

Angel went back to ignoring him. There was the parked Continental, no sign of the other woman. He didn't like that. Then he studied the big open belly of the power wash and the battered facade of the motel. Lots of angles. Good angles. He could work with that.

A fat raindrop spattered against the windshield. Then another, drizzling down from the roiling, darkened sky. Storm clouds were gathering fast, billowing through the starless night like smoke.

The rain was coming down now, cold and steady, as Dom scrambled uphill in the dark. One shoe slid in a furrow of fresh mud, the other catching on a rock. She cradled her rifle case with one hand and pushed against a slick, grassy outcropping with the other, forcing herself along a slope gone close to vertical.

Then the grass evened out, turning to brambles and bare roots. Thick, stout trees became pillars of onyx in the dark, drawing hard black lines between patches of moonlight. Dom kept her ears perked. Eyes open. Hunting now, her breath slow and steady.

I don't care how good you are, she thought. *You've only got one pair of eyes. Even if you saw us pull into the lot, you can watch me, or you can watch Beckett and Charlie. Pick one.*

Either she'd draw Nina's fire, or she'd be the one doing the firing. If it kept her friends safe, she was good either way. All the same, she wasn't looking to get shot at tonight. She kept low, moving in a loping crouch, and froze behind a fat tree trunk to get the lay of the land. Cold rain matted her hair and ran an icy finger down the collar of her shirt. It pattered off the foliage, cloaking her footsteps under a steady wet percussion.

The overlook gave her a perfect view of the truck stop down below, even with the rain in her eyes. She set her case down and flicked the plastic hasps. Her Remington 700 nestled inside, gray as a storm, with all the fixings. She unfolded the support struts of a bipod and slid it along the barrel.

Then she lay down flat in the grass and mud, dragged the oilcloth tarp over herself until only the tip of her rifle's barrel was peeking from cover, and adjusted her long-range scope.

"Show yourself," she murmured. "I've got all night, and I'm not going anywhere."

THIRTY-NINE

"Still open?" Charlie asked the waitress as she stepped into the diner. The woman's deep-lined face offered a weary smile.

"We're awake as long as you are, honey. Twenty-four hours a day, twenty-five on weekends. Sit anywhere you like. I'll be right over."

They had their choice of seats. It was late enough for all the road warriors to retreat to their RV bunks and sleeper cabs. Beckett nodded to a round table in the corner of the room, draped in a red-and-white-checked tablecloth. The diner had a southern aesthetic, a down-home atmosphere with the scents of apple pie and strong black coffee mingling in the air. Charlie's duffel bag thumped down on the floor at her feet.

"Empty house tonight," Charlie said as the waitress came around the counter, order pad in hand.

"It's the dang motel," she said, shooting a withering glance at the window. Raindrops plinked against the glass and ran down, drawing slow, rolling streaks. "Summer's our peak season, so when does the owner decide he's gonna renovate? Summer. Normally we'd have three times this much traffic."

"Must be boring."

"Let's just say I'm getting real good at sudoku. What can I set you up with?"

"Coffee," Beckett said. "How's the pie?"

"We have apple, cherry, and peach cobbler. Cherry's fresh."

"Cherry," he said.

"Same for me," Charlie said.

"Nice and easy," she said, not even jotting it down. "I'll bring that right over for you."

Charlie didn't ask *what next*. She knew what was next. Next was waiting.

Next was staring at the western-style clock on the wall, the dial framed by rearing wooden horses, and watching the second hand crawl by. Next was listening to the rain pattering on the long picture windows and the burbling of the coffee maker, the occasional clatter of cutlery ringing out beyond the swinging kitchen door.

The waitress swung on by, dropping off their coffee and pie. She headed back behind the register to slouch on a stool and scribble numbers in her puzzle magazine. Charlie dug her fork into her slice of cherry pie, the buttery crust flaking off, sliding down in a river of red.

"Why is she doing this?" Charlie glanced over at Beckett. "Making us wait. We have what she wants."

"How do you feel right now?"

"How do I feel?" Charlie reached for her mug. "Stressed. Angry. Worried."

"That's why," he said.

His fork, laden with a scoop of glistening crimson pie, went motionless halfway to his mouth.

"Beckett?"

He was staring out the window. Transfixed.

Charlie followed his gaze. In the dark, in the rain, she could make out a figure standing under the hard, stark light of the gas pumps. A woman, hood pulled down and dripping wet, draped in a leopard-print coat.

"Vienna," he murmured. "I bought her that coat in Vienna."

"I see her. *Just* her." Charlie glanced down to the bags at her feet. "I don't care what kind of games she's playing. She doesn't get a damn thing until I see my dad. Alive."

Beckett pushed his chair back.

"Sit tight; guard the loot," he told her.

"What are you going to do?"

He rose, took a deep breath, and turned to the doorway.

"Long overdue reunion," he said.

Dom's scope tracked Beckett as he stepped out into the rain. The cold droplets rolled off his glistening scalp, soaking his suit jacket.

She adjusted her aim. Now she was tracking the woman in the leopard-print coat. She adjusted for distance and bullet drop, factored in the shifting night wind.

"Give me a reason," she murmured.

She watched Beckett approach the gas pumps. His hands were open and empty at his sides. He raised his chin, called out, his voice swallowed by distance and the downpour.

The woman turned on her heel and ran.

The rain washed out the world, washed out everything but the gas-pump lights and Nina. Beckett watched her pirouette and bolt, dashing away from him. He chased her. Had to. He knew she was playing with him, drawing this out, leading him somewhere he didn't want to go.

As he darted between parked semis, on the heels of her shadow, he thought about an old folk story. Marshlights, masquerading as lanterns in the belly of a swamp, luring unwary travelers into deadly bogs and quicksand.

There was a chance Nina was going to play it straight, give Charlie's father back safe and sound, and go in peace. There was also a chance she was planning to murder them all, and leading him into an ambush was a great way to kick off the fireworks. Divide, isolate, terminate.

You taught me that, he thought.

He circled the side of a camper van. She was gone.

He put his back to the aluminum, eyes sharp, ears perked. The drumming of the rain against the black asphalt echoed over the diesel thrum of parked trucks, their engines idling through the night. The windshield of a semi flickered with blurry images, reflections from a portable TV playing inside the sleeper bunk. Beckett stayed out of the light. He moved like a panther, fast, with hungry intent.

There she was, tail of her coat flapping as she ran toward the open and darkened bay of the power wash. Beckett went the long way around, avoiding open ground, using the parked trucks for cover as he closed in on her.

Sitting ducks, Cobb thought. *We're sitting ducks out here.*

He was a sitting duck, down in the parking lot, out in the open and just waiting for a state trooper to roll on by. Angel had left him here, posted on sentry duty, while he went to set up his gear. Angel still thought a buyer for the coke was on their way, and Cobb could guess why he was holding back until they showed: he wanted the snow *and* the money.

He was dreaming. Impossible to find a buyer this fast. Not a real one.

But you can sure as hell find an undercover DEA agent posing as a buyer, he thought. *Which means it's not just the cops on their way. The feds are coming. A bust this big, they'll send a small army.*

Christ, I've got to get out of here.

He watched the big man leave the restaurant. That left Charlie McCabe all alone, sitting at a corner table with a million dollars at her feet.

Cobb patted his jacket, feeling the comforting bulge of his stolen gun. Angel could do whatever he wanted. He was done waiting.

He steeled himself and moved in for the kill.

Beckett hovered at the edge of the power-wash bay. He narrowed his eyes and hunted for movement. The rain pinged down off the sheet metal roof, mad steel drum percussion, stealing the sound of his footsteps as he crept through the shadows.

Machinery whirred, an engine groaning to life. He spotted Nina's shadow just before the overhead nozzles unleashed a fire hose torrent, painting the belly of the bay in a waterfall curtain. Big orange brushes began to spin, sweeping out slowly on mechanical arms. Beckett ducked under one, a nozzle spritzing white foam against his sleeve, and held up an arm to shield his eyes from the torrent. Wax and soap pooled on the concrete under his unsteady feet, painting oily rainbows.

Ambush. His other hand snaked under his coat and drew his gun. He crouched down, grabbing cover behind a whirling pom-pom brush, and he moved along with the mechanical arm as it swept across the bay.

"*Nina,*" he called out, voice bellowing over the machinery and the rain. "Nina, damn it, don't *make* me do this."

She darted past on the far side of the bay, out the other side, into the rain. He chased her down. Around the corner was a block of private showers, a spot for long-haul truckers to get refreshed and changed. She hauled on a door handle. It rattled, locked.

Beckett almost stopped cold in his tracks. He watched her move to the next door, desperately tugging on it. Then she hammered her fist against the wood.

He brought up his weapon, framed her in his sights, and moved in slow. Sidestepping, angling to get a better view of her face under the hood. A lamppost stood halfway between them, the light bending down, catching the rain in a spotlight glow.

She turned and pressed herself flat against the locked door, palms pressed to the wood.

"Don't kill me," she whimpered. "Please, don't kill me."

It wasn't Nina.

He'd known it the second she'd tried to pull open a locked door. Nina would never make that mistake. She always had an escape plan and always tested it twice.

"I'm not going to hurt you," he called out. He holstered his gun and approached her, easy now, showing her his empty hands.

"The woman," she stammered. "She didn't say you had a gun. She told me this was a prank. That you were a friend of hers. She said you'd think it was funny."

"I'm sure she did," Beckett said, gentle.

He got a better look at her now, on the far side of the lamplight. A lot lizard, maybe nineteen or twenty, wearing Nina's open coat over a crocheted halter top and a denim miniskirt. The rain turned her heavy makeup into a horror show smear.

"She gave me fifty bucks and said I could keep the coat."

"She gave you something else," Beckett said. "For me."

The kid nodded, remembering. She jammed her hand deep in the left pocket. It came out gripping an envelope.

"Get out of here," he told her. He watched Nina's coat vanish into the rain. He stood under the eaves of the shower building and peeled open the envelope.

Inside was a card. Nina had drawn a map. The highway, the ramps, the truck stop laid out in spidery lines, arrows showing where to go. The real meeting place was a backwoods road, maybe a ten-minute walk from here.

He flipped the card over. She'd written a note, for his eyes only.
You tell her to come alone, Little Duck.
XOXO.

Charlie had lost sight of Beckett. The rain blotted out the world beyond the diner windows. She drank her coffee and hoped and stewed in silence.

A crash rang out beyond the kitchen door, the sound of plates shattering on tile. The waitress slapped her magazine down and sighed. She raised her voice as she looked to the door.

"Comin' out of your paycheck, you know that, right?" She turned to Charlie. "I swear, that man's a fine cook, but he's a capital-*K* klutz. Can't go one night without breaking something."

The door swung wide. Charlie expected the cook, emerging to deliver his apology.

It was Cobb, leading with his gun.

FORTY

Riley burned down the highway, flashers lit on his unmarked car, painting the forest with strobes of burning neon. He crested the ridge above the truck stop and killed the lights. He didn't want to give anyone a warning in advance.

The cop who Cobb had shot was dead. He'd bled out in Riley's arms.

Riley wasn't giving any warnings at all tonight.

His hands still felt sticky on the wheel. He'd washed them, scrubbed them until his skin was pink as a newborn, but he could still smell the blood. Riley was off the clock, out of his jurisdiction. He wasn't even supposed to be carrying a service weapon, not until he'd waded through the endless red tape attached to an officer-involved shooting. He needed to talk to IA, get his mandatory counseling.

That would keep. Charlie had told him where they were meeting Nina. Security-cam footage from the harbor showed Cobb and Angel teaming up, tearing off in Angel's Jeep in hot pursuit. Good chance they might have found their way here. If they did, more blood was going to spill tonight.

As far as Riley was concerned, some people needed to bleed.

Cobb strode through the kitchen door, gun high. Charlie was half a second faster on the draw. She kicked her chair back, sidestepping as she drew her piece, slipping from his line of fire in one smooth motion.

He faltered. Panicked. He grabbed the waitress by her wrist and yanked her close. In a flash he was behind her, muzzle of his stolen automatic pressed to the side of her head.

"What now?" Cobb said, shifting from foot to foot, head bobbing behind her. "What now, bitch?"

Charlie closed one eye and trained her iron sights on his face. The waitress held her breath.

"You won't do it," he said. "I remember the hotel. You won't take the shot."

He taunted her, weaving from side to side, ducking behind the terrified woman and popping out again. Charlie leaned into her training, cloaking herself in steely cool. She didn't say a word. She just tracked him, aim steady, and waited.

"What now?" he said.

"You tell me, Cobb. You're the one with the hostage. How do you see this situation panning out?"

"First, put your gun down. Kick it over here."

"No," Charlie said.

He squinted at her.

"I've got a hostage."

"I can see that."

"I'll kill her." He jostled the waitress's head with the muzzle, drawing a whimper. "You don't think I'll do it?"

"Oh, I know you're a killer all right. Racked up a hell of a body count on Saratoga Street. But here's the thing: If I throw away my gun, nothing's stopping you from murdering both of us. If I hold on to it, maybe you shoot her. At which point nothing is stopping *me* from emptying my entire magazine into your body, all seventeen rounds, starting with your balls and working my way up to your lying face."

The arrogant smirk withered and died on his lips.

"I can promise you a closed-casket funeral," Charlie said. "So. How about you do yourself a favor and let the woman go?"

He gripped her more tightly. A life preserver, now. At least Charlie knew he wouldn't shoot her, which was exactly the reaction she wanted. The more valuable the waitress was to him, the safer she was.

Charlie was plotting. She found a strategy lying at her feet.

"You came here for the coke, right?" she said. "You're a wanted man. You've got to disappear, and not the way you were planning. Not the easy way."

"You ruined it. I had the perfect plan, and you ruined it."

"We have a saying at Boston Asset Protection: our clients tend to create their own worst problems. But hey, looks like a solution in the making, right here." She kept her eyes on him but nodded downward. "I'll trade you. One bag for the waitress. She goes free, you get your ways and means, and everybody lives to see tomorrow."

As far as Charlie was concerned, Cobb wasn't leaving the truck stop in anything but handcuffs or a body bag. All she had to do was make him believe otherwise. He bit down on the bait. He was too desperate not to.

"Bring it over here," he said.

She kept her gun trained on him as she reached down with her free hand, hoisting the bag by the handle. It was heavy. Unbalanced. And he only had two hands. Cobb wouldn't put his gun down, so he'd have to let go of the waitress to take his reward.

She stepped around the table, slow, careful not to spook him. A gust of wind sent the rain pelting the window at her back, hard and cold as a hailstorm.

Then the sound of thunder as the glass exploded.

Bullets tore through the shattered window. One hit the clock above the counter, blasting its face off, leaving springs and electronic guts dangling. Another cracked through the diamond window set into the kitchen door. Charlie threw herself to the floor. She kicked her table and knocked it over, mugs and dishes sliding, crashing, sending cold coffee and porcelain shards splashing across the tile. The table gave her a flimsy wooden shield against Cobb.

At least for a second or two. She was pinned between two shooters, one inside, one outside, and they both wanted her dead.

Angel had been perched on what remained of the motel's second-floor balcony. Prone, shielded from the rain by the concrete overhang, his ArmaLite patiently trained on the diner windows. McCabe was just out of sight, her corner seat at a bad angle. Then she stepped into view, reaching for one of the duffel bags.

He took the shot. A three-round burst tore through the night air and blew out the window in a flurry of broken glass. He waited, holding his breath—

Damn. Missed. She went low, down below the window frame, hiding behind a table.

Need a higher angle, he thought. Angel jumped to his feet and back into the gutted motel, racing for the stairs to the third floor.

From her windswept perch, at this distance Dom couldn't see anything inside the diner. She saw the window implode, though, and heard the rifle's report—three sharp, staccato bursts echoing over the storm. Her scope swiveled toward the sound.

Just in time to catch Angel's back retreating inside. Her finger brushed the trigger. Just a brush. He was too quick, slipping out of reach before she could be sure of her aim.

She scanned the motel's face, slow and methodical, moving from darkened window to window. Hunting for him.

Beckett had been jogging back to the diner. At the sound of gunfire, he broke into an open run. The front door and the big wall of light from the windows were a suicide play. He circled around instead, where a back entrance had been propped open with a brick. Good for smoke breaks, bad for security.

Bad for the short-order cook, who was limp on the kitchen floor in a puddle of fast-drying blood, right next to the cast-iron frying pan somebody had brained him with. Beckett slowed down, moving on light feet to the swinging door.

"Sorry about that," Cobb called out, the smirk back in force. "Guess I forgot to mention I brought a friend along."

Charlie had her back to the wall, just left of the broken window. She calculated the angles, studying where the bullets had hit. The shooter was outside, elevated. Only point of elevation in close firing range was the motel balcony. If she stayed left of the windows, she should be out of reach. If. If she wasn't wrong, if he didn't change tactics. If Cobb didn't shoot his hostage and then storm her position, hunkered down behind the table.

What's he packing? Charlie thought, trying to place the sound of the shots. *Carbine?* She was thinking about effective ranges. Then she was thinking about optics in a rainstorm, putting together the shreds of a plan on the fly.

She rose from cover, slow, preparing herself. If Cobb aimed his gun at Charlie, she'd have to take the shot, hostage or no. She was relieved that he still had the waitress gripped tight in his hand, gun pressed to her temple. They were all safer that way, for the moment. The waitress had her eyes squeezed shut, face locked in a grimace like she was on a carnival ride and wanted off.

"That friend of yours," she said, aiming down the barrel at him. "Angel Strickland?"

"That's right."

"You do know he's the guy your former partners hired to kill you, right?"

His expression faltered. Just for a second, just long enough to give the game away.

"Did you really think he just swooped in out of nowhere, your personal guardian angel?" Charlie laughed. "Let me guess—he offered you a deal to take us out and split the coke."

"That's right," he said.

"He's using you, Cobb. The second me and my friends are out of the picture, you're next. No chance he lets you live."

"I can handle Angel just fine."

"You really can't," Charlie said. "See, he kills people for a living. Actual grown adults who can fight back. Not stoners and teenage girls, like you."

Cobb was shifty now, easing to one side and pulling the waitress with him. Subtle, but Charlie saw exactly what he was up to.

You want to force me out of cover, she thought. *Get me back in front of the window so Angel can take another shot.*

She pretended not to notice.

"Smartest thing you can do is run," she told him. "Get out of here right now; put as much distance between you and Angel as you possibly can. He's got his own problems. Odds are he won't chase you down. My offer still stands. One bag of coke for one waitress."

"Sure. Yeah." He lifted his chin. "Bring it over here."

A glimmer of movement caught Charlie's eye. Beckett stood on the other side of the kitchen door, his face blurry through the bullet hole in the diamond of glass. He was craning his neck, trying to get a visual on Cobb. Charlie made a subtle gesture with her free hand, waving him back. *Wait for it.*

She picked up the duffel bag. She was about to become a moving target.

FORTY-ONE

Angel eased out onto the third-floor balcony. The railing was intact up here, sturdy old iron, but the eaves had been torn away, along with most of the roof. The air smelled musty, like black mold, the icy rain free to whip through the gutted motel rooms and stain the concrete. He didn't mind. He'd done harder work in worse weather than this.

He gave the railing an experimental shake. It held fast, rooted firm to the walkway. Satisfied, he leaned his weight into it. The wet iron held him steady as he brought his weapon up.

"First things first," Charlie said.

She felt the duffel's weight, her arm straining. She was calculating ranges, sight lines, probability. The waitress was paralyzed, frozen with fear, and Charlie was going to have exactly one chance to save her life. If she got this wrong, the woman was dead. And Charlie would probably be right behind her.

Angel would move after his first shot, she reasoned. *He's ex-military. He's been taught the rules of a gunfight, same as me: Unless you've got solid cover, you shoot and then you move. You move or you're dead.*

There's no cover on those balconies. He would move on instinct.

She could guess he'd go higher, third floor, so he could get a better line of sight. In fact, she was counting on it.

"First things first," Charlie said again. "I need you to take five steps to your right."

Cobb squinted at her. "Why?"

"Because where you're standing, I can't bring you the bag without stepping in front of that window." She nodded back over her shoulder. "Move right, and I can stay out of Angel's scope."

Which was exactly his plan, but he couldn't admit it. Or argue. He gave the waitress's arm a grudging yank and pulled her to his right.

Closer to the kitchen door, where Beckett was waiting. But he wouldn't make a move as long as that muzzle was pressed against the waitress's temple. Opening an opportunity was Charlie's job.

"We have to be careful, okay?" She took slow, careful steps along the wall, closing the distance between them. "It's really important that we all stay calm right now."

"I'm calm. I am *calm*." The gun rattled in his hand.

Five feet between them. Time to gamble.

"I want you to be perfectly calm," Charlie said. "So I'm putting away my weapon, all right? Watch me."

She slowly pulled back her jacket and slipped her Beretta back into its holster. She held her hand up and open for him as she took another step closer.

In a heartbeat, he turned into a wolf. He pulled the muzzle from the woman's temple and started to aim it at Charlie, smelling an easy kill and a chance to cover his tracks.

Just like she'd known he would.

Beckett burst through the swinging door and grabbed the waitress, tearing her from Cobb's grip. He wrapped his arms around her and pulled her down, shielding her with his body. The surprise startled Cobb, buying Charlie a second to drop the duffel bag and bat his arm aside. He yanked the trigger, and the pistol fired blind, blasting away a chunk of the fallen table. Muzzle flash in her eyes, Charlie hauled Cobb close, spun him around, and gave him a hard shove. He staggered back into the heart of the diner.

Another thing Charlie knew: There wasn't any protection from the rain up on the motel's third-floor walkway. And sighting a target with a carbine from that distance, blinded by a downpour, was next to impossible. The best Angel could do was shoot at anything that moved.

Like Cobb.

The carbine roared as Angel fired off a three-round burst. Then another. Round after round punched into Cobb's spine and his shoulder, spinning him around and ripping into his belly and dropping him to his knees on the bullet-riddled floor. The last shot tore out his throat.

He pitched to the floor onto his face, eyes wide and glassy and dead, his stolen pistol still clenched in his hand.

Out on her overlook, nestled deep in the muddy grass, Dom laid eyes on her target. She saw Angel emerge from the ragged hole where a door used to stand, soaked from the rain. She watched him test the railing before he braced against it.

She'd only get one shot. She dialed it in, checking and double-checking her distance, judging the movement of the rain. She issued a prayer to the Goddess of Superior Firepower as she zeroed in on Angel's heart.

Then she had second thoughts.

Their Nina problem, one way or another, ended tonight. That didn't take care of their Jimmy Lassiter problem. Someone still needed to take responsibility for Grillo's .38, to get the bookie off Charlie's back.

"You'll do," she murmured. She dropped her aim, just a little.

Angel opened fire. So did she. One feather-light squeeze of the trigger. The Remington bucked against her shoulder with a polite cough, delivering her love letter by airmail.

Angel saw blurry movement through the diner window. A perfect shot, framed in the heart of the glass like a painting. He couldn't tell if it was McCabe for sure. Could have been Cobb, but honestly, it wasn't like he was letting Cobb live either. He'd take out as many targets as he could from here, then go in and mop up at close range.

The carbine kicked, rattling as he fired off two bursts, one right after the other. A body dropped in a spray of red mist. Satisfying.

Then he heard the distant crack of a rifle. And the crack of his left leg, two inches below the knee, as a round tore through flesh and muscle, shattering bone.

The world was red now. He screamed and fell to the bare concrete, skinning one arm bloody as he hit the floor. His brain struggled to process what had happened, to function through the searing pain and shock. His pant leg was torn, sodden, leaking a slug trail of scarlet as he pulled himself into cover.

He dropped the carbine and hauled himself up along the wall. He leaned on it with his shoulder for support and hopped on his good leg. He had to get out. Escape was all that mattered, and he'd figure out the rest once he got clear. The Jeep. He had to get to the Jeep. He could drive fine with one good leg. He left the gutted room and hopped out into the pitch-dark hallway. The rain poured down from an open chunk of ceiling, washing his vision in an icy blur.

A clenched fist hit him like a pile driver, splitting his bottom lip open, jarring a tooth loose. He stumbled back and fell. Then he landed on his broken leg and shrieked until his breath gave out. Rough hands grabbed his shoulders and rolled him over, pinning him to the bare concrete on his stomach.

The hands wrenched Angel's arms behind his back. A steel cuff ratcheted around one trembling wrist.

"Angel Strickland," Riley said, locking the other cuff in place, "you are under arrest."

"I'll talk to the waitress," Riley said. He held Charlie's hand tight in the slanted light from the diner windows. "Something tells me, considering you saved her life tonight, she'll be willing to suffer some short-term memory loss."

He took a step closer to her. Broken glass crunched under his heel. Charlie had one of the duffel bags, her shoulder aching under the nylon strap. Beckett carried the other. Dom sent a text; she was on her way down the hill, and she'd meet them at the car.

"But you have to get moving," he said. "Right now. I called a bus for Strickland, and state and local cops are already on their way. Campers in the lot heard the shots and phoned it in. They'll be here any minute, and you need to be gone."

"What are you going to say?" Charlie asked.

He looked from the corpse in the diner to the balcony and back again.

"A CI gave me a tip, said he heard Cobb planned to run north. I followed on a hunch and stopped here for gas. Clearly, Strickland turned on Cobb and assassinated him. As for the bullet in Strickland's leg, well . . . there are deer in these woods. Maybe it was a hunter trying to take down an active shooter, playing hero. Understandable that they wouldn't want to turn themselves in. I guess it'll just be a mystery for the ages."

Charlie looked dubious. "That's . . . a lot of lucky breaks. Are your bosses actually going to believe you?"

"Probably not," Riley said, "but you'd be surprised what people are willing to *pretend* to believe when you get results. Bagged a professional killer tonight. That should buy me some generosity from the brass."

"Strickland's not going to play along with your story," Beckett warned him.

"Oh, I don't know." Riley glanced back over his shoulder. "He's going down for killing Cobb, for opening fire at the marina, for attacking you at the Crowne Plaza . . . even if we can't prove anything else, that's more than enough to send him away for a good long time. Whatever he says under interrogation won't change a thing. And even if he does tell some crazy story about a million bucks in stolen cocaine—"

Charlie's anxious hand gave the duffel bag a protective caress. "Yeah?"

"No one is ever going to find it, are they?"

"Not one stray speck of powder," she said.

"That's what I thought." He let go of her hand. "Go on. Get your dad back."

She leaned in and kissed him on the cheek.

Charlie walked fast at Beckett's side, cutting across the parking lot. "Where are we headed?"

"You," he said. "Just you."

He showed her the card, the hand-drawn map. Charlie saw the faint outline of a note on the opposite side. Whatever Nina had written, he didn't share it with her.

"Should I be worried?"

"Would you like the truth," Beckett replied, "or a comforting lie?"

She took that as his answer.

Charlie walked down the back-forest road, alone.

She carried a sagging duffel on each shoulder. They dragged at her arms, making her back ache, every step teaching her the weight of Cobb's sins. Everyone's sins, really. The moment Hector Ibarra had decided to steal from his employers, he'd birthed something evil into the world, and it had ruined everyone who'd touched it.

Everyone in that house on Saratoga Street was dead, save for one teenage girl condemned to carry the memories of a massacre for the rest of her life. Lieutenant Gimondi and his crew were headed for life in prison. Angel Strickland wasn't far behind, and it looked like Pembrose, the corrupt lawyer who'd hired him, had ended up tortured and killed for the secrets he'd been guarding. ADA Felton might have covered his tracks—might have—but even if he got away clean, he'd be looking over his shoulder every waking moment until his dying day, waiting for the hammer to fall, living in fear. Might have been kinder to put him down.

And Hayden Cobb, the man with the perfect plan, had bled out on the floor of a truck stop diner with no one left to mourn him and no one to avenge him.

The duffel bags were packed with raw chaos, swaying and seething against Charlie's hips as she walked. They'd come into the world sowing destruction and loss everywhere they went, and now it was time to send them back where they belonged.

Charlie mounted the crest of a muddy hill. Around a bend in the road, headlights from a parked car, a sporty coupe, blinded her. The engine was purring. The rain had slowed to a steady drizzle, icy and shivering through the forest boughs.

And beside it, standing out in the middle of the road, was Nina. The apex predator. She wore a long olive rain slicker, the birdlike hood pulled down low over her eyes. It cast her face in shadow, all but the lopsided curl of her midnight-blue lips.

Charlie trudged up, hands curled around the nylon straps of the duffel bags. She stopped fifteen feet away, at the edge of the headlights.

"I want my father," she called out. "You get nothing until I see my father."

Nina raised her left hand off to her side. Her fingers curled in a beckoning motion.

Her father stepped out from behind the coupe. Slow, uncertain, but alive. Her father was alive. Charlie's hands clenched tight on the duffels' straps. She wanted to run to him, to hold him, to take him home—

Not yet.

He stood at Nina's side. Her beckoning hand lifted, turned, curling and latching on to the back of his neck. A mama cat holding a kitten's scruff.

Charlie took deep breaths. She walked forward, slow, closing the gap between them. She stopped halfway.

She let the duffel bags fall. They thumped against the muddy road. She was lighter now, light enough to fly. Then she walked backward, liberated from her burdens, back to where she'd first stood.

Nina gave her father a tiny shove and let him go.

He walked toward Charlie, unsteady, looking confused. Then he ran. He ran, and she pulled him in and held him tight, hugging him in the rain.

"I'm so sorry . . . ," he started to whisper, burying his head against Charlie's shoulder.

"No, hey. No. You didn't do anything wrong."

Charlie caught movement in the corner of her eye.

"Get behind me," she whispered. "Right now."

Her father stood at her back. Nina was moving, casually hoisting the duffel bags, tossing them into the trunk of her car. The lid swung down. It slammed shut like a coffin.

Nina circled the coupe. She opened the driver's side door and stood there, suddenly motionless, staring at Charlie.

Charlie couldn't see Nina's hands. She felt the weight of her own gun against her ribs, so close but a million miles away. She held her breath.

Nina tilted her head, silent. One corner of her mouth crinkled. Amusement, at some private joke.

Then she sat behind the wheel and shut the door.

"Did she hurt you?" Charlie said, her voice soft.

"No, but . . ." Her father's voice drifted into silence.

"What?"

He leaned close, one hand on Charlie's shoulder. She felt his palm shake.

"What *is* she?" he whispered.

The coupe started to roll. Its tires rumbled against the forest road, digging into the gravel, drawing muddy furrows. Then it stopped again, right next to Charlie and her father. Now Charlie could see it was some kind of Italian model, all sinuous lines and bulbous curves like a lamp of delicate blown glass. The windows were tinted as black as the paint job.

Charlie could hear the muffled car stereo playing. Jangling guitars, some seventies rock anthem, and then she placed it: Steppenwolf. "Magic Carpet Ride."

Charlie knew the answer to her father's question. She felt it down in her gut, in her heart, feeling the music ebb out on a wave of raw malevolence. Whatever rode inside that car was alien to Charlie's world.

Nina was a genie. She came into the world in a gust of smoke and granted dark wishes, twisting them around. The stolen coke was a bit of stray magic from the places she called home, and now she was taking it away with her. Restoring order.

The lock of the passenger-side door went click.

And Charlie understood.

Come with me.

Nina wanted to know her. Nina wanted to teach her. Nina wanted to change her, to show her things, to show her the world she walked in and the secrets that only people like Nina knew. For a moment, just a moment, Charlie felt the pull of temptation. She almost reached for the door handle.

Instead, she curled her arm and put her hand over her father's shoulder.

The lock clicked a second time. They watched the sedan pull away, rolling slowly down the forest back road, until the taillights vanished around a bend.

"Is it over?" he asked her.

"Almost," she said.

FORTY-TWO

"When I started my career as a prosecutor," Poole said, "the first thing I learned was the value of pragmatism."

Sunlight streamed through the arched windows of her office, shining off a wall of bookshelves, making the hardcovers gleam. Charlie sat across from her. Just Charlie. She'd been called for a meeting, alone, and the first thing Poole had done was close and lock the door.

Charlie held her silence. It was a warm summer day outside, but in here, the ice under her feet felt a tenth of an inch thick.

"Pragmatism," Poole said. "You only go to court with the cases you can win. You plead criminals out on lesser charges even when you know they're guilty of bigger crimes, unless you're absolutely certain you can sell your case to a jury. Not prove it but *sell* it. Because those are two different things, and don't let anyone tell you otherwise."

"I . . . think I understand," Charlie said. She didn't, though.

"Idealism is for interns. Compromise and efficiency keep the wheels of the law in motion. When I see a report like . . . this one, from the desk of Detective Glass"—she held up a sheaf of hand-typed pages held together with a binder clip, gave it a wriggle, and dropped it back onto her desk blotter—"an idealist might be driven to seek the truth of the story. Because it sure as hell isn't to be found anywhere in Glass's account."

"Ma'am, if you called me here expecting me to dispute his story—"

"Hardly. You know, something interesting happened this morning."

"Oh?" Charlie said.

"Mm-hmm. I was . . . not pleased when I heard about Hayden Cobb's death. Whether he was just the informant or the fourth man on Lieutenant Gimondi's crew, Cobb's testimony was essential to sealing the case against the East Boston Three. I needed him alive."

Charlie's head bowed, just a bit.

"I know. We let you down. And I'm sorry for that."

"Well, that's the funny thing." Something almost mischievous glinted in Poole's eyes. "A young woman named Mila Huerta came to see me, along with her mother. It seems she's an even better witness than Cobb ever would have been."

"That's a lucky break," Charlie said.

"It is. Detectives originally tried to talk to her after the massacre, but the family was afraid of reprisals. It seems someone visited their house late last night, explained that they were safe now, and encouraged them to come forward."

"Even luckier," Charlie said.

"I arranged around-the-clock protection. Mila and her family won't have anything to fear, especially once I win this case. And I will win this case. One curious thing: they didn't want to discuss the woman who visited them, wouldn't give me a name," Poole said. She locked eyes with Charlie. "Do you know the second important thing I learned as a young prosecutor?"

"No, ma'am."

"How to get people to reveal more than they *think* they're revealing." She waved her open hand. "That unknown person has my gratitude. Anyway. The good news is my case against Gimondi and his men just grew that much stronger. When all is said and done, the East Boston Three won't be seeing sunlight again for a very long time."

"And our city is a little bit safer."

"Mm. And as such, I can hardly be angry about what happened to Hayden Cobb. Rest assured I'll be giving Boston Asset Protection my highest commendations. You and your team delivered exactly what I needed."

"Thank you, ma'am. I'll relay that to—"

Poole held up a finger, silencing her.

"*And*, because everything worked out so well in the end, I wanted you to know that I see no need for a thorough and rigorous investigation of the circumstances. My people will be looking into things, of course, just . . . not that deeply. We have more important things to focus on."

"I'm sure that's best for everyone, ma'am."

Poole saw her to the door. She had a firm, dry handshake.

"There's an election coming up," Poole told her. "Don't forget to vote."

Charlie's next stop was the Nashua Street Jail. At least she was on the right side of the bars. And the right side of a Plexiglas shield, bracketed by curling booth walls, down in the visitation gallery.

Stone-eyed guards escorted Angel Strickland into the room on the opposite side. He hobbled along on a crutch, his leg sheathed in a plaster cast. He got one look at Charlie, and his lips curled back, baring his teeth like a wounded animal.

He took his time to settle into a cheap plastic chair, staring her down. Finally, he reached for the phone receiver. The protective wall swallowed his voice, but the receiver carried it down the line, a breathy gust against Charlie's left ear.

"The hell are you doing here? I got no reason to talk to you."

"You've got years of reasons," Charlie said.

He gave her a dangerous squint.

"I need a favor," Charlie said. "And not only are you going to do it, you're going to thank me before I hang up this phone."

"Or else what?"

"It's not an 'or else.' I come bearing gifts, Angel. One of the many, many charges pending against you involves the Pocono Motor Inn. First time you tried to murder Cobb. They've got you dead to rights on that one: the tollbooth transponder in your Jeep places you coming and going from the scene, and you were caught on security camera at a nearby gas station right before the shooting."

"Circumstantial," he said.

"Sure it is. But with all the other charges against you, do you really think any jury is going to let you slide? *Oh, sure, we know he tried to kill the same guy on multiple occasions and eventually gunned him down at a truck stop, but maybe that* one *time wasn't him.* Do you really think it'll play that way?"

She read the answer in his scowl. "So?"

"So here's what you're going to do. You're going to tell the police about the .38 revolver you brought to the scene of the crime. You bought it on the black market; clearly someone stole it from the registered owner, but you don't know anything about that."

The furrows on his brow got deeper. "What .38? I use a—"

She waved her hand like she was performing a Jedi mind trick.

"You're going to tell them about your .38, which you dropped when you fled the scene. And I'm going to tell the Southborough police where to find a .38 slug buried in the motel wall. The ballistics will match, and the revolver was only fired once. Ergo, you *couldn't* have been the person who fired through the motel-room window. A jury might go for circumstantial evidence, but they can't argue with the laws of physics. And since that means there was a second shooter on the scene, well . . . a competent lawyer, if you're lucky enough to get one, could spin that into all kinds of reasonable doubt."

Charlie leaned back in her chair, cradling the phone receiver in her bone-dry grip.

"Let's be clear," she said. "You're going away for a long time. But you cooperate, and that's one less charge on your jacket. A few more years of life as a free man, on the far end of your prison stretch."

He studied her like she was an algebra textbook.

"What's the catch?" he said.

"No catch. Free gift. Thank me."

He stared at her a little longer. Then he snorted and hung up the phone.

On his way out, bracketed by a couple of guards, he turned and gave her the faintest nod of respect. It was the closest thing to gratitude Charlie was going to get. That was enough.

Outside, walking to the train station and drinking in the summer sun, she took out her phone. She called Deano's.

"Put him on," she told the bartender.

She heard a rustle, quick footsteps, the phone being rushed over to Jimmy's booth in an anxious hand.

"Lass, for what it's worth—" Jimmy started to say.

"Don't talk. Listen. Angel Strickland is going to take responsibility for the .38. Grillo is free and clear."

She hung up the phone and kept walking.

Charlie made her way back to headquarters. There were reports to file, a follow-up meeting with Jake and Sofia, and then a date on the shooting range with Dom. She'd made the unwise choice of getting into an argument about two competing brands of sport pistols; now she had to back her words up, with twenty dollars riding on the line. Charlie had already written the money off as a lost cause. She'd try her best anyway.

She stepped into the women's restroom. Like the rest of HQ, it was utilitarian at best: three unpainted stalls, a row of porcelain sinks with exposed plumbing, and a bare halogen tube over the mirror that buzzed like a swarm of flies. She stepped into the stall on the end. She hung her jacket and holster on the curling peg inside the door and sat down.

The washroom door opened. She heard casual footsteps. One of the sinks turned on, flowing for a moment as the new arrival washed their hands.

Then they walked over and stood in front of her stall door.

All Charlie could see were the toes of her shoes, sapphire-blue pumps. Motionless.

A chill spread through her veins, rippling in a slow concussive wave. Charlie looked to her hanging jacket and her holster, wondering if she should lunge for it.

"Who's there?" she said, breaking the silence.

Pointless question. She knew exactly who it was.

The figure crouched. A slender hand set a brown accordion folder—fat, almost bulging, tied off with a length of black string—down on the white tile floor. Then she rose and gave the file a kick. It slid across the tiles and came to a stop as it thumped against Charlie's shoes.

The woman turned and walked away, taking the winter chill with her. Charlie sat there, still frozen, until the bathroom door drifted shut.

She bent over, picked up the folder, and tugged at the string until it opened up. There were documents inside, a rainbow of carbon copies, transcripts, photographs. Maybe three dozen microcassettes, sheathed in plastic pouches and labeled with names and dates. Slowly, the realization of what it was dawned on her.

A wish, granted.

◆ ◆ ◆

This is fine, Felton told himself. This time, he believed it.

Everyone who could put him in danger was in prison or dead. Mostly dead. All was well that ended well. He'd gone through the dark of the woods and emerged a new man, free and clear. He had taken an early lunch today, strolling along a bustling city street, savoring the sunshine. Freedom had a beautiful taste to it.

Then, in a heartbeat, it all went wrong.

Someone was following him. He noticed the men when he stopped to check out a store window. Two of them, dark glasses, square-toed shoes, hustling fast along the sidewalk and making a beeline straight for him.

Police, he thought.

The understanding rode in on a kick of adrenaline, and when the fight-or-flight instinct hit him, Felton had only one option. He broke into a run, frantic—

Straight into the hands of Riley Glass, who had circled around to cut him off. Riley grabbed him by the forearms, spun him around, and shoved him up against a rough brick wall. Cold steel bracelets ratcheted tight around his wrists. Riley hauled him away from the wall, turning him toward the waiting back seat of an unmarked cruiser.

"Funny story, counselor. See, Oscar Pembrose is still missing, presumed dead—"

"I had nothing to do with that," Felton squawked. He struggled, digging his heels into the pavement as Riley shoved him along. "You can't prove a goddamn thing. Get your hands *off* me. Do you have any idea who I am?"

"As I was saying, he's missing, but a very interesting collection of files was just delivered to the DA."

Riley patted his shoulder and leaned in, close to Felton's ear.

"Pembrose's poison pill," Riley said. "Which includes recordings of your private phone calls, like, for instance, the one where you agreed to set Hayden Cobb up to be killed, and documentation of every bribe you ever took from him. I hope you had a good lunch, Mr. Felton. Because I'll tell you right now, you are *not* going to like the food at Nashua Street."

Felton was still screaming when they drove him away.

That night, a second storm rolled in. It shook the windows of Beckett's apartment, rattling bony fingers against the tempered glass. He rolled on his futon and sank deeper into slumber. He always slept like a baby when it rained.

His eyelids snapped open.

The only light in the room came from his bedside clock: *1:14 a.m.* hovered, luminous green.

He didn't know why he was awake. He'd had a dream about a kiss. Soft lips brushing against his cheek. Now he was awake, alert, battle ready but all alone in the dark.

He slid back the covers and rose, bare feet touching down on smooth, dry planks. He padded across the span of wood, glancing to the front door. A second light glowed from his security system's console. Green light, all secure.

He went back to bed, and that was when he saw the token on his pillow. He picked it up, gingerly, turning it in his fingertips.

A bullet. A sniper's round, long and jacketed in bright metal, like the stinger of a mechanical wasp.

Beckett stepped into his bathroom. He flicked on the light. He looked to the corner of the mirror, where a message was waiting for him. A smiley face, drawn in blue lipstick.

Beckett smiled. He almost laughed. He clicked off the light and spoke to the darkness, though he knew she was already gone.

"Love you too, Mama Duck."

FORTY-THREE

The next week brought a fresh assignment. Charlie had been looking forward to this one.

"So," she said, "we're doing this?"

Dom gave her a wicked smile. "Oh, we are doing this. We have Jake's and Sofia's full blessing, as long as their names don't come into it."

Beckett glanced over at her. He was driving today.

"Discretion is part of the service package. Everything's set up?"

"Our little helper has been very cooperative," Dom replied.

They picked up Lincoln Gable at his estate. He was dressed to the nines, fidgeting with his silk tie as he squirmed in the back seat.

"I have to impress upon you," he said, "how amazingly important today is to me. I mean, there have been some . . . hiccups along the progress of this book tour, let's be honest—"

The rest of his nervous spiel slid through one of Charlie's ears and out the other. She'd held her silence about what she knew, about how he and his publicist had set her up, and focused on keeping a plastic smile on her face. No cracks in her armor, not today.

Today, their client was moving up to the big leagues. They drove him to the TV station. A real one this time, for a show more than a few hundred people actually watched. *Sunrise Boston* was a variety show, the regional answer to *Good Morning America*, and the live broadcast would put him in front of the biggest audience he'd ever had. Thousands of households, all tuning in to hear the wit and wisdom of Lincoln Gable.

The publicist met them at the studio gates. No protesters, not yet at least. Charlie kept her smile fixed firmly in place. The network had even given Lincoln his own private dressing room, with his name written on a dry-erase board. He was moving up in the world.

"One moment, sir," Dom said, blocking them at the door. "I need to check the room first."

She stepped inside alone and emerged a minute later, giving him the all clear. Then there was nothing to do but wait while he was primped and primed, made up for the television lights. They escorted him to the soundstage, a long and lavish affair that was half news studio, half kitchen, all set up for a food demonstration later in the show. He joined the show's two hosts in comfortable-looking easy chairs, and they sat him down next to a propped-up copy of his book.

The cameras rolled, and the interview began. Lincoln didn't take long to make the hosts visibly uncomfortable. He was going for broke, milking his act for all it was worth. Charlie could see his angle: he was aiming to present himself as a righteous truth teller, and if he could antagonize the hosts into throwing him off the show, so much the better. The footage from the interview would blow up overnight and cement him as a controversial sensation.

Would have.

Charlie spotted movement. A shadow scurrying along the catwalk twenty feet above the stage. Incoming threat.

She didn't do anything about it.

"And there are people telling me," Lincoln bragged, "and I mean every day, they're telling me, 'Sir, you ought to run for governor.' Because they know that I am the only man who could restore common sense and *nobility* to—"

That was when the figure on the catwalk flipped over a plastic bucket, and ten gallons of yellow mustard came pouring down. The

Day-Glo torrent hit Lincoln like a waterfall, dousing him from head to toe, splashing across the soundstage and spattering the hosts. Studio security sprang into action, shouting and pointing to the catwalk, rushing to catch the kid before he could escape.

Charlie leaned back and crossed her arms. Now her smile was genuine.

"How'd you get him to agree to help?" she asked.

"Oh, we had a talk about the importance of proper nutrition," Dom said.

"Proper nutrition?"

Dom nodded.

"Vitamin C, Charlie. Never discount the amazing power of vitamin C."

The interview was officially over, especially after Lincoln—jumping up, mustard spatters flying as he flailed his arms—unleashed a torrent of obscenities unfit for live television. His publicist raced to the rescue, pulling him off the set, and they vanished behind the door of his dressing room. A smeared yellow handprint marked the wood just below his name.

Dom took out her phone, angling it so Charlie and Beckett could watch over her shoulder.

"And now, the real fun begins."

She tapped the screen. A window blossomed, showing the feed from the tiny camera she'd hidden during her "security check." Lincoln was scooping at his ruined suit and sluicing gobs of mustard from his silk tie while his publicist paced.

"What the—" Lincoln flailed, sending more mustard flying. "What was that? Huh? I just looked like a complete idiot out there!"

"That wasn't supposed to happen. That's *not* what I paid him for." The publicist made easing motions with his hands, trying to calm Lincoln down. "He was supposed to use the bucket just outside the studio doors and make it real obvious this time. Your bodyguards see it coming, they do their job and stand in the way, it looks like a Three Stooges gag, and you don't get a drop on you."

He winced as Lincoln grabbed him by the collar, hauling him nose to nose. Rivulets of mustard rolled down onto his upturned face.

"Listen. You. Little. Shit. It's real simple. I pay you. A lot. You stage a few little incidents; you get some funny viral footage; everybody ends up talking about *me*. They're not going to be talking about me today— they're going to be *laughing* at me."

"Honestly, I don't know what went wrong. I don't know how he even got into the studio."

"Why the hell do you think I wanted a veteran in my entourage in the first place? She gets attacked, it sets the narrative: if you hate Lincoln Gable, you hate the troops. It's a stupid, dipshit, mouth-breather narrative, but my books are *for* stupid dipshit mouth breathers, so it works. This isn't complicated."

"And to think I questioned his sincerity," Charlie murmured.

"And . . . boom," Dom said, saving the clip. She was tapping out a message as they closed in on his dressing room door. Charlie looked up to Beckett.

"You do the honors," he said. "Think you earned it."

Charlie knocked on the door.

"Mr. Gable?" she called out. "Are you all right in there?"

"Not now," he bellowed through the door.

"Just wanted to tell you that Boston Asset Protection is officially canceling your contract, effective immediately. It's been a pleasure working with you, and we wish you the best of success in your future endeavors."

Dom showed her the phone. *Upload complete.*

"Also," Charlie added, "check YouTube. I think you're about to go viral."

◆ ◆ ◆

"We should go out for drinks," Dom said. They were out in the sunshine, the three strolling through the studio lot, headed home.

"It's ten in the morning," Beckett said.

"Victory mimosas. Charlie? Victory mimosas?"

"Actually," she said, "I've got to go pick up my dad. Until he gets a new ride, I'm pretty much his chauffeur. Can we do dinner?"

Dom looked to Beckett. "Victory *whiskey*."

"I'll make the reservations," he said.

She drove back to the quiet streets of Spencer, to the gray clapboard walls and bell spire of the Presbyterian church. She paced the sidewalk and waited. Then the doors opened wide, and a handful of attendees shuffled out, going their own ways. Some looked crestfallen, some quietly hopeful. Each one of them carrying a private story, fighting a private battle.

And there was her father. His eyes lit up when he saw her. The sun glowed down against his weathered face.

"Guess what," he said.

"What?" she asked him, though she already knew. She wanted to let him surprise her.

He held up a key chain.

"I told 'em, I thought we got *chips* once we're clean for thirty days. They said that's AA. And I said, well, then shouldn't we get bottle openers?"

She pulled him into a hug and clung tight.

"Feels like a lucky key chain." His voice quavered around the edges like it was about to break. "Think I'll hang on to it for a while."

It was a sentimental moment. She couldn't be sentimental. Charlie had a soldier's eyes, and they were looking over her father's shoulder while she held him, scanning the street, breaking the world into pie slices of data as she performed a threat assessment. Threats like the one parked at the end of the block, a sedan with a dented hood and windows tinted like amber.

Grillo was out of jail.

The leg breaker slouched behind the wheel. Just sitting there, engine humming, hitting her with a prison-yard stare. He knew he'd been made. He didn't care.

"Come on," Charlie said. "Let's get you home."

Behind the wheel, she adjusted her rearview. She eased out into traffic. So did Lassiter's man, keeping a careful three car lengths back. Dutch's warning at the bar came back to Charlie's ears: *You ever train a dog, Charlie? You get the behavior you reward.*

The obvious tail was a message, from Jimmy Lassiter to Charlie. He'd worked her pressure points, used her father as leverage, and he'd gotten his reward. Now he was telling her that he could do it again, anytime he wanted.

She didn't say a word to her father about it. They talked about sports, the incoming cold front, small talk to fill the rolling miles and the backwoods roads. She knew that his one-month chip was just that; getting clean was a lifetime marathon, and he was barely out of the starting gate. The last thing he needed was more stress, more pressure.

That was fine. She could look over her shoulder for both of them, could take the pressure. And when she decided how to solve her Jimmy problem, if it meant lacing up her boots and getting her hands bloody, her father would never need to know. He had his own battles to fight.

So did she.

Acknowledgments

The first book in a new series can be tricky. There are a lot of introductions: getting to know new characters, the challenges they face, and the streets they live on. Book two is where we can pick up the pace. The mysteries get twistier and the stakes grow higher. And of course, looming on the horizon, the specter of an inevitable showdown yet to come.

That's how I try to do it, anyway.

As always, thank you so much for reading, and I hope you had a good time with Charlie and company! And on the subject of thanks, this is a shout-out to the people who made this book possible: Jessica Tribble, Carissa Bluestone, and Laura Barrett at Thomas & Mercer; Clarence Angelo (developmental editor extraordinaire); Riam Griswold and Sylvia McCluskey (copyediting, so much copyediting); Susannah Jones (best of audiobook narrators); and Morgan Blake (assistant who kindly puts up with me).

If you'd like release notifications when my books come out, I have a newsletter over at http://www.craigschaeferbooks.com. If you'd like to reach out, you can find me on Facebook at http://facebook.com/CraigSchaeferBooks or on Twitter at @craig_schaefer, or just drop me an email at craig@craigschaeferbooks.com.

About the Author

Photo © 2014 Karen Forsythe

Craig Schaefer writes about witches, outlaws, and outsiders. Whether he's weaving tales of an occult-shrouded New York in *Ghosts of Gotham* or the gritty streets of Boston in the Charlie McCabe thriller series, his protagonists are damaged survivors searching for answers, redemption, or maybe just that one big score. To learn more about the author and his work, visit www.craigschaeferbooks.com.